9\17

UNDER A SARDINIAN SKY

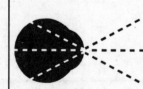

UNDER A SARDINIAN SKY

SARA ALEXANDER

THORNDIKE PRESS
A part of Gale, a Cengage Company

GALE
A Cengage Company

Farmington Hills, Mich • San Francisco • New York • Waterville, Maine
Meriden, Conn • Mason, Ohio • Chicago

LIBRARY OF CONGRESS CIP DATA ON FILE.
CATALOGUING IN PUBLICATION FOR THIS BOOK
IS AVAILABLE FROM THE LIBRARY OF CONGRESS

ISBN-13: 978-1-4328-4046-4 (hardcover)
ISBN-10: 1-4328-4046-0 (hardcover)

Published in 2017 by arrangement with Kensington Books, an imprint of Kensington Publishing Corp.

Printed in the United States of America
1 2 3 4 5 6 7 21 20 19 18 17

*For Pietruccia and Carmela,
wheresoever they dance*

PROLOGUE

London, England — 2007

In Zia Piera's wardrobe I can find anything from a fluorescent paisley dressing gown from 1963 to a pair of dejected Baghdad trousers with a jarring 1980s print. Hipsters would salivate over the latter. I've never grasped the concept of ironic dressing. I'm not a girl who could spend a day with that geometric noise on me. I like the anonymity of my half-dozen washed-out T-shirts and two pairs of jeans. It makes packing for my travel writing a swift affair so I can use my time for more fulfilling tasks like eating food I don't recognize and can't pronounce or sniffing out the local inebriation haunts in whichever nook of the globe my work has zapped me to.

I catch my reflection in the mirror on the inside of the wardrobe door as I open it. My body is straight as a board. My head is topped with a mass of rebellious black curls perched above a "thinker's" nose, as my uncle calls it, with little to ogle at in between. The mirror and I are fair-weather friends. My ancestral line suggests a predisposition to ample bosoms, a pert ass, irresistible olive skin, and those gooey chocolate eyes guys fall into, just like any prime example of a Sardinian female. My sister, not I, received such gifts at birth.

I'm inept at ironing, blow drying, and nail painting. I don't lick my floors clean, wipe the sink with bleach after use, or stash half a pharmacy of feminine hygiene washes. I escaped those Italian manias. Doesn't mean I can't cook the best *gnocchetti* I've ever tasted, roast a suckling pig to perfection, and tell you the year any particular Cannonau red wine was barreled — just by the smell. I also give up very, very rarely, on anything. Ever. This alone proves I am not, in fact, adopted.

I peel off Zia Piera's tailored jacket, which, out of respect for my mother, I had borrowed for the service this morning to disguise myself as a bona fide Italian grown-up. I reach inside the wardrobe for a hanger. The five decades of hoarding clothes means there are suitable outfits for all occasions — whether it's a solemn day, like today, or a frivolous night at my best friend's house when she's ordered me to play a Russian duchess, complete with mink stole and sequins, at one of her murder mystery parties with her Shoreditch actor mates. I prefer necking espressos and whiskey, just the two of us, but her thespy darlings are good company when all is said and done, even if they spend too much time arguing over which locally brewed botanical spirit deserves supreme worship. I fit the jacket around the hanger and squeeze it into a narrow space on the burdened rack. Then I grab my tobacco out of my pocket and walk into my parents' spare room, slumping onto the bed to roll up.

Zia Piera's funeral this morning has emptied my tank. My aunt died five days ago. We had all taken turns to sit by her throughout the day and evening that led to the night she passed. She was skeletal, disappearing into the bedsheets. My ten-month-old nephew had refused to settle down to sleep in the next room; my sister was over to help and looked gaunt with worry and frustration. Sometimes Zia Piera's expression reminded me of my sister during labor. The pain, like contractions, seemed to come in waves. In between, she would settle, the thin skin on her cheeks hollowing into her face.

When my mother entered, not long before midnight, she'd taken one look at her sister and asked me to call for the doctor. I did. We'd helped Zia Piera onto a chair beside the bed when he arrived. He spoke softly, as if he was interrupting, like someone shuffling along a full row of seats in the middle of a play. "I'm going to ask you a few questions, Piera," he'd said.

She nodded.

We looked at him.

"Can you tell me where it hurts?" he'd asked.

Mum and I turned back to Zia Piera.

In the second it took for us to do so, she had taken her last breath.

The doctor offered condolences. We all began talking in whispers. He started filling out forms. My mother had tapped into her nurse background and performed all the necessary procedures with clinical calm. My sister's baby finally fell asleep, as if he had intuited the release in the room next to his. My father brought up a bottle of *mirto*, an aromatic elixir, which my aunt had made some months ago by soaking wild myrtle berries in *aqua vitae*. We toasted her carcass. That is what it seemed to me. She was somewhere else now. Not there, in that skinny frame.

10

My Piera had fat fingers stacked with sparkling, semiprecious-gem rings that she'd bought after fierce haggling with the Senegalese beach sellers hawking the crowded Sardinian coast. My Piera wore rhinestone-encrusted sneakers and visited her sister, who now lives in my late grandmother's house, inland of those beaches, with cases full of curry powder, dry-roasted peanuts, and pyramidal British tea bags as exotic gifts. My Piera could cook for twenty-five people with the ease another would fry an egg. She had a tongue to cut through any bullshit and a razor-sharp memory that filed every wrong, every triumph, and every little beige moment in between — from the pope's visit to her hometown of Simius when she was three to what socks the local north London bus driver wore two weeks ago.

Now Zia Piera smiles at me, like she always does, from the photo on the bedside table of this tidy room reserved for guests or itinerant offspring. We took the shot at our favorite Sardinian cove on the last day of our stay at the summerhouse, when we knew she'd only ever return to her island as ashes. Cancer was rippling through her lungs even though, at seventy-three, she miraculously had come out on top after

11

surgery and chemotherapy for pancreatic tumors. All the pictures of her during her final summer are resplendent. She'd gone on a last-minute retreat near Bologna with a friend and, in her words, "met the angels." She reconnected with her long-lost cousins in southern France.

In short, she did what I'd urged her to do one wet afternoon in Edinburgh, when she visited me while I covered the city's theatre festival for a broadsheet. I asked her then if she was scared. She responded with a quintessential Sardinian shrug. Could mean yes. Could mean no. Could mean I don't know; the universal body language for I can't give you words for that, or the Sardinian for I *won't* give you an answer to that. Why commit to a thought, a stance, when we could hover in the vagaries of a purgatorial no-man's-land?

"You are in a way really lucky," I'd said at the time, once again clawing out of the earthy pits of realism toward delusional optimism. "You've been given a warning. It's a chance to do everything you've always wanted. Don't waste it."

Her tears finally came — the first I'd seen since the ordeal started the previous year. In that condensation-thick Scottish café, Zia Piera and I sobbed into laughter, leaving little pools on the dirty floor for the impish shadow of Death to frolic in.

The only other time I'd seen her cry was when she talked about her beloved sister Carmela.

I stick my head out of the spare room window and inhale. I was with Zia Piera when the doctors diagnosed her pancreatic cancer. When they asked her if she exercised she answered them with a gruff "No!" Then they laughed — I explained she walked three miles daily because in the next neighborhood she could buy bananas two pence cheaper per kilo. When they asked her if she was on medication, she replied, "Yes, I take ibuprofen if I have a toothache." They didn't understand her at first, her thick Italian accent always elicited either condescension or bafflement from the listener. Once I had repeated it, they laughed at that too — at that sweet, old Italian lady with the funny voice and the dancing hands, whose number was almost up. Grimness and comedy twirled a dance — the perpetual symbiotic pair, like fish and chips, tea and cake, pasta and *parmigiano*.

I breathe out my smoke and watch it waft over my mother's prize-winning back garden. My boyfriend — I use the term with some hesitation — drifts into my mind. I

13

stayed over at his place last night so I could cry loudly. Then we made love all night. He likes having sex to music. Last night it was the opening track of *Astral Weeks*. It played the first time we did it. That was the night I fed him nearly comatose with my family's guarded recipes: homemade *gnocchetti* with sage butter and a liberal, fresh grating of Sardinian *pecorino,* followed by braised lamb with fennel and green olives. Then I revived him with a truck driver's portion of very alcoholic tiramisu and a large pot of espresso to accompany my aunt's home-made *mirto.* Only then did he finally loosen his guard and perform a fine demonstration of unbridled British passion; much like the crackling of a suckling pig roast, if you have the time, it is worth the wait. Only I prefer to have sex without the music. I like to hear nothing but the charged breathing of a lover, his sweat on my throat, the squelch of his hand hot in mine as we lift off into the ether. I hate an underscore. It feels con-trived.

That's why I know it can't last. He's a romantic, and his instinctive approach to seduction is like that of any true Brit: crab-like. Couple this with the fact that my fam-ily can leave even the strongest soul bull-dozed and it leaves little hope of a future

14

together.

My father is my Jewish mother. He's armed with a colorful spectrum of passive aggression, an unstoppable zest for life, and bombastic meltdowns that are devastating and fortifying; after growing up with him, the newspaper editors I work for feel like puppies on Valium. He was born to Russian-Polish Jews, grew up in a leafy suburb of north London, and fell for a demure Catholic girl from a then-little-known rustic island in the Mediterranean. I went to a Catholic school with all the other local Italian, Ghanaian, and Irish families. I learned the Bible stories by heart. I chose favorite saints, dependent on which names I liked best rather than good deeds.

At home, however, I'd pore over my dad's collection of books about Atlantis and listen to his after-dinner lectures about space, or spirits being frequencies that we might tune into like a radio antenna — radical thinking for a nice Jewish boy from Golders Green. When my elementary school teacher asked me to draw God, I did my best scribble of a mesh of yellow and blue light in the center of my page, because that's how my dad would describe Him/Her/The Universal Source. I remember my teacher's arched eyebrow, but nothing more came of it

15

because I went to mass every week and my grades were good.

My family speak over one another. We overfeed. We argue for fun. Loudly. I watched my boyfriend at the crematorium, even though I had insisted his attendance was a punishment he didn't merit. I saw him look desperate to feel comfortable — and fall short despite his best efforts. No doubt he's in love with the idea of charging at this fairly successful, London-born, Sardinian-Jew (ish) travel writer with boy hips and a Medusa mop. But the reality must be exhausting, I'm sure.

I look down at the yellowing tip of my forefinger. It reminds me how deeply my smoking disappoints my mother. I start to sob again. My mother is halfway through her own course of chemotherapy for breast cancer. The two women I love most in the world have been out to battle for months. One has fallen.

Now I wade through the first stages of grief while watching my mother battle on. I feel helpless, except for the odd misplaced joke I can offer here and there to lift spirits. I've sat next to Mum as the chemicals drip into her vein. I've given a mouthful to the mincing male matron reigning over the night staff in the hospital, who had mistakenly taken her blood pressure on her arm when her notes explicitly said not to, due to the removal of several lymph nodes. I've watched her sleep through the thick panes of a solitary room when her white cell count was dangerously low and contact was unadvised because of the high risk of fatal infections. I've watched her hair fall out. We've laughed at her shiny new head. We've chuckled when strangers compliment her fashionable new hairstyle, because we know it's one of her wigs. We've clutched those snatched moments of happiness in all the small things, for each dinner she manages to cook on the good days. But there is still too much left unsaid. Too many questions I haven't had the courage to ask. At night I cry in the bath. I sob until it hurts.

I cry on her behalf, for losing the sister who held me first while my mother rose to consciousness after a general anesthetic for a C-section during the heat wave of 1976. Zia Piera had lived in the house since that day. She had cooked for a small army every night. When we left for university she sent food parcels to my sister and me. Each delivery contained enough dried ramen to make you never want to set eyes on a noodle again, a lifetime supply of homemade biscuits, and tiny packets of *saporita* — a blend of spices, which, after much coercing, she had reluctantly revealed was her secret ingredient in tomato sauce, then dispatched them in wholesale quantities. I cry for two sisters facing a life without the other by their side.

When the tears fade into numbness, I feel a familiar, cold terror well up inside. I just let it drift through me, like a passing gray cloud. The worst has already happened. Zia Piera, who no one could imagine living to anything younger than 102, is dead. Yet the world plunders on. The sun rises, the weeds ramble, the universe squiggles into infinity. Mum and I have no choice but to face life and death with awe, fear, and joy.

I stub out my cigarette on a small ceramic dish and walk back into Zia Piera's room next door. I open the wardrobe again and nuzzle my face into the dresses. They smell of her. There's a bag hanging on a hook beside the mirror. I pull it down and run my hands over the soft leather. I like to imagine her fingerprints on the worn indentations along the front flap. I will take it everywhere I go now. There will be a warehouse amount of such vintage appendages to trawl when Mum and I feel ready to clear her room. What we will do with the 700 matchboxes and large collection of sugar sachets she'd pinched from every place she'd ever had a cup of tea in, ever, escapes me. In the end we'll manage to let those go too, I imagine. The top two shelves of her bookcase are lined with a collection of porcelain dolls, forever looking at a hypnotic apparition on the horizon. In the bathroom next door, which she had the sole use of, on account of the folks having a cheeky en suite put in, her colorful, glittery nail polishes still sparkle on the skinny glass shelves inside the mirrored cabinets, a miniature cross between a pound shop and Aladdin's cave.

I sit down on her bed. Mum changed the sheets after the private ambulance took Zia Piera out of the house on a stretcher, surrounded by a black body bag. I look at her pillow. That's where I watched her toss and turn, every now and then mumbling inaudible mutterings. The last few words we exchanged echo in my mind. She had turned to me, eyes half closed. "Carmela?"

"No, Zia, it's Mina, your niece."

"I want to go with you to fetch the thread."

"It's all right, you can rest now."

I took her bony hand in mine. It was cold. My heart lurched.

"Carmela, where are you?" she asked,

"Come back, Carmela. . . ." Her pleas faded into shallow breaths.

Carmela's life has been retold to me in barbed whispers. Sometimes, at the mere mention of her name, family members' and friends' eyes still well with tears. A palpable sadness tinges even the happiest of times. It has always seemed that my mother and her three siblings neither laugh with all their bones nor cry like no one is watching. As I consider how the two women I love most in the world have battled cancer, it strikes me that the stifling of unexpressed, unresolved pain over their eldest sister manifested as life-threatening illnesses. The past eats at the women I love most on this planet, and I'll be damned if I'm going to let those haunting memories do any more damage. No dignity in being that passive bystander, harboring their pain to pass on to the next generation. The responsibility of breaking this cycle falls to me. I won't watch my mother lose the fight.

Only one way to expose the real Carmela. Only one way to release her hold over my mothers. It's what I've always done.

I write.

CHAPTER 1

Seven years had passed since the roars of V-Day before the Sardinian town of Simius flung off its ashen veil of world war and threw an Assumption Day fiesta full of spectacle and hope. Children squealed beneath the strings of lights that rendered the stark, dusty central promenade unrecognizable. The narrow houses that lined the square, crushed together like skinny matriarchs pushing against one another for attention, boasted long strips of red and green fabric hung beneath their weary shutters. Benevolent, rosy-cheeked men butchered nougat. Farmers sold their pungent *pecorino*. Women flogged slabs of bitter almond brittle. And yet the Simiuns would never throw their hands in the air with the abandon of the singsong Neapolitans or caterwaul into the night with the joie de vivre gesticulation of the Romans.

Carmela looked over at the portly accordion player, who squeezed life into his instrument and bellowed a *ballu tundu,* a traditional dance performed in a circle, heralding the start of the festivities. A troupe from a neighboring town, south of Simius, swarmed the piazza. They interlocked arms in a tight line and began to dance. The accordion player's fingers raced up and down the keyboard as the tune whirled into a fast ditty.

Carmela admired the female dancers' costumes, and not simply because she and her colleagues at her godmother's tailoring studio had made them. Their starched white headscarves were wrapped around their heads in a complicated crisscross pattern, held in place with gold pins on either side. The scarves framed their faces, drawing attention to the dark twinkle of their almond eyes, much like a Spanish mantilla or the veils of Arabian princesses; historic invaders from both places had left their mark on her island's history and traditional dress. They wore billowing white blouses with intricate laced cuffs and collars. Over these were very tight-fitting, sleeveless bodices in bright red satin with gold embroidery, which cinched in their tiny waists. The neckline was cut low to allow the ruffles of the collars to show. Their plain, long black skirts with angular creases were topped with narrow aprons festooned with vibrant needlework depicting flowers, birds, and patterns in primary colors as bold and joyous as their expressions were inscrutable. Around their necks were velvet chokers from which coral and turquoise crucifixes hung. In their ears, garnets and cornelians, with intricate gold settings as delicate as fine lace, swung as they bobbed into their steps. At the yoke of the neckline each dancer had a brooch, made from two flattened, golden conical shapes, like tiny Bronze Age shields, set with coral or turquoise at their centers.

The men, dressed in long black woolen waistcoats despite the balmy August evening, glided in white shirts with sleeves that ballooned toward tight, starched cuffs. The black tunics below flared out like skirts, reaching down to the middle of their thighs, where the tops of their white cotton trouser legs underneath puffed over the rims of their high black boots. The length of their velveteen black hats flopped over to one side, like a hare's ear.

The dancers stared out into the distance, their shoulders perfectly level, as their feet shuffled, syncopated and synchronized. Despite the joyous melody, their expressions were cool with indifference, as if their feet moved involuntarily. Their torsos were held bolt upright; they wove in and out of formations like ornate planks. Carmela would have liked to lose herself in the colorful beauty of the display but couldn't help dissecting their costumes with the mathematical eye of the seamstress who had crafted them over the past year. Each autumn brought a slew of commissions for the numerous summer festivals in which the dancers would perform. As she tried to commit any improvements she would make to memory, there was an urgent tug at her elbow. "We're a girl down!" Carmela's sister Piera was flushed with panic. It made her look wirier than she was already.

"What?"

"Ripped her ankle. You're on!"

"Nonsense!"

"Here's her costume," Piera said, shoving a mass of color in front of Carmela. With that she grabbed Carmela's arm and dragged her down into the warren of darkened streets in a frantic search for an abandoned doorway to change in.

"This is ridiculous!" Carmela cried out, trying to catch her breath. Piera cut a sudden turn downhill, passing their Zio Raimondo's shoe shop. Then she jerked to a halt beneath the arches of The Old Spanish House, a high-walled diminutive fortress left by the sixteenth-century Spaniard invaders her islanders were so proud of.

"Just ask one of the Nugheddu girls!" Carmela said, trying to fight off her sister's quick hands scrambling over the buttons on the back of her dress.

"I'm not asking any of those trollops from the next town!"

"Then tell the dancer's partner to sit it out too, for goodness sake!" Carmela snapped, quickly reaching to catch her own dress as it fell over her slip toward the cobbles. "Piera!" she gasped, seizing her sister's hands. "Have you lost your mind?!"

"I let you out of my sight for two seconds and you're down an alley getting undressed!" a voice called out. The spidery silhouette of Carmela's fiancé, Franco, crept round the corner. She yanked her dress up high over her front, covering as much of her body as she could, though the warm night air still brushed over her bare shoulders.

"Perhaps you can knock some sense into my sister!" Carmela cried.

"Impossible," Franco replied. "She won't let any man in spitting distance." He leaned against the wall of the house that flanked the steps.

Piera didn't mirror his grin. "Carmela's

25

got two minutes to save us from disaster," she huffed, stuffing Carmela's feet into the black underskirt and yanking it up. "Turn around!" Piera ordered, spinning her to face the wall, throwing a blouse over her head, and beginning to squeeze her into the bodice.

"This dancer's half my size," Carmela muttered.

"Not everyone's been blessed with your curves. Take this shawl," Piera replied, throwing it over Carmela's shoulders and knotting it at the base of her back. "It'll hide the gap at the back."

Franco stood watching. Carmela felt her cheeks flush.

Piera whipped a scarf around Carmela's head and began fastening it at the back of her neck. Franco looked her up and down. "I've never liked those old-fashioned head things till now."

He sauntered down the last few steps and planted his lips on Carmela's before she could brush him off.

"Franco . . ." she said, smoothing the embroidered apron Piera was wrapping around her so it would lie as well as it might.

"Piera's almost my sister-in-law. Not the last time she'll see me kiss you."

"Not if I can help it," Piera piped from

26

the hem of Carmela's skirt, where she crouched down to pick it out from under her square heels.

Franco smirked. "Tomboys make fine spinsters, Pie'."

"That's enough, you two!" Carmela said, feeling the heat of embarrassment and increasing nerves.

"Franco! *Vieni subito!*" a voice called.

The three looked up toward the steps.

"Cristiano?" Franco yelled up to his cousin as he came panting down toward them. Franco pulled away from Carmela. "What in God's name?"

Cristiano stood, breathless and giddy with liquor. "You must come — the boys have got the Americans in a drinking competition. We'll lose if you're not there!"

Carmela willed Cristiano's eyes to tear themselves away from her body.

Franco gave him a shove. "Where's your manners, you cretin? That's how you look at my fiancée?"

Carmela winced. She felt like a gormless mannequin wearing the wrong clothes.

"Come on, you imbecile," Franco said, giving his cousin a kick as they set off. "You watch this, Carmela," he called back with the malevolent bristle of an adolescent, "we'll show those G.I.s what Sardinians are

27

made of!" With that they bounded around the corner to inebriation.

Before Carmela could take a breath, Piera grabbed her wrist and led her in a gallop back up through the alleys. Their footsteps ricocheted off the thick walls of the houses, which huddled along the *viccoli* barely wide enough for a loaded donkey. They reached the main square just as it was time for the local troupe to begin their performance. The injured dancer's partner moved toward Carmela and wrapped his arm around her waist. Before she could compose herself, she was spun around like a top, shuffling into the middle of the long line of dancers, hoping she didn't look as much the deer before a hunter as she felt. She adored creating the costumes, and her deft work attracting admiration, but being the center of attention in this way was something Carmela loathed. The entire dance was spent holding one side of the skirt down with her thumb so that it wouldn't ride up to her chest.

Carmela had watched every rehearsal, using the time in between choreography calls to give each of the performers their fittings, adjusting their costumes accordingly. By tonight, she was as familiar with the routines as threading a needle, though she had never planned to perform them. During the bridge, the dance mistress had chosen a few measures for the now-fallen dancer and her partner to perform alone while the remaining members of the troupe jigged upstage in a line. It was a scandalous departure from the military patterns of these traditional dances, and one Carmela had hoped to enjoy from the safety of a crowd.

Now she found herself led this way and that. The world whirred. She aimed to stare at a spot directly in front of her, to maintain balance in the fog, just as the dance mistress had instructed the dancers during rehearsals. Her eyes couldn't focus with the sea of faces ahead of her. She lost her footing. Her partner would have almost spun her horizontally had he not had the forethought to shunt them into a retreat and rejoin the line — a measure too early. The troupe, counting in their heads, was thrown off beat. The remainder of the dance was a ramshackle version of what they had spent months preparing for. Carmela could feel the hot glare from the dance mistress on the sidelines.

As soon as the accordion wheezed its closing chord, Carmela fled the square, grabbing her own dress and retreating to the secluded changing spot. She didn't wait for

Piera. It was too painful to look anyone in the eye, even her own sister.

In the quiet, Carmela began to slip out of the costume she had spent hours making and back into her own. She brushed away embarrassment with each stroke of her ruffled hair. Why should she care what she looked like anyway? A betrothed woman had no place worrying about her appearance. Her job was to prepare for marriage, to portray a wholesome image to the world. To look good enough for a fiancé to invite her to be his wife, she supposed, but not so much that it would seem she chased attention elsewhere.

"Everything all right, ma'am?"

Carmela twisted around to the American voice, grasping the top of her dress and pulling it up to cover as much of herself as she could.

"Apologies, ma'am."

She squinted up toward the steps, at the unfamiliar silhouette. The man's voice was clear and warm, silky even, very different from the timbre Carmela was accustomed to hearing from the soldiers. Or perhaps it was her comprehension that had improved.

"I caught you running. I wanted to make sure I needn't be chasing after someone on your behalf," he continued, with a polite turn of his head away from her, signaling that he had noted her state of near undress. What must he be thinking of her skulking in the shadows this way? The fading light from an oil street lamp streaked across his eyes for a brief moment. "You can't be too careful at these fiestas."

"Yes," Carmela replied, struck by something more startling than the blue of his eyes. She was half dressed down a darkened alley speaking English with a perfect stranger. He was a soldier, no less, and they weren't well known for their manners. Despite all of this, she felt something peculiar in the presence of this man she didn't know: safe. It was more disarming than fear itself.

Carmela recalled how she and her sisters, as young adolescents, had run down to the piazza when these corporals had arrived eight years ago. She imagined that those V-Day hero cheers from the mainland were still ringing in their ears as they swaggered into her town, victorious. They liberated the island from the decay of war with gum and smiles. The shoeless poor still ambled the white roads of neighboring villages, farms crumbling in the crags of the ancient valleys inland, and for many, hunger was entrenched in quotidian life. But the fatal sting of malaria had finally been eradicated, thanks to the Americans, and this alone was cause to celebrate. Carmela and her sisters had returned home that day with their pockets bulging with hard squares of pink, covered in wrappers they couldn't read, to be pummeled with their grandmother's vitriol against those devils incarnate. She had confiscated their loot, placing it into the glass urn filled with candy reserved for visitors.

"I'm fine, really," Carmela said at last, feeling as if she owed a decent reply to a genuine concern for her safety. "It is a long and silly story."

He smiled. "Your English is better than my Italian. Compliments."

"I work with people from London some-times," she said. The little English she knew, she had learned from an adventurous London family, the Curwins, who took residence in a Victorian villa every summer since the war ended. Carmela and Piera worked for them as seasonal domestics. Because of the eradication of malaria, Simiuns had felt the first blushes of tourism.

The soldier stepped back into a shaft of light, casting his shadow through one of the arches and onto the stucco wall beside him. He had an open, handsome face. Carmela had seen many handsome faces since the foreigners settled. Their tall, pale beauty was so different from the small, dark men most girls were promised to at a young age. It made the soldiers somewhat of a novelty, one that many local girls chased after but that always left Carmela cold.

She realized she must have been staring straight up into the light, because he had morphed back into a silhouette. Carmela shifted and grasped the tip of her dress tighter to her chest.

"Good night now," he said, breaking the silence.

With that he placed a cigarette onto his lips, turned on his heels, and climbed back up to the fiesta. She watched his smoke spiraling up into the night air.

After securing every button on her dress and clutching a carefully folded pile of costume, Carmela began her ascent toward the piazza. She placed the dancer's costume on a bench by a neighbor's sweet stall, relieved to find everyone's attention directed toward a new event taking place in the center of the piazza. She joined the throng, bristling with anticipation ahead of a live performance. The audience surrounded a smaller, impenetrable circle of an all-male choir. No danger of being asked to substitute this time.

Carmela noted the starkness of their expressions, that characteristic Sardinian stare that would not let on whether it loathed or loved what it saw. For a fleeting moment she perceived that hard, diffident shell for which her islanders were infamous, but also the molten center that it protected. Maybe this is what it felt like to stand close to a range of volcanoes.

Her eyes drifted over the American soldiers, dotted among her neighbors. For a split second she thought she caught sight of the alley soldier. She squinted. He was fair-haired, with the same white skin flushed with a rosy pallor. But even from this distance, she could see that the way he moved as he spoke with his colleagues was jerky and juvenile. He was a blond pup, with none of the understated grace of the man in the *viccolo.* She brushed away the futility of the thought without taking her eyes off the young soldier. Instead, she considered how different the Simiuns were compared to the prim Milanese, the refined Turinese, or the girdled girls who these young American men might have left behind before their journey to her craggy, crystalline-coved isle.

There was a rumble from the bass singers. A hush fell, so swift, so thick, that the night sky itself seemed to grow darker and the scatter of shimmering stars glistened brighter. Carmela couldn't remember the last time such a great number of Simiuns were so silent. Even in church, there would always be the echo of stray toddlers exploring the side chapels, followed by the tireless footsteps of their mothers, or older men who thought their whispered gossip couldn't be heard from the back pews.

The singers upheld the silence.

Finally, the bass singers took a breath, in perfect unison, as if they shared a set of lungs among them, and intoned several measures of percussive humming. Their voices rose as if from the earth underfoot, trembling the crust of the land, like the first warning of an impending earthquake or the distant rumble of a thousand wild horses thundering toward Simius from the parched plains that surrounded it.

Carmela could feel the vibrations on her chest from where she stood. Now the other singers joined in. A column of sound rose. The ancient harmonies mesmerized the crowd. Carmela allowed the honeyed notes to wash over her, as rich and deep as the burnished red of the naked trunk of a stripped cork tree. The melody was sonorous, full of loss and longing, somewhat at odds with the unadulterated joy of the surroundings.

The music described a long-lost antiquity. The chords crushed together, dissonant almost, sweeping Carmela back to a time when the Neolithic settlers sheltered in those caves carved into the rocks on the outskirts town. Where those peoples once saluted the sun and venerated pagan gods of fertility, her family now celebrated May 1, with picnics of homemade cheese and bread. She and her sisters would gaze out over the valley that looked like an enormous emptied lake. They ate, sat upon that same stone, smooth with an age of travelers' steps. She pictured those Neolithic men now, beneath fat moons, wrapped in animal skins, singing these same melodies into the night. Carmela lived for these stolen moments of pleasure, a respite from arduous monotony, transported by the music in churchless worship.

Her eyes landed on Franco, on the opposite side of the outer circle. She watched him, glancing over the milieu, giving half nods to any of his father's compatriots at the town council office. His eyes returned to rest on her. He smirked, mischievous, then peeled the dress off her shoulder with his gaze. His smile was unchanged from the adolescent chimp she had acquiesced to during the cherry harvest in the early summer of their sixteenth year. Her breasts had had a growing season of their own, something that hadn't escaped the attentions of a young Franco. He was the son of one of the most influential landowners — a heavyweight on the town's council — a burden Franco carried with neither ease nor grace. Carmela watched him run a hand through his thick black hair, sharing a joke with his cousins, who shifted about him like the hungry stray cats that skulk along Simius's narrow *viccoli*.

A solo tenor's voice lifted up and over the group as he recounted the Sardinian tale of the deer woman who could settle for no man. The lyrics were plaited with fierce longing. He wailed his highest note, consumed with his song, as if this deer woman he sang of were his own lost love. It pierced the inky night, a lost sheep's bleat down a starlit valley.

The hairs on the back of Carmela's neck prickled. Franco's trysts, though exciting, never brought her this rapture. This heightened passion could only ever exist in song, surely, those fables of poetic love. This was not the real feet-in-the-dust, earth-in-your-hands love that Carmela could expect from joyful married life. A good wife would be rewarded with life's honest pleasures — food on her plate, babies with fleshy thighs at her breast, and wine to drink to her family's health.

The singers closed with a glissando and a final rich, hummed chord that hovered, golden, in the air. Then the night erupted with applause. Carmela listened to the hands pounding with pride, but her eyes couldn't tear themselves from Franco. She remembered how it felt when his salty mouth had made her heart pound and his body felt like an unchartered universe to touch, taste, and discover. Like the choir's song, at once stirring yet distant, this boy, with his cherry and wild fennel kisses, felt like someone she once loved in a dream.

CHAPTER 2

The cottage on Carmela's family's farm stood camouflaged against the boulders of the surrounding hills. A low wall made up of roughly chipped rocks undulated from the house over to the near distance where it gradually broke off, stone by stone, till there was no wall at all. In the middle of August the grapes on the hundreds of vines — lines of gnarled soldiers — grew plump with juice but remained green, awaiting the ripening autumnal sun. Dozens of tomato plants hung heavy with their second round of lustrous red, plum-shaped fruit. Beyond those were the almond, cherry, and plum trees. The cherries had long since been devoured, sold, or bartered in exchange for staples such as sugar or coffee. The June harvest of nuts had been dried, toasted, ground for marzipan, and then rolled into coin-shaped *sospiri* — bite-sized sweets dipped in white icing. They stored well for months and were given as gifts on feast or saint days. Only the plums remained to be picked. Their sweet, jamlike flesh, destined to fill hundreds of jars as preserve, would glaze the family's breakfast breads throughout the winter.

Carmela's father, Tomas, and his younger brother, Peppe, joined forces on the farm. After the war, and the division of land that followed, the two had found themselves owners of this narrow idyll. There was produce to feed their respective families and enough left over to barter for anything they didn't, or couldn't, grow themselves.

The two brothers had built a roof over the ruins of the home they found there, using mismatched terra-cotta tiles salvaged from crumbling villas on the outskirts of town. After several months of sweaty work, they had converted the stones into this two-room cottage. One room had the skeleton of its original hearth resurrected. This was where Carmela's mother, Maria, performed her culinary spells when the women joined them from town to help. The other room had several cots for sleeping, though it was usually only the men who would stay there overnight. The women would return to their Simius homes, where their day-to-day lives were anchored and the children schooled.

Tomas paced the stone floor, hot in the middle of a rant, his sun-parched skin creasing into sharp lines. "Fire-and-brimstone-thunder-lightning-heavens-and-hells!!!!" The two-year diet of sugar, lemons, and bananas during his time in Africa, building roads for Mussolini, had left him with a mouth of rotting teeth that caused him considerable pain. "Cross-the-devils-heavens-above!" he cried, stomping his dusty boots and clenching his fists. The bronzed muscles on his wiry forearm bulged.

One end of a thread was tied tightly around the metal door handle and the other around the culprit. Maria stood beside him, her alabaster face serene, unruffled by the frantic tirade of her husband; her black eyebrows didn't furrow, and no worry creased her forehead. Maria's white skin, unlike the tawny olive of her siblings, had earned her the nickname of Spanish princess. Genetic surprises were not uncommon in Simius. Maria's cousin was born to a small, dark woman with thick, black locks but grew to be almost six feet tall, topped with a mass of copper hair and bright blue eyes — a nod to the area's Norman, rather than Spaniard, history. The tone of Maria's skin was set off by the jet black of her hair, the color and sheen hinting little to her forty years. Only on rare occasions did Carmela spy it liberated from the bun wrapped in a tight knot at the base of her mother's head, cascading in thick, natural curls down to the middle of her back.

Carmela had inherited the same lustrous locks, though hers were less cooperative. They fell in erratic waves by her shoulders, creasing into tighter curls depending on the weather, or sometimes, she supposed, her mood. She gave up trying to tame it into a bun and swept it off her face with a scarf tied around her head instead, or a pin or two clamped around a few strands as an afterthought. Carmela's skin was several shades lighter than her sisters' also but had little of her mother's porcelain quality. Where her mother guarded her thoughts and feelings, Carmela's every emotion rippled across her face despite any attempt at concealment, the deep ochre of her eyes revealing each flickering thought. On certain days, Carmela noticed marbled flecks of her father's green in hers. Piera swore this happened only when her sister was trying not to lose her temper, or if she'd cut a pattern wrong or burned the garlic.

Carmela sat at the wooden table before the wide stone hearth and stopped kneading the dough for fresh *gnochetti*. She admired the tender stoicism her mother radiated, the way her soft wrinkles underlined an innate wisdom, especially when her father was mid-fury. It was an occurrence Carmela would have wished unusual, for her mother's sake. If it wasn't a painful tooth, Tomas ranted about the onion being cut incorrectly for red sauce — eventually Maria placed it in whole for the duration of cooking and removed it before serving — or that the cauliflower had boiled too long and fumigated the house with the smell of sewer. It was a blessing that he had found someone as exacting as he was but who managed to keep her attention focused on minutiae with apparent ease.

Maria's sister-in-law, Lucia, sat on the opposite side of the table and shifted her glance from her baby, asleep in his wooden cot at her feet, oblivious to the drama. Tomas took a breath, gave the door a defiant slam, and let out a guttural growl.

The familiar tinkle of a dead tooth tapping on the wood restored a short-lived peace.

Maria wrapped a strip of old sheet around her two fingers and dipped it into an enamel bowl of water. She held it out to her husband. He flicked her hand away.

"Water's for washing!" Tomas whistled through the new gap. "Give me the bottle!"

"Tomas," she implored, "you need to clean it first."

He stomped over to the wooden dresser and yanked out the *aqua vitae* from the lower cupboard. The women watched him rip a fat strip off the old sheet in one motion and douse the frayed material in the alcohol. His mouth opened wide. Tomas stuffed the sodden cotton inside. His jaw clamped down. He winced. Then he straightened, his cheek bulging with cloth.

Carmela saw the steely determination for which he was infamous flash in his green eyes. Her father could plough through agony of any sort like no other. A dogged stubbornness marked everything he turned his hand to. Tomas could dig his entire farm without stopping, not even for a sip of water. The first time the younger hired hands had worked at the farm, they raced ahead of him, ridiculing his grandfather speed, as they called it. An hour later, they succumbed to paralyzing hunger and thirst. Under the relentless sun that day, they guzzled their water and inhaled Maria's homemade bread and cheese. Meanwhile, their eyes fixed on their swarthy, bare-chested boss, twice their age. They gawked

44

at him with admiration as he lifted and dropped his pick into the rich soil with slow, mechanical movements, an unyielding ox, till the pink sun dipped down into the hills, its fading rays streaking in through the branches of the cork oaks. They never teased him again.

Tomas threw the door wide open. Carmela looked out of the small window of the hearth room, watching her father charge back out to his fields. Beyond the ploughed earth, the yellow grasses swayed in a breeze, offering little respite from the midsummer sun. Inside, the stone rooms allowed the women to work in the comfort of the cool temperatures, unless it was cheese-making day, like today, in which case the milk simmering on the wood fire in the hearth raised the temperature.

Beyond Tomas and his younger brother, Peppe, sweating over the long rows of tomato plants, Franco's family's parched land lay dotted with cork oaks. Their trunks had already been stripped. The cork bark hung, maturing, in one of the two adjacent huts, later to be boiled, flattened, and sold.

These two circular huts were the oldest structures on the farm, left by solitary shepherds, whose century-old footprints, some said, could still be found, untouched, on the floors of virgin forests where autumnal gatherers dug for truffles. One hut was used for drying out cork and cheese, and the other, with a fire pit dug into the center of its earthen floor, was used to smoke their homemade sausages, which swung high above the flames, suspended from the conical thatch. It was here that Tomas, his brother, and any occasional worker would gather at the end of the day to sip their pungent wine out of tiny *ridotto* glasses. As night fell, they would grieve for times gone by and argue over whether America's sidewalks were truly covered in gold or if all of God's riches were right there, under their noses, among their beloved Sardinian wilderness.

Carmela loved the light, space, and fresh air of the farm, a world away from the cool darkness of their town home. The latter was built with the small fortune with which Tomas had returned from Africa. In its inception, he had favored size over finesse. He cared little for fancy fixings or elaborate plaster moldings. Where his neighbors had ornate columns that upheld covered terraces on the top floors of their narrow, old homes, his new creation had a veranda closed in with large, square glass panes. He erected a practical construction large enough to keep his family warm and dry. Tomas chose not to paint over the stark gray of the concrete with the pastel earthen hues of the homes that surrounded it. To his mind a house served a purpose, no more. It was neither an extension of his artistry nor something to gawk at, admire, or covet. He grew up shoeless, darting along the dirt alleys before his family's one-room cottage. Now his children had a large terrace of their own, granite stairs, concrete walls, and a kitchen with a table that sat twenty. Tomas sweated several times his own weight in Africa for it; his pride was justified and unabashed.

On the farm, it seemed like everything and everyone grew. Carmela attributed this, in part, to the fact that Nonna Icca, her father's mother, never joined the women there. She preferred to remain in town and guard the house. In Nonna Icca's mind, the walls had hidden chinks through which all the towns' gossips would peer at their lives like vultures, waiting to peck at scandal.

She had lived in the house since Carmela was born on a stormy Christmas Eve night in 1930. Icca's screams overpowered her daughter-in-law's as she cried out to God to forsake them from the oncoming apocalypse. Although thunder rumbled the house, the first sounds Carmela heard were that of her grandmother banging her bony fists on the wooden doors to ward off what she deemed to be Lucifer's battalion. Being surrounded with four hard-working sons, a manicured daughter who was spared manual work of every sort, and a gaggle of, mostly, obedient grandchildren did not allay Icca's bitterness. She sat, day after day, atop her raffia stool by the front entrance of the house, strategically placed to witness all incoming and outgoing human traffic, clutching the rosary in one hand and her broken heart in the other. By now, she ought to have been in the Promised Land. Instead, her husband had returned from the Americas, gold in his pockets, Panama Canal dirt under his fingernails, whereupon death visited him with appendicitis. A month shy of their departure for New York, he was playing cards with the angels while she bit back her tears.

Carmela tore her gaze away from the window. Lucia had begun industrious production of *gnocchetti* from the lump of pasta dough, big enough to satisfy several herds of farm help.

"Icca's a tyrant and that's the end of it, Mari'," Lucia began, as she pinched tiny pieces of the dough and rolled them over a corrugated metal plate. It left circular indentations over the small pasta shapes. "She can stick her snide remarks where the sun don't shine — and I don't mind saying that to her face, dried-up old sow."

Maria never commented on gossip, neither admonished nor agreed. This morning, however, as Lucia preached, Carmela noticed her mother's white cheeks flushed the pale pink of crushed rose petals. Maria heaved the oversized copper milk pan off the wood fire. Carmela stood up and grabbed one of the round handles from her. They placed it down on an iron stand in the middle of the room to begin preparation of salted ricottas.

"I told Peppe," Lucia continued, flicking the little pasta shapes that dropped onto a floured tray like raindrops on a tin roof, "I didn't marry you to be anybody's serving girl. I'd go to a lady's house and get paid for that. Six children he has from me. Six little piglets that need feeding. Who in Jesus's name is supposed to do all that and look after mother hen up at yours as well?"

"Lucia . . ." Maria interjected, as a feeble courtesy. On the subject of Icca, Lucia would never have her opinions altered.

Carmela brought the wooden cheese molds to her mother, and together they soaked their forearms in a bucket of water and patted them dry with care.

Lucia went on. "We move to our own house, and Icca's asking me to do her washing! 'Too many dirty sheets coming out of your and your daughter's quarters,' I says. 'Stained sheets have no place in a spinster's house.' Unless, she shits herself in her sleep? Don't know how you stand for it."

Lucia's baby squirmed into a hungry cry. "Jesus, that child is never satisfied, greedy like his father." She pulled him up and, in one brisk motion, flipped up her shirt and attached him to her ample bosom. The room tipped into silence but for the contented suckling of his tiny lips. Carmela and Maria dipped their hands into the warm whey till it reached their elbows. They filled the small, bowl-sized mold and gently raised it to the surface. Carmela had performed this ritual with her mother since she was a child. Working alongside Maria set a high standard for becoming a wife herself. Carmela's discipline supported her well — any dress she made would be finished with impeccable precision and an eye for detail.

Lately, though, the force with which her imagination swept over her, and her inability to settle on one task for too long, unsettled her. She attributed her distracting daydreams to wedding flutters and tried her best to think little on it. Over the past few weeks, at her godmother's studio, where she had apprenticed since she was thirteen, she was bombarded with ideas for dresses and trousseaus. The pictures flashed in her mind as clear and colorful as those in a high-gloss magazine spread. Her hand could barely keep up with the pencil careening over her notebooks. It raced across the page, trying to manifest those visions, with the frantic energy of a child leaping to catch the swinging string of a beloved balloon before it floats up into the clouds, forever out of reach.

Carmela looked back down into the pan, lifted out the full mold, and squeezed out the excess liquid. Then she placed it upon the stone ledge by the back wall and topped it with a circular piece of sanded wood and a slab of granite to press the ricotta down into shape.

"Love a man with appetite, Mari'!" Lucia boomed, breaking into laughter. The fat of her arms jiggled. "I could feed half the town with this left tit. Given up on the right, the little devil almost bit her off, I told him straight — you bite me one more time and I'll bite you like the wickedest donkey on the farm and you'll know it, all right."

"He's two months old, Lucia. . . ." Maria

51

said, reaching back down into the warm pan.

"You got to be strong to a man, Mari', or he'll walk all over you. Mark my words, Carmela — you fill a shirt and have a waist as narrow as a new olive — best listen to your Zia Lucia before your fiancé fills you with ideas!"

To Carmela, Maria was strength personified. Her mother never tired but devoted herself to the work of providing for her family with a very private, near religious ardor. There was not a minute in the day when her mother's hands lay idle. Even in the deep quiet of the afternoon, her fingers would be racing over some skirt or shirt to be mended. From the time the sun rose, her mother glided from one task to the next with a grace that Carmela could not even begin to imagine imitating. When Tomas exploded over the hot topic of any particular day, Maria listened, unswerving, letting his rancor wash over her like water, suffusing his steam with wordless patience, neither intimidated nor defiant. If that was not strength, then what was?

Lucia threw her head back when she laughed, sung like no one was listening, cared little for what anyone thought of her. She would jump up and twirl at the first sound of music; life danced through her. She told Peppe what she thought and could scream into a fight at the slightest provocation. She drove her truck to and from the local markets, unafraid of the rough roads, happy to roll up her sleeves and fiddle with the engine as needed. She appeared to be her husband's equal. Her childhood began in the orphanage, but Lucia refused to let life swallow her up. She was a survivor.

But was all this passion, this vociferous philosophizing over the battle to be won, a testimony to strength? Wasn't finding the beauty in the everyday rhythms of life, committing with an open heart to one man and the children he helped a woman bear without jostling for control, true strength? Wasn't this the faith that everything was built on? After all, Carmela thought, how ridiculous it was for humans to fight off God's plan, succumbing to the illusion of control. Why then, in that very union of marriage, made under God's eyes, was control so important? Was not this grappling ungodly? Sinful, even? How far could love take you if, in the end, it was a battleground? Few years had passed since everyone agreed that the futility and horror of war was not to be forgotten or repeated. Why, then, invite it into your own home?

It seemed to Carmela that striving to put a man in his place was a refusal to acknowledge that different members of a household had different roles. Although Tomas would scream and shout over the tiniest detail, it was Maria who held the domestic reins. It was she who saw that everything ran like the well-fitting cogs of a flour mill. A church was not built with two steeples. Was the tiny gold crucifix upon the altar any less important than the tall spire? A family, like a church, is built over time, each new member drawing and feeding strength to those who came before, like the construction of Simius's gold-tipped cathedral, which rose up toward the stars, brick by brick, over decades.

Carmela did not want to think she'd ever stand up to her fiancé, Franco. The playful anarchy of Lucia's home was entertaining and joyous, from afar, but Carmela longed for the delicate treasure of a home and a marriage honed with care, gentleness, and devotion. How could she stand beside Franco at the altar if she believed the reality of their life together would be a constant wrangling of wills? Lucia lived for this, fought hard for the thrill of winning every little argument with her husband.

Carmela had never played like this with

Franco. Their love began in a blush. A sideways look from beneath the mottled shade of a cherry tree. Carmela and her siblings were helping her father with the harvest, along with several aunts and uncles. That June's heat had lacked the oppressive beams of August or the scorch of July. A breeze blew. The children and adults sang, making the plentiful work light. Against the cloudless blue of early summer, Franco caught her eye. Of course they had known each other since they crawled the dirt of their farms, but that day it felt as if they had met each other for the first time. His face had creased into a mischievous grin. It was as if he could read the playfulness inside her, which she denied herself. The firstborn, studious apprentice to her godmother had little time for distractions. And yet.

Later that afternoon, as they waddled the weight of the luscious red berries in their heaving baskets, he'd spoken to her about his dreams. He had ambition. His eyes lit up when he talked about his soon-to-be burgeoning empire. He spoke like a prince, not a whisper of doubt in his voice about his trajectory toward wealth and responsibility. That's how it had felt that day, when his eyes lingered on hers past the end of sentences, between thoughts, in the silences percussed only with the crunch of their feet on the hot earth. To a sixteen-year-old Carmela, it was all she could do not to think that he had just met the most beautiful woman in the world. In his eyes she saw the future. It was bright. Filled with possibility. And freedom — an intoxicating promise of something beyond her own world.

Floating through these memories now felt like a half-remembered dream. Her thoughts hovered in the narrow space between sleep and waking. It was nearly impossible to know if any of them had happened at all. Perhaps Franco had only been that sixteen-year-old for one day. Perhaps it had taken all these seasons since for Carmela to realize that he might never have been that boy at all. Like her aunts always said, "Sun and fruit remove sight."

She had felt as if he once had the power to offer her something different from the certainty of small-town life. But as the days passed, it became harder to ignore the little voice in her head whispering that this was little more than her own brittle illusion, stitching made in haste without a knot at the end of the thread. Over time, his ambition had begun to curdle into a stubbornness of someone beyond his years. His excitement about the future ebbed into a subtle paranoia that he may not have the responsibility and riches gifted to him. There were other siblings whom his father adored more. In place of his breezy swagger germinated the near imperceptible seeds of bitterness and jealousy. He was a slightly bruised cherry — altered but little, yet marred nonetheless. Carmela wiped a tiny wisp of hair from her face with the back of her hand, and with that these fruitless shoots of thoughts.

Lucia rolled the last squeeze of dough into a final *gnocchetto*. Her impatient hands rested for a moment, till the one that wasn't cradling the baby swirled through the air to punctuate her speech. "One good thing about milking — I don't have to put up with the curse every month."

Maria looked up from the pan. Her cheeks had returned to their vanilla white.

"Tit's out again!" Peppe exclaimed, striding in to fill a glass with water from a terracotta jug.

"Just jealous it's not for you," Lucia answered, without missing a beat.

"They're the mismatched mountains of the North."

"You and me, more like!"

Carmela watched her aunt and uncle chuckle, wondering if she too would dance around her husband like this after six children and uneven, milk-laden breasts. Is this the kind of wife she would be? It was hard to imagine Franco teasing her like this, almost as hard as it was to picture him stamping his feet over rotting teeth. Carmela took her sudden impatience to know where her life would take her as another painful reminder of her immaturity. A wise woman like her mother never let her thoughts race headlong into anything.

Another wave of energy bubbled up inside. She dropped a second mold into the whey, dipping her hands into white warmth. As she lifted it out of the pan, Carmela felt the liquid streak down her forearms. All her simmering thoughts evaporated into the milky air.

The sun began to hit the height of afternoon when the clatter of a vehicle brought everyone out from the back of the house, where lunch was drawing to a reluctant close. It wasn't a sound any of them were accustomed to hearing there. A cloud of dust rose from the dirt track leading to the farm, which was set back almost a kilometer from the main road. The family would travel the three kilometers from town on foot or in Lucia's fruit truck. The brothers paused to scrutinize, squinting into the near distance. As the vehicle reached the rusted gate, it stopped.

The engine fell silent.

Tomas marched over to the driver.

The family's distrustful Sardinian glares scissored across the scorched earth. A serviceman got out of the jeep with one lithe jump. Nothing about the crisp white of his shirt, or sweat-free brow, suggested he had traveled from the base in a roofless vehicle under the unforgiving August heat. Tomas shook his hand and gave him a welcome pat on his back. Everyone shifted.

"*L'Americano! Venite!* Gather round!" Tomas called out, as the two turned and began their walk toward the group.

"And that," Lucia muttered under her breath to Carmela, "is what tourists call a breathtaking view."

Carmela flashed her aunt a disapproving frown.

"What? You don't make babies sitting on the back pew."

"This," Tomas announced, "is Lieutenant Joe Kavanagh. He's from the base." He gestured to the mob. "Got a bit up here," he said, tapping his temple. The officer flushed.

"He's promised to help me get my hands

59

on some equipment. Wants to see how we do things."

The bashful lieutenant smiled as if he had understood every word of Tomas's Italian. Although he appeared to hold substantial rank, judging by the appendages on his jacket, there was something about the way his knowing eyes swept over the land that suggested he was no stranger to farming. Carmela glanced at the faces around her but gathered little from their inscrutable, unblinking expressions. Tomas reached a warm arm around the soldier. "Is this how you treat a guest?" he called out to everyone. "Pour the man a drink!"

Maria, Lucia, and Carmela hurried back to the house as the men joined Tomas. Maria covered a tin tray with *ridotto* glasses and a green bottle of garnet-colored wine. Carmela placed a slab of *pecorino* onto a chopping board, uneven and scarred with scratches from years of use. Then she filled a basket with roughly torn strips of *pane fino,* the large circular flat bread for which the town was famous, along with a handful of small *paniotte* rolls she and her mother had baked that morning.

Tomas led the visitor toward the long wooden table under the shade of a gnarled vine canopy at the back of the cottage. Its legs were made from two wide oak trunks, a rugged altar at which feeders worshipped Maria's cooking.

"This is the man you told me about?" Peppe whispered to his brother, as they sat down.

A handful of local young men, hired for extra help that week, straggled behind like a pack of dogs salivating for a treat.

"Play our cards right and we could do very well," Tomas replied.

Tomas gestured for the American to sit. Carmela noted the lieutenant's posture. He seemed so at ease, or else created an impeccable performance to that effect, even among this group of strangers intent on force-feeding him and making him drink into a fog. The men took their places on the benches and thrust a glass into Kavanagh's hand, filling it to the rim with Tomas's wine. Their glasses raised skyward. *"Saludu!"* Tomas called out.

"Salute," the lieutenant replied.

That silken voice unlocked a memory.

Carmela stood by the door that led into the house, hovering between participation and service, the chopping board and basket still in either hand. She watched as the men coerced him into drinking in one gulp so they could refill. Peppe signaled to Carmela to pass the *pecorino,* made from their own sheep's milk. She walked over to him and placed both board and basket before him, allowing him the honor of slicing the cheese. He carved out a generous slab, wrapped *pane fino* around it like a blanket, and bellowed across the table, "*Tieni!* Take it, Americano. God bless our sheep! God bless America!"

The men clinked to America and long life. Kavanagh was fed a sample of their ricotta too, and several slices of their homemade sausage, fragrant with fennel and thyme, balanced with just the right amount of salt. The group made easy work of polishing off three of them. When four bottles stood empty and the lieutenant still appeared intact, Tomas called down to Maria at the other end of the table. "Got ourselves a professional, Mari'. Bring out the hard stuff!"

She disappeared into the house, followed by Carmela and Lucia.

"Going to take more than wine to make this one dizzy," Lucia whispered, frisky. "I'm going nowhere until that collar is undone and I get myself a look at more skin than just a neck. And those eyes, no? Clear like the Chia coves."

Maria reached into the bottom of the

wooden dresser and shook her head with a reluctant smile. She passed up glass bottles of homemade liquor to Carmela, for the tray; *aqua vitae* and Tomas's fragrant *mirto,* an aromatic, potent after-dinner drink made from their native myrtle berry.

"Give it here!" Lucia exclaimed. "I'll do the pass with the *mirto,* Mari', get me a closer look!" With that she whisked the bottles out of Carmela's hands before she could get them onto the tray. Carmela followed Lucia as she flew back out of the door, laying out fresh *ridotto* glasses before each man.

"Oh, here she goes," Peppe said, as Lucia sidled up to the table. "Why must you always nosey about the men, woman? You stay in there and I'll stay out here, and we'll all go home happy!"

"Someone's got to protect her beautiful nieces from you lot!" she replied, flashing Kavanagh a toothy grin.

The men laughed at the couple's familiar repartee, which accompanied the end of most meals. Peppe fidgeted in his seat.

"Americano! Which one for you?" Lucia asked.

"Mirto, per piacere."

A stunned pause fell over the merry group. His Italian impressed them. Mumbled surprise rumbled into clinking glasses. The men slurred wishes of good health as the initiation fast approached completion. The afternoon trickled through another bottle of each digestif, alongside plentiful servings of Maria's *seadas,* thin pastry-encased slices of cheese, pan fried till crispy on the outside and oozing on the inside, topped with a drizzle of the neighbor's acacia honey.

The setting sun cast its ruby glow over the men as they cajoled in a soup of half languages that everyone appeared to understand. The *Americano* started to gesticulate in Sardinian. Carmela noticed his hands were worn, those of a man accustomed to hard physical work. The way they moved smoothly through the air, however, was more akin to an artist describing a new work than that of a worker discussing the fluctuating prices of milk and cheese. His sleeves were rolled up now, exposing his muscular forearms, much to Lucia's delight.

Tomas looked over to his daughter and signaled for her to bring out yet another bottle. She moved to clear the empty ones first, when her father took her hand. "Americano!" He hiccupped. "You'll forgive me, I haven't introduced you to my daughter. This is my eldest, Carmela. Not just a pretty picture — inherited my brains too!"

Kavanagh's eyes widened, his head cocked slightly. "Actually," he replied in English, stretching out his hand, "I think we've already had the pleasure."

Carmela flashed a brief half smile in return and gave his hand a perfunctory shake.

"She speaks English too, you know?" Tomas began.

Carmela stiffened. She was no stranger to being put on the spot by her father after he had drunk too much. Her face reddened in spite of herself.

"Go on, Carmela, say something!" Tomas cried, swinging his arm up like a ringmaster announcing the headlining act.

Carmela felt the glare of a dozen eyes. What was this fixation with her knowledge of English? It was a skill, but she was not an acrobat who lived to hear applause for her tricks. Carmela had a heightened sense for when her father would perform such turns and now berated herself for failing to escape in time.

"*Attenzione,* everyone!" Tomas called out, "My firstborn is going to speak like an English!"

The blood thumped in her ears.

"Please, don't put yourself on the spot on

65

my account," the lieutenant said, undoing the top button of his collar. The blue of his eyes deepened. Carmela would have liked the warmth that shone in them to relax her, but it only made her unease swell. Her eyes darted up and down the table, scanning the remnants of the food, a gourmet graveyard. She raced around in her mind for something simple to say, but it was like a bare white room. Her eyes lifted. They met her mother's, reminding Carmela it would be no great pain to humor her father. She found her voice.

Carmela muttered something about welcoming the lieutenant to Sardinia and the Chirigoni farm, but the applause drowned out the end of her sentiment. Her eyes flitted over a sea of sun-cracked smiles. Kavanagh flashed her a grin, as warm and wide as hers was taut.

She beat a swift retreat inside.

The cicadas serenaded a fat moon by the time the group bid each other reluctant good nights. Carmela stood in the shadows of a cork oak beyond the house, scraping food off the plates and into a trough for the pigs. She looked up as her father and Peppe creaked the gate shut. The lieutenant strolled to his jeep, jacket swung over his shoulder, a satisfied sway to his walk.

She watched his taillights zigzag into the blackness of the hills.

CHAPTER 3

The long windowpanes of Yolanda's dressmaking studio reached up to fresco ceilings,
but its clouds were cracked, and the sanguine *putti* — happy harp-playing angels —
now had several bare plaster patches where
rosy cheeks once grinned or chubby thighs
bent into flying arabesques. The business
took up the entire third floor of Palazzo
Grixoni. The building ran almost the length
of the narrow street, Via Santa Lucia, a
brutal incline from the main Piazza Cantareddu ending at Fontana Grixoni. This
marked the center of town. From here, Simius sprawled up and around like a funnel.
The icy mountain water gushed out of the
marble lions' mouths, ensuring Simiuns had
access to fresh water, unlike some of the
neighboring villages. Its Victorian black-
and-white marble base, topped with busts
of the Grixoni family, who had commis-
sioned it, flanked Palazzo Grixoni. In the

halcyon days of the mid-nineteenth century, when the valley had been christened with the proud title of *Logudoro,* land of gold, Palazzo Grixoni had been home to the wealthy merchant family of the same name. Now, as Simius blew away the ashes of war, buildings like these had been divided and rented out as separate quarters.

Carmela sat at her worktop by the farthest window from the entrance and lifted her eyes from her stitching. Her gaze drifted out toward the fountain. She watched the women below as they swayed, balancing long, terra-cotta jugs upon their heads filled from the flowing faucets. Yolanda insisted on keeping the shutters closed against the heat, especially at this time of the morning, but today there was intricate work to be finished and the girls worked better in natural light. Besides, any money she might save on electricity would result in increased profits.

Carmela unpicked her stitching for the third time. Yolanda walked over to her. "You feeling all right, Carme'?" she asked, leaning on the worn wood of the worktop.

"Yes, of course."

"Look at me, *tesoro.*" Yolanda lifted Carmela's chin with a gentle hand. "You're distracted today, my darling. Your skin is

69

almost white." As Carmela's godmother, Yolanda reserved this tone for her alone; all the other girls worked in fear of her biting tongue and fierce intolerance for careless mistakes. This was the place every woman with taste traveled to from along the entire coast. Sometimes customers even came up from as far as the capital city Cagliari, half a day away on the south of the island. Carmela's deft hand and incisive eye for cut and current trends owed much to the business's success.

"Your London lady from the villa has made an appointment for today," Yolanda said, trying to appear relaxed. "I need you to be at your best."

Carmela, of course, was aware that her godmother had a feral sixth sense for when her thoughts were drifting. In truth, she hadn't been able to concentrate since Piera told her that posters announcing her official engagement to Franco were plastered on the walls of the houses by the cathedral. She'd spent most of the morning trying, and failing, to contain her excitement over the fact that her name was in large black letters for all to see, only steps from here. At the same time, Carmela knew how important Mrs. Curwin's appointment could be. The wealthy family from London would pay double that of the locals. Mrs. Curwin bought most of her attire from the dressmakers of New Bond Street, central London, a place she described with broad brushstrokes but that remained a misty picture of a faraway land in Carmela's mind.

Yolanda rallied. "Do your magic and she may order an entire wardrobe. Good news for this young woman who'll be standing in my shoes one day, no?" Yolanda reached into the leather pouch hanging from her belt, beside her coiled tape measure, and pulled out three coins. "Take these lire and buy yourself a *spremuta* at Bar Svizzero. Tell Antonio to give you magnesia too, yes? Then come back looking like the Carmela with the bright eyes and fast hands."

She was more than ready to heed her advice. Her legs ached to race her down the street and take a swift glance at her temporal fame. The dry heat, toasting the cobbles outside, beckoned. She looked up at the sharp face of her godmother. It was crease free despite her fifty years, with feline eyes that rose ever so slightly up toward her temples, imbuing her with a permanent air of sage curiosity. Carmela struggled to picture herself even half as shrewd. The studio's success lay in the perfect balance between Carmela's artistry and her god-

mother's quick head for figures and unfal-
tering leadership. Over the past few months
Yolanda mentioned Carmela's inheritance
of the business more than usual. It filled
Carmela with a rush of excitement and
ideas, but if she was destined to take over
one day, how would she summon the steel
to captain all these seamstress girls, so
happy to smile to your face, then sending
daggers at you from behind closed doors?
She reached up for Yolanda's coins, thanked
her, and left the room, knowing the kind-
ness did not go unnoticed by the other
young seamstresses.

Carmela wound down the darkened staircase. Suffused light shafted through, in
ornate patterns, from the decorative metal
grate above the main double doors. Behind
the wooden banister, the paint looked as if
it had been dragged downward by a powerful force, streaking the wall where it had
clawed to try to remain attached. Her
footsteps echoed off the marble steps. They
were wide enough to show off the dazzling
ball gowns of the original owners, not the
worn shoes of a seamstress.

The white sun beyond the heavy door
blinded her.

"Congratulations, Carme'!" a woman
called down to her from the fountain. "Just

72

read about the soon-to-be-newlyweds in the piazza. Not every day you get your name posted on the wall, you know!"

"Thank you! I'm going to see it now!" Her voice bubbled like an overexcited adolescent.

"It's next to Ignazia Cau's death notice," another chimed, hoisting a jug up onto her head. "God rest her soul. . . ."

The women muttered a blessing and set off in opposite directions. Carmela stood and listened to the water as if the sound itself might cool her down, but she knew that even the unforgiving ice of February would not have that effect on a special day like today.

The pitter-patter feet of her youngest sister, Vittoria, drew Carmela round.

"Aren't we in a hurry?" Carmela called out to her.

"Nonna made me say the rosary twice!" Vittoria said without slowing her trot. "She's angry because Zia Rosa is late home. And now I'm late for the sisters!" Her candlestick legs propelled her downhill. With a quick turn she disappeared into a narrow *viccolo* that led to the back entrance of the cathedral, where the summer session of the children's church group was held. Vittoria had been in the Cherubs for several years. Last night, as Carmela had tucked her into the bed Vittoria shared with Gianetta, she had, with much exhilaration, relayed that the nuns had finally graduated her to the Angel's class. Then, Vittoria had carried on, without pausing for breath or punctuation, that if her dream to become as good a seamstress as Carmela failed, she would follow her second calling to the convent.

Carmela watched Vittoria's dress flap as she ran and made a mental note to add a trim from some of the off cuts back at Yolanda's. A flamboyant woman from the next town had ordered an elaborate floral pattern for a light overcoat. Carmela could patch together the scraps and make her sister the happiest ten-year-old on the street.

Carmela continued on down to Piazza Cantareddu, passing a slew of *tzilleri.* The pungent smell of damp barrels and wine-stained stone floors wafted out from those darkened cantinas, while outside men stood around sniffing their *ridotto* glasses, arguing over everything and nothing. A voice called out to her.

"There's my bride!" Franco swung in beside her.

"What are you doing here?"

"I can think of a nicer way to greet your

fiancé — only we don't want to shock these old men."

"Sorry, I've only got a little while —"

"We made the wall, Carmela. You should walk around town like you own it. Which you will, in a few months."

He took both her hands in his and turned her to face him. "Not so bad for a farm girl, no?"

Her mind flitted to the stack of embroidery to complete at the studio. His phrase grated. He used it often, and always as an expression of endearment; after all, their first tentative trysts were under the cover of her father's vineyard. There was no shame in being a farm girl. That very earth had borne their love, in every sense. Carmela and Franco were grafted together there, twisting around each other like new vines. She looked into him. The sun shone into the darkness of his eyes, picking out the hidden chestnut flecks, invisible in all light but that of the blinding midmorning beams. He took her elbow and drew her over toward one of the upturned barrels, where several men she didn't recognize stood, sipping wine.

"This is my fiancée, Carmela."

She nodded. From the look of their shirts, Carmela hazarded a guess they were men of some influence.

"These signori are here from the council in Tula. I'm showing them our sights."

Carmela flashed Franco a quizzical look. Why would men from a town thirty kilometers away be in Simius for sightseeing?

"You are welcome to use Carmela's English however you see fit, gentlemen." Franco's face unfolded into one of his winning smiles, which few people could resist.

"Yes, Signorina," the oldest of the three men said, his cheeks red with sun and wine, "your fiancé has promised us that you can be our interpreter in future meetings between us and the *Americani*."

Carmela tried to rein in her confused frown before it creased her forehead, and failed. Franco never cared about her English. To him it seemed little more than a puzzling pastime. Now he was peddling her basic knowledge of it?

"We've heard they're about to start looking for land," a second man, shorter and rounder than his colleagues, piped in. "They've got some rockets they want to shoot up into the sky. My cousin's son works at the base sometimes. People are talking. They're going to fly planes and play war games. Plenty of dollars to give us landowners in return."

Carmela opened her mouth, hoping something half intelligent might come out, but before she could speak, the last man, the silent of the three, wrapped his fingers around the plate loaded with cubed cheese and sliced smoked lard. He lifted it and offered it to her. A lazy fly heaved itself off the side of one of the rinds and landed on his knuckle, long enough for Carmela to note the black under his nail.

"Thank you, gentlemen, it all sounds very interesting, but if you'll excuse me, I've been sent on an errand to Bar Svizzero for my godmother, and I really ought to get along."

"Piacere," the first man said, holding out his thick hand. Carmela shook it, out of courtesy, wishing she didn't feel that it bound her to him in some way. Then she turned to Franco and kissed each cheek. His eyes drifted past her on the second kiss. She had disappointed him. These men must be more powerful than she had guessed. It would have been polite to partake in some food at least. A sweaty piece of cheese or a tiny nibble of greasy lard wouldn't have been such a great sacrifice in order to place Franco in a favorable light.

Bar Svizzero became a welcome oasis on the other side of the piazza. Carmela headed straight for it — the poster would have to wait till after work. A couple of ladies eating dainty balls of gelato out of glass cups looked up and gave her a polite nod, then readjusted their hats. She smiled back, having the vague sense they had been into Yolanda's several times for small alterations. What must it be like to have the biggest choices in your day be which hat to wear or whether to try the local honeyed nougat or toasted hazelnut gelato?

Franco was holding court at Bar Nazionale, where men played cards and smoked. He felt most comfortable doing his business there. Bar Svizzero, in contrast, prided itself on attracting the wealthier female clientele — wives of traveling merchants, landowners, or fallen aristocrats with Savoyard money left over from the days when Sardinia was its own kingdom. The owner, Antonio, had once spent a summer in Switzerland with a distant aunt. On his return he had changed his bar's name, ordered an ornate counter from Turin, and doubled his profits. The valley wasn't called *Logudoro* for nothing, after all.

"*Buon giorno,* Carme'." Antonio smiled as Carmela entered the cool of his bar. The low vaulted ceilings gave the impression the room had been chiseled into the rock.

"Caffè?" he offered. His crisp white jacket was spot free even though he was the only one manning his barely tamed, highly polished chrome espresso machine.

"No, Anto', I'll take a *spremuta, per piacere.* And some magnesia."

"Wedding jitters already?"

Carmela smirked. He was almost convinced.

"My sister was the same," he said, reaching for three lemons from the basket on top of the empty glass display cabinet where Antonio kept the fresh breakfast pastries. The scent of vanilla sugar still powdered the air, alongside the toasted nutty caramel from the morning's roaring espresso trade.

"Lost ten kilos before the big day," he said.

"She was a beautiful bride, Antonio."

"Thanks to you. No one else could have made her look half her width and twice her height!" He sliced the fruit in half on a pristine marble chopping board and twisted the lemons on a glass juicer. "Mother was lucky to get her married off when she did."

The fresh smell of citrus had the desired effect.

"There you are, Signorina." He poured the juice into a flute, then stirred two generous spoonfuls of sugar into it with a long, slim metal spoon, and finally topped it with sparkling water and a tiny spiral of rind. "I'll run next door for some more magnesia. I'm clean out." With that he parted the bead curtain. Carmela watched them tip-tap to stillness.

She took a sip of *spremuta* and her tongue tingled sour and sweet. She emptied the flute and glanced over the rainbow of cordials behind the counter. Their labels fascinated her, intricate works of art, embellished in gold, with elaborate, decorative lettering. All that pomp and polish for alcohol. It was beautiful, maybe a little frivolous? Across the piazza, men were pouring wine out of plain green bottles. Would her father's gruff concoctions taste better if they were decanted into one of these bottles?

From where she sat, she could just about see Franco's tiny head through Antonio's delicate lace curtains. She watched him holding court. She and her fiancé existed in different, yet parallel, worlds. What of it? This was a good thing. A strong couple was not a marriage of similarities. Would she have wanted Franco to sit by her and admire Antonio's collection of liquor? Discuss her morning or Mrs. Curwin's appointment later that day? Did he wish Carmela had stayed by his side for the rest of that meeting with those three shirts? Even though the answer to all of the questions starting to swirl in her mind was a resounding no, Carmela took more than a moment to shake off the brief wave of uncertainty that swelled. She berated herself for letting a careless faux pas affect her longer than necessary. She watched Franco reach out his hands to the men. He looked happy, as did they. What harm she thought she may have done was already forgotten. Her etiquette was not going to clinch or lose a deal after all. There was comfort in that, at least. And plenty of time to hone the art of being a wife to one of the most influential men in town.

Dressing the many women who came through Yolanda's doors was the exaltation of God-given gifts. To some, it was deemed simple, sinful vanity. But to Carmela, the presentation of anything revealed the respect a person had for it. A dirty plate with cheese and lard slapped on in haste offered less physical and spiritual nourishment than a simple basket laid with a few homemade bread knots upon a starched square of linen. One revealed and revered the time and effort of preparation, where the other displayed a scant respect. A perfectly cut skirt, suit, or wedding gown exulted the wearer and gave permission for the onlooker to feel uplifted too. There had to be power and purpose in beauty. Why else was the earth strewn with breathtaking sights? What could be the purpose of the penetrating azure of her island's sea, the fire red of May's poppies, the intoxicating fuchsia of a prickly pear's fruit, if not to exhilarate a soul?

Antonio prided himself on importing obscure concoctions from far corners of the continent, especially Paris. Though so far, by the look of the unopened bottle, no one in Simius had acquired a taste for violet liqueur. Did Antonio's love of all things foreign reveal a worldly attitude? His curiosity about life beyond the parameters of their small town was something she respected. No one gossiped about the fact that he still lived with his mother. If he had been a woman, he would have been labeled a spinster, an unwanted, an unlovable. But as a man in his early forties, he had simply earned a mixture of respect and pity from his peers, having sacrificed his own life to take care of his mamma.

At the end of the counter was a copy of *Vogue* that Antonio kept on display. He said it attracted the ladies who had an eye for fashion and the purse to match. Some such must have been leafing through it, because it was folded open at a beach spread.

Carmela thought about her grandmother's expression if she imagined any of her grandchildren at the beach dressed in short puffy shorts, pulled in tight at the waist and attached to a bodice that left little to the imagination. The model in the shoot played with a multi-colored paper balloon that floated just beyond the tips of her fingers. Carmela was moved by the buoyancy of the moment that the photographer captured.

She picked up the magazine and turned its pages, convincing herself it was preparation for Mrs. Curwin's appointment, even though no doubt she would arrive, as always, with a small shipment of dog-eared magazines to show the outfits she adored. Carmela would then work out accurate patterns from sight and match them to Mrs. Curwin's measurements, re-creating the designs of the fashionistas with ease.

Audrey Hepburn looked out at her on the page, sitting on one hip on a studio floor, a mass of layered tulle cascading about her. Carmela took in the pure embodiment of effortless grace, a modern-day princess. Her heart ached; she spent hours re-creating such things for others, but she knew there would be few occasions for her to do anything close to it for herself. Besides, the generous curves of her silhouette were a world away from the elfin figure in the magazine. Sometimes she'd imagine herself at a fitting. She'd picture the dressmaker, dreaming up ways to taper her wide shoulders, her athletic arms — which she always wished were more like her mother's than her father's — and how to divert the eye to her narrow waist instead. Franco and his family were one of the wealthiest in town, but they cared little for the frivolity of parties or unnecessary expense. After all, Franco would preach, one didn't accumulate wealth by spending it, like a peasant. It was a patter that accompanied their Sunday promenades, after mass, when she, Franco, and the rest of the town's younger generation would congregate in Piazza Cantareddu and admire the elaborate window displays of the closed boutiques that lined it.

Flipping the magazine cover shut, she pushed it back over to its place. The model on the cover puckered her red lips into an expression of faux surprise. Her hair flew in the wind, beyond her was the sea, and in her hand she held a camera.

Perhaps Franco would be open to considering a honeymoon after all? Somewhere on the island where no one from Simius would know them. Somewhere Carmela might slip into a skimpy bathing suit to feel the wind caress her bare stomach, hair twirling a wild dance on the breeze, and not a soul around to remind her it was not the done thing of any respectable Sardinian woman. A part of the coast where only chic Parisians, classy Florentines, or royal Spaniards would strut for the summer, with little regard for propriety, their heads full of poems and sultry cigarettes. Perhaps Franco would swim with her, trace down her neck with his warm lips as the poppy red sun dipped into the pink water.

Antonio flung the bead curtain open before she could indulge herself further.

"She changes prices on a whim," he moaned. The grocer next door was a distant cousin of his. Her narrow shelves ached with card boxes of pasta and vats of olive oil. Although she had barely enough room to fit more than three customers at a time, she made ends meet in part, Antonio would insist, by not offering significant discounts to her neighbors. "She's still bitter about my father breaking his engagement with her, is all," he said, opening up the large jar of milk of magnesia with a pop. The coy maid on the label flashed a saccharin smile.

Antonio took a teaspoon and ladled a generous helping of the white granules into a tumbler, then lifted the beaded linen doily off a ceramic jug on the counter and poured water from it. Carmela watched it fizz together, transfixed for a moment by the bubbles racing up to the surface.

"Take a good siesta this afternoon. If I was your mother, I'd be worried." He smirked, half joking.

"Of course you would," she said, taking a gulp. "Here, keep the change."

"Someone's on the road to partnership, then?"

"Just trying to thread needles straight."

The sound of laughter blasted in from outside, followed by a group of soldiers bursting into the small bar, filling the space with uniforms. Antonio grew an inch taller and began his well-rehearsed patter. With little convincing they ordered a dozen *caffè corretto,* espresso spiked with *aqua vitae.* Carmela thought it strange that they would be drinking at this time of the day, and in uniform. Perhaps the addition of coffee to the liquor made it somehow permissible. There was an excited jitter about the men, as if they had little time for a big celebration. Antonio was a tornado, powering out the large order from his beloved coffee machine that whooshed into production.

The beads swayed again and another officer walked in, to deafening cheers.

"To be sure, sir," one man shouted out, "back in my family's Ireland, we'd be wetting the baby's head with Guinness, not coffee!"

The pack laughed.

"Three cheers for Mr. and Mrs. Lieutenant K!" another called out.

Carmela's ears pricked.

Her eyes darted to the gilt mirror in front of her, but she couldn't make out any of their faces; the bottles were stacked too high. As their bellows vibrated Antonio's little cave, Carmela took a snatched glance over to the crew. The corporals looked young. She saw them take turns patting an officer on the back. He laughed with them, relaxing into the celebration but still keeping rank. Then he was ushered into the middle of a circle they formed around him. The men clinked their tiny cups of creamy espresso, topped with enough hot water to make it palatable to the American clientele but pungent with Antonio's generous shot of alcohol.

She didn't need to see his face to know who it was, because the voice gave it away. When he turned around toward the bar, she caught a flash of his aqua-blue eyes and felt a short, sharp twinge of vanity — a brief wish to have spent a little more care on her appearance that morning. She silenced the sudden hurricane of jumbled thoughts with one swift, polite smile. He returned the pleasantry, but Carmela wasn't convinced it was a new father's joy she read in his eyes.

She twisted back round to Antonio, but he was thick in the onslaught of more orders, pulling another round of shots, delighted for the profitable morning. She slid off her stool and flew out of the bar, wind on her heels.

CHAPTER 4

Mrs. Curwin swished into Yolanda's studio, sparkling with the same charisma with which she shimmered at the center of her parties. Carmela had no memory of Mrs. Curwin ever waltzing into rooms, conversations, or relationships, without the kind of ease and grace most could never aspire to, let alone achieve. This British lady of the house made no secret of the fact she had been raised among the poor of London's East End Jewish immigrant community. She often reminisced about those early days, without feigned nostalgia, rather to express a deep appreciation for her new position. Carmela loved the way Mrs. Curwin neither succumbed to a maniacal fear of losing her riches nor flaunted it, as others from similar backgrounds did. She enjoyed her wealth with neither guilt nor condescension, but with respect for the husband who had accumulated it from his hanger factories that supplied most of London. She was married to a man she adored and bore him two boys with ease. To Carmela, it seemed that her life was but a dance.

Yolanda rose from the fabric desk and cut across the room in one smooth, direct motion, like a sharp scissor blade slicing material. She offered a warm handshake. "*Piacere,* Signora Curwin, *sono* Yolanda."

"*Piacere,* darling," Mrs. Curwin replied, extending her hand. "I insist you call me Suzie."

Yolanda smiled, trying to follow.

"Signora asks you to call her Suzie," Carmela translated, moving toward them from her table on the other side of the room.

"Yes, do talk for me, Carmela," Mrs. Curwin added. "My Italian is worse than I think!" She waved her hands in the air with a giggle. "Carmela, darling, be a love and take my hat, will you? You have that wonderful look of fresh air about you today — even more than usual."

Carmela smiled and hung the red, wide-rimmed hat on the stand by the fitting area. The space was separated from the seamstresses' stations by three full-length mirrors framing a small square rug. Across the width hung a rail with a heavy navy velvet curtain ruched to one side, held together with a plaited cord. Mrs. Curwin glided toward the three mirrors, opened her pocketbook, and powdered her nose. "It's positively sweltering out there!"

While Yolanda and Carmela stood a polite distance away, waiting for her to finish, Carmela scrutinized Mrs. Curwin's dress. The front bodice was cut on the bias and gathered at the upper edge to a yoke emphasizing her tiny waist. The extended shoulder seams formed cap sleeves in a deeper shade of red cotton. The full skirt was gathered at either side of the front waistline. It was the perfect summer dress — cool, alluring, and elegant.

She turned back to face them, her cheeks flushed with excitement. "I'm throwing a party next week, and nothing I've brought from London seems appropriate — too formal, too black tie. I'm looking for something light but suitable for evening. Decadent but understated. I know dear Carmela has magic hands — and eyes that cast spells." She flashed Carmela a twinkling smile. "If your sewing creations are half as good as the lamb and fennel you made for lunch the other day, my dear, I'll be belle of the ball!"

Mrs. Curwin reached into her woven bag and pulled out some magazines. "Let me show you what I'm thinking."

"*Caffè,* Signora?" Yolanda asked.

"*Sì,*" she replied, like a child in a *pasticce- ria. "Latte poco, grazie.*"

"*Macchiato,*" Carmela explained to her godmother.

Yolanda replied with a smile. Carmela could tell she was trying not to appear too desperate.

Carmela pulled over a high-backed chair for Mrs. Curwin and sat on a small wooden stool beside her. Several pages of her magazines were dog-eared. "Now, Carmela, I adore this halter neck," she said, flicking past the first few pages and pointing to a model on a Parisian street, "and doesn't every woman feel irresistible in a pencil skirt? But I'm not sure I like the way they work together in this dress here, do you?"

"We can do anything, Signora."

"A delicious dilemma!" She laughed, leafing through to the next dog-ear. "You see, I adore the off-the-shoulder —"

"Signora, *ecco il caffè,*" Yolanda said, arriving with a wooden tray with the two-cup coffeepot she had set to rise just ahead of the appointment. She placed it on a low, wooden stool beside them. Carmela noticed that Yolanda used her best espresso cups, white bone china with fine, gold-painted trim. Yolanda placed one cup and saucer in the center of a square of embroidered linen and poured coffee into it from the metal pot. To this she added warm milk from a china jug. An oval plate lay beside it, painted with bright pictures of traditional Sardinian dancers, topped with fresh pastries from the *pasticceria* down the lane; *copulette* — paper-thin pastry cases filled with sweet almond paste, topped with smooth, white icing that looked like small diamonds of virgin snow. Alongside lay *tiricche* — pastry cut with delicate scalloped edges, filled with fig jam and rolled into horseshoes. Carmela breathed in their fruity sweetness as she lifted the plate to Mrs. Curwin.

"Darling, how could I possibly refuse?" she said, reaching out a manicured hand for a *copulette*. Carmela noticed how the girls at the nearest stations eyed Mrs. Curwin. None of them ate sweets in the daytime. They were strictly for weddings or fiestas, not morning breaks.

Mrs. Curwin took delicate bites with relish, careful not to spill any of the crumbling icing. Then she stirred some sugar from a ceramic caddy into the tiny cup. "Why, oh why, are the streets of London not lined with espresso bars?" She took a sip and moaned with pleasure. "I'll talk to Marito about it. Soho would be the place, of that I'm certain."

Since the Curwins' first visit to Sardinia five years ago, Mrs. Curwin had stolen sporadic words from Italian and peppered her English with them. She now referred to Mr. Curwin as Marito, Italian for husband. "If I could convince Marito to open the first one, I could bring a little bit of Sardinian paradise to the London drizzle — but only if you'll come and prepare the sweets, Carmela! We'd have all those fashionable city boys queueing up to gawp at you besides."

Carmela smiled, flattered — the creamy, marsala-spiked *zabaglione* she made for the family last night had not gone unappreciated. Then she thought about Piera, at this moment likely returning from the market in the unforgiving heat, loaded with produce to prepare the Curwins' dinner.

Over the next hour Mrs. Curwin showed Carmela several other magazine spreads. Carmela took her sketchpad and a length of charcoal from the drawer underneath her desk and returned to the fitting area to begin a quick outline of some initial ideas. Her hand skimmed over the page at great speed. The other seamstresses began to tidy their stations for their three-hour lunch break. Carmela could feel them glancing over her shoulder at her sketch as they passed on their way out.

She began with the outline of a pencil skirt but added some extra bounce just below the waist. A bodice rose up above it. The neckline was off the shoulder. Two sweeping curves overlaid one another to form a heart shape by the collar bone and extended slightly wider than the arms. The border was accentuated with a lighter fabric. On the side of the waist she drew a jeweled clasp. It was dramatic and imaginative. Exactly what Mrs. Curwin had hoped for.

"I love it, darling!" she said. "Those sharp lines are stunning, coupled with the softness over the décolletage. It's just beautiful. Yolanda!" she called, leaning toward her with a conspiratorial twinkle. "If I were you I would tell you to offer her partnership in a heartbeat — only make sure she keeps her summers free to carry on feeding my family to distraction!"

"What does she say?" Yolanda asked Carmela, barely masking her panic.

"She likes it."

Carmela walked along the only road out of town that led to the Curwins' rented summer villa. Huddles of houses gave way to parched countryside. The town's hills were dipped in the rusty hue of the fading sun, rising and falling in crags down toward the crystalline coast. Wild fennel sprouted in tufts along the side of the dusty, white road. Carmela yanked at one of them and chewed it; the refreshing taste of anise cooled the inside of her cheek.

The road was punctuated with grand Victorian villas. Their porticos rose above Corinthian columns, with verandas wrapped around the width of the houses. High arched windows were framed with granite cornices and hung with heavy, dark green shutters. Several were now rented out to inquisitive tourists like the Curwins, who paid handsomely for their month stay and appeared to take pleasure in the faded majesty. The families who owned them were descendants of the island's aristocrats. They took responsibility for arranging local staff to undertake all domestic duties.

The Curwins' villa belonged to Franco's uncle, one of the reasons Carmela and Piera could rely on being hired each year. Domestic work was seen as the mainstay of orphans or immigrants, but working for the British held a certain cachet. The positions were sought and fought over.

Carmela turned to the driveway and

walked through the tall iron gates. She passed a fountain carved into the rock, which trickled with water from an underground spring. Beside it, wide lily pads floated upon the green surface of a pond. On the opposite side, a small stone chapel stood, where the original owners attended private masses, joined by neighboring families so as to avoid the necessity of traveling into town and mixing with folks of lower class. The four rows of pews were polished weekly, but outside, ivy threatened a coup and the wrought iron cross rising from the tiny steeple was fighting a losing battle against the elements.

Carmela carried on past the high, wooden double doors of the entrance, terra-cotta pots of blooming geraniums lining the side of the house, and reached the side door of the kitchen. Piera had her hands deep in preparations for dinner. Carmela was greeted with an earthy whiff of sautéed garlic with warm spinach wilting in a skillet upon the stove.

"Nice of you to stop by," Piera huffed, grating a snowfall of nutmeg into the pan.

"I'm sorry, I was cutting patterns. Mrs. Curwin came in today. She loved my design."

"Wonderful. Now work some magic here,

please." Piera moved to the floured surface of the marble counter; picked up a long, wooden rolling pin; and began thinning a sheet of pasta dough. "Sauce won't cook itself, you know."

Carmela washed her hands under the iron faucet of the large ceramic sink. An enamel bowl next to the stove was already filled with tiny cubes of carrots, celery, and onion. Carmela placed another skillet on the stove top, drizzled some dark green olive oil into it, and lit the gas ring. She peeled the clove of garlic that Piera had left beside the bowl, crushed it with one quick blow of a knife, and placed it into the warming oil to infuse. Beside Piera, a metal crusher clamped onto the worktop had a large bowl of fresh tomatoes beside it, pulped into *passata*. Carmela cranked the handle a few more times to squeeze the final tomatoes into the bowl.

"Daydreaming again?" Piera piped. "Or do you like burned garlic?"

Carmela snatched the skillet off the flame and poured in the diced vegetables, trying to brush away the pique of irritation. She took a deeper breath. Their aroma was sweet and earthy, unchanged from her earliest memories of dancing around the hem of her mother's apron. Others found peace in the chilled silence of church. For Carmela, it was in the kitchen. The excitement of today, the short-tempered mood of her sister, would give way to an inner peace. To prepare a meal with success required the cook to devote her complete attention to it — mental, physical, and emotional. It was a well-known fact among the Simiuns that an angry, distracted, or lazy cook produced only bitter food.

The sisters' culinary duet was well oiled. If Carmela was a little late, though, like today, it took a few dishes before Piera would settle back into their combined rhythm.

"Hard day?" Carmela asked, stirring the *trittata* so that the olive oil glazed all the small pieces evenly.

"While you were dreaming up dresses, I had to shunt in and out of town like a donkey. Nonna was on fire all day."

"I heard. Vittoria came running past the studio today, flapping like she'd been stung."

"When Zia Rosa finally got home, she bossed me around like a slave. Never been happier to get to work, I tell you."

They slipped into a familiar silence. Carmela let the vegetables soften before adding the tomatoes. She sprinkled a small spoonful of sugar over them, a pinch of *saporita* — a blend of nutmeg, paprika, and cumin — and then reduced the heat to let the sauce thicken.

"You know that woman from Pattada came again the other day," Carmela began. "There are some off cuts enough for me to make you a new summer dress."

Piera pummeled the dough as if it were an old enemy. "Pass me the spinach."

Carmela grabbed the woolen potholders and lifted the skillet off the stove, then picked up another chopping board — a slice of an olive tree trunk — and placed it underneath. Before Piera could ask her, she moved to the wooden icebox and grabbed a slab of salted ricotta. She sliced a generous amount and crumbled it into the warm spinach. Then she threw a pinch of salt and ground some pepper into the mixture. With two teaspoons she carefully cupped small balls of green and placed them at even spaces along the rolled-out dough.

"I look ridiculous in those dresses — like a boy in a skirt."

"Not when I make them, you don't. Smells delicious, Piera," Carmela said.

Piera lifted the second pasta dough sheet and laid it like a blanket over the balls of spinach and ricotta.

"Here." Carmela took the wooden wheel out of Piera's hand. "I'll finish. You won't cut straight if you're thinking about Nonna." She rolled the serrated wheel along the length of the pasta and then along the widths, cutting out perfect parcels of ravioli. Then she dusted them with flour and placed them on a tray.

"Did you see your poster?" Piera asked, brightening at last.

"Almost," Carmela replied, wishing the image of that tired plate of cheese and lard didn't flash in her mind, or the coolness in Franco's eyes as they kissed good-bye. "We didn't stop for lunch today."

"It's nearly six," Piera said, brushing down her apron. "You know they eat early."

Carmela never paid much mind to the usual time Simiuns ate their dinner before she worked for the Curwins. Few were the Simiun families who dined before nine o'clock, and it certainly would not include pasta. At home, Carmela and her siblings would be lucky to get more than a cup of warm milk and bread. Feasting at night was deemed gluttonous excess, particularly in their household, an indulgence reserved for special occasions only, like Christmas Eve.

Carmela lifted the loaded tray to the stove and gently dropped each parcel into a deep pan of boiling water. The ravioli bobbed as if reluctant swimmers gasping for air.

"Ladies, that smells absolutely divine!" Mrs. Curwin said as she sashayed into the kitchen wearing a two-piece swimsuit in a tropical flower print, a halter-neck bikini top, and tight shorts to match. An oversize white linen shirt hung over her bronzed shoulders. "I've been taking in the last rays on the back terrace. It's glorious at this time."

She reached into the icebox and removed a jug of water with sliced lemons floating inside. She poured herself a drink. "I think we'll eat out there this evening, Signorine."

"Of course, Signora," Carmela answered, as Mrs. Curwin floated out of the room to change for dinner.

Piera scooped the ravioli out of the pan. She layered them gently on a wide, flat dish, spooning sauce in between as she went. When all the pasta was on the dish, she grated a generous amount of *pecorino* over the top. It oozed into the hot sauce. Before she placed the cheese back into the icebox, she pulled off a tiny hunk to nibble.

"I saw that," Carmela said.

Piera grinned.

The sisters filled another bowl with paper-thin slices from a fresh fennel bulb and narrow wedges of orange. They squeezed the remaining juice from the inside of the orange peels into the bowl and sprinkled salt and freshly ground pepper over the top. With a generous splash of olive oil, the salad was complete. They tore some *pane fino* and placed it in a basket, then topped it with a few sheets of *pane carusau,* thin sheets of crisp bread they had warmed in the oven and drizzled with olive oil, a little salt, and some fresh rosemary. A carafe was filled with their father's wine. They laid two large, wooden trays with all the dishes and carried everything outside.

The terrace at the back of the villa was paved with large terra-cotta tiles, framed with a delicate marine mosaic of waves and fishes. Overhead, passiflora and clematis wove a thick, fragrant canopy. Piera and Carmela took out a linen tablecloth, four plates, and four heavy green glasses from the wooden sideboard that stood against the wall of the house and laid the table with them. On each plate they positioned a rolled linen napkin wrapped around a knife, spoon, and fork. A thin bottle of dark green olive oil, a small pot of grated *pecorino,* and a pepper mill were placed in the center of the table, along with all the plates of food and breads. On top of the sideboard was a basket of velveteen peaches and purple-green plums, for after dinner.

Mr. Curwin came out first, holding a glass of cold, white *vermentino,* a book tucked under his arm. "*Buona sera,* ladies, this looks wonderful." He pulled his linen trousers up an inch as he took his seat and then he straightened his collar. His skin was not as bronzed as his wife's. Mr. Curwin preferred the cool of the shade in which to read historical accounts or biographies to the dazzling rays in which his wife and children basked. His eyes were small and light brown, bright with an intelligence he reserved for well-timed, dry quips. The boys raced up from the back of the garden, where they had been playing around the lemon and fig trees, and hopped into their respective seats.

"Hands, boys," Mr. Curwin said. They marched inside.

Mrs. Curwin made her entrance in a simple, yellow cotton crossover dress that was tied in a bow at the back. It showed off her sun-kissed skin. A cluster of citrine sparkled in each ear. "How we will ever go back to English food escapes me, Marito, really."

"Yes, you remind me every time we come, dear," he replied, reaching forward to snap off a crisp of *pane carusau.*

"Then take my advice and buy these girls plane tickets!" She smiled, half joking.

Carmela imagined Franco's expression if she were to tell him she had packed for a London life. Her mind flew back to the time an uncle had asked her whether she would accompany him on one of his salesman's trips to the south of the island. He had been trying to earn commission on the sale of sewing equipment and told Carmela she would be the best person to demonstrate how good such and such a needle was, and so forth. She remembered sitting on the front step outside the house before daybreak the following morning, clutching a small overnight bag. When the morning sun slit across the violet dawn and he still hadn't shown up, she realized he had been teasing. How foolish she had felt to even think her grandmother would have let her go, or that her uncle would have seriously thought about taking her. What kind of impression would he have made traveling alone with a young, unmarried girl, only sixteen at the time, even if she was his niece? Piera hadn't stopped laughing at her until they fell asleep that night, probably relieved, Carmela had since realized, that her sister hadn't left her alone, forgoing the predictability of a Simius life for the adventure of life on the road.

"Now, ladies, before you go and the night girls take over," Mrs. Curwin said, "have a think about our party, yes?"

"Party?" asked Piera.

"Yes. Next week. Marito has invited about thirty people. Fellows from the base, mostly. The charming captain introduced me to his chief lieutenant — even Marito had to admit he was a darling American —"

"I used that word?"

"Absolutely! He's the most marvelous specimen either of us had clapped eyes on. They're pretty new around here, so they told me — how Americans do love to talk — and we thought we'd give them a proper welcome, if you like."

She lifted her glass, and Mr. Curwin filled it with *vermentino*. "In truth, it's a bit of a belated birthday bash for me, actually. Wear your dancing shoes, won't you, girls? Everyone needs a break sometime!" She raised her glass toward her husband. They drank. Carmela pictured her grandmother watching, agog, as two of her grandchildren left for work in their best shoes.

"We'll talk about the menu over the next few days," Mrs. Curwin continued, running a swift hand through her hair, lifting it higher off her face. "Just thought I ought to mention it now in case you need to order anything special from the salumeria, and so forth."

"Of course, Signora," Carmela answered.

"Suzie, darling, please. Now head on before it's too dark."

Carmela and Piera turned back to the kitchen and laid the skillets to soak in the deep ceramic sink. Two young girls came in to take over for the night shift and exchanged a perfunctory greeting. Piera and Carmela stepped outside and began their winding walk back to Simius in silence, under the canopy of a starlit, purple dusk.

"Ticket to London?" Piera asked after a while, kicking a stone.

"Tickets."

"Franco's always wanted to meet the Queen, no?"

The daydream brought a broad smile to Carmela's face. Considering even the slightest possibility of a life beyond her shores was seductive. She breathed in the cool, scented air of the evening, aromatic with sun-toasted juniper and thyme. In the near distance, the lights of Simius twinkled; beyond it, the cobalt sea. Franco was right, of course; this island was the perfect place for them. Paradise was underfoot. How foolish to even entertain the idea of chasing dreams in London, or Marseilles, or Munich, like many of their contemporaries, running after invisible riches.

The sliver of a moon crept up over the distant hills, jagged silhouettes of the surrounding valley. Carmela thought about the woman playing on the beach in Antonio's magazine. That life was nothing more than a photograph, after all.

CHAPTER 5

Carmela and Piera reached Simius just as their family prepared to sit for dinner. They washed their hands and took their respective places around the long wooden table, a formidable island in a narrow strait.

"Nel nome del padre, e figlio, e spiritu santu," Grandmother Icca intoned from her chair at the head of the table. She crossed herself.

"Amen," Maria and her children echoed.

Carmela looked down at the tiny piece of meat in her bowl. It lay adrift at the center of her bowl, surrounded by a thin red sauce, the reluctant survivor of a shipwreck. All flavor had been simmered away. Wilted runner beans floated about it with a scant helping of potato pieces. Carmela returned to the Curwin villa in her mind, imagining the satisfied couple relaxing on their terrace after their meal, bellies full of fresh ravioli, moon rising to the underscore of cicadas' serenades as they savored their way through the bowl of plump, fresh fruit.

"Admiring your reflection or waiting for the cow to raise from the dead?" Icca asked.

Carmela looked up. It took a moment for her to realize the comment was directed at her. "It's delicious, Nonna."

"It's overdone." Icca switched her gaze to her daughter-in-law, at the opposite end of the table. "Maria, take greater care over my recipes."

"Yes, Nonna," Maria answered in the placid tones she'd mastered to deflect Icca's criticism. Carmela tore some *pane fino* from the small pile on the table.

"Plenty of time to fatten up after you're married," Icca said, reaching out her hand. Carmela knew better than to do anything other than place the entire piece in Icca's hand. The family returned to silence but for the percussive tinkle of their spoons against the enamel bowls.

Vittoria, sitting on the opposite side of the table, had almost devoured her entire helping. It would seem graduation to the Angels had finally given her an appetite. *"Buonissimo, Mamma!"* she squealed, searching for remnants of sauce with a lick of each corner of her mouth. Gianetta, two years Vittoria's senior, sat beside her and had separated each of the vegetables. She chewed every studious mouthful several times, her mane of straight, jet locks motionless, relishing having the family's meat dish in the middle of the week as opposed to Sunday. Tore, Maria's only son, sat on Carmela's left, hunched over his plate under the weight of his adolescent world, brooding over his stockpiled bread beside his glass. No one would rob him of it on account of him being the only boy of the house and apt to need the extra energy to help his father at the farm the following day. Tomas was spending the entire week out at the farm, thus tightening Grandmother's stranglehold. Piera, on Carmela's right, wiped her plate clean with a slipper of *pane fino.*

Carmela glanced over at her mother, enjoying her meal. It was hard to imagine her as the young woman described to her by Lucia, defying her father and marrying Tomas. One day, when they found themselves alone in a snatched moment between chores, Lucia had recounted the tale of Maria's father, how he had warned his daughter that she would cry every day of her life if she went ahead and married a man he did not approve of. Days after the wedding, which only a few of her siblings attended, Maria lost her mother. Carmela imagined a newlywed Maria, honoring her duties as a wife while stepping in to become her siblings' substitute mother. Her mother lifted her eyes from her plate. Carmela watched their chestnut warmth glisten despite the pallid light of the bare bulb overhead.

Icca bore into Carmela. "She gets her faraway from your side of the family, Maria. Spends all her day looking at those magazines with the customers. Fills a girl with foolish ideas. My boys' bones are for working." A tiny spit of bread flew out of her mouth and landed in Carmela's bowl. "This house wasn't built on air."

"I am sorry, Nonna. I'm dreaming up food. Mrs. Curwin plans a party."

"Indeed? The wretches south of here have no shoes and under our noses we fatten up the foreigners."

Maria turned toward her firstborn. "I can see you have little appetite, Carmela — I'm sure Vittoria and Gianetta will be glad for a bit extra. Why not go upstairs to finish your sewing work." She followed her instructions without reply, sliding off her chair and stifling the guilt she felt for her escape. As she climbed the granite stairs to the bedroom she shared with Piera, Icca's voice echoed, "You'll be sorry you raised her with a soft hand, Maria, you mark my words."

■ ■ ■ ■

On Mrs. Curwin's insistence, the driveway to the villa had been lined with glass lanterns. The candlelights flickered in the early evening, leading the guests toward the main doors. Tore stood before them, assuming the role of butler, but summoned up little more than a begrudging half nod to the invitees as they entered.

First to arrive were the Villanova family from Milan, who pounded up the gravel drive like they had a train to catch, noses pointed in the air as if a bad smell followed them. Signor Villanova was the director of a bank back home and was careful to make sure everyone knew it. His wife Gironema, descended from Piedmont aristocracy, had a bouncing gait, emphasizing her short-waisted frame. Her eyes traced over Tore as she approached, then dismissed him like someone looking at a poor imitation of a famous sculpture. They considered themselves intrepid explorers by visiting the undiscovered villages of Sardinia for their summers, though a small army of domestics made sure their rented villa was pristine and all meals were prepared in timely fashion.

"*Buona sera,* darlings!" Mrs. Curwin

exclaimed, throwing her arms high in the air. A drop of her gin and tonic fell onto Signor Villanova's bald patch. "Do come on in, please, I'm so glad you could make it." She placed a welcoming hand on the small of Signora Villanova's back, leading them through the dining room to the terrace.

The Fadda clan followed soon after. They lived year-round in the next villa, but the two daughters' translucent skin revealed a life spent indoors. Their black locks were scraped away from their faces and knotted into a severe bun at the base of their necks. Their dresses were simple, without ostentation, and made of dark cotton that did little to add any form to their bony frames. Signor Fadda waddled close behind, almost a foot shorter than his wife, with the portly belly of a man who had come from poverty and ate his way through his newfound riches.

In the kitchen, Piera and Carmela performed a frantic dance. All the pans were off their hooks on the white stone wall and in use. Piera reached over Carmela, who was laying out thin slices of sausage on the inside of a small length of cork tree bark that formed a natural tray. Piera tasted a small piece of poached calamari steaming in a ceramic serving bowl, adjusted the seasoning, then butchered a handful of parsley and threw it over them. She mixed in a glug of olive oil, a crushed garlic clove, and the juice of half a lemon.

"Antipasti should be out by now!" Piera puffed. "Stay in front of what you're doing and you'll get it done faster."

Carmela was unruffled, not allowing Piera's frenzy to distract her from the care she took over her dish of cold cuts.

"Gianetta! Vittoria!" Piera called. Her sisters dashed into the room.

"Signora Villanova has got a ring the size of my eyeball!" Vittoria exclaimed, pantomiming the woman's strut around the table.

"That's enough," Carmela said. "Take these two trays and offer all the guests. No dropping!"

Vittoria and Gianetta balanced the cork in their hands and gazed down at the load with hungry eyes. They breathed in the salty olive oil of the warmed *pane carusau,* the herbs of the sausage, the pungent cubes of *pecorino,* the paper-thin prosciutto ribbons. It was barely resistible.

"I've saved you both a plate. For later. No fingers."

"*Sì,* Carmela," they replied in unison before turning on their heels for the terrace.

Outside, Mrs. Curwin held court and

poured the drinks. Mr. Curwin engaged in serious conversation with Signor Villanova, over a salad of broken Italian and English. The Curwin boys were the first to accost Vittoria and Gianetta, grabbing handfuls of cheese at such speed that Vittoria nearly dropped her entire tray, before they dashed back out to the darkened fruit trees. The boys were followed by Salvatore, Peppe and Lucia's middle boy, here at the party to be an assistant to his father, in charge of roasting, though no one had pinned the child down since their arrival. He shoved a fistful of salami into his mouth and another into his pockets before he too disappeared toward the brush beyond the garden.

A caravan of lights appeared, snaking round the bend in the near distance.

"The party has arrived!" Mrs. Curwin exclaimed, glancing over to the silhouette of the hills. "Excuse me, everyone." And with that she sauntered to the front door. The dress that Carmela made cinched at Mrs. Curwin's tiny waist and skimmed her hips in a pencil skirt cut to accentuate their toned curve. The smooth bodice drew attention to her bare décolletage with a delicate sweep of heart-shaped trim that extended beyond the shoulder line. She had opted to experiment with a deep purple fabric rather than a traditional black, which Carmela decided added a royal flair to what might have been a more conservative cocktail dress. Mrs. Curwin completed the outfit with purple suede open-toed shoes that rose to her delicate ankles, finished with gold trim and a tapered golden heel on which she perched with effortless balance. Her hair was curled away from her face, drawing attention to her bright green, almond-shaped eyes and the bronzed glow. An amethyst circled by tiny diamonds sparkled in each ear.

When Mrs. Curwin reached Tore, American G.I.s were already crammed into the vaulted lobby like a litter of excitable puppies. Bobbing above their heads was the wide horn of a record player, its base held in the crook of a soldier's arm, while another soldier balanced a heavy card box up on his shoulder, filled with records.

"Welcome, gentlemen!" Mrs. Curwin flashed them a painted smile. "You may help your sisters now, Tore," she said, adding sotto voce, "these are the last of our guests." She wafted back out, leaving the scent of violet in the air. The soldiers followed their pied piper and filled the terrace with noise. The Fadda sisters straightened, gawking at the mass of testosterone. Signora Villanova followed close behind her husband, who took great pains to shake each of their hands. Mr. Curwin was quick to fill glasses for each of the men with a generous measure of sparkling *rosato,* a local, crisp wine with a rose blush. They held them up to the star-dusted sky. "To Sardinian summers!" Mrs. Curwin yelled above the throng. They replied with a bellow and celebratory clinks.

As Mrs. Curwin made a second sweep of the fast-empty glasses, one of the soldiers cleared an area on the sideboard and placed the record player on top of it. Another pulled over a chair on which to rest the box of records. Moments later, as Al Martino sang about his heart into the inky night beyond the blossoming canopy, the soldiers polished off two trays of antipasti and three bottles of *rosato.*

Vittoria and Gianetta entered the kitchen with their empty trays. "There's thousands of them!" Vittoria squealed. "Do you think they have gum?"

" 'Course," Gianetta answered, sober.

Carmela lifted a basket of warm bread. "Vittoria, take this. Gianetta, you'll do the shrimp." Carmela doused the hot skillet with *vernaccia* — an earthy, aged wine — and shook it over the pink shells till the alcohol evaporated and filled the kitchen with garlic- and wine-scented steam. "Tell Signora Curwin that the risotto will be out soon, understand?" And with that she tipped the shrimp into a ceramic dish, sprinkled a handful of parsley over it, and sent the girls out.

"When you've done that, go out and give Zio Peppe some water," Piera called after them. "He's in the garden, by the fire." Gianetta nodded as the girls marched back out.

"Where's Tore, for the love of God?" Piera said, shaking her head, ladling chicken broth over the rice with one hand and stirring it with the other.

He shuffled in. "I'm here."

"Could have fooled me," Piera answered, drizzling another ladle of liquid into the risotto. "Pass me the Parmesan!" She reached out a hand into which he placed an enamel bowl of grated cheese. She grabbed a fistful that became melted ooze in the hot rice. Piera took the pan off the heat and spooned it into a terrine.

"I'll follow Tore with this," Carmela said. "Then I'll let Mr. Curwin know we'll carve the meat soon."

Carmela followed her brother onto the terrace, dodging the dancing couples to reach the table of food at the far end. One soldier grabbed onto the younger of the

Fadda girls, who giggled in spite of herself as he swung her like a dervish. Signora Villanova, thrilled with her dance partner, looked up at the young man, though from the looks of her unsteady jerks she was not the easiest dancer to lead.

Mrs. Curwin glided across the tiles. With the gentlest touch to the small of her back or wrist, her partner sent her swirling in and out of his arms, then back and forth through the crowd. They spun to the center of the terrace, and the guests gathered around and cheered. As the young man jitterbugged with her, she threw her head back with abandoned laughter, never once missing a beat or falling out of sync with him.

"I taught her everything she knows, ladies and gentlemen!" Mr. Curwin shouted over the music, smirking.

"Of course, my darling!" she answered back, beaming, then reached out her hand to him. The two men spun her between them as she basked in the raucous applause of her guests.

Tore returned to the kitchen with the empty trays of antipasti. "They're drunk already."

Piera focused on the steaming dish of cauliflower she spooned into another terrine, catching out of the iron skillet the final pieces of tender olives and tomatoes she had cooked them with. "I don't care if they're dead — just get this out!"

"When do I get to eat?" Tore asked.

"When I say so!" Piera shooed him out with the cauliflower dish in hand.

The bell marked ENTRATA rang in the glass-fronted service box hanging over the door.

Carmela looked up from the radicchio leaves she had just begun to pat dry.

"Hurry," Piera said, "God gave me only two hands."

Carmela took off her apron and placed it on the back of the chair, then smoothed her hair. She flew through the living room, past the ornate rococo settee, the velvet ottoman, and the somber portraits of Franco's uncle's ancestors. Mrs. Curwin's laughter bubbled above the twirling dancers and Perry Como. Carmela caught glimpses of the party through the square holes in the crotchet lace curtains of the living room windows. She tried to imagine how it must feel to be swung around your terrace by young, visiting soldiers while your husband enjoys you from afar.

Reaching the main doors, Carmela turned the fat, gold knob with two hands and heaved them open. The silhouette of a man stood before her, blackened against the candlelit path behind him.

"*Buona sera,* Signore," she said, politely.

"*Buona sera,*" he replied, removing his hat. "I hope I'm not too late."

"You're fashionably late, Lieutenant, that's what you are," Mrs. Curwin cooed as she glided in behind Carmela, flushed with dance and *rosato.* "And handsome as a button." She laughed, breathless. "No dueling for my heart, though, do you hear?"

The lieutenant smiled, bashful.

"Beauty is beauty is beauty," she continued, "to be appreciated at all costs, don't you agree?"

"Yes, ma'am," another man answered, stepping in behind Kavanagh. He was taller, with a strawberry tinge to his blond locks and the beginnings of gray creeping in at his temples. His face was dotted with freckles, which Carmela tried not to stare at. His eyes were closer to slate than the luminous blue of Kavanagh. They raced over Mrs. Curwin's outfit in one swift move.

"Captain Casler, I am honored you could make time to stop by!" Mrs. Curwin said.

"Just trying to do the proper thing for a pair of proper Brits." His face creased into a sharp smile.

"Lieutenant, Captain, this is the inimitable

Carmela."

She felt their eyes on her, followed by the flush of her cheeks.

"Her talents are utterly wasted here," Mrs. Curwin continued. "Look at what she made me!" She twirled, hands on hips, inviting their gaze. "Ought to have her own studio on Fifth Avenue, not Piazza Cantareddu! I want her to come work for me in London, but she's intent on getting married to her dashing childhood sweetheart! A horribly pretty pair. If you are looking for anyone to help you with interpreting work, this is your lady!"

Carmela felt her cheeks turn a deeper shade of plum.

"Shall we?" Mrs. Curwin asked, with a coquettish tilt.

"Yes, ma'am," the captain answered, offering her his arm. The pair left for the terrace, where Mr. Curwin headed toward them with a welcome glass of *rosato*.

"Third time's a charm, right, Carmela?" Kavanagh said.

Carmela looked at him, blank.

Kavanagh cleared his throat. "It's the third time we've been introduced."

Carmela smiled, feeling her head give an involuntary nod instead of words finding their way out. He tipped his head and walked away. She liked the way her name sounded when he said it.

A pound at the door startled her. She opened it.

"Franco!" she gasped. "I thought you weren't getting back to town till tomorrow."

"You never told me there was a party," he said, stubbing out the butt of his cigarette on the gravel. "I got to hear about what my fiancée is doing from strangers?"

"What?"

"That why you're dressed like that?"

Carmela stepped forward and planted a soft kiss on his mouth. It tasted like ash. "Is your uncle coming, too?"

"His house, isn't it? Madame invited us last week. Your little secret, eh?" He reached forward, took her chin in his hands, and ran his tongue over her top lip, then strutted down to the terrace.

Carmela watched him disappear into the throng, then turned back and walked out through the door and along the front of the house. She carried on past the side of the house toward the fragrant herb garden, flanked with the last of the summer's plum tomatoes and bell peppers. Peppe sat by a pile of hot coals placed at the center of a dusty circle, a safe distance from the foliage, turning the spit. His flat cap sat at a jaunty angle, and his tiny wooden stool ached under the weight of him.

"Almost ready?" Carmela asked as she watched him dip a tied bunch of rosemary into a terra-cotta pot of olive oil and run it across the caramelized crackling of the suckling pig.

"Americans come, everyone wants now. Rush life, die quick."

Carmela smiled. Peppe's face was burnt ochre in the glow of the coals, emphasizing the deep creases of his face. They watched the spit turn without talking for a moment, with a cicada chorus in the blackened brush and echoes of laughter rolling up in waves from the terrace.

"Gianetta brought you water?" she asked.

"I wait till Sunday for my wine like a priest?"

She grinned. "Depends. Have you said confession?"

"You grow a mouth on you like Zia Lucia, no one will want to marry you," he answered with a benevolent twinkle. As the first child born to the brothers, it sometimes seemed to Carmela that Peppe was as much her father as his brother Tomas.

"Let me share a glass of the good stuff with my favorite uncle!" Franco yelled, appearing at the kitchen door and sauntering over with a bottle of wine and a couple of glasses.

"There's the vagabond!" Peppe replied. "You'd do best not to travel till she's got that ring on her finger, if you know what's good for you." He chuckled.

"Gonna keep my treasure safe, don't you worry."

Franco's eyes planted on hers. For a fleeting moment, they slit with a passion that Carmela would have liked to describe as love. She was his *treasure*. Had he ever described her this way? Perhaps. So why did her mind claw the word just now? There was so much still to do inside with her sister, as the party was dancing into life. Yet the word pricked, a minuscule spike from a cactus fruit that can't be seen to be removed but sharpens into the skin with even the gentlest brush of fabric. Treasure? Hold on to *precious,* she lied to herself. Treasure: something to keep hidden under lock and key. Something to covet, gaze upon. Own. Carmela had followed Franco into the muddy distance between love and ownership. She had become his possession after all. If he wasn't assured his father's empire, if his brothers would usurp him in the end, then Carmela was the one thing in his world that would belong only to him. She had promised him as much. A mist of quiet doubts fogged her mind. Her gaze lowered toward the fire. She willed her thoughts to whip up into the dark night with the flames.

By the time Carmela returned to the kitchen, Piera was reaching boiling point faster than the pan of linguini. "Russian army at the door, or were you having a cocktail?" she asked, heaving a huge tray of roasted potatoes out of the oven, then lifting up her apron to wipe the sweat off her brow.

Carmela lifted the pasta off the heat and drained the salty water into the sink. The steam blinded her for a moment. "Franco's here."

"I don't see him helping." Picra darted to the large wooden dresser that took up almost half the length of one side of the kitchen. She opened one of the upper glass-paned doors with such ferocity that the lace curtain inside nearly swung off its hook. "Oh, for crying out loud! Tore!"

"Take it easy," Carmela said, trying to smooth her sister's ruffled feathers. "They'll think we can't cope."

Piera stomped back to the other side of the table and reached into the wooden icebox for a small jar filled with *bottarga,* dried fish roe. "We can't! I said three simple courses. But no! You had to turn Mrs.'s ear with a menu fit for a godforsaken royal wedding! Which, in case you didn't know, is not what I like to be sweating over on a hot summer's night!"

Tore entered. "Please bring down that top bowl, Tore," Carmela said, trying to keep her tenuous grip on calm. He reached up, then carried the large bowl over to her. Carmela tipped the linguini into it, covering the hand-painted circle of traditional dancers. She reached for the bottle of olive oil, then waved a generous amount across the steaming heap of pasta, while Piera attacked the potatoes with a metal spatula. Tore snatched a small piece from the corner just before Piera made to swat his knuckles.

"Franco found a soldier to dance with, then?" Piera snipped, punctuating each syllable with a scrape.

"He's with Zio Peppe." Carmela sprinkled the cured fish roe over the linguini and stirred the strands so that each piece was coated with an even, salty glaze. "Am I like Zia Lucia?"

"No. Your breasts still point to heaven."

Carmela smiled.

"Now for the love of God, let's get this out!" With that, she snatched the hot bowl from Carmela's hands and shoved it at Tore, who beat a hasty exit, wincing at the heat of the potato ricocheting about his mouth.

Carmela returned to the radicchio leaves and laid them in a glass bowl. She shaved slivers of cucumber and placed them on top. Then she took a handful of *ruccola* from an enamel bowl filled with pickings from the garden and tore them onto the other leaves, releasing their metallic aroma. Finally she peeled a couple of long radishes and sliced them. Piera threw a generous sprinkle of salt over the salad. "Here, take the salt cellar out to Zio Peppe," she said, placing it on the center of a large slab of cork lined with myrtle stems. Carmela thought about leaving Piera with a line to soothe, but the way her sister stabbed the enormous watermelon in preparation for the fruit tray persuaded her it was best to wait till later.

Outside, Peppe's cheeks had reddened, and the bottle of wine Franco had brought was half full. He had set the pig atop a large wooden butcher's block beside the embers and was carefully peeling the meat off the bones, its juices trickling down onto the large flat bread placed underneath. He took a spoon to the pig's eye, scraped out the jelly, and swallowed it.

"Let's not waste the best bits on those

Yanks, eh, Carme'?" he said, splitting the pig's head in two, using the same spoon to scoop out the brain. He tore a piece of flat bread from the cloth bag beside his stool and smeared the spoon across it. "You want?"

"No, Zio, you enjoy."

The brain-laden bread disappeared in a few bites.

"Piera's having a baby in there," she continued, trying to stay on top of the task at hand.

"Doesn't take after your mother, that's for sure."

Carmela held up the cork while he placed the white meat upon the myrtle stems, balancing the two halves of the pig's head at the center. He topped the entire tray with coarse salt from the cellar. "Start with this, Carme'. Come back for the rest."

Carmela turned back for the house, balancing the heavy load. The parched earth crunched underfoot. The aroma of the roasted meat heralded her entrance and made all the guests turn toward her. She passed through the crowd, catching the Fadda girls look at the tray with longing, leaving her wondering whether the rumors of their eating meat only once a week, despite their wealth, were true. Grandmother was always quick to remind Carmela and her siblings that the way to wealth began with not squandering the little one started with.

She placed the tray at the center of the food table and took a moment to admire the spread. In between the dishes she had placed small *ridotto* glasses filled with sprigs of fresh herbs. Upon the tablecloth she had laid strands of bougainvillea in deepening shades of pink and purple. The aromas hung together in the air above the colorful table. It was a culinary celebration of which Carmela was proud. How indebted she felt to Mrs. Curwin, the woman who allowed her creativity to take flight without criticism or censorship. Her mind flitted back to her grandmother at the house, most likely sitting on her solitary throne at the head of an empty table, dipping toasted bread into warmed milk. How she would have scoffed at the whimsy of the table decoration and hissed at the excess of food!

Mrs. Curwin swung in beside her. "You've done me proud, my darling," she whispered in Carmela's ear, then she turned toward her guests. "Dinner is most definitely served!" she announced, a ringmaster opening the show.

As the guests moved toward the table, a

piercing scream shattered the night.

Someone scratched the needle off the record.

"The mines!" a child's voice yelled, warped with agony.

Quiet panic froze the group.

Several soldiers moved toward the garden and shone their flashlights.

"Help!" the voice cried again, desperate.

Carmela raced forward. "It's Salvatore!"

"Wait!" Kavanagh yelled from the other side of the terrace as he lurched forward to stop her before she could run out. "Private Johnson," he called, turning to one of the soldiers while holding Carmela, "no civilian is to follow me. That is an order!"

"Yes, sir," the private replied, snapping to attention.

Kavanagh ran out toward the trees.

He was swallowed into the night.

The group became statues of fear, waiting for him to reappear. A sliver of light caught his face. A limp Salvatore came into view, draped in Kavanagh's arms. The Fadda girls gasped. Patches of red were smeared on his thin legs. They were a sculpture of the Pietà in church, a lifeless Jesus collapsed in his mourning mother's arms. Vittoria dashed to Carmela and clung to her hip. Peppe bounded through the group, ashen. He tore his son from Kavanagh's arms.

"Carmela, boil some water and clear the kitchen table," Kavanagh said. "This is his father?"

"Yes."

"Tell him to follow me."

"Zio Peppe, come," Carmela said, but her words fell flat against her uncle's sobbing. He swung round from foot to foot, lost in terror, clutching his child.

Carmela grabbed his face. "Zio! This way."

When they reached the kitchen Piera was on her way out to see what the commotion was. She saw her cousin's bloody body and froze.

"Bring a pot of water to the boil. Lieutenant needs help."

"Clear and clean this table! Cut up a tablecloth!"

Carmela opened the dresser drawers. She had assisted her mother during the labors of several of her neighbors. The sense of urgency and copious blood was not unfamiliar, but this time it took an almost insurmountable level of determination to keep her panic at bay. Kavanagh's hands worked quickly. He cut part of the cloth into strips, then laid the largest piece on top of the wood.

"I will take the boy now," he said, turning

to Peppe, whose tears were smeared across his weathered skin. Kavanagh cradled Salvatore and laid him upon the table. Mrs. Curwin ran in. She saw the blood and turned pale. Mr. Curwin moved in behind and steadied her.

"Ice to stop the bleeding, please. Is the water almost ready?"

"Nearly," Piera replied.

Carmela ran to the icebox and chipped at the inside. She wrapped a pile inside a muslin. Kavanagh placed Piera's hand where he wanted the ice pack held. He ripped a strip of tablecloth to make a tourniquet around Salvatore's shin. It slowed the flow of blood out of the open wound near his ankle.

"I'm going to suture the wound on his head first, Carmela."

She nodded.

"Mrs. Curwin," Kavanagh said, without taking his eyes off his patient, "I need you to take care of the father."

"Of course," she answered, pulling a chair out from the table and sitting Peppe down on it.

Two soldiers burst in and unbuckled two tin medical cases. Thin boxes of supplies lined the inside side by side, labels on their spines like books on a shelf.

"Tourniquet and forceps, Williams," Kavanagh said, steady.

The private reached into the case and pulled out the first box and began to open the package.

"Carmela, in a moment Private Kendricks will place an ammonia inhalant under his nose. This should bring the boy into consciousness. He has a strong pulse. This is good. When he wakes we're going to need something for him to bite down on."

Carmela grabbed a dishtowel and twisted it thick.

"Williams, get a couple of boys in here to hold him down. Kendricks: inhalant, swabs, gauze."

It was hard for Carmela to imagine these unflappable men caterwauling into the night but moments ago.

"The water's boiling, Lieutenant," Piera said, her voice wavering.

"Take it off the heat. I'll clean the wound before I suture."

After the lieutenant had mopped Salvatore's wound clean, he covered most of his face with the remnants of tablecloth to focus on closing the wound. A couple more soldiers entered and moved directly to Salvatore's head.

"Kendricks, ammonia."

The private waved a small vial under the boy's nose, and Salvatore gave a confused whimper, eyes still shut.

"He's coming to," Kavanagh said. "That's enough. We have to work quickly."

Kavanagh leaned over his bloody head and examined the wound. "Tell the father it appears superficial. The skull is intact. The damage must have been caused by flying shrapnel. He escaped the direct hit."

Carmela moved to Peppe and relayed Kavanagh's information in whispers. Meanwhile Private Kendricks dipped several needles into the pan of boiling water and fished them out with forceps. Kavanagh used his own pair of forceps to handle the needle while Kendricks threaded it. Kavanagh leaned over Salvatore and swabbed at the wound with several layers of cloth dipped in the sterile water. Then he began to pierce the skin around his temple. Carmela watched his wide fingers move with delicacy. No tremor of nerves or adrenaline.

Salvatore's semi-conscious state lasted two stitches before he jarred awake with a shriek that Carmela felt at the base of her spine. The soldiers held him still, as ordered, their faces void of emotion. Peppe wrapped him arms around himself and clawed at his sides, muttering to Jesus. Mrs. Curwin turned to Tore, who was hanging at the doorway, immobile. "Whiskey," she said. Tore left, then returned with a tumbler for his uncle. Peppe's hand shook so much when he handed it to him that Tore decided it best to place it up to Peppe's lips himself. Peppe took a few sips before his head began shaking.

"Carmela," Mrs. Curwin whispered, "tell your uncle his boy is in safe hands."

Carmela took her uncle's head in her hands and rocked with him. *Tutto andrá bene, Zio.*"

Salvatore's screams rose with each pierce of the needle.

Kavanagh spoke. "Kendricks. Gauze, compress, muslin." And with that, both wounds were covered and Salvatore was slowly pulled up to sitting. "This is a lucky boy. Undetonated mines are almost unheard of these days."

Piera and Carmela ran to his side trying to get him to breathe through his sobs. Peppe jumped up from his seat and wrapped his fat hands around his skinny boy, thanking Mary and Jesus, letting his tears drop onto the boy's shoulders.

The operating theatre was cleared as quickly as it had appeared. The privates made their way back out to their vehicles.

Franco entered.

Carmela looked at him. For a flash it seemed as if he were a complete stranger.

"The Americans save the day again," he said, slurring.

"*Buona sera,* Signore," the lieutenant replied in Italian, catching Franco off-guard. "Carmela, please tell this gentleman — I understand the house belongs to his uncle — that we will be taking a full reconnaissance of the land tomorrow from 06:00 hours."

"The lieutenant says they're coming in the morning to — er . . ." She turned back to Kavanagh. "Reconnaissance?"

"We will look everywhere in the fields for mines," he explained, his eyes glinting a deeper blue, complementing the darkened timbre of his voice.

"Marito, darling, it could have been any one of us! The boys!" Mrs. Curwin cried, unable to contain her panic.

"Suzie, darling," Mr. Curwin soothed, clasping her into him. "Undetonated mines are extremely rare. This area was one of the first to be swept clear. The boy is going to be fine. You heard the lieutenant, he had a lucky escape."

Carmela turned to Franco. "The soldiers are returning to check the fields. I think he means to apologize for having to walk the property."

"Tell him the allies should finish what they started."

"Lieutenant — Franco says that's fine."

The men shook hands.

"Carmela," Kavanagh began, his face warming with the start of relief. "Please tell your uncle I would like to take the boy to our hospital on base. I'd feel better if I could keep a close eye on him. We have antibiotics too to keep any infection at bay."

"Zio, Salvatore should go with the soldiers to their hospital."

He nodded. "Carmela, you go with him, yes? I will get Zia Lucia. You stay with him. You can understand what they say."

"Yes, Zio." She turned back to Kavanagh. "My uncle will get his wife from town and meet us there. I will go with my cousin. Is that all right?"

"Of course. We'll ride in my vehicle."

"What's going on?" Franco asked, stepping between them.

"I'm going to the military hospital with Salvatore."

"Says who?" Franco replied.

"I do!" Peppe bellowed, a lion protecting his cub. "If I say she is to go with my son, she is to go with my son!"

Mrs. Curwin took a step toward the group. "We're indebted to you, Lieutenant. I am so sorry, Signor Peppe. Carmela, you go. I can help Piera with everything here."

Kavanagh lifted Salvatore. Carmela followed the two of them through the darkened living room and out through the house. Kavanagh placed him onto the backseat of his open-top jeep. He turned to Carmela. "You're to keep him awake back there, you understand?"

"Yes." She longed to allow the sobs that gripped her throat to release.

The engine jerked to life, and soon they careened through the night. The moon shed little light on the craggy landscape. Carmela wished the enveloping blackness felt comforting, but as the jeep started along the winding descent all she felt were dread and the hard thumps of her heart. She clung to her cousin's bony shoulders, asking him questions to keep him talking.

The dread swelled to anger. If she had insisted he play closer to the house. If she had been less concerned about the look of the table, maybe all of this could have been averted. If she had forced him to help his father or Vittoria, he would have been spared this. A matter of inches had lain between Salvatore's survival and obliteration. We're like harried ants, the lot of us, she thought. How much time we waste in the belief of control over our destinies. How God must laugh at us, racing down here to nowhere!

And where had Franco been when everyone was crowding around the table? Carmela imagined he'd been taking care of the guests, but her heart intimated otherwise. Surely he wouldn't have been drinking through the screams? How long had he waited after she had gone to drink some more?

The cluster of lights from the base rose into view by the bay below.

Her heart lurched.

She convinced herself it was because of the task at hand and not because her eyes had caught the piercing blue of Kavanagh's in the rearview mirror.

Chapter 6

The ward gleamed a disinfected white. Several nurses floated across the polished floors. Their starched caps, perched at the center of their impeccable locks, caught the dim light of the lamps clamped on the bed frames. Carmela sat by Salvatore as she watched a nurse apply fresh dressing. He winced when she swabbed close to the wound. As she finished, the nurse looked at Carmela, flashed a brief, sympathetic smile, and left.

Kavanagh sidled up to the opposite bedside, holding his hat in his hands. "I'm so sorry, Carmela. God knows it could have been a whole lot worse."

"Yes."

He looked down at Salvatore, who turned his head, a few breaths from sleep. Kavanagh's skin flushed, his short blond hair gilded in the lamplight. He lifted his gaze back toward her. It was not the deep blue of his eyes that struck her as much as the dignity that shone there.

"We thank you. So much," she said.

As Kavanagh took a breath to reply, an older man in uniform stepped in.

"Captain," Kavanagh said, snapping to attention.

"Lieutenant," Casler answered, followed by a perfunctory nod to Carmela. "You've done a fine job on the native. Not bad for a med school dropout." He flashed an arch grin.

"Thank you, sir."

"Pity. Was turning out to be quite the party. . . ." His eye tracked a nurse walking by.

Carmela caught a whiff of whiskey on his breath.

"Who's this?" he barked. "The mother?"

"No sir, a cousin. Carmela."

Her eyes met Casler's.

"Ma'am," he said, with a sweep across her body as if it were the first time they'd met. He looked back at Kavanagh. "I thank God every day for stationing me in paradise with a wife back home who won't get on a plane or boat. Hot savages everywhere you look, for Chrissake," he said with a sideways glance. "Get hard just looking at them."

Carmela pretended she didn't understand.

Kavanagh masked his embarrassment with an awkward smile. "Sir, with your permission I would like to lead a reconnaissance and full sweep of the area tomorrow."

"Of course," the captain answered, his eyes planted on Carmela's neck.

"May I talk to you, sir?"

"That's what we're doing."

"In private, sir?"

"Farm girl's a red spy?" he answered with a guffaw that nearly woke Salvatore.

Carmela stared at her hands.

Casler's eyes narrowed. "What's the matter? You don't tell jokes down south, Kavanagh?"

The double doors at the ward entrance flung open before Kavanagh could answer. Lucia charged through them like a crazed bull, Peppe close behind. Carmela ran to her aunt. "He's fine, Zia, he's going to be fine."

Lucia brushed past her niece to Salvatore's bedside. She slid her arm underneath him and pressed him to her chest.

"Signora," Kavanagh said, "*piano* — Carmela, please try to get her to let him rest."

"Zia, *l'Americano* says he needs sleep."

Lucia ignored them, burrowing her face into her son's hair and rocking him, her tears running down her cheeks and falling in fat drops. He began to wriggle awake.

Carmela placed a gentle hand on her aunt's shoulder and a chair by her side. "Here, sit, we can stay for a while."

A nurse at the adjacent bed drew a curtain around a young officer in traction. "Excuse me," Captain Casler said, catching her eye as she disappeared behind. "I need to continue my rounds. Be sure the family does not stay long, Lieutenant."

Carmela watched him leave, returning her gaze to Kavanagh for a moment, who, though holding a polite distance from her family, seemed to be looking at Salvatore with a warmth she would not have anticipated from anyone other than a relative. The memory of him being celebrated at Antonio's bar floated into her mind. She found herself wanting to know how he must feel with his new baby being so far away. It seemed that this was not a man who might bear the distance with ease. The start of a tender smile faded as he straightened.

"How long does Salvatore need to stay, my aunt is asking," Carmela asked.

"Certainly overnight. I'm afraid visitors cannot stay."

Carmela's expression dropped.

"But I'll speak with my captain," he said,

fumbling a little for words. "It would be better if Salvatore wakes and someone familiar is nearby."

An hour later Lucia and Peppe had been wrenched from their son's bedside and led out by Kavanagh. Carmela watched her cousin's chest rise and fall until sleep overtook her as well. She drifted in and out of restless dreams till she was jarred awake with a bolt. It felt like the dead of night. The witching hour, her mother called it, when the souls of the dead slipped out and the babies slid in. It took a moment for her to realize her hands were wet from the upturned glass of water trickling from Salvatore's bedside table onto her palm, not the river in which she had dreamed she was drowning. She must have flicked it over somehow, by mistake, in her sleep.

"Would you like a drink?" Kavanagh whispered.

Carmela looked up, on guard. No words came to her rescue.

"I'm having trouble sleeping," he said, handing her a small glass of water.

"Thank you." She reached over to Salvatore's glass and straightened it. "Sorry."

He walked over behind her chair and mopped up the spill with a tea towel. "Bad dream?"

Carmela shifted with unease. Surely he hadn't been watching her sleep? She took a sip. Her swallows sounded louder than usual. He folded the wet towel and returned to the other side of the bed. They sat in the quiet of the shadows.

"My baby is four weeks old today," Kavanagh said, breaking the silence. "Times like this I'm reminded of the distance."

"Boy?"

"Yes. Seymour. After my grandfather."

"I was supposed to be named after my grandmother. Only thing we would have had the same," she said with a smirk. Kavanagh smiled, seeming somewhat surprised at her sense of humor — a quality that Carmela knew most of the local girls were not known for, among the soldiers at least.

"It will be nothing like that feast at Mrs. Curwin's, but we've got a kitchen with supplies — can I fix you something?"

She should refuse politely — after all, he was already manipulating the rules by allowing her to stay. To take food seemed a step too far.

"I don't know about you, but I'm starving. I've got to take this wet thing back too," he said, throwing the tea towel from one hand to the other. He gestured for her to follow him. "Come on, it's just up here."

She hesitated for a moment. Her stomach rumbled. Then she stood up and followed him.

They made their way along the length of the ward, passing a couple of nurses. Carmela liked to think their eyebrows didn't raise as she walked by. She realized she was still wearing her apron and that the jeep most likely left her hair looking as if she'd dived through a hedge backward. She berated herself for caring and for feeling a little too excited to be spending a night in this foreign world.

They arrived at the kitchen, a small galley of white cabinets and shiny lemon Formica countertops. At the far end was the largest refrigerator Carmela had ever seen. Kavanagh moved over to it and pulled the chrome handle. She saw a stack of sliced cheese in perfect squares and a line of fat, sausage-looking shapes in colorful packages. A nurse entered with a tray of empty glasses. Carmela turned, feeling like a trespasser.

"Good evening, Lieutenant," the nurse said, flashing him a bright smile. As she filled the glasses with water from a large jug, her eyes slit sideways to Carmela. "Is there anything I might help you with?"

"No, Kelly, that's fine. Just fixing a snack."

"I'm happy to do that, Lieutenant, just as soon as I've given out these."

"That won't be necessary, Kelly, thank you though."

Carmela watched the peachy-skinned nurse leave, imagining how beautiful she would look in the cotton summer dress she had sketched a few days ago. It struck Carmela that the female staff could bring a lot of business to Yolanda. She wondered if they had shops on the base, or if they spent the entirety of their days dressed in various combinations of white starch, like novice nuns.

Kavanagh placed two slices of bread on a couple of pale blue plastic plates and laid two slices of cheese on top. The deft, steady hands she had seen at work in Mrs. Curwin's kitchen now looked hesitant. He pulled back the wrapper of one of the fat sausages and smeared a pink slab of the contents over another slice of bread. Then he pressed them together.

"It's a sandwich, Carmela," he said, on the back of her quizzical look.

She looked down at the plates, wondering what animal had been pureed for the purpose of this meal.

"Your first?"

"Sorry?"

"Am I the first person to make you a sandwich?" He sounded like a young boy for a moment. Carmela felt a great urge to ask him about the story of his life up until the point where he found himself alone in a small, clinical kitchen with a Sardinian woman. He was looking straight at her. She realized she hadn't answered. "I suppose, yes," she said, smiling with three o'clock delirium. Somewhere between the accident, the roofless ride, and the lack of sleep, she had let her guard slip. The image of Zio Peppe screaming at Franco surfaced, but she buried it. Reality could wait till tomorrow.

Kavanagh lifted up both plates, and Carmela followed him back down the hallway to Salvatore's bedside. He pulled over a small table on wheels and set a chair from another bedside for Carmela to sit on. He sat opposite. She picked up the soft, white square.

"It's not homemade pasta — which was unbelievable, by the way — but it's also not as bad as it looks. Honestly."

She smiled. He had enjoyed her food at the party. She watched him look at her, expectant, as she bit into the bread. There was a whisper of taste from the square cheese, followed by the overpowering saltiness of the mystery sausage spread.

"Well?"

An awkward pause, as Kavanagh waited for her to swallow her tiny mouthful.

"American," she answered.

He laughed. His shadowed face lit up as he did so. "You speak English well, Carmela."

"Thank you."

"Why is that?"

"Mrs. Curwin. We have worked there for five years. She gave me records, books. I like it very much."

They chewed in silence for a moment. He devoured the food without wasting a crumb, not chewing openmouthed like the young men who helped at the farm. The way he still looked as if he'd just arrived at the party rather than having dealt with a medical emergency and the hysteria of Carmela's family impressed her. Had she ever even known a man with a cool head?

"That's good," he said, wiping his mouth with a white napkin. "Especially now."

"Now?"

"I probably shouldn't mention it before it's official," he said, lowering his voice and leaning in close enough for Carmela to pick up his woody scent, "but we've had word from our senior officers that the base is considering opening up positions for locals in the near future."

"Positions?"

"Clerks, front desk work, administration, that sort of thing. No point us being here if the local people don't benefit."

His singsong lilt was difficult for Carmela to decipher when he spoke at such speed. He seemed to intuit her thoughts, because he stopped for a moment. "I'm racing?"

"A little."

"Sorry," he said, wiping the corners of his mouth again. "I'm trying to say that I may be able to offer you some work."

Carmela wasn't sure whether to allow herself to feel excited or maintain a cool appearance of professional calm.

He appeared to mistake the absence of any reaction for rejection. "Only if you're interested, of course," he added, hesitant.

Carmela put her sandwich back onto her plate. What little appetite she had evaporated.

"I have work. Yolanda, Mrs. Curwin."

"Yes. This kind of work would not be full time. I'd figure in your commitments."

"I don't understand."

He cleared his throat again. If she didn't know better, she could have mistaken it for nerves.

"How would you like to be my interpreter, Carmela?"

She froze, hoping she'd understood. "Interpreter?"

"Yes."

Excitement rippled through her. A door swung open onto a whole new world. This man was offering for her to work beside him? Was she even qualified for the post? What on earth would be expected of her? Not *an* interpreter. *His.* She pictured herself beside him, and chose to ignore the dizzying swell in her chest. In but a few words he had made her feel chosen. Special. And not because of how she did or didn't look, whose daughter she may or not be, but because of a skill she had almost taught herself. Other girls had records from America and England. Other girls had worked for English families, but only she had committed to learning more than what was expected or needed. Only she had sought to bite into another culture with everything she had, to understand, educate herself, expand. How many girls in Simius were blessed and cursed with this curiosity? She had been looking past the horizon of Simius for longer than she realized. The further it took her, the smaller her hometown became. Kavanagh was so capable, so calm, yet he needed her in some way. It was an honor. Her mind convinced her she felt nothing more than flattered. It was shock at the surprise offer, nothing more. She was overwhelmed only because of the night's events. It was the only way to explain this exhilarating rush in her chest, like a child darting down the grassy bank of a hill, sun streaming on her, wind whistling through her fingers.

"I don't understand —" she fibbed, heart still running.

"I'm heading a project in the area. We're under orders to involve local workers — a mandatory requirement from the Italian government. Sort of in return for letting us be here in the first place."

She straightened, her back lengthening like an alert, wide-eyed cat scanning a townscape from a high window.

"We've got to become part of Simius, Carmela," he explained, though Carmela couldn't shake the feeling he was trying to convince her, more than make her an offer. "I'm about to start paying visits to all the local farmers, like I did your father, and landowners too. You're the first person I've met whose English comes anywhere close to what I would need." His cheeks flushed again. "My Italian . . ."

She smiled, smoothing a strand of hair that bounced straight back up into a frazzled curl. "Enough to ask for pasta, no?"

"First thing I learned."

A brief silence. Even under the angular shadows of hospital equipment, his eyes beamed. "Before the base was established, Casler and I did a reconnaissance of the island. Parts of the wilderness took my breath away — forest-lined gorges, waterfalls fighting out of the rocks, untouched lagoons. Have you ever seen them?"

"No. I've never left Simius."

"We traveled far south too, to your capital, Cagliari, of course, but also to Chia and the surrounding bays."

She licked her lips. "My uncle travels south often. He told me he wouldn't have believed the sea could be that color unless he had seen it with his own eyes."

"I stood on those jagged cliffs, gazing out toward Africa, wishing I was an artist or a writer, just so I could describe it with the majesty it deserved." The timbre and rhythm of his voice changed as he painted her island with his words. He spoke with the light of someone describing a new lover.

"He's told me many stories of those places — my uncle is a traveling salesman."

"I'll be traveling back there and, of course,

connecting with the locals here."

"An adventure."

He cleared his throat. "Sure. But I can't do it alone. If fellow Simiuns saw a familiar face, they'd feel comfortable."

The wilderness was a mystical place she had always dreamed of exploring, and the capital, a day's travel away on the south coast, conjured up images of an exotic metropolis. She pictured herself beside Kavanagh, rattling through the rocky hills in his jeep, sporting a crisp civilian uniform, the wind in her hair, as they wove through the valleys visiting local farmers and shepherds. She thought about the wide plains inland, dotted with crumbling ancient fortresses. She pictured them climbing the untouched expanse of Barbagia to the center of her island, majestic home to Mount Gennargentu and a cluster of isolated towns infamous for squat, mustached women who dabbled in magic. Her breath quickened with anticipation.

He shifted in his seat a little. "The food here is everything they told me it would be too."

"I'm sure you have good food at home, no?"

"I'd be lying if I said I wouldn't go for some of my Virginia's fried chicken!"

"Your wife?"

"Yes."

Carmela watched his eyes darken. He missed her — that much was obvious. For a moment it seemed as if he was about to elaborate, but then he straightened his collar and sipped his water. She admonished herself for prying; he was inviting her to work for him, and she needed to prove her professionalism.

"Will you think about it, Carmela?"

Think about it? She wanted to ask when her first day would be. Then her mind crashed back to her duties at Yolanda's and Mrs. Curwin's. She hoped the waves of nausea were thanks to the pink sausage and not the thought of Franco's face when she'd tell him of her possible new role. It was impossible to imagine him excited at the prospect of her working alongside this handsome stranger, impossible to picture Franco wrapping his arms around her, congratulating her on the unexpected job offer. Now that she thought about it, she couldn't remember when he had ever praised her work. She didn't remember ever needing this from him. Why now? Vanity? Ambition she had kept secret from everyone, even herself? It was unnerving. She pictured Franco's face folding into a glare after she

revealed the news. She heard his bombard-
ment of questions, woven together with
mistrust, affront. He'd pretend not to care
about the extra money they might save for
their wedding. He would think only of his
pride, of how it would look to others. And
for the first time she acknowledged that he
would always put that ahead of how she felt.
These foreign thoughts were disorientating.
Her hands felt cold. She decided not mention it to Franco for the time being. After
all, didn't Kavanagh say the orders had not
yet been made official from his senior officers?

"I will think about it, Lieutenant."

"Please call me Joe."

"I will think about it — *Joe*," she answered, feeling like someone high above was
either having a joke at her expense or shining a sunbeam down on her.

CHAPTER 7

Carmela and Salvatore stepped out onto the hot tarmac outside the military hospital doors. Antonio waved from the opposite side of the parking lot. He walked over to them and took Salvatore's hand in his. "Gave us quite the scare, boy," he said, pinching Salvatore's cheek between two fingers. "Though not as terrifying as what your mamma is going to do to you after you're completely healed!"

"Are we your first passengers?" Carmela asked, pleased to see a familiar face. A month or so ago, Antonio had revealed his plans to become Simius's first taxi driver, on top of running the bar. She had teased him at the time, reminding him how most places were reachable on foot, but he had reassured her that the growing tourism would bring in good business.

"It's not quite the girl's maiden voyage," he said, tapping the hood of his Fiat, "but

no one ever built up a taxi business overnight. When I heard what happened, I drove
to Mrs. Curwin's in case anyone needed
rides over here. She wanted to pay me to
pick you up this morning. Of course I told
her no."

Carmela was touched. "I hope you let the
woman at the desk know about Simius's
premiere taxi service."

"You're the sister I never had — 'course I
did. They don't walk any place, those Yankees. I never forget your grandfather telling
me about the motor cars over there, God
rest his soul."

Antonio opened the back door for Salvatore and Carmela. Salvatore shunted along
the polished seats, breathing in the smell of
new leather and gawking at the chrome
dash.

"Listen," Antonio began, his entrepreneur
eyes bright in the rearview mirror, just
above the swinging rosary, "there are imbeciles who still don't want them making a
base here, but this could be the making of
our town, Carme'. Let those bigots stay in
their hillside huts following sheep around
all day moaning to one another — I'll be
busy building my sea-view villa with Yankee
dollars."

"I'm starving!" Salvatore squawked, fingering the window lever. "They gave me hard square bread in there and crunchy pebbles with milk."

"We can stop in at my bar on the way if you want, Carme' — on the house?"

"I'm sure Zia Lucia's cooking enough for a small army," Carmela said with a smile, gently taking Salvatore's hand off the knob and placing it on his lap.

"Are they going to have a party at my house this time?" Salvatore asked, eyes wide.

Carmela smoothed his hair. "I think we've had enough excitement for a while, don't you?" she asked, though it felt good to see the beginnings of Salvatore's mischief rosy his cheeks again.

Antonio pulled out onto the main road back to town and began the climb. Carmela peered down out of her window at the steep drop down to the sea, shimmering bright azure in the morning sun. Along the craggy coast, rock rose and old juniper scrubs clung to the ancient stone, the sand a dazzling white under the unforgiving beams.

"Life *is* exciting, boy, don't you listen to her," Antonio said, negotiating a bend. "You don't let anyone tell you otherwise, do you hear me? You die happy only if you dream big."

■ ■ ■ ■

The cool quiet of the house was a great relief after the hot drive and the exhaustion of the past few days. A pot of sauce sat upon the stove in the deserted kitchen. With lunch just about prepared, Carmela entertained the idea of an indulgent nap before the family returned from cathedral mass. Grandmother lived for Sunday mornings. Priest Vaccari was her personal favorite. She preached that his command of Latin was good for the girls' souls.

Carmela headed toward the stairs when the creak of a floorboard overhead stopped her in her tracks. She looked up, as if her eyes might bore through the wood into Zia Rosa's room. Rosa was the apple of Icca's eye. All love lost on Icca's grandchildren was showered on her only daughter, who took residence in the largest master bedroom as if it were her own private wing in a palace. There was the low rumble of a man's voice. Carmela's heart pounded.

Footsteps.

She shot a panicked look to the door.

Then a woman's laughter rippled down the stairwell. Carmela froze behind the kitchen door, left ajar. Through the slit between the door and the frame Carmela saw Zia Rosa.

Carmela caught Rosa's head fling back as she flicked her tousled locks off her face. Signor Rossi, the local doctor, followed soon after. What she saw next nailed her to the spot before she had a chance to move around and greet them. Her eyes widened.

Rosa and Rossi's arms raced around each other. They locked together in a clamorous embrace. Rossi raised the lace hem of her aunt's slip. Carmela's ears committed the sounds of their hungry kisses to unwanted memory — her aunt's gasps as he lifted her up against the wall, his moans as her slim thighs wrapped around him. Unsure of what to do, or how to breathe, Carmela decided to escape through the main door out to the terrace. After only a couple of her steps, the lovers fell silent. Carmela stopped, wobbling on the tips of her feet.

In the shuttered shadows three hearts beat a fast dance. Each chose their lie.

How the doctor had pulled up his trousers, smoothed his hair, and swallowed his guilt in the short time it took for him to appear around the door Carmela would never know. Nothing about his crisp, white linen shirt or fitted suit trousers painted anything other than the perfect picture of decorum.

Once more the pillar of the community, the father to three well-dressed children, faithful and stylish husband to a porcelain-skinned wife who need not crease her hands in the fields.

"*Buon giorno,* Carmela," he said, without even the faintest whisper of embarrassment.

Carmela thought she answered but couldn't hear herself for the blood pulsating in her ears. "Please tell your grandmother I'm sorry I missed her. I'll be sure to stop by during the week, instead. I'll see myself out, please don't trouble yourself." And with a half nod he walked by her.

Carmela watched him cross the terrace, then disappear down the far steps to her mother's garden on the lower terrace.

The gate clicked shut.

He was gone.

Rosa appeared in the doorway. Her face was darkened against the light in the hallway behind her, where the sun streamed in through a tiny window facing the terrace. She reached an arm up onto the frame in a languid stretch. The third button of her shirt was in the second hole. Her lipstick was eaten away. Her pencil skirt, clenching the delicate curve of her hips, was creased.

"I'll let Mother know the doctor stopped by for her," she purred. "I'll rest now. No one's to wake me, do you hear?" She pivoted away from Carmela and left.

Carmela, trembling with disbelief, listened to her aunt's heels tap up the granite stairs and across her bedroom floorboards. When all fell silent, Carmela shuffled to the kitchen table and pulled out a chair. She sat down, pale. An avalanche of thoughts tumbled into a mess of white noise.

Soon enough Piera returned home, her lean legs pacing across the kitchen before she dropped down into a chair. "You look like a ghost! Anyone would think *you* had sat through Vaccari's five-hour sermon!" She flopped her head onto her forearms.

"Where are the others?" Carmela asked.

"Stopped at the bottom of the hill. Nonna is getting the gossip from number twenty-three."

Carmela grabbed Piera's wrist, yanked her out of the kitchen and into the darkness of the sitting room reserved for visitors on the opposite side of the stairwell.

"What are you doing?"

"Shhh!"

"Whatever's the matter?"

Carmela's breath became shallow. "I can hardly believe what I'm about to say." Her voice came out in choked whispers, which

Piera mirrored.

"What's happened? Is it Americans? Any of them laid a hand on you?"

"Worse."

Piera's forehead creased into a severe frown. "That wild light in your eyes is scaring me."

Carmela shut the door without a sound. "Rosa and the doctor are having an affair."

The whites of Piera's eyes doubled.

Carmela nodded. "I saw them."

Piera stared at her without moving.

"On the other side of this door. I don't know who's going to hell first. Me or her."

A smile began to unfurl the corners of Piera's lips.

"What's that for?"

"Thinking about the look on Nonna's face when she finds out."

"She won't find out!" Carmela's chest tightened.

"We don't all have a Franco waiting for us."

"What's Franco got to do with this?"

"You'll be married before her. It's killing her. A handsome man gives her attention, 'course she'll take it."

"In the house?"

"Would it make it any different if they were down an alley?"

166

Carmela's mind darted back to the shadowy *viccolo* where Franco watched her being stuffed into a tiny costume. "He's married!"

"She's desperate! We should feel sorry for her." Piera reached up and clasped Carmela's face. "Pull yourself together. Everyone's coming in."

"What are we going to do?!"

"Nothing."

Carmela shot Piera a frantic look.

"This is what we'll do, Carmela: We go back to the kitchen before Nonna finds us hiding in the dark and gets suspicious. We talk like we would normally, understand?"

"I'm shaking."

"Pretend you're fine. Come on."

Piera opened the door and began an impressive performance. "The Angels and Cherubs at the convent youth group are having an early San Giovanna celebration. Gianetta gets to sit at the High Table, apparently. You should have seen them, had ants up their bottoms!"

Piera glanced back at her unsmiling sister, then plowed on. "We stopped in on Lucia on the way back from church. Salvatore's already running around. Zia said she was going to tie him to the chair with a belt so he would eat his lunch."

Piera's chuckle was not reciprocated.

"Hard at work, I see?" Icca announced, crashing through Piera's patter. Carmela stiffened. Then she followed Piera's lead as she began preparations for lunch. A fistful of *gnocchetti* per person was measured out into a pot of boiling water, plus an extra one in case Tomas made it back from the farm in time. Sunday was the one day Icca could be a little more lenient on portion size. As Carmela tipped the dried pasta shapes in, however, several of them missed the pot and rattled down onto the floor. Piera shot her a look.

"I enjoyed Monsignor Vaccari's sermon immensely today, didn't you, Maria?" Icca asked as the women untied their black head scarves.

"Yes, Nonna, very much." Maria answered, walking over to Carmela. They gave each other a kiss on either cheek. "Thank you for taking such care of Salvatore. God bless him."

"She looks pale as a spirit!" Icca cried. "This is what a night in America does. See that? The devil came over with cigarettes and gum. We should have known that was just the beginning. I'll not see my land become an American colony!"

"Nonna, they took great care of Salvatore,

168

of me. It was clean," Carmela said, stirring the water with a little too much vigor so that it spat out onto the flames. "They were kind. Really."

"Brainwashed already. Listen to that. One night is all it takes, Maria!"

The door to the stairs creaked open. Rosa slid in.

"Are you feeling better, my dear?" Icca asked, kissing her daughter on the forehead.

"I have rested," she answered as she bowed her head. The pot boiled over and splattered onto the stove. Piera walked over and took it off the heat. "Act normal," she whispered.

Carmela stared down into the pool of salty water, longing to lose herself in the bubbles, disappear for a moment to stop the room from spinning. Piera placed a firm hand on Carmela's elbow to steady her.

The bell of the front gate rang. Carmela flew out of the kitchen before anyone could ask her. She raced across the terrace and looked over the wall down to the *viccolo* below. Never had she been so happy to see Franco's face. Her feet pelted the stairs, then she wove round, under the wisteria canopy of her mother's garden, till she reached the gate and flung it open. She wrapped her arms around him. They held each other, feeling the rise and fall of their chests against each other.

After a few breaths Franco pulled away. He traced Carmela's face with a gentle finger, rubbed his nose along her cheek. "You still smell of that first summer. I look at you and see that crazy sixteen-year-old who loved to dance and race me along the figs." He placed his warm lips against hers. "I see my life, Carmela."

"Franco," Carmela murmured, shuddering into tears. She wrapped her arms around him again and then clasped him. The tears rolled. Over two days, so much about her life had become unfamiliar: the party, Salvatore's accident, being catapulted into the world of the base, the offer of an opportunity to work alongside Kavanagh, and most damaging, most painful, the shattering discovery of her aunt's brazen infidelity. It was almost too much to bear.

Yet here, in her arms, was the man who promised her a life of stability, wealth, and passion. Here was her anchor. The person to keep her feet planted in reality, in the hot, fertile, igneous earth of her motherland. Their roots would drive deep, entwining in a web of stoic, tireless ancestors. Their babies would be boys: fat, hungry, irresistible. Deep chocolate pools for eyes, a lifelong love of their mamma, and unwavering respect for their papa. They would grow into tree trunk men, build roofs for their parents, hand them rosy-cheeked grandchildren, honor them at the head of their lunch tables, salute them with wine. Those grown babies would hold the translucent skin of their parents' bony hands, when death would creep upon them, like a silken sheet, sending them slipping back to their creator without fear, pain, or fight.

Franco pulled away again and looked into her eyes. She searched his eyes for the boy she had fallen for, but her sight seemed skewed, as if she had walked into the darkened kitchen out of the blinding white morning sun outside, not the other way around. He held out a small bunch of wildflowers. She lifted them up to her nose, but their scent was at once unfamiliar. Carmela knew this wash of uncomfortable feeling would fade soon enough, along with all the excitement of the past few days. She clung to this thought as her hand slipped into Franco's, silencing the little voice inside that proclaimed it impossible.

CHAPTER 8

A silence spliced the seamstresses' chatter as Carmela stepped into Yolanda's studio the following day. Carmela felt her colleagues' glares follow her as she walked across the room to her worktop. She pulled out her chair and sat down, pretending it was any other Monday.

"I suppose this is all very pedestrian after your weekend, Carmela," Agnes said with a sneer. Her table flanked Carmela's. Though she almost matched Carmela for skill and experience, she floundered when it came to grace, tact, or charm. It was the precise reason Yolanda sat her far from the clientele, even if she took on the majority of the more intricate assignments.

"Thinking about becoming a nurse too, in between being a slave to the Jews?" Agnes asked with a smirk. Carmela looked straight at her. The snide remarks were unsurprising. Five years after the fact, Agnes still

refused to relinquish her bitterness toward
the girl she deemed had stolen Franco's
heart from her.

"Salvatore is a lucky boy," Carmela answered without rising to the bait.

"I'll say," another piped in from the other
side of the room. "Got himself a night with
those Yankees — those boys aren't too bad
to look at neither!"

The room frothed with girlish laughter.

"Carmela wouldn't know anything about
that, would she now?" Agnes chimed. "Only
got eyes for her husband-to-be, isn't that
right?" One eyebrow lifted into a provoca-
tive arch.

"Go on, tell us, Carme', what were they
like?" the youngest worker called out from
the far wall.

"Perfectly nice." Carmela pictured herself
at the end of Salvatore's bed, eating Kavanagh's sandwich.

"Take me next time! We're not all brides
in waiting, you know!"

More cackling.

"If you concentrate on actually reaching
puberty, you might have something worthwhile to look at," Agnes cut in. "Carmela
likes to think those Yanks are drooling over
her English, but she knows a man is interested in the size of something other than

your brain. Think she'd have been asked to go if she had a washboard for tits like you?"

The girls turned, stunned. Agnes usually reserved her sting for Carmela, not the starlings of the group.

"Been working those extra shifts at the post office again, Agnes?" Carmela replied. "You're even more bad tempered than usual."

In the brief silence Yolanda swept in, fixing a pin into her heavy bun at the base of her head. Her eyes scanned the girls. "I pay you to be statues at the cemetery?" she barked. The women returned to their work.

"There's a word for girls who stay out all night with strangers, you know," Agnes whispered out of the side of her mouth, without taking her eyes off the embroidery she was finishing along the hem of an A-line skirt. Carmela spied Yolanda, who was pouring water from a small metal watering can into the lustrous begonia by the main door, and felt thankful when she signaled for her to go to the fitting area.

"We have a full morning," Yolanda began as Carmela reached her. "I need you with the customers today. Word's got out about your little episode at the base — won't hurt to have our very own celebrity convince the women to try out some of the newer, more expensive fabrics, no?" She glanced down at the appointment book. "By the way, what did I interrupt?"

"Sorry?"

"The girls looked like I'd just stepped in on a secret. What's Agnes brewing?" she pried, without taking her eyes off the wide page of the ledger.

"Nothing."

"Hard to believe."

"Hoping for an American husband, I imagine."

"There's one who'll never find happiness. If she keeps turning over rocks, she'll only find scorpions."

There was a tentative rap at the door.

"Ah, Signora Rossi, she's early. Wouldn't expect anything less from the doctor's wife," Yolanda said.

The words shattered like a jam jar on cold tiles.

Yolanda nodded to the door. "See her in, won't you?"

Carmela stood planted to the bare boards. Her palms were clammy.

"Today, Carmela."

Before she had a chance to compose herself, Carmela opened the door. A wan woman stood before her. A sorrowful oil portrait, were it not for the fact that she nodded her head and muttered a quiet hello. Carmela gestured for her to sit down on the settee. Signora Rossi took her place and glanced around the space as if intuiting from which wall a wild beast might leap out and consume her. Carmela tried to quash the image of Rosa's tryst with this woman's husband, but it kept lighting up, like the flame of a candle that flickers in a breeze too weak to snuff it out.

"*Caffè*, Signora?" she managed, clinging to etiquette.

"That would be nice. Thank you."

Carmela fled for a moment's refuge into the sliver of kitchen just off the main room. Yolanda was already preparing a pot.

"I'll watch the coffee, Zia. It's probably best you speak with Rossi."

"Nonsense. What on earth is the matter? You've been on pins since I got in."

"What?"

"Get out and get talking!" she hissed.

Carmela turned back. She took a reluctant seat beside Rossi. "Please feel free to take a look through any of these magazines, Signora."

"Thank you."

Carmela ignored the galloping in her chest as she watched the woman's thin fingers creep across the pages. "Is there something

176

in particular you had in mind?"

"Not really, no," she answered, sails lowered. "I am to accompany my husband to an important dinner with professors from the university in Sassari. I suppose I would need something elegant but not brazen. He hates it when I wear anything too revealing."

Carmela glanced at Rossi's cotton blouson, wondering how she could stand to have the top button fastened in this heat.

"He finds modern fashions cheap."

The pale woman's hair was pulled back off her face in an elegant chignon, drawing the eye to a delicate nose and full lips. Despite the ochre of her eyes, they remained cold, void of expression. Carmela had no idea where to begin dressing a woman who portrayed herself as invisible.

"Are you an admirer of Audrey Hepburn?" she asked. It dawned on her that her flair for design might be a way of turning this woman's husband's head back in the right direction. She brushed off the thoughts, disgusted for thinking that the only thing a man is drawn to is the picture of a woman. Sadness followed soon after; perhaps Agnes's words were not as far from the truth as Carmela would like to believe.

Rossi shrugged.

"You have a similar bone structure, madam, if I might say. Perhaps something like this?" Carmela flicked open the magazine to a shot of the star in a pretty pastel summer evening gown, straight, with a high neckline, delicate tulle layered skirts widening from her tiny waist.

"That is pretty, yes." Rossi's cheeks flushed with a memory of color.

"I think a pale yellow would work with your skin tone, Signora. But we needn't rush a decision. I'll begin with your measurements."

Her client stood.

Carmela drew the velvet curtain. "When you have dressed down to your slip, let me know. I'll be waiting out here."

Yolanda arrived with a tray of espresso. Her eyes widened as she gave an inquisitive nod toward the curtain. Carmela forced a reassuring smile. Rossi called her in. Carmela took the tray from Yolanda and placed it inside the cubicle upon a stool.

"Sugar, Signora?"

"Three. My husband says I take too much." She studied her reflection, as if disappointed.

Carmela stirred the tiny cup with care and handed it to Rossi. From her pocket Carmela pulled a tape measure and a small leather-bound notepad with a tiny pencil pushed through the top. She held the tape at Rossi's nape and pulled it along to her shoulder. Carmela scribbled down numbers, stretching the measure around every angle of Rossi's body with fast, confident hands. Carmela clung to her well-practiced routine, hoping it might quiet her racing mind. The woman watched her, expressionless. She reminded Carmela of the sheep that came into milking, indifferent to the men squeezing their udders and relieving their loads. What had come first, Rossi's sallow demeanor or the doctor's infidelity? Her skin felt cool to the touch as Carmela held the tape to her, despite the relentless summer heat outside. She was the perfect mannequin; even her breaths moved her little. Carmela finished and left Rossi to slip back into her clothes.

Without ever intending to be, Carmela had been shunted into the lie. A passionate man like Dr. Rossi would always seek out a woman whose blood pulsed as hot as his. It was unsurprising that a sullen woman like Signora Rossi couldn't satisfy him for long.

Signora Rossi pulled back the velvet curtain.

Carmela admonished herself for even beginning to justify Dr. Rossi's unforgivable behavior.

"The dress on page four will be fine," Rossi announced.

"Very well, Signora. We will schedule a second fitting for the same time next week."

"Yellow will be acceptable," she said, giving a mechanical powder to the tip of her nose. "My mother always said it was the color of envy. No matter now. She died the night before my last child was born." With that, she, and her golden vanity, clasped shut. "Good day."

Carmela watched her slide through the doorway and down the steps. "Good day, Signora."

"Did she go with the new season yellow?" Yolanda asked.

"Certainly."

"If he doesn't fall in love with his wife all over again I'll eat my hat."

Carmela faintly smiled.

Then Yolanda whisked around to crack the whip at an unsuspecting seamstress.

And Carmela caught Agnes's glare.

It was early afternoon when Carmela arrived at the Curwin villa to find the lady of the house lingering over an espresso in the kitchen.

Mrs. Curwin stood up to give Carmela a

kiss on either cheek. "Good heavens, it feels like an age since the fiasco! Piera was just telling me how well the boy is doing."

"Yes, Signora. A miracle."

"Indeed." Mrs. Curwin took a final gulp, then reached for the pot resting on the table upon a crotchet doily and poured herself another cup. "I'm morose. Holidays here go so ghastly fast. I can hardly bear it. September looms. What will I do?"

"You'll eat my *fregola,* Signora," Piera joked, lighting the stove, then placing a skillet upon a flame to gently sweat tiny cubes of carrots, onions, and celery glossy with olive oil.

"Goes without saying! It feels rather flat to finish our holiday with a party that ended in near tragedy." The tar-colored coffee swirled around her spoon. "I know!" she exclaimed, slamming down her cup. "A marvelous idea! A picnic! Goodness knows the boys could use a change of scene. They've been terrified to run around since the fact. It will be a special thank-you to Kavanagh, and the captain, of course, for their heroics. Could you ask Antonio to be available to take us all to Tharros on Friday?"

How would the whole family fit into his cab? "Gladly, Signora."

181

"Wonderful. Think carefully about what you'd like to prepare. I'll send Tore to pick everything up from the *salumeria* in town, yes? You two will come with us, of course. The boys will need supervising, obviously."

"Very well, Signora."

"How many times, child? Suzie! Please call me Suzie."

"Sorry, Signora."

"I'll run and tell Marito right away. He just loves that magical place! Bravo, girls! The world is bright once again!" She took off for the terrace, leaving a scent of rose cold cream in the air. But before she reached the door she twisted to a sudden halt. "Girls, you're to come and find me as soon as the sauce is ready. Marito and I will dine late. We'll let the evening staff finish up here. I'll have an invitation ready for you to take to Kavanagh now, yes?"

Carmela and Piera nodded.

Her second visit to America in three days; Agnes's tongue would be on fire.

"Grandmother's going to kill us," Piera said, the golden evening rays slanting on the road, catching the twinkle of mischief in her eyes.

"*After* the picnic, I hope."

"I've never seen Tharros."

"Antonio told me it's beautiful."

"How long does it take to get there?"

Carmela shrugged. "A long time. It's on the opposite coast."

"You think Grandmother will let us go?"

"Perhaps Grandmother won't know we're going."

Piera took a slow burn to her sister, unaccustomed to this secret rebellion. "I'm a bad influence on you."

The clatter of a vehicle climbing the hill drew the sisters to a standstill.

An army jeep snaked around the corner and then screeched to a halt.

"Evening, girls! In need of a ride, I see." Captain Casler flashed them a wide grin, revealing the startling white of his teeth.

The women offered polite smiles in reply.

"C'mon in, now. You headed to town?"

"No," Piera answered, unblinking.

"Hot date, ha?"

The girls stared at him.

"Suit yourself, missy!"

He accelerated away, leaving the girls waving off the cloud of white dust from their eyes.

"What was that?" Piera asked.

"A wolf in man's clothing."

The blond receptionist at the base looked

surprised to see Carmela. "It's you. Everything okay?"

"Yes. We have a note to give."

"Oh?" the receptionist answered, as if it was a surprise that any of the locals might write.

"For Lieutenant Kavanagh."

"I see." Her eyebrows rose a little, as if accustomed to the lieutenant receiving hand-delivered fan mail. "I'll be sure to give it to him when he arrives."

Carmela, unnerved by the disappointment of his not being there, reached into her pocket for the envelope. As she looked back up to hand it over the desk, a warm voice interrupted them.

"There she is!" Kavanagh said, bounding over to the women, offering a firm handshake and two polite kisses on both sisters' cheeks. Piera looked taken aback. She straightened her skirt, shifting from foot to foot.

"Come to give your answer?" he asked with a broad smile, his eyes alive with enthusiasm.

Carmela ignored her sister's perplexed stare. "We've been sent by Mrs. Curwin."

"Everything okay? I assured her we had concluded the sweep this morning. Nothing more found."

"Yes, fine. She sent us to give you this."

Carmela handed the envelope to him. He reached out a hand and took the lilac package. Carmela noted his scrubbed nails. As he began to unseal the invitation, the doors opened. Kavanagh looked toward the sound. His face lit up. The girls spun round. A slight woman with an elfin, heart-shaped face stood in the doorway. She had a neat auburn bob, a spray of freckles on her white cheeks, and a baby dangling on her hip.

Kavanagh ran. He wrapped his arms around her delicate frame. Then he took her cheeks in his big hands, gazed deep into the languid green pools of her eyes, and ran his lips all over her face. She laughed and whispered his name. Carmela, Piera, and the receptionist looked on, moved by the unbridled joy of the couple's reunion while feeling like awkward trespassers.

The baby caught Carmela's eye, bemused, till he was swooped up in Kavanagh's arms. He bowed his head in, inhaling the infant. Carmela remembered doing the same when she had been handed new baby cousins for the first time. Few things came close to the innocent pleasure of a baby's warm, oaty smell. She bent down to retrieve the envelope from the floor and handed it back to the receptionist, wondering when it would reach the recipient. Then she hooked her arm in Piera's, signaling their exit.

Kavanagh disappeared into his baby son and wife. He did not notice the sisters step out into the crimson dusk.

Chapter 9

In the early morning of the picnic day, Kavanagh pulled into the Curwins' villa driveway and parked his jeep beside Antonio's polished taxi. He stepped out and ran around to the other side, took the bundle of baby in his arms, and reached his hand for Virginia, who grasped his fingers and stepped out. She looked up at the house, taking in the bougainvillea blooms creeping around the arched lobby of the huge wooden door. "You'd do well to convince Captain Casler to put you up in a palace like this, Joe. I'm not sure I can put up with the deathly gray of the base for too long! You're a family man now."

"If anyone's moving off base to a home like this, Ginny, it'll be Casler."

"I saw how he looked at you at dinner last night. He adores you. You're the son he never had."

Seymour squirmed. Kavanagh adjusted

his blanket and rang the bell.

"Buon giorno," Carmela said, opening the door and welcoming the couple in.

"Carmela, this is my wife, Virginia."

"Piacere," Carmela said, shaking Virginia's hand, noticing how delicate her fingers felt. Before Carmela could gesture for them to make their way to the terrace, Mrs. Curwin breezed in, her magenta chiffon beach gown billowing behind her.

"My darlings, welcome! You must be Virginia. I'm Suzie." She stretched out her hand and placed the other on the small of Virgina's back, leading them through to the terrace. "Marito! Here's the lieutenant's first lady, bright as a button!"

"Good morning, it's a pleasure," Mr. Curwin said, as he placed his linen napkin on top of his plate, scattered with the crumbed remnants of breakfast. He stretched out his hand for a polite shake of Virginia's.

"Your home is simply stunning." Virginia smiled.

"If only it were ours!" Mrs. Curwin said, pouring a tiny porcelain cup of coffee for Virginia. "Now I really have something to worry about, a Southern belle with eyes like those. I shan't get a sensible conversation out of Marito all day!" She placed the saucer in Virginia's hand with a breathy giggle.

"Do excuse my wife, won't you, dear," Mr. Curwin said with a sardonic smile. "Picnics make British women a little overexcited. We so very rarely get to see the sun long enough to eat under it, you see."

Kavanagh pulled out a wooden chair for Virginia. She took a tentative seat.

"Please do give me that package, Lieutenant. I haven't smelled a baby's head in far too long." Mrs. Curwin wrapped her arms around Seymour and took him just beyond the terrace on a tour of the lemon trees, heavy with summer fruit beginning to glow in the rising sun.

"Carmela, please see the boys are ready to leave," Mr. Curwin said. "Antonio will help you load the car."

"Yes, Mr. Curwin." Carmela turned toward the kitchen, catching Kavanagh's eyes as she did. He took a breath to speak, but Mr. Curwin raised the coffeepot, offering a drink, and his attention shifted.

Carmela found Antonio and Piera already packing three large wicker hampers up on the kitchen table.

"She's like a fairy," Carmela said, setting down the breakfast tray upon the marble

189

counter by the sink.

"What's she done now?" Piera asked without taking her eyes off the large, stuffed loaf she was swaddling in cotton cloths.

"Not Mrs. Curwin, the lieutenant's wife."

"Perhaps she can magically move the food here, then?"

"Tell your sister to go half the speed and we'll get this in quicker," Antonio pleaded, looking at Carmela. "I say the same thing to my nephew — he's Papa of the bar for the day, I'm trying him out."

Piera waved her hands in the air as if swatting flies. "Gas about the Americans all you like, I have work to do."

Carmela took her place beside them and loaded another hamper with peaches and plums wrapped in brown paper. She wanted to mention the fashionable mint green of Virginia's immaculate linen dress, or the fact that nothing about her delicate frame suggested it had produced another living being only months ago, but thought better of it.

As Antonio heaved the hampers and several canvas sun umbrellas into the trunk of his taxi, Carmela and Piera tried to round up the Curwin boys — who found great pleasure in hiding at the precise moment their cooperation was required. They were eventually discovered cowering in the bathtub of the upstairs bathroom. Roger, the golden boy, both in looks and personality, was hiding behind Vernon, his elder sibling. The latter teetered on the precipice of pubescence; his matt of dark locks flopping over his black eyes, forever bright with scheming mischief. Their cheeks were bronzed with a Sardinian summer, several shades darker than their usual pale skin. Carmela reached in a hand and hauled them out. "Come on now, you have a brand-new Sardinian taxi to ride in!" They leaped over the side of the tub and scuttled downstairs, sniggering, bundling into the backseat of Antonio's taxi. Mrs. Curwin was sitting there already, too excited about the trip to let the boys' escapades fluster her. Mr. Curwin slid onto the front seat beside Antonio.

"Must we ride with the help?" Virginia asked, as Kavanagh helped her up into the passenger seat of the jeep.

"It's the least I can do in return for the scare the other night. Besides, an extra set of hands will come in useful with Seymour, don't you think? They're good folk."

Virginia looked down at her son's sleepy face. "It's hardly the romantic drive you promised, Joe."

"Just you wait. The views where we're going even make me believe in God."

"If your father could hear you now, Joe," she said with a flirtatious grin, "the most blasphemous son of a preacher man I ever did know. I praise the Lord for every irresistible drop of devil in you."

Carmela watched as the two kissed. She caught herself noticing the fullness of Kavanagh's lips. Piera stomped in behind her carrying a leather sack of water and a cloth bag of *formagelle,* sweet cheese tarts. "If Grandmother could see us now," she whispered.

The sisters locked eyes, twinkling conspirators, and took their seats in the back of the jeep.

The party began the descent toward the coast, winding through the hills on the outskirts of Simius. Each bend revealed neighboring villas. Cypress-tree-lined drives led off the main road toward small crumbling palaces, postcards from the glory days of the valley. Nestled high in the hills tiny, private stone chapels faced a copper horizon. Beyond the military base they turned west and climbed toward the Gennargentu forest, inland. The pavement gave way to white roads that wound through the alder and yew woods, the air aromatic with lavender, myrtle, and thyme. The road grew steeper. Carmela and Piera could feel their ears popping. Seymour gave a jerk and began to wail.

"Honey, pull over!" Virginia shouted over the rattle of the jeep.

"I know a spot a little farther up," Kavanagh called back, zigzagging to miss a pothole.

The road narrowed. Carmela looked into the thicket as they passed ancient oaks and craggy corks — a place untouched, somewhere fairy tales were born.

Kavanagh turned onto a narrower dirt track, the trees' branches almost brushing against the side of the jeep. Moments later he reached a standstill by the edge of a tiny pool. For a brief moment, the hidden lagoon and the sound of the fresh water trickling over a cluster of low, shiny boulders beside it silenced even Seymour before he returned to his hungry lament with a frantic crescendo.

"Mrs. Kavanagh, please, I can take baby while you get ready to feed," Carmela offered, accustomed to helping her aunts with their newborns.

The expression Virginia flashed her lay between confusion and affront.

"Thank you, Carmela," Kavanagh said, taking Seymour from Virginia. He twisted back to Carmela, passing Seymour over as if he were a delicate china cup. Kavanagh's fingers brushed against her wrists as he pulled away. Although Seymour was red with fury and impatience, Carmela decided his cheeks were still edible, the blue of his eyes the absolute mirror of his father's.

Kavanagh opened the door for Virginia and then moved back to the trunk. Antonio pulled in beside him, his backseat vibrating with bickering boys squawking about nothing.

"The ride didn't seem quite so long when the children were smaller." Mrs. Curwin sighed, stepping out and stretching. "But could we have asked for a prettier rest spot? Well done, Lieutenant — you know these back roads like a native!"

Carmela looked up trying to see where Virginia had chosen to sit and nurse her boy, expecting to spy her on the smooth rocks a little way from the group, but a noise drew her around. Virginia was searching deep in the baggage for something. It was the first time she had seen the hint of a flustered new mother in the woman who, till now, appeared a young girl playing with a doll. A moment later she returned clasping a glass bottle with a decorative picture painted along the side. Carmela watched her unscrew the lid and flip it over to reveal a brown, rubber nipple. She placed it under her arm. Kavanagh, meanwhile, took out a small can and began to open it. A cream-colored liquid was poured from it and into the bottle. Virginia resumed her place upon the passenger seat, waiting for Kavanagh to hand her Seymour. He reached his arms out to Carmela, taking the screaming bundle for his wife. The nipple touched Seymour's lips. His cries came to an instant halt. The sound of the water had to fight for an audience no longer.

It came as no surprise that the whole operation had been orchestrated with well-rehearsed, military precision, though Carmela couldn't help but wonder how on earth the woman scrambled through the nights if this dance had to be performed every few hours in the moonlight. She thought about Lucia, who took but seconds to loosen her shirt and cradle her babe to suckle at her breast.

"Stop gawping and help me hand out the refreshments," Piera said, hopping out of the jeep.

Carmela followed her sister toward the water's edge. They placed a small linen cloth upon one of the flatter rocks, opened up the cloth sack, and laid out a handful of the *for-*

magelle, small cheese tarts sweetened with honey, candied orange, and raisins. The Curwin boys descended upon them as if they hadn't eaten since Christmas.

"Boys! Wash those hands! And don't go too far. This is just a quick pit stop!" Mrs. Curwin yelled. "Let the guests help themselves first." She walked toward Virginia. "Honestly. One summer running wild and all manners simply evaporate. You'll forgive them, won't you?"

"I am the youngest to five brothers, Mrs. Curwin —"

"Suzie, please."

"I know boys all too well, *Suzie.* They need to eat a small house-load of food. My mama had two cooks just to keep up with them. This one's halfway there already!" Virginia looked down at her son's mouth. Carmela saw an expression flicker across the new mother's face. It wasn't the warmth of a maternal gaze she might have expected. Something more stilted, awkward even.

"Good heavens, Suzie," Mr. Curwin said, stepping toward the women, "there arc ladies who really do speak like Scarlett O'Hara after all. My inner adolescent is performing celebratory somersaults as we speak."

Mrs. Curwin rolled her eyes. "Marito! Do

ignore him, won't you?"

Virginia giggled.

Kavanagh approached the rock where Carmela and Piera were arranging the tartlets. "Do you ladies cook all day?"

"You want?" Piera asked.

"Sure!"

Carmela crouched down and folded one in a cloth napkin. He took a bite. His expression made the sisters swell with pride.

"Ginny, you've got to try these," he called back to his wife. "It's like cheesecake. Only better!"

Virginia looked up for a brief second, squinting as if she hadn't heard, before returning to her conversation with Mrs. Curwin.

"I'll take another," he said. "There's my ruin right there!" He chuckled with a glint of playfulness that Carmela hadn't seen since the night he had described the island to her, in the half light by Salvatore's hospital bed. Her eyes were drawn away for a moment, toward Virginia, who she now realized was waving her over. Carmela walked to her. Seymour had inhaled the contents of his bottle.

"You may wind him," Virginia said. "I must stretch my legs."

She handed the baby over to Carmela like

a package delivered to her by mistake and walked to the edge of the water to join Kavanagh. Seymour was not a light package either, despite his tender age. Carmela felt his tiny heart galloping against her shoulder and rubbed her hand up and down his back, enjoying the intimacy of holding Virginia and Kavanagh's child. A baby felt like the distilled version of the people who created it, a tiny, concentrated version of them in part, even though his personality was entirely distinct. Seymour jerked his head this way and that, trying to understand everything about him. It reminded her of the way his father would study those around him. As she reached the waterfall, Seymour let out a deep belch, more appropriate for an overfed grandfather holding court at the head of a crowded family table. Then his face creased into a scowl, his eyes narrowing in the same way Virginia's had a moment ago.

"Carmela, I saved us one," Piera said, walking over to her and holding a couple of tartlets. "Not bad for a Yank is he, eh? We've lived here all our lives and no one ever took us here! It doesn't even seem real, does it?"

"Heaven-sent."

"Baby's got you all poetic."

"Look at those cheeks, Pie'."

"He's a fat bugger," Piera said with a grin, taking a wide bite of her tart.

There was a rustle a few paces away. The sisters froze. Their gaze darted toward the thick of the trees. It wouldn't be unusual to come across wild boar in these parts, and if she was with her babes she may not think twice about using her tusks. Piera's eyebrows furrowed. The sisters began silent steps back toward the group, taking shallow breaths. What they saw next stopped them in their tracks.

A wild horse, its coat a lustrous chestnut, slunk out from behind a large oak. Its tail swished. Its ears moved back and forth, as he intuited whether the two women and baby before him were friend or foe. Piera turned toward Antonio on the other side of the pool. She caught his eye and pointed toward the horse. Antonio touched Mr. Curwin lightly on the arm. He turned toward the trees. The remainder of the herd revealed themselves. The party stood still, gazing at the diminutive animals. They were the size of ponies, but their build was that of a full-grown horse. A few were black, but most were the deep brown of the Sardinian brush. Everyone watched in silence, even the Curwin boys, as the animals bent down to chew on the damp, herb-covered ground.

Virginia, however, powdering her nose, was the last to notice the silence. When she did, she let out an involuntary gasp, startling the herd so that several reared back on their haunches and raised their front hoofs. Seymour followed his mother's lead and broke into unstoppable shrieks. Kavanagh ran to Carmela and took his baby in his arms. All the while Virginia stayed rooted, in panic, to the ground beside the vehicles.

Mrs. Curwin put an arm around Virginia. "It's all right, darling girl, the boy is fine."

"Where in Lord's name have you brought us, Joe?! What other wild animals are there, for Chrissakes?!" Everyone shifted, unnerved by Virginia's sudden contemptuous snarl.

Mr. Curwin stepped forward, armed with British etiquette. "Dearest Virginia, I too was most alarmed the first time we came across the wild horses of Giara. They are usually to be found on the plains just beyond here. Perhaps the heat of the morning brings them to this cool drinking hole. Much like us, I dare say. I can assure you that they are perfectly harmless. Like the natives, my dear, they appear far more formidable than they in fact are."

The horses' ears twitched. With a flick of their hair they beat a retreat and were swallowed back into the brush.

"Well, now I feel quite the fool." Virginia's swift recovery was as alarming as her launch into hysteria. "It's not what I had expected in these parts, is all."

"Perfectly understandable, my dear," Mr. Curwin reassured her. "Though I'm sure a lady such as yourself is no stranger to equine pursuits."

Her face lit up. "Absolutely."

Carmela moved to the jeep and poured some water from the leather flask into a small enamel cup. She handed it to Virginia, though from her expression it was clear that Virginia suspected the contents to be contaminated. She refused it with an unconvincing smile.

"Thank you, Carmela," Kavanagh said, stepping in beside her. "I'll gladly take some."

Carmela reached out for the baby so that Kavanagh could drink easier, but Virginia swooped in. "That's quite all right, I'll take the boy, thank you. I'm sure Mrs. Curwin will be needing you."

Carmela walked away and then bent down to rinse her hands in the shallow pool. The cool of the water felt good. Antonio moved in beside her. "Someone's got a dynamite stick shoved where it oughtn't, eh?"

"*Shhh,* you'll get us in trouble."

"I'm not the one who nearly got her child flattened by a pack of wild horses," he said, eyes smiling with mischief.

"Stop it," Carmela replied. "Your nephew must be doing a good job of running the bar, then, if you're relaxed enough to tease me."

"Chauffeur for the day — make more than a week's worth of espressos."

"You're not in this just for the money, surely. You're in it for the gossip."

"Seeing how the other half lives is what I call an education. We've lived by the horse and cart too long, Carmela. I'm Sardinian, but I'm no savage. Look around you, girl. We were born in paradise, and we don't even know it. Those morons who sit at my bar and curse the foreigners don't see the gold mine beneath us." He looked up toward where the horses had appeared. "Antonio Comida is going to show our countrymen that there's a difference between pride and diffidence. I love my island, Carmela, and if I can make my fortune by sharing it, I will."

"And if that doesn't work, you can always consider a life on the stage."

Antonio chuckled.

"Come on, let's head back, Anto', before any more ambushes from the wild."

A short while later, they left the forest behind them, and the road continued uphill toward the expanse of the Giara plains. Here, under the white midmorning sun, the grasses swayed in the fragrant thyme and rosemary breeze. The valley opened up, the formidable slopes of the Gennargentu mountain range stretching as far as the eye could see. Trees fought for survival over a blanket of rocky brush, shunting out in improbable angles from the cliffs, raising their branches as if delivering prayers of gratitude. In the near distance a waterfall spouted from behind a rock into three small pools, cascading down into a larger one below — a natural bath for anyone who would ever dare clamber up the sheer rock face to reach it. Onward they drove toward the west.

As they left the majesty of Gennargentu behind them, the wide, wild, aquamarine expanse of the Oristano coast opened into view. Virginia squealed in delight.

"What did I tell you?" shouted Kavanagh over the clatter of the engine and the wind. His pride in sharing the island was something Carmela would have expected only from a local.

"My God, Joe, that is the most beautiful water I've ever seen!"

The road curved slightly, unveiling the rocky ruins of Tharros, a small, ancient city sprawled along the hillside. A pair of Corinthian columns gleamed white, triumphant remnants of ancient Roman domination. Carmela gazed, wide-eyed, at the antiquity. It would be but moments before she might stand where Phoenicians once ruled the crystalline waters of her Mediterranean. Kavanagh slowed down and let Antonio drive beside him. Mr. Curwin wound down his window.

"It's just up here, Lieutenant — *poco minuti!*" Antonio shouted.

Kavanagh followed Antonio's taxi till he turned in and parked in the shade of a cluster of pines beside the ruins. A narrow path led off from the edge of the stone city and snaked down between dunes toward a deserted stretch of beach. It swept into the sea in a wide curve beside a fortress rising at the farthest point. The travelers stepped out of their vehicles and into a salty breeze.

"Glorious, Lieutenant — simply breathtaking!" Mrs. Curwin called out, stretching her arms up into the welcome relief of the cool air off the sea. A cluster of rocks and a strip of pine trees sheltered the cove. Once the cars were parked, Mrs. Curwin and Virginia were the first to step out. The crystal clear water beckoned; the Curwin boys ran through the faded mosaic-lined streets of the ruins, ripping off their clothes as they ran, sliding down the sandy banks and diving headfirst into the shallows. Mrs. Curwin and Virginia, holding Seymour in her arms, sauntered between the columns, gazing up at their crumbling stone, with the same hushed awe as those walking into a huge, deserted cathedral.

"Let us cool off in the water, then I'll be glad to explore, won't you?" Mrs. Curwin asked.

"Certainly — I've never seen anything like it!"

Carmela, Piera, and Antonio met at the trunks, unloading the hampers, umbrellas, and the couple of Windbreakers Mrs. Curwin had insisted on bringing for the new mother and child.

Kavanagh reached Carmela as she grappled with the last basket. "Here, let me," he said, taking both handles in his hand. "Don't want the master chefs to hurt themselves, do I?" He flashed her a wide grin, bristling with the enthusiasm of a little boy. "I don't think I'm the first American to be dumbstruck by something so old."

"I don't think I'm the first Sardinian either," Carmela replied, overcome by the silent majesty of the place.

It took little to imagine these streets, now sustaining their battle against moss and weeds, humming with merchants and sailors. The atmosphere was thick with stories. She had never been to a place where such history was so palpable. The caves near the farm were even older perhaps, but theirs was a darker, more remote history. The deep holes in the rock where those Neolithic people sepulchered their dead didn't share this atmosphere. Here, in the delicate moldings of the Corinthian columns, were the traces of the beginnings of the new world — a physical link to modern civilization, where poets and philosophers were prized.

"I've been wanting to come back here," Kavanagh said, gazing along the stones of what looked like a wide avenue. "I'm glad it's having the same effect on you as it did me the first time I saw it!"

Carmela tore her eyes away from the white stone to watch him heave the load up on his head and negotiate the sandy banks down to the shore. She took a deep breath of the crisp air and began her own walk through the ruins, listening to the sound of her heels ricochet off the sides of buildings that were most intact. She pictured those ancient ships sailing to the busy port at the foot of the bay, loaded with kings and their riches. She imagined this hillside teaming with workers and dark-skinned Phoenician princesses, dripping with ruby-encrusted gold necklaces, their light robes dancing on the sea breeze.

Shrieks of laughter drew her eye back down to the cove, where Mrs. Curwin frolicked with her sons, diving in and out of the sea, a staggering azure backdrop to the blanched bricks of the ruins and the white sand. She splashed her offspring. The light played upon the dappled water, tracing undulating flecks of sun. Carmela watched Mrs. Curwin run her hands through her hair, sweeping it off her handsome face. She wished that one day she too might swim as lady of the house, with a halter-neck suit of floral fabric clinging to the voluptuous curves of her own hips and bosom. One day she too would bring her children to this magical place. She would teach them the richness of their isle, instill a deep pride in the abundance of its natural beauty and colorful history.

Piera tore Carmela out of her reverie with the frantic waving of her arms from behind one of the breakers, no doubt already laying out the lunch spread for after the Curwins' swim. Carmela took big strides down to her, feeling the powdery sand fall away underfoot, marveling at how this day would ever be deemed work.

CHAPTER 10

Just as Carmela and Antonio finished unfolding the last of the wooden deck chairs, the rumble of a vehicle drew the gaze of the group up toward the dunes. Captain Casler appeared at its peak, grinning like an intrepid explorer on the precipice of an insurmountable mountain. His hands were fixed on his square hips; the wind blew his reddish locks off his freckled face. "I'm no church man, Kavanagh," he boomed down to the party, "but this sure as hell makes me think there's a guy upstairs after all!" With wide strides he barreled down the slope toward the group.

Mrs. Curwin jumped to her feet and raced to meet him, planting kisses from her sea-cooled lips on each of his cheeks and hooking her arm in his. "So you made it after all, Captain! We are honored."

"Honor's all mine, ma'am. I brought me some locals along to help. Nice to have company on a long ride, but it looks like you already thought of that."

Carmela glanced up at the girl in Casler's jeep.

"The Chirigoni sisters are the finest cooks in town, you must know that. Wouldn't want anything but the best picnic for our final jolly before we head back to London, Captain."

"You could feed me bologna, ma'am, I wouldn't notice. Not with you dancin' around in that swimsuit."

"Marito, darling! You're to save me immediately. I fear the captain's intentions aren't entirely wholesome after all. . . ."

"For once," Mr. Curwin called up to them from where he had disappeared into a deck chair, eyes masked beneath the tipped rim of his Panama hat, "your instincts are perfectly accurate. Luckily I made a pact with the lieutenant. He has agreed to protect one and all from my violent fits of jealousy."

A ripple of laughter.

Mrs. Curwin ushered Casler toward Virginia. "I assume the two of you are well acquainted."

"Good afternoon, Captain," Virginia answered with a wide smile.

The captain guffawed with a lascivious twinkle. "Good God, Kavanagh, you want to ruin me altogether, man? I can't be responsible for my actions this afternoon. Tell me what man could be with these visions before me."

"Come now, Captain," Virginia cooed, "it's just like what Mama taught me about food. Enjoy the look of it, but you need only take one small bite."

"Sure. Which piece do I try first?"

The group's cackles flew out to sea on the welcome breeze. Carmela glanced at them as she smoothed the linen tablecloth upon the low folding table, weighed down into the sand. It pleased her to see that Kavanagh's smile seemed a little forced, strained into coercion, by his senior. Carmela caught a fleeting streak of raw ambition in Virginia's eyes. From her outburst by the water it was clear that she was used to playing the lady of the house. Carmela noticed Kavanagh's protective gaze drifting toward Seymour throughout the conversation, while his wife's was fixed firmly on the one man responsible for any possible promotion of her husband's rank.

An undulation of envy swelled in the pit of her stomach. Carmela tried to concentrate on the tiny, white ripples of the water as they lapped at the powdery sand, willing them to wash the feeling away.

"Carmela?" Antonio strutted over to her. "Your grandmother keeps you girls under a tight fist, eh? One hour in the sun and you look as pained as a white Brit!"

Carmela squinted back at him.

"She can look after herself just fine."

The familiar voice pulled Carmela's view back into sharp focus. "Agnes?"

"Why am I surprised you're not happy to see me?"

"Play nicely, girls," Antonio said, turning to go help Piera. "Some of us are here to work."

Carmela shifted and smoothed her skirt. "To what do we owe the pleasure?"

"You think you're the only girl in Simius who gets to hang on the arm of an American?"

"Pardon?"

"Heard Blue Eyes is looking for a translator. My cousin works at the hospital, told me a certain local had made quite the impression, but I'm sure he would be open to other candidates offering themselves for the job. Those who have more time to help. Those less greedy, maybe, who don't have two jobs already, say."

"What are you doing here?"

"Captain invited a few of us to join the party. I don't waste time with the lower ranks myself."

"A married man, Agnes."

"Just can't help themselves."

Carmela turned and began to walk over to the hampers. "I have lunch to serve."

"That's how those Yanks like their women, right? Bending over for them?"

"Some of us have pride," Carmela said, whipping around. "Look at the beauty around you, Agnes. *That's* something to be proud of. Not how quickly you can seduce a married man!"

The suggestion of a smile curled the corner of Agnes's mouth.

Carmela, off-guard, felt the fire rise in her chest and flush her cheeks. For a moment Agnes had the same smug furl of her lips as Rosa did the day Carmela discovered her affair. "Hang off a uniform like a bad smell all you want, but don't you ever, *ever* talk to me like that again!"

"Hot breath from a bride-to-be."

Agnes turned and sauntered toward the captain, who introduced her to the other women with the roving hands of a dubious uncle.

"What in Jesus's name is Agnes doing here?!" Piera piped, arriving with a parcel of stuffed bread.

"Headed to slaughter."

"Go put your feet in the water for a bit. Antonio said you looked pale. I'll finish up here."

Carmela took the loaf from her sister and began cutting it into thick slices. The smell of *mortadella* and ham mixed with the marinated peppers and eggplant that she and her sister had stuffed it with drew her back to the start of the day: the cool, clean of the kitchen, the safe order of her world. She arranged the slices on a wide plate, then cut thin lengths of chicory and made a green nest at the center before trimming a couple of stalks of celery and placing those on top. "I'm fine."

Carmela's thoughts drifted to her mother, as they often did when she prepared meals. She pictured Maria at the family meal, un-flustered by her grandmother's rants and stream of criticism. In the same way, Car-mela focused on the salty slab of *pecorino* upon the chopping board, hoping that each neat cube she cut would etch away the pulsating. She didn't dare look up at Agnes, bouncing without a care in a polka-dot bikini. She didn't want to notice the gentle wave of her thick hair or her porcelain thighs or the way the women looked at her. Nor did she care to notice Mrs. Curwin and Virginia take in her thick eyebrows, wolf eyes, plump lips, with a mixture of admiration and masked disdain. They were unaccustomed to socializing with the local women in any capacity other than domestics.

Agnes's pidgin English appeared to impress them, though Carmela wondered whether she had mastered it enough to tell a joke, or if the laughter was at her expense. Either way it shouldn't have mattered. What did Carmela care if Kavanagh flashed Agnes the same winning grin he had to her earlier? What did it matter that Agnes played into the cheap stereotype of the local girl, an easy target for the dazzle of American dreams?

But she did care. Somewhere along the drive here, she had begun to care. Somewhere between watching Kavanagh's tender gaze at his babe in arms and the pleasure with which the lieutenant had eaten her food, she began to care. Carmela tried to concentrate on the fresh, sea-salted air, the whisper of pine sap in the breeze, her daydreams of those Phoenicians, but her mind wouldn't shift. It stayed fixed on that gentle face bathed in sunlight. Kavanagh looked back at her. He was about to call to her. Carmela's chest tightened. Before he could speak, Virginia hooked her arm in his, led him to the water's edge, and waded into the shallows. The sea would feel like a warm bath at this time of day.

What of the palpable change that had taken place just in the few hours' drive from the base through unchartered lands of her own island? What of the dull pang of sorrow creeping in, as she felt something close to coveting another woman's man? Another woman's life? What of those deep, blue eyes, bright with intelligence and curiosity and respect and gentleness that could make another forget their beginnings, futures, or plans? That could make a girl dream bigger than she'd dare and cry for an eternity — with happiness, with pain. What about Franco? What of it all? This is life, thought Carmela. We are to live, not chase, not run about without aim, nor gallop toward hell, nor catch the bait of provocateurs like Agnes. There was cheese to serve and bread to pass.

She watched Virginia holding Seymour on her hip and began to imagine herself slinking into beautiful summer gowns a few months after delivering her own baby, not a trace of her travails on her body. Would she leap off her mother's bed like her aunt did, running down to the fountain within hours of her cousin slipping into the world? She tried to imagine Franco with his arms wrapped around her sweaty body, after she had pushed out a beautiful soul. But she could not feel the heat, found it impossible to imagine him holding her in that raw state. She tried to think about them making love in the days that followed, celebrating the unstoppable pulse of life, but the pictures felt forced, contrived, the figures acting out the scene like unconvincing amateur players.

"Carmela, dear, that smells wonderful!" Mrs. Curwin waved her over toward the group.

Carmela balanced two plates in each hand, hoping her racing thoughts were not streaked over her face for all to see.

"What time is it, Joe?" Virginia asked.

Kavanagh looked up at the sun. "I'd say almost midday, least my belly tells me so!"

The women laughed. Agnes was the loudest.

"Seymour's nap time," Virginia announced.

"He looks happy to me, don't ya, fella?" Kavanagh jiggled him up and down on his hip, besotted.

"Ask Carmela to put him down for his sleep."

Kavanagh took Virginia by the arm. "Just

excuse us a moment, Carmela." They moved off toward the Windbreakers. Carmela strained to follow their whispered conversation above Mrs. Curwin and Casler's chatter.

"Carmela is not our help. She understands English. Don't speak to her like an illiterate servant."

"Your boss is on the brink of promoting you and all you want to do is talk about some dumb local's language skills, for Chrissakes!" she spat. "Joe: champion of the downtrodden — cute, but not the time!"

She stomped back to the group.

"Carmela, take Seymour to his carry cot and lay him down," she said flatly, someone asking another to pass the butter dish.

"Here, Captain," Mrs. Curwin interjected, ever the sublime hostess, "let me offer you a slice of this." She took the plates from Carmela. Her boys dashed toward her from the water, shaking their heads like dogs after a dip. "Boys! You're getting us all wet!"

"Good-lookin' fellas they are too, ma'am. A credit to you," Casler said.

"Perhaps, but I fear their appetite somewhat overrides their manners. I apologize. Do try this cheese, Captain, it comes from the Chirigoni farm!" She took the wooden board. "To die for!"

Mr. Curwin wandered over to them, handing out glasses of white *vermentino.* "When you get tired of my wife's effervescence, Captain, I'll do my duty and pretend I'm listening."

Glasses clinked. More laughter. Agnes shot Carmela a look, which she ignored. Seymour was placed into her arms, and Carmela wandered under the shade of an umbrella to lay him inside his cot. He looked at her, perplexed, staring wide-eyed at the blue sky beyond the umbrella. Carmela was unaccustomed to laying babies down at the beach, or at all. Her infant cousins had always been appendages on her aunts' bosoms till they collapsed into sweet, milky sleep. To tear Seymour away to a separate area while still wide-awake seemed peculiar.

At first he enjoyed the freedom of letting his tiny feet explore the air above him, his legs kicking invisible targets, then running with zeal to nowhere. The bright aqua of his eyes was lighter than his father's but had the same open quality. Then his brows furrowed, and Carmela thought she could see the scowl of his mother. His tiny mouth opened wide. He let out a wail to raise the dead. She picked him up and held him to her chest, but his legs and arms flailed in rebellion. Cradling him, she began a hesitant move toward the group. Virginia stood at the water's edge sipping her wine beside Casler.

"Excuse me, Lieutenant," Carmela said, tentative.

Kavanagh turned. On hearing his son's cries he raced up to her. "What a lot of noise, sir!" he said, taking his boy in his arms. A droplet of seawater ran down Kavanagh's temple, off his chin, and onto Seymour.

Virginia looked back for Kavanagh. "Joe? What are you doing?" she called up from the water.

"Where are the bottles, honey?" he shouted back.

"It's nap time, Joe. No bottle."

Virginia turned back to Casler, hanging on his every word, her green eyes fawnlike in the sun — something he appeared to be enjoying a great deal.

Carmela stood, waiting for direction, unsure how much of her own instinct she was expected to act on. If she were Seymour's mother, she would sit upon a rock, her feet in the water, and let the hungry baby suckle at her bosom. She thought about her own mother. When babies from up the street were fussy and their mothers were out in the fields or too exhausted from broken nights, Maria would feed them. There were several adolescents who still called her their Milk Mother with affection.

Seymour's face was red with fury now.

"Joe! Captain has a wonderful story you just got to hear!" Virginia shouted out, waving Kavanagh down to her. For a moment Carmela could see the lieutenant fighting his own instincts to cradle his screaming child. Virginia was not someone he made the habit of contradicting.

"He will be fine, Lieutenant."

"Yes." Something flashed in his eyes. Apology? Embarrassment?

"Joe! C'mon! No baby died of crying!" Virginia called.

He slipped off his shirt and ran down to the shore.

Carmela noticed the way his back muscles rippled.

"You're to lay him down!" Virginia bellowed before she slipped her slim arm around her husband and placed a protective hand on his bare chest. Carmela hoped to enjoy Mr. Curwin's anecdotes from where she sat, but nothing could be heard over Seymour's wailing.

"Don't worry," Piera said with a grin as she reached her with an empty plate ready

221

to be refilled. "In a little while you'll be barking out orders to your own house girl. Franco will make sure you won't have to wipe any asses, no?"

Carmela reached back and placed Seymour against her chest. She hummed a made-up tune. It didn't take long for him to acquiesce to sleep in her arms, even if he put up a good fight. She listened to his galloping heartbeat and decided that if anyone would be feeling the thump of her own baby against their chest, it would be hers alone. Seymour's fingers unfurled and then clasped around her forefinger. Was this how Franco had seen their lives? Had he planned to make her a kept woman? Produce babies for others to lull to sleep? They hadn't spoken of this openly, and it wasn't a thought that had crept up before today. She watched the party frolic in the shallows, her eyes on a brazen Agnes while she sat holding a stranger's baby. An icy bolt of jealousy scored through her, followed by the bitter taste of guilt. She realized, at this precise moment, that there was only one of those women laughing by the shore whom she longed to be.

CHAPTER 11

The following morning, the Curwins' residence reverberated with the cacophony of departure. Antonio loaded the last of the cases into, and on top of, his cab. The boys dashed around the house, a final marking of their territory. Once Mrs. Curwin had organized her vanity for the third time, she returned to powdering her nose in the hallway mirror. Mr. Curwin, an island surrounded by frenzied waters, stole a moment of solitude in the bright morning sun by the back table on the terrace, savoring his final espresso, breathing in the hot, fruity air.

"*Buon viaggio,* Mr. Curwin," Carmela said, clearing the remaining dirty dishes.

"Yes. Thank you," he answered, placing his cup down onto his saucer with a sigh. "And there it is. Another year, gone. Sardinia has seduced once more. She's like a mistress you simply cannot live without, costing one a small fortune to keep her in the manner to which she has become accustomed."

"I am glad."

"Back to the real world."

"Yes."

"I suppose this is all too real to you."

Carmela let his words hang, unsure whether he was enjoying the wistful rhetoric or inviting conversation.

"Once again, you and Piera have been astounding." He stood up, returning to business.

"Thank you," Carmela replied.

"For the two of you," he said, handing her a small envelope.

Carmela always felt a twinge of embarrassment at the ritual, unchanged in all the years she had worked for the family. "Signor Curwin, there is no need."

"Certainly," he replied, placing the envelope inside her palm. She knew that inside there would be half a week's pay, enough to buy most of the fabric for an entire trousseau — or partway toward an airplane ticket, perhaps? Mr. Curwin turned on his heel and walked toward the front door. Carmela stood for a moment, listening to the chorus of crickets and the echoes of the Curwin family's voices from inside, bouncing off the stone walls and terra-cotta tiles.

Heels approached. Carmela turned. Mrs. Curwin stepped out onto the terrace, radiating elegance in her crisp, white linen suit. Carmela felt like a barefoot farmhand.

"The next time I see you, you will be a beautiful newlywed." Mrs. Curwin placed her hands on Carmela's shoulders. "I wasn't nervous in the slightest before I married Marito. Goodness knows how many tried to push me up that aisle before him. But once I met Sam, everything was clear. And that's the way. Enjoy each other, Carmela." She seemed to search Carmela for something. Carmela bowed her eyes, embarrassed by the maternal outpouring.

"And laugh," Mrs. Curwin added. "Promise me you'll laugh!"

Carmela met Mrs. Curwin's eyes again, willing the feeling in the pit of her stomach to be something closer to excitement. "Of course."

Mrs. Curwin planted a polite kiss on each of Carmela's cheeks, her lily of the valley cologne stronger than usual. "*Arrivederci,* then!"

"*Sì, arrivederci,* Signora."

Mrs. Curwin turned back to Carmela. "You will be a radiant bride. You'll hate me saying this, I'm sure, but your beauty is something rare. It's like a light. Pure. Bright.

225

Utterly irresistible, as far as I can tell! And the best thing about it, Carmela dear, is that you won't believe a word of what I've just said" — she gave a breathy laugh — "and I'm not being flippant about my invitation to work for me in London, you know that, don't you? Just say the word."

Carmela, embarrassed by Mrs. Curwin's outpouring and invitation, could but smile in reply. It seemed like Mrs. Curwin wanted to impart a further nugget of bridal wisdom but then thought better of it, much to Carmela's relief. They looked at each other, unspoken thoughts hovering, until Mrs. Curwin turned away, and Carmela followed her and the rest of the family to the door. Piera left the stripping of the beds upstairs to join them. The sisters stood on the stoop, waving the clan farewell.

"I'll be back for you two," Antonio yelled to them as he walked around to open his taxi doors for the Curwins.

"Thank you, Toni!" Carmela called back.

The taxi started down the driveway. A few minutes later, all that was left of the English and their summer of 1952 was a cloud of sun-toasted dust.

"I'm almost done upstairs, won't take me long," Piera said, shuffling inside.

Every year, the Curwins' departure would

herald the onset of a brief melancholy, soon followed with the excitement of the summer that would follow. This year it was different. Next summer, it was likely Carmela would receive the guests as mistress of the house. She couldn't imagine that Franco would allow her to work for them once she became his wife. His honor would prevent him from allowing her to do so, in his own uncle's villa. "Pie', do you ever think about London?"

"What do you mean?"

Carmela billowed a dust sheet and watched it land over one of the armchairs. "I mean, do you wonder what our lives would be like somewhere else?"

The cold truth of her thoughts chilled her. Once she was too young to chase after her dreams, and now, watching the Curwins for the last time as a young bride-to-be, it was likely she would never get the chance to explore any other life beyond her own in Simius.

"I think people are happy when they're on holiday," Piera said.

"You really think they would be so different over there?"

"Tie your shoes tighter."

"What?"

"They keep itching your feet. Don't suppose you'll be planning on dancing the polka at your wedding?"

"Of course. Naked. While I howl up at the moon."

Piera cackled.

The white sheets draped over the furniture formed the craggy angles of a mountainous, foreboding land. "I just want to know if you think about it, Pie', that's all."

"No one feeds a family on dreams."

"But you do think about it, don't you?"

"I can just picture Franco now, leaving all this behind to go wash Mr. Curwin's car every weekend," she answered, flippant, but there was the spark of sincerity in her eyes. Carmela forced a smile and covered a second chair. Another pang of sorrow. What was this dull ache? The fact that she would be sharing a marriage bed soon, no longer curled alongside her sister as she had been for the past twenty-one years? Why, this morning, did ripples of uncertainty rise and fall, like the ebb of a wave as it creeps up to gloss the dry sand on the shore? Carmela waded in these new and uncomfortable sensations, a sea of silenced, wordless doubts. Trying to decipher or articulate the foreign feeling, even to herself, was futile. The more she tried, the quicker the thoughts spiraled away, like water down a drain.

Carmela tried to convince herself that these feelings were rooted in the fear of how her relationship with her sister would change after she married Franco. Then the gray mist of doubt clouded her thoughts. Once married, London would be a pipe dream after all. These fluttering conversations with Piera would never happen again. A sadness swelled inside. In her heart she couldn't say that she had ever truly longed for a life elsewhere. But at the same time, she didn't truly long for a life in Simius either.

Kavanagh's work proposal had confused her. It was the first time somebody had treated her as an adult and offered her a responsibility unrelated to whatever she had done before. It was exhilarating, more so, even, than becoming a married woman. Those responsibilities now felt overwhelming, crushing. It was time to grow up, but all of a sudden, watching the Curwins leave, the adult Carmela had decided to become seemed like a cold stranger. That dull, nagging feeling had resurfaced. Her thoughts broke off in tangents, sprouting new questions and doubts. She had never hidden anything from her sister before now. It felt wrong. Worse, even, than allowing the whispered second-guessing of her marriage to spiral in her mind.

"And if I did think about it," Piera answered, finally, "I'd picture you by my side."

She ran up the stairs, closing the conversation before Carmela could reply.

The beady eyes painted on Franco's great-grandmother's portrait pierced Carmela from across the room — a gaunt, stony-faced matriarch wearing pearls and a high-buttoned, dark shirt. Who could blame her for despising her great-grandson's choice of wife?

By the time Antonio returned, the heat had reached midday ferocity. The beds had been stripped, the sheets boiled, scrubbed, wrung and hung to dry, starched in the sun, folded, and stored in the linen closets. The shutters were locked tight.

Carmela hesitated before climbing into the cab. "You two go on ahead, I need to take a walk."

Antonio's and Piera's eyebrows rose.

"You'll be prosciutto by the time you get back," Piera said.

"She's right, Carme', let me take you uphill," Antonio offered.

"No, really, if it's all the same with you, I need a little time alone."

"Our cousin was the same a month before her wedding. Started writing poetry and everything," Piera quipped.

Her teasing landed flat.

"Take some water, at least," Antonio said, handing Carmela his leather pouch flask.

"Thank you, Toni. I won't be long, Pie'."

Carmela headed toward the trickling fountain by the gate to fill up the flask. The cool water was soothing, but did nothing to silence the thoughts racing through her head as the car pulled away.

"Is Lieutenant Kavanagh expecting you?"

"Yes," Carmela lied, marveling at the tight platinum wave of the receptionist's hair.

"Take a seat."

Carmela wandered over to the plastic seat by the glass doors. The cool of the waiting area was a welcome relief to the inferno outside. A small bead of sweat trickled down her temple. Her heart raced. What if she had walked all this way for nothing? What if Kavanagh found her bravado at turning up uninvited, unannounced, inappropriate? How had she become the kind of woman who tricked receptionists? She reached into her pocket for a handkerchief, pretending not to notice the tremble of her hand.

"May I use the bathroom?" Carmela asked.

"Certainly," the receptionist answered.

Inside the gray-tiled space Carmela splashed her face with cold water. Her reflection gazed back at her. The same strong jaw, wide shoulders, and smooth, olive skin, but a change flickered in her eyes. A steel she had not noticed before. The naked ambition she saw yesterday was not Virginia's after all. It was her own. It was she who longed for promotion from her own life. Carmela smoothed the mass of her wavy hair, which did little to tame its rebellion. The image of the portrait back at the house floated into her mind again. It had eclipsed her thoughts the entire walk while the sun beat down on her. It had felt like the entire army of Franco's ancestors had wafted behind her, spying her every move, hovering in her thoughts and haunting her. And yet, her feet kept walking. The sea below beckoned her onward.

She didn't expect Kavanagh to be waiting for her by the time she came out of the bathroom. The expression she read was of pleasant surprise. It put her somewhat at ease.

"To what do I owe this unexpected pleasure?" he asked, his face widening into a warm grin.

Carmela's eyes snapped to the receptionist, hoping she hadn't heard.

She took a breath. "I can start the job."

"The job?"

"I'm ready to help you."

His pause seemed to last an age. Had he changed his mind? Chosen Agnes? Why had she waited so long to give her reply? Had she been so terrified of her feelings from the moment she had met him? Of course she had. Kavanagh blew through her like the maestrale wind from the north. He whipped up the dust and debris of her life, sending shards of habits and memories swirling. But unlike the maestrale, he didn't leave destruction in his wake. Unlike Franco, he didn't seek to contain or control her. She thought about Agnes, imagining her jealous sneer, recalled her barbed whispers telling Carmela that Kavanagh paying for her services was no different to the better known skills that girls offered soldiers. The imagined insult hovered for a moment, soon overtaken by the image of Kavanagh's smiling eyes when he'd hear her acceptance. His face would light up with bright warmth, openness, and a generosity of spirit that never had been showered on her before. At no other time had she felt this exhilarating pull between earthed safety and liberty. Since that night in the hospital the little girl inside her had not stopped careening down her hill with abandon. Kavanagh propelled her into the world, forced her to see beyond the confine of her own expectations. Was it possible not to fall into the person who offered you the most precious gift of all: freedom? Kavanagh ignited a fire that Carmela had allowed Franco to keep sheltered, embers of possibility starved of air to whip up into flames. The room tilted.

"Well," he began.

What? No, thank you? Go home? Don't ever come here again?

"That's the best news I've heard all day."

Excitement rippled up her spine. "When do we start?" she asked, impressed by the way her voice came out without the tremor she felt in her abdomen.

He smiled. "Seymour has taught me a lot in a short time — teachers come in many different sizes, you know? I'm going to take a leaf out of the little fella's book — how's about right now?"

"Now?" Carmela said, eyes wide, a child at Christmas.

"I was just on my way out to a farm nearby. Signor Bacchisio Lau is the name."

"Yes — his son sometimes delivers wool to the studio."

"I'll grab my hat."

Kavanagh disappeared toward the back offices. Before she could change her mind, think about what was happening, remind him that at this lunch hour any visit might prove fruitless, as everyone would be taking their siestas, they were sitting in his jeep, rattling up the familiar hills of Simius. Only now, they looked like the terrain of a brand-new world.

CHAPTER 12

Bacchisio Lau's remote farm lay tucked into the hills at the end of a dusty lane lined with trees as gnarled as their owner. Kavanagh pulled the jeep up in front of a tiny stone house, shutters firmly sealed against the heat. A solitary wicker chair that had seen better days stood beside the door, the last remnants of its green paint clinging in patches. A stray chicken clucked by. The scraping of paws heralded the crazed dash of a sheepdog, from behind the house, that howled a frantic cry. Try as he might, Kavanagh's charm fell flat on the animal.

"You stay, Carmela, until Rover and I have become acquainted."

"Lieutenant, Signor Lau is not known for being too friendly."

"I'm sure the sight of your face will change that."

He jumped out of the jeep. "Come on, boy," he called down to the dog, walking toward the house. "Let's go find your master, yes?" The dog ran circles around Kavanagh. After a few soft knocks, Kavanagh looked back at Carmela. "I'll go round back, you wait there."

Carmela nodded. She looked up at the spaces left by missing roof tiles and the dried-up geraniums in the window boxes. Bacchisio's wife had died just after the end of the war. There had been whispers of foul play from some of the more imaginative gossips in town, stories that were mostly ignored. Bacchisio had had several boys in town work for him as farmhands, but no one would last too long here. The remoteness, and their boss's eccentricities, were more than most could handle.

A cat slinked toward the jeep. It looked up at Carmela with bright yellow eyes, flicking her tail into the air, sizing up the competition. Then she gave a defiant turn, walked back toward the house, and sat upon the slab before the door, on guard.

"She doesn't like anyone but us," a little voice wafted out from the mottled shadows.

"Paolo?" Carmela called, turning toward the sound. A dark face poked out from behind a tree. The boy's hair was matted, his cheeks tawny from hours spent alongside his herd of sheep. "Is your father inside?"

"Maybe."

"I have an important lieutenant here who would like to speak to him."

Paolo shrugged. His clothes hung on his skinny frame like tattered curtains on a rickety pole.

"He's a nice man. I think you'll like him."

"Papa told me stay outside."

"You in trouble again?"

Paolo tugged at his sleeve, trying to cover a weeping wound on his arm. "Lost a sheep."

"Did you get the belt?"

He shrugged again. His eyes shifted side to side.

There was a scrape. The door of the cottage opened.

"Signor Lau?" Carmela called, getting out of the vehicle, thinking how rude it would appear to be yelling at the farmer from the jeep. She looked back at Paolo for a moment, then decided it better to pretend she hadn't noticed him. The slight space between the frame and the door widened to reveal a black eye and half a crinkled face.

Carmela stopped several feet away before continuing. "*Buon pomeriggio,* Signor Lau, so sorry to disturb you at this hour. . . ."

"Chirigoni girl?"

"Yes, Tomas's daughter."

"I won't sell to him, or any of his godforsaken brothers neither."

The eye withdrew and the door slammed shut. Carmela stood for a moment. The cat looked up at her, triumphant.

How naked she felt, standing in the middle of his dusty front yard, one arm as long as the other — bearing no gift, no polite token, no symbol of respect whatsoever. Had she stopped to ask some questions beforehand, she might have prepared something by way of an olive branch. Why on earth hadn't she found the confidence to educate Kavanagh in basic customary etiquette? To turn up like a vagabond, rattling in with an officer?

Carmela took a breath and walked toward the door, ignoring the feline yellow eyes boring into her from below. "Signor Lau, I am not here on behalf of my father. I can assure you my only business is to introduce you to a kind American lieutenant. He is helping some of the farmers in the area. He's promised to fix my father's plough, in fact."

Silence. Paolo shuffled out from behind the tree into the light.

Kavanagh reappeared from the other side of the cottage.

"I'm sorry, Lieutenant. I don't think Signor Lau is going to talk with us."

"Well, hello there, kid!"

Paolo looked at him without blinking.

"This is Paolo, one of his sons," Carmela said. "The older boy is probably out with the sheep."

"*Ciao,* Paolo," Kavanagh called. The boy stood motionless, a scrawny statue.

"He takes a while to answer sometimes, Lieutenant."

"Is Signor Lau here?"

"Yes. But he does not think too much of my father. He saw me and now he won't come out."

"I see." Kavanagh moved toward the door. "*Buon giorno,* Signore?"

The cat wound herself around Kavanagh's legs.

For a moment it seemed their first call was nothing short of a complete failure. Then the door cracked open. This time, both black eyes squinted into the light. Signor Lau stepped out toward Kavanagh. He looked into him, then offered a bony hand to shake.

"*Piacere,* Signore," Kavanagh said with the same fresh smile he had beamed at her father not so long ago. Lau reciprocated, though his lacked several teeth.

"*Io,* I, and Signorina Carmela, here to

speak — save me any time you want, Carmela."

"Signor Lau, the lieutenant would very much like to talk with you," she said, slipping in as if they were accustomed to crossing over one another's speech. Lau nodded without looking at her. Then he pulled his flat cap farther down on his head and started to hobble toward a smaller hut beside the cottage. "Paolo! Glasses!" he yelled. The boy dashed into the house, then ran out clutching a couple of *ridotto* wineglasses. Lau signaled for Carmela and Kavanagh to follow.

There was a huge sawn-off trunk inside the tiny hut. To the side were rough shelves made from untreated wood. Upon one was an enormous, dark green bottle of wine and a tall jar filled with what looked like orange paste. Lau reached into his pocket and flicked open a knife, something he was famous for crafting, and using, especially to conclude disputes. He flashed the lieutenant a crooked smile. Kavanagh stiffened a little until Lau reached up for the jar and placed it onto the trunk. He twisted the lid off. A pungent, salty odor filled the little hut. Lau dipped the sharp blade inside. When he lifted it back out it was covered in a thick, cheesy spread, alive with skinny, white maggots. He shuffled over to a sack on the upper shelf and pulled out some flat bread. He ripped a strip. Carmela noticed Kavanagh take in Lau's blackened nails and callused fingers. Lau smeared the bread with the moving cheese, rolled it up, and handed it to Kavanagh. Then he poured two glasses of wine. *"Saludu,"* Lau murmured.

Kavanagh clinked and looked down at his wormy bread.

"It's delicious," Carmela whispered. "Those worms only grow inside the cheese. It's a delicacy."

"He doesn't eat?" Lau asked, turning his palms up to the thatched roof.

"Yes, yes, of course, he just wanted to know how you made it," Carmela replied.

"So tell him."

"You must eat it, Lieutenant."

Kavanagh took a polite bite.

Carmela and Lau watched.

Kavanagh chewed.

"This stuff is sublime," he said at last, relief sweeping across his face.

"The lieutenant says thank you, it's absolutely delicious, Signor Lau."

Lau shook his head. " 'Course it is. I'm the only one in the valley who knows how to make it. Your father thinks that salt is the only thing that adds flavor. Wouldn't know his sage from his ass — tell him. More to cheeses and smokehouse than just heat and salt."

"What did he say, Carmela?"

"You're the perfect guest, Lieutenant."

Kavanagh pointed outside the hut toward the fruit trees. "I would very much like to take a look at your farm, Signor Lau, *vedere campagna . . .*"

"Eh?" Lau asked, looking at Carmela. "Not selling cigarettes and gum, is he?"

"No, Signore, the lieutenant would like to see your land."

"Don't need a farmhand."

"Can I tell Signor Lau why you'd like to look around, Lieutenant? I think it would help."

"Of course. I'm looking for farmers who would be interested in renting us some land."

"Doesn't look like a farmer to me," Lau answered, slugging back his second glass of wine.

"Would it be for farming?" Carmela asked.

"I'm not at liberty to go into details. I just want to gauge if he would be open to the idea. Please explain we have a large budget to spend on this endeavor."

"Signor Lau, the lieutenant tells me they have a lot of money to pay for some land."

" 'Course they do. But I don't want to be an American colony."

"I don't believe he's interested in money," Carmela said, turning to Kavanagh.

"Would you tell him I'd love to take a quick look at his land?" Kavanagh asked.

"He really would like to look at your farm, Signor Lau."

"Dirty dollars can't buy me a thing. My wife is dead. Waiting for me up there — God rest her soul. Upset stomach? I chew on my wild fennel. Tired kidneys? I pick the asparagus that grows on the hillside. I suck a lemon every day in the summer, chew on chestnuts in the autumn, eat broad beans over winter, and kill a pig once a year. My children don't chase me salivating after my money, pretending they love me. One day I will die and my bones will grow another tree."

Carmela turned to Kavanagh. "He says no."

"*Molto grazie,* Signore," he said, offering his hand, which Lau shook after a pause. "Carmela, please tell him that he is welcome to come and see me at the base anytime."

Lau replied with a silent nod that made it clear to Carmela that he would never set foot beyond the end of the path leading away from his home. "Tell him stick to

American. He speaks it better."

"*Arrivederci,* Signor Lau," Carmela said.

Lau led them out of the hut. "Not if I can help it. And don't forget to tell your father what I said."

With that he shuffled back toward his house and disappeared into the blackness within. The door closed behind him. The cat and dog flanked it, like breathing gargoyles.

"I'm so sorry, Lieutenant."

"No fault of yours."

"I should have explained about Lau. He's particular."

Kavanagh rubbed his forehead. "I dragged you out here without a proper briefing. My God, what must you think? I owe you an apology. I just . . ."

"Lieutenant . . ."

"It's Joe. That will be the last time I remind you." He leaned back onto the hood of the jeep. "I'm really sorry. I got overexcited to get going. You see, Carmela . . . how can I put this?"

He looked down at his boots for a moment. When his eyes lifted they met hers. "I've fallen in love."

Carmela didn't move.

"No other way to say it. I've fallen in love with Sardinia."

There was a rustle from behind a tree. Carmela's eyes darted toward the brush to spy Paolo disappearing behind a trunk.

"The herby smell of it," he continued, "the look of it, the people who stare at me as if I've just landed from another world. The food that makes me realize my first thirty years on the planet have been utterly wasted." He looked across at Carmela, and his face crinkled into a bashful grin. "You must think me a big kid chasing after a new toy."

Carmela noticed how the sun highlighted the natural blond of his hair.

He shook his head. "It's been tough with only a phrase book and pidgin Italian. I'm sure everyone's enjoyed quite the joke at my expense."

"My father was very impressed. As were all the men. They'll never tell you that."

"Right."

A brief silence. Carmela watched Kavanagh trace his fingers across his knuckles.

"May I be honest with you?" she asked.

He squinted. "Always."

"You won't charm all Sardinians with dollars. Especially the ones who live in the hills and couldn't spend it even if they wanted to."

He shook his head with a smile. "I can see that."

"We're islanders, Lieutenant. We've not had much luck with invaders in the past. Not everybody is in love with the Americans. Even ones who speak like you."

Carmela bit her lip. She hadn't meant to make a personal remark. Something flashed across his face; he was not offended, quite the contrary.

"Here's the thing, Carmela," he said, standing up and fixing his eyes down on her. "I need you. A beautiful, intelligent, articulate woman who knows this world is far more irresistible than some Yank. That much I know. I'm under considerable pressure from above to find the right place."

"Lieutenant, it's the first farm. There are many others. May I suggest something?"

"Yes?"

"Let's not talk about money and land when you're trying someone's food. It makes them think you're not concentrating on what you're eating."

"Concentrating?"

Carmela took a breath, trying to find the right words to articulate her thought. "When someone gives you their food," she said at last, "they are giving you a piece of themselves."

That naked feeling crept up again. Carmela shifted. She curled a stray wisp of hair behind her ear. Her face creased into an embarrassed smile. Their eyes met. For a fleeting moment he looked as stilted as she felt. It was of little comfort.

Then he straightened, ran his hands through his own hair, returned to a familiar composure. "We'll head back," he said, confident. "I'll show you the map of the farms and people I would like us to meet. I'll schedule a meeting before our next excursion so that you and I know what we can expect. We can pack food for the day and cover several places at once. Make the best use of both our time."

At the mere mention of it, Carmela began scrolling through her list of favorite dishes she might make to impress him.

"I ask you to forgive my impetuosity with regard to our first trip," he said, once again the cool professional. "It was brash. I saw an opportunity and seized it. Time is of the essence. I'll be sure to clarify our payment rates too."

He turned toward the jeep and opened the door for her. She stepped up and sat down.

"Wow, I've really done this all backward, haven't I?" He sighed.

Carmela watched his wide chest rise and fall. It felt as if they were the only two souls in the wilderness. Two floating lights.

Kavanagh nodded and closed Carmela's door. He leaned an elbow on the side. "I hope you won't change your mind about the position."

She smiled. Nothing could be further from the truth. Her eyes followed him as he moved across the front of the jeep and climbed in with one graceful leap. He started the engine. She felt a spark of fearlessness. Or was it recklessness? The soft caress of pine-scented breeze lifted the strands of loose hair resting on her shoulders. Dappled sunlight sparkled in her eyes.

Carmela turned to meet Kavanagh's gaze, his eyes rich blue in the golden rays. "Sardinians very rarely change their minds."

CHAPTER 13

Carmela arrived home late in the afternoon. Franco and her parents looked up at her from the kitchen table as she stepped inside. The surprise gathering caught her off-guard. She felt a pang of self-consciousness as she walked over to Franco, planting a polite kiss on each of his cheeks. His skin felt hot, clammy even.

"*Buona sera,* Franco, Mamma, Papa," she said.

Her parents nodded.

"Your father has some important news, Carmela," Franco said. "You'd better sit down."

Had some tragedy befallen one of her sisters or brother? Nothing else would warrant an unexpected gathering such as this. "What's happened?"

"Everyone is fine," Tomas began, his voice gruff. "But we have some difficult news."

Carmela braced.

250

Tomas shifted in his seat. "It's about the wedding."

"The wedding?" Carmela's gaze shot to her mother, but her eyes were lowered.

Franco stepped in for his future father-in-law, now taut with embarrassment. "We have no choice, *tesoro.* We cannot be married before the spring."

"The spring?" Carmela asked, wishing the feeling in the pit of her stomach was closer to disappointment.

Franco looked between Carmela's parents and stiffened. "A family matter."

"What's happened, Franco? Is your family all right?"

"Everyone is fine. Your father has spoken his wishes. We will not celebrate in September as planned. We will marry next summer."

"Papa? This is what you want?"

Tomas cleared his throat, as if the truth were sticking to the back of it. "We decided this is for the best."

Her breaths became shallow. Tears welled. Guilt? Relief? "I see."

"My darling, *tesoro,*" Franco cooed, reaching for her hand. "It's only a few months. It will pass quickly. Another winter, is all." The words washed over, didn't penetrate. The last of the afternoon light fought in through the tiny window of the hallway, but nothing about the chocolate glow it cast on him moved her. She looked at him like someone staring at a snapshot of another's life. A tear trickled down her cheek. Carmela's mother stood up and put an arm around her.

"Leave us for a while, Franco," Tomas said, also standing now.

"Carmela" — Franco planted a soft kiss upon her forehead — "I'll call for you tomorrow." He gave a polite nod to Maria and Tomas and then left.

Carmela felt pale.

She didn't move from her chair.

Several minutes passed before anyone spoke.

"I'm going to stop in on Peppe," Tomas said, walking out onto the terrace and easing the door closed.

In the silence, Maria took a chair next to her daughter. She placed Carmela's cold hand in hers. "I married against my father's wishes. The day I left he told me I would cry every day of my life. He died a week later. Be grateful for your father's blessing, Carmela."

"I am. Of course. But . . ."

Maria took a breath to reply, but the staggering footsteps from upstairs brought her to her feet. There was the loud clang of a bedpan. Rushing upstairs, they threw open the double doors to find Rosa on her knees over the pan, Grandmother Icca holding back her hair. She heaved again and again, until her stomach produced nothing but yellow bile. Icca looked up. Her eyes hardened. "We leave tomorrow, Maria."

Maria looked away. "I will prepare everything."

As she closed the doors Carmela caught sight of her aunt's swollen abdomen. How could she have not noticed? So lost in the world of the Curwins, the promise of her new position alongside Kavanagh, the abundance of the summer, she had failed to spot the signs. This was no sickness.

Maria moved quickly. She drew out a large trunk from underneath her bed and began filling it with linens and her mother-in-law's clothes. Carmela, close behind, bombarded her with barbed whispers: "Mother?! Is this why? Zia Rosa is being sent to the farm to grow her baby out of sight? Does Franco know? What is happening?!" Carmela grabbed her mother's shoulders a little too hard.

"Carmela!" Maria shot back with uncharacteristic fire. "We will not speak of this. We will do what we need to do so you can be a bride."

"I'm not the one having a baby!"

A thorny silence. Maria looked at her firstborn, her eyes glistening with what seemed to be remorse and panic. She fought for a deep breath, and straightened. "In a few months you will be the wife of the most important young man in town. Your children will want for nothing." She wiped her eyes with the back of her hand, determined to stop the tears from falling. "You have a great life ahead of you. Don't be a slave to your passions. Do this, and the world is yours."

Carmela hoped for comfort through her mother's words, but all she felt was a chasm open up between her and the woman whose tireless family devotion she had always admired. Rosa was having the doctor's baby, and the family would be forced to bury the dirty secret. Her aunt would flee to the wilderness, labor in silence, and relinquish the babe to willing adoptive parents, no doubt. The woman about town, now fleeing to the hills she had always despised. The woman draped on the most dapper arm in the valley behind closed doors, now slinking into the mud, mired by her passion, burned by desire.

Carmela's shock turned to pity. "Very

254

well, Mamma," she answered.

She would never be trapped by lust, Carmela vowed. Unlike Rosa, she would play victim to no man.

Yolanda's studio was alive with activity. Most of the girls were busy clearing their station or folding and sorting scraps and patches from ends of fabric rolls. Carmela sat by her godmother as she read out the inventory from the store cupboard, essential work for the oncoming September, when business was at its height in preparation for the winter wardrobes of the wealthy.

The bell rang. They stopped what they were doing and moved across the room to welcome the unexpected guest. Carmela opened the door. There, looking pinched, was a diminutive Virginia. For a flash Carmela panicked that something had befallen Kavanagh, then berated herself for even thinking it; the first port of call for his widow would not be a seamstress of Via Dante with dreams beyond Simius.

"*Buon giorno,* Signora," Carmela said, wanting to sound neither formal nor familiar.

"One of the girls at the base said to come here. You make dresses, correct?"

"Yes, of course, come in."

Virginia stepped inside, looking tentative, as if she might tread on something untoward. Yolanda swept in, thrilled to have an American come to call. Her godmother's expression brightened with ambition; she hoped this American customer might be the first of many.

"*Buon giorno,* Signora!" she exclaimed a little too loud.

"Yes," Virginia replied.

"This is my godmother, Signora. This is her studio. I work here."

"I can see that. I want this dress," Virginia answered, pulling from her clutch a picture that she had ripped out of *Vogue.* Carmela caught sight of the magazine's name on the top right-hand corner of the page.

"There is a dance at the base in a week's time," Virginia said.

"Yes, Lieutenant Kavanagh mentioned something about invitations for all the farmers!"

Virginia bristled. Carmela wasn't sure if it was because she had mentioned Kavanagh's name like that of an old friend, or because the idea of sharing a hall with a handful of elderly shepherds was not Virginia's idea of high society.

"Is that so?" she replied, with an arch of her eyebrow.

"We will be delighted to help," Carmela added, off Yolanda's urgent look.

Carmela caught Agnes spying on the group from the other side of the room and counted a few seconds before she whisked herself over, greeting Virginia like an old friend. Yolanda stiffened. It was obvious she found her approach vulgar, and she was quick to send her back to her table. Yolanda pressed the importance of making new customers feel unique and appreciated, welcome, not stifled.

"Signora — *caffè*?" Yolanda asked.

"Ice tea would be just fine."

Yolanda shot Carmela a glance.

"Just a moment," Carmela said to Virginia, walking a few paces away to whisper to her aunt. "Zia, she wants iced tea. I'll run down to Antonio and fetch some?"

"Get one of the girls to do it — you stay and measure her before she changes her mind."

"Really, Zia, I don't mind."

Yolanda's eyes narrowed. "Anyone would think you didn't want her business!"

Carmela leaned in closer to her ear. "This is a woman with little patience. Trust me. If things aren't just the way she wants them we'll have our name smeared. Get this right and she'll bring in more lire than you can dream of!"

"Fine. I shall begin, then."

Carmela walked back to Virginia, who was leafing through a pile of magazines, looking bored.

"My godmother, Yolanda, will measure you now. When I return with your drink we can talk about fabric?"

Virginia nodded as she turned to the mirror to check her teeth for lipstick and readjust her hat.

Outside the sun was unforgiving, but Carmela preferred the hot air to the glare of Kavanagh's wife. She reached Antonio's bar and stepped into the welcome cool. It took a moment for her eyes to adjust.

"If it isn't the world-famous interpreter! The brains and beauty of Simius! To what do we owe the pleasure?"

"That's enough, Anto'."

"Everyone's talking about it. Had one in this morning from his farm out east, telling me he heard about some dance at the base being thrown by that handsome lieutenant fellow."

"Did *he* call him handsome?"

"And Giuaneddu from the dairy farm stopped in, says you and Blue Eyes were quite the pretty pair, sat side by side in his veranda trying to get him to give up a piece of his land to the Yanks."

She sat on a stool. "Rent, Anto', not give up."

"So they say."

"Will you be at the dance?"

He toweled off the counter in front of her. "Running the bar."

"Don't even tell me how much you're charging."

"More than they have sense."

Carmela shook her head with a smile. "Well, right now I need an iced tea."

"For you?"

"No. Kavanagh's wife."

"I didn't know you two were friends," he chirped with a grin.

Carmela rolled her eyes. "She's at the studio being measured for a gown."

"I see," he said, reaching up for a tumbler. "Going to make her belle of the ball?"

Carmela liked to think that Virginia's visit hadn't raised her own expectations of how she herself would dress for the evening. Nothing uglier than vanity, Carmela reminded herself. "She hardly needs any help from me, Anto'."

"True," he answered, opening the wooden door of his icebox to chip at a block of ice. "I saw her next to naked at the beach picnic," he carried on. "Like she had her own spotlight follow her."

"You're no better than Casler."

Antonio set a small paper coaster on his marble counter and placed the glass on top of it. Then he sliced three rings of lemon and dropped them inside. "Only a fool allows himself to feel superior. If Casler's manners have a lot to be desired, who am I to say mine are any better?"

"You keep your eyes to yourself — for the most part — that's why."

Antonio reached over for a large jug of tea and poured it into the glass. The ice clinked. "And there I was thinking that mass twice a day was making me a good person."

Carmela reached into her pocket for some coins.

"Wait," Antonio said, reaching for a small vial of simple syrup. "The Yanks like their drinks — and women — sweet." He drizzled the clear liquid into the glass and gave it a stir with a metal rod.

Carmela rushed back to her office, careful not to spill any of Virginia's cool drink. She placed it down on top of the low table Yolanda had cleared in the changing area. Most of the measurements were already done, and Virginia was slipping back into her pale yellow linen dress.

"Here, let me," Carmela offered, reaching

for the buttons at the back. She noticed how transparent Virginia's skin looked and the way the muscles in her shoulders rippled underneath, like the sinew of a new colt. Her neck was long and slim, a delicate perch for her heart-shaped face. Virginia leaned forward toward the mirror to reapply her lipstick. Her mouth was small and looked like it was almost, or had just been, puckered for a kiss. On another it might have lent the face an overall impression of someone sensual, ready to be touched at any time. On her it painted permanent disappointment. Carmela was a head taller than Virginia. She felt like an awkward prepubescent playing with an oversized doll.

As far as Carmela could tell, Kavanagh was curious about people and generally inquisitive. His wife, on the contrary, appeared to despise anyone who might not be of use to her. Try as she might, Carmela couldn't stop the slew of images floating into her head —Virginia and Kavanagh dining, dancing, making love. She wondered whether this woman was someone who ever caved in to raw lust. Or whether there would always be a part of her kept locked away, protected, cold. Was this a woman who would die for her mate? Unlikely. But what would be the sense in feeling like you would sacrifice yourself for another? That was not love. That was not marriage. Would someone like Kavanagh even crave that sort of woman anyway? Of course not. His was a measured life. The consideration and gentility he displayed toward her countrymen was of someone who, in the words of her mother, was not a slave to their passions.

Carmela reached the top button. "Would you like black for the bodice, or try something else?"

"I want this dress. It is black. Joe convinced me you were more than capable of cutting the exact match of anything I chose."

Carmela felt a swell of pride. Kavanagh deemed her talented enough for his wife. Why had she said it had been one of the girls to convince her to come? He couldn't have paid Carmela a bigger compliment if he tried. She would hate to disappoint him. Now it was her job to make his wife dazzle, though she couldn't help feeling that Virginia stepping into a room dressed in a burlap sack would turn as many heads. An image of herself, standing in the gown she had been asked to make Virginia, pierced her mind. Carmela pictured Kavanagh casting a glance down the length of her own body.

"Yes, I want this dress," Virginia said,

clipped, snapping Carmela back to the room. "I shall be back in two days for the fitting."

With that, Virginia rose and left. Not so much as a thank-you or farewell. Carmela and Yolanda watched the door close.

"They all like that up there?" Yolanda asked with a frown.

"What do you mean?" Carmela pretended she hadn't scrutinized Virginia, didn't feel the tide rise and fall in her stomach or the cold ache of guilt.

"Barely looked at me," Yolanda said. "I haven't felt like that since I was an apprentice to my own godmother down in Cagliari. Never seen skin like that, though, have you? China. White like the sands of Sant'Antioco."

Carmela disappeared into her work, using the picture as a guide for a pattern. Never had she been asked to make anything so dramatic. As fashionable as they liked to feel, the gentry of the surrounding areas were marked in their conservative attitude to high fashion. Off-the-shoulder dresses would be built up to cover a little more flesh. Inches would be added to lengths. Décolletage was covered with discreet swathes of tulle perhaps. But the vision before Carmela was one of pure drama. A tight bodice, barely leaving room to breathe, clung to the model's slim waist, rising up to a deep plunge toward the cleavage in a heart-shaped rim. From the waist a three-tiered skirt fell to the ground in swooping layers to a gentle train. The fabric — a rich, black velvet — added to the aching decadence. The model stood with a foot upon the first step of a sweeping marble staircase, looking back toward the camera as if she had been interrupted at the start of her flight to a secret lover, hidden perhaps in the upper rooms of the palace she found herself in.

Of course Virginia would be the belle of the ball.

CHAPTER 14

Local women lined the walls of the dance floor at the base, doing their best impersonation of demure, eyeballing the uniformed men while masking their excitement with apparent nonchalance. Carmela knew that, despite their best efforts, they felt as swept away as she did. No party in town had been anything like this. At best, they might expect a twirl around an uncle's cement terrace, if they had any who were lucky enough to own a gramophone. Carmela knew that none of these girls had ever heard a brassy swing band howl into the night like this one, nor had they twirled beneath a sea of star-spangled banners or sipped from bottom-less bowls of punch served in squat glasses with dainty handles. This was as close to America as any of them might hope to get.

A trumpet player at the podium took to his feet and screeched out a riff. Every fiber in her body willed her to dance. She skimmed the crowd for Franco. He was lost right after they entered, accosted by one of his cousins hovering over a table with booze. There was a cackle of laughter. Agnes was at the center of a small group of girls beside Carmela. "If we don't get lucky tonight, girls, I'll eat my own dress!" she gasped, stifling a girlish giggle. Her eyes landed on Carmela's. "Don't we look fancy tonight?"

"Evening," Carmela replied.

"Fiancé left you to fend for yourself?"

Franco slipped in and hooked his arm around Carmela. Agnes's smile faded. If she wasn't so full of malice, the fact that she was still in love with Franco might have made Carmela feel sorry for her.

"I was just getting my bride a drink," Franco purred, slipping a glass of orange punch into Carmela's hand. "Sounds like you need one too. Might be the only thing to wipe the sour puss off your face."

Agnes turned on her heels and disappeared into the throng, her clique of young girls close behind like a line of ducklings.

"Just jealous because I'm standing with the most beautiful woman in here." Franco ran a finger along Carmela's jaw. "Did you wear this so I wouldn't be able to think about anything else but being inside you?"

he whispered.

Carmela met his gaze.

"Let's go out," he said, "for air."

He slipped his hand into hers, grasping it a little tighter than she would have liked.

"Carmela! Franco! Welcome!" Kavanagh called, wading through the dancing couples, stretching out a hand to Franco. "Quite the turnout, right?"

They shook hands. Franco's smiling eyes glinted with an undecipherable twinkle, which Carmela wished was closer to warmth than threat.

"I'm so glad everyone made the trip down here. *Benvenuti,* yes?" Kavanagh was shouting now, as the band had hit a raucous bridge. In her periphery, Carmela spied Piera being twirled by Luigi, a local optometrist who had recently set up a tiny photo studio in his back storeroom. She hadn't seen her sister smile like that in a while.

"This party is wonderful!" Carmela beamed. "We've never seen anything like it!"

"Great," Kavanagh answered, a little bashful. Carmela noted how the tone of his voice shifted when talking of anything beyond the comfort of work. "I know the girls in the offices had a great time fixing it. Most of them haven't been to a dance since they left home. I'll call for you when I make my speech, if that's okay?"

"Of course."

Franco shifted. "What he say?" He never failed to intuit when Kavanagh spoke of her interpreting.

"He says I'm going to help with his speech later."

"In front of everyone?"

In the slight pause, Kavanagh's gaze lifted from Carmela to scan the room.

"Well, you two have a good time, now. Please excuse me."

Carmela watched Kavanagh walk away, noticing how his jacket tapered at his slim waist, emphasizing his wide shoulders.

"Where's his wife?" Franco asked. Carmela's eyes scanned the crowd. The sea of people ahead parted. There, at the end of the narrow aisle, the delicate frame of a woman appeared, her alabaster skin luminous beneath the folds of the black velvet of her ruched bodice. The sweeping décolletage led the eye to a polite hint of cleavage. Her hair was gathered up and away from her face, drawing attention, like a magnet, to those unmistakable green eyes. They sparkled as bright as the diamond clusters in her ears.

"There she is," Carmela replied.

Virginia's beauty was not lost on Franco.

Carmela admired her work, if not the person wearing it. She hated to admit it, but Virginia was a woman who knew how to wear a dress. Some time ago, during the early days of Carmela's apprenticeship as a young teenager, she had learned that a seamstress could only do so much. It didn't matter how well she cut or finished a gown. If a customer, however wealthy and well bred, chose to shuffle with self-consciousness inside it, she would never be as beautiful as the model in the magazine she hoped to emulate. There were other young girls, however, who had visited Yolanda's studio, sometimes for the first time, to have a gown made for them as a gift from a benevolent aunt or godmother, who might have walked in from the hills. Their lives in the relative wild, as opposed to the girls brought up in marble villas of counts and countesses, had instilled a feral royalty. Their backs were straight and proud. They moved with ease. Carmela marveled at their instinctive, unaffected grace; Virginia fell into this camp.

Carmela suspected the woman's beginnings were more humble than she would like to have known. It wasn't hard to picture her with long copper tresses, running barefoot down a creek, dangling a younger sibling upon her hip. Or out at dawn in the cowshed milking beside her older brothers. The vision that stood before the throng now, however, was grace personified: radiant and regal. All the rough edges were masked beneath a fragile veneer. There might have been a gasp or two, but Carmela couldn't hear them. She ought to have felt proud to have everyone look at the gown she had created. But all she felt was piercing regret for having done such a good job. She caught the light in Kavanagh's eyes as he gazed upon the gown and his wife. He studied her work with admiration. The feeling was akin to having him look up and down her own body. The dress was the best work of her career. Would he think of her every time he looked at his wife? A fizz of delight corroded any guilt.

Kavanagh passed through the crowd and took Virginia's hand. Carmela wondered if his felt as hot and creased as Franco's. He kissed her. Virginia lit up as if a lantern above had its cover lifted. Kavanagh leaned into her ear. Carmela doubted his whisperings involved slipping inside her under the cover of the moonlit pine trees. No, he would be telling her how proud he felt to have her by his side. Franco's fervent desire for Carmela had once made her bristle with excitement. She clung to that memory as she watched Kavanagh coo over his bride, but the feeling slipped away, like water through her fingers. The beauty of the American couple filled her with the prickle of jealous heat and a brutal emptiness. It was impossible to shrug away the feeling that every part of her life now seemed meaningless, senseless even. She was beside the wrong man. A man whom she no longer desired, of whom she was no longer proud. Before her stood a woman who did not know the value of her husband. How could a Virginia love a Kavanagh the way he deserved? They were not kindred spirits. Neither were she and Franco. And maybe a life is wasted if it's spent chasing the one soul, Carmela thought, that complements your own with startling, simple perfection. She longed to stand next to Kavanagh now, to feel exulted in his presence. Franco's desire had little to do with helping her become the woman she deserved to be and everything to do with self-gratification. This was not love. This was ownership. That word again. It left her mind very little these days.

Why had she allowed herself to be acquired? Why could she not find the strength to object? And for where? For who? For a pipe dream. For a fantasy. The illusion she magicked in her mind was just as damaging as misunderstanding Franco's fervor for love. There was no difference between her and the silly girls around her, gawking at Kavanagh's handsome colleagues. No, she was worse. She fed her delusions before everyone, playing the part of the obedient fiancée and talented seamstress while basking in the light Kavanagh showered on her. How insipid, thought Carmela. How weak she felt now, having woven these lies to herself without the courage to repair the damage. Franco slipped his hand into hers. It was difficult to know whom she disliked more, him or herself. She took a breath and straightened her back. She would live the lie for one more night. It wasn't hard to imagine it was Kavanagh's hand in hers. Her chest felt tight and hot. It was reckless. She forced herself not to care, for a few hours more at least.

Virginia waved to the crowd, as if a kind queen to her people. She hadn't earned that wave. She hadn't visited one of the farmers or their families. She had done nothing to even attempt to communicate or ingratiate herself with the locals. And yet Carmela watched her fellow Simiuns fall under her spell, helpless subjects. The couple sashayed toward a table beside the podium where Casler sat.

"Fuck me."

"Cristiano!" Franco chided his cousin, who stood, salivating, beside him. "Watch your mouth! Is that how you speak in front of Carmela?"

"Sorry, Carmela, only I can't see shit with Elizabeth Taylor here."

Franco playfully pushed his cousin's cheek with the palm of his hand. "No Yankee wife is going to give you a second glance — roll your tongue back into your mouth."

"Can you make Maddalena a dress like that, Carme'?" Cristiano asked, breathless.

"Tell your girlfriend to come and see me. She's the prettiest girl on Via Dante and you know it."

"Ain't no princess, though. Jesus, I think I just died."

"Give me a Sardinian over a white Yank," Franco piped. "I like my women with fire, not ice."

Plural?

Cristiano shuffled toward the band to get a closer look.

"Where was I . . . ?" Franco said, sliding his hands over Carmela's waist. As he leaned in to kiss her, applause erupted from the crowd. Carmela and Franco turned toward the podium. Kavanagh stood behind a large chrome microphone, his wife a few steps behind. He wasn't as comfortable in the spotlight as she, that much was clear. She remembered how he had cocked his head to the side slightly when he spoke his pidgin Italian, an embedded modesty that had ingratiated him with the local farmers quicker than the arrogance of a Casler. There was simply something about his presence alone, assured but not arrogant, confident but not proud, that was enough to make the people around him want to help, impress him even. It struck Carmela that a lieutenant such as Kavanagh held the power to make or break the success of the base. And it was a man like this, so admired in such a short time, who had placed his whole-hearted trust in Carmela to act as his voice. She felt a surge of pride.

"Buona sera, tutti," he began. His cheeks flushed a little.

The crowd roared back, holding up their glasses.

"Per favore, chiamo, Signorina Carmela Chirigoni."

The people before Carmela turned around. Now it was her turn for the blood rush to her cheeks.

"Best obey Mr. Sergeant's orders," Franco

whispered, tapping her on the small of her back.

Carmela handed Franco her glass and began a cautious walk toward the stage as people moved aside for her. The lights were a little dazzling, shining behind Kavanagh much like the first time she had met his silhouette on the *viccoli* behind the piazza. Carmela summoned the coolness of professionalism, the way she would when a particularly difficult customer was exacting in the fitting cubicle. She reached the top step and turned to look at the sea of Simius's faces below. Only then did she feel the earth rise up beneath her feet again, though her chest still rose with shallow breaths.

"Here, Carmela," Kavanagh said, standing back from his microphone and placing a second one in front of her. She caught Virginia's eye over his shoulder, but Carmela's polite smile was not reciprocated. Kavanagh's eyes caught the light of the side lanterns. The color reminded Carmela of the August sea, the day an uncle had taken her and Piera off the coast in his rowboat, the aquamarine water so clear you could see the sporadic tufts of seaweed and rocks at the bottom, like looking through glass.

"I'll begin and leave spaces for you to do your magic, yes?" he asked.

"Yes," she replied, letting the excitement of standing onstage, before a familiar crowd, in the most glamorous dress she had ever dared make for herself, ripple through her. It had taken hours to prepare, stitched in the twilight after the close of business, or before the doors of the studio opened as the sun slit pink across the valley for the dawn chorus. She'd cut the pattern from a picture of a French design in one of Mrs. Curwin's magazines. The partial off-the-shoulder gown had a fitted bodice, for which she had used black satin. On one shoulder Carmela added a partial shoulder drape, ruched at the top of her arm and falling into a scarf that swung down her back. She ornamented the semi-fitted sheath with another draped panel that accentuated her hips and then swooped down to the hem.

With every stitch that pierced the heavy silence of the studio, she pretended not to rival the gown she created for Virginia. Her fingers raced over the fabric running away from her thoughts. In the quiet of that deserted room, she had stood before the three mirrors for clients in the half-made gown. She'd gazed hard at the woman who looked back at her. Sometimes she recognized the stare. Sometimes she saw the young woman everyone expected her to be.

Most nights she saw a stranger, a woman who chased the shadows she fled. Even the cherubs on the frieze overhead seemed to mock her, their happy grins turnings to grimaces, their chubby hands playing harps to taunt her.

Now she felt the lights hot on her cheeks. When would she ever get this close to feeling like a star again? Might as well enjoy this fleeting moment. It would be nothing but a hazy memory before too long.

Kavanagh told the crowd how grateful he and his senior officers were for their hospitality. How the party was a meager offering in return and, he hoped, the first of many. He told them how he wanted to share some of their American traditions with them and how he couldn't wait to help in the *Vendemia* in the coming months — the vineyard owners had been joking when they'd invited him to assist in the grape harvest, but Kavanagh was determined to show goodwill. Carmela had to pause her interpreting at this point for the crowd's laughter. At the end of his speech, Kavanagh invited the crowd to applaud Carmela for her untiring assistance throughout the past month. She felt embarrassed at this and more than a little awkward when she caught Franco's crooked smile beyond the applauding guests. If Franco had anything to do with it, hers was a position she would not keep for long — that much was clear. It didn't matter that she was working with a decent, married man and not a desperate, oversexed Simius singleton. Kavanagh was a man: That was threat enough.

She was lucky, she knew, to have held the job down this long, somehow having dodged Franco's uncertainty, shielded by the cachet her work with the base had given her. For a month she had reassured Franco that she was his personal link to the base, one way he and his family could keep careful taps on the Americans' intentions and, more important, know how best to exploit them. Both her and Franco's families owned several acres of land that had drawn particular interest from Casler and Kavanagh, and they were ready for some steep negotiations on how much they would charge the Americans to rent it. Carmela consoled herself with the thought that in the four weeks of working alongside Kavanagh, they had visited all but one farm and forged friendly relations with all of them. Even if her interpreting didn't go beyond tonight, she could look back on this month as one of the happiest of her life, topped with this grand finale of sharing the spotlight, facing the adoring expressions of the people who had known her since she was toddling the cobbled streets of Via Gallura.

Surely that was enough. Enough to pass on beautiful stories to her children, who would feel proud that her mother was instrumental in facilitating wealth and regeneration for their town and beyond. She wasn't performing life-saving surgery, or flying a plane solo, granted, but she would leave a soft imprint on the town's history. A sliver of immortality was hers.

Kavanagh signaled for the band to resume. A brassy jive began, and the bodies on the dance floor leaped back into action. As Carmela walked down the steps, she caught sight of a private rushing in from the back doors, waving what looked like a telegram in the air toward Kavanagh. She watched the lieutenant hurry toward the private, unfolding the paper with haste. His face dropped. The private left. Kavanagh turned toward Virginia. Carmela looked back up at the podium to see Virginia being helped by Casler down the steps, both basking in one another's glow. Kavanagh interrupted their joke and led Virginia by the elbow toward the quieter end of the room. Beyond the spiraling revelers Carmela caught sight of a frantic Virginia and a tussled Kavanagh. In between twirling skirts, Carmela watched a gray Virginia being ushered out through the doors that lead to the hospital wing. An anxious Kavanagh followed close behind. The doors swung shut behind them.

"Quite the performance, my love," Franco said, turning her away from the back of the hall toward him. "Don't be getting any ideas about Hollywood. We need you to be the star of our family here!"

He planted a hot kiss on her mouth. His lips were fleshy. It was one of the things she had first loved about him. No sixteen-year-old Sardinian girl could resist lips like those pressing up against her own in the shade of a laden cherry tree. He tasted a little like ash tonight, but it didn't matter. Carmela pulled away and looked into the dark pools of Franco's eyes. She ached to know what news had befallen Kavanagh, but her adrenaline was fast shifting to desire. "Let's go outside."

When Carmela hung her gown the next morning, she made a mental note to repair the tiny tear to the lower end of the skirt. A souvenir from Franco, from when he had pressed her up against the trunk of an ancient oak. She hadn't fought the image of another man when it flashed in her mind, nor Franco's racing hands. This time, she had allowed herself to undulate toward ecstasy imagining this other. Carmela knew, as Franco slipped his fingers away and led her own down into his trousers, that he believed it was her shuddering desire for him alone that had brought her to tears.

CHAPTER 15

On the following Monday, there was a hint of autumn in the sea breeze that swished the parched brush. Carmela took large strides, clopping downhill in her red leather shoes that scuffed against the white dust. Her uncle Raimondo, Tomas's younger brother, had made them for her twenty-first birthday. He had let her choose the color and the style. She loved the smell of leather inside his narrow shop beneath the cobbled arches just beyond the piazza. When they had been young children, she and Piera would often hover at the back of his store where he kept the scraps. Raimondo would set down a small crate full of them and let the girls play. Sometimes he might give them some to take home to make garments for their dolls, only Grandmother Icca would confiscate them and put them in a large box above one of the kitchen cabinets to keep them safe. From what, Carmela never found out. As a child she succumbed to the belief that transparent elves hid beneath their high, metal-framed beds and snuck out at night to plunder their home. The same fate befell the candied delights cousins would bring over on feast days.

This morning, those shoes filled her with childlike energy. She felt light, expansive. The world was in her grasp. She and Kavanagh were to visit the last farm on their list, the Toiedda family, several miles away. She cast aside the little voice reminding her that after today she may never again ride beside Kavanagh in his rattling jeep, with the wind flying through her hair, while the high summer sun blazed down on them.

Instead, she remembered the numerous times she had walked past the Toiedda land with her family, during the annual pilgrimage to Castro, a medieval church that stood high upon a hill in the middle of the plains. The walk would begin before dawn. Hundreds of Simiuns would trek under the stars, come rain or shine, until the pink sun rose and the spring wind swept through the valley. When the pilgrims finally arrived at the summit, they would huddle in and around the church, most of them in the courtyard, for the stone sanctuary only accommodated a minuscule congregation. They would murmur the rosary in unison, as they had throughout the ten-kilometer pilgrimage from Simius. After celebrating mass, the women would unwrap packages of fresh bread and cheese. The men would eat and drink together on one side of the church. The women would sit and swap tales of past pilgrimages on the other, drawing inventories of how many elderly had perished during the arduous walk in the past, who had given birth upon the hill, and what kind of summer they could expect based on the direction of the wind that day, the blossoms, or the hue of the sunrise. The walk back felt shorter. Carmela's sleep on those nights was always deep and dreamless.

These pictures replayed in her mind as she reached the main entrance to the base, once again a place of work, no longer ringing with festivities. She pushed open the glass door and greeted the receptionist. Although she had heard Kavanagh refer to her by her first name on several occasions, Carmela felt it an imposition to assume such familiarity. "Good morning."

"Good morning, ma'am," Mary-Anne replied, flashing her white teeth in a smile that lit up her platinum-hair-framed face.

"I'm here for Lieutenant Kavanagh."

"He's not here."

"It's okay, I can wait."

Carmela walked over to the gray plastic seats. She smoothed her linen skirt down. Piera had commented on her outfit that morning. It was impossible to share a small room and not expect her younger sister to offer unwanted opinions. Besides, this might be her last outing for some time. Why not wear an impeccable linen two-piece suit? Who cared if it got dirty on the farm? Who cared if the Toieddas would wonder what on earth she was doing wearing her Sunday best on a Monday morning? Kavanagh might take a moment to notice the cut, her fine embroidery along the front of the skirt of delicate bougainvillea and vines in a cream palette. He might enjoy the way her olive skin was enhanced by the crisp white of the linen. He might even think her lips suited the deep coral of the lipstick she had borrowed from Aunt Rosa's dressing table. After all, what would Aunt Rosa want for lipstick where she was? Idling at the farm in quarantine, passing her secret confinement with only her mother for company. Rather be kidnapped by bandits and tied up in a damp cave, Carmela thought, than sit with four bare walls, an unwanted baby gnawing at your insides, and a mother before you to make sure you couldn't bury your guilt. A shiver zigzagged down her spine.

"Miss, I believe you misunderstood me," Mary-Anne said.

"Sorry?"

"Lieutenant Kavanagh. He's not here," the receptionist replied, slower this time, overenunciating the way many of the Americans did for the Simiuns.

"Yes, you said. Many times I've waited."

"No, miss. He is gone."

Carmela drew a blank.

"Home," Mary-Anne continued, reduced to single-word sentences. "America."

Carmela opened her mouth to speak, but the words caught at the back of her throat.

"Left last night."

"When does he come back?"

"Twelfth of never, if his wife has anything to do with it."

"God-damn it!" Casler's voice boomed from around the corner. "For Chrissakes, Mary-Anne, what in the Lord's name have you done?"

"Sir?" Mary-Anne stood up to attention.

"The godforsaken report I dictated to you about Kavanagh for the Lieutenant General in DC?"

"Yes, sir. Did I make a mistake, sir?"

"Yes, you made a god-damn mistake!"

"Sir?"

286

A vein pulsed at the side of his head. "You wrote every fricking word I asked you to write!"

"Yes, sir."

"I'm holding you solely responsible for robbing me of my best man! DC told me they're keeping him stateside. Indefinitely! Don't you ever do that to me again!" He swung open the door and flew out. "Son of a gun!"

The women stood. Carmela's heart galloped. The rest of her body was numb. She looked at the rosy-cheeked receptionist, who was flushed with embarrassment. Carmela willed her expression into something close to breezy, but her face wouldn't cooperate.

Gone. The word stuck like a thorn.

It was only when Carmela was halfway up the hill beside the base that she realized she hadn't said as much as a good-bye or thank you to Mary-Anne. Hadn't stopped to ask her whether she was expected to visit the farm without Kavanagh and report back. She had turned and left, and that was all. Holding on to her last scrap of pride. Holding her breath till the base was out of view. Giving into the sobs only when she was sure no one would see. Seething with disgust for wailing like a woman who had just lost a child. Balking at her self-pity as she rocked beneath a cork tree, raped of its bark. Her cries vibrated against its ochre trunk.

And for what? A shabby silhouette of another life? Some man she was terrified to admit to being in love with? Some man she had loved the moment her eyes had landed on his mere shadow, a man who made every fiber in her body stand at attention and vibrate with life — a made-up man. When had she become so spoiled? When had she looked her destiny in the face and chosen to lose herself in some young girl's fantasy? It was beyond pathetic. She was a simpering mess, an embarrassment to herself, to all Sardinian women.

She could run away from the pointless-ness of existence for only so long, after all. Kavanagh was a delightful diversion. That was all. And so was Franco, she supposed. And so was the work she loved. And so was everything. In the end we die and spend a lifetime running away from the fact. Being alchemists in the kitchen to make gold out of root vegetables, manna out of tomatoes, for what? A fleeting moment of pleasure. A desperate act of worship for the beauty all around us. We wake the next day, realizing death inches closer, so we do it all again. Throw our hands in the air, dance for no reason, succumb to frivolity, illusions, flattery, vanity — all to buy precious time. Creating the illusion of memories till we are dust. And for what?

How stupid we all are, she thought, little ants scurrying around to nowhere. Some Greek or Roman said it better. Laid it out on stone or scrolls; pointlessness was their specialty. She was no philosopher. She was just a withering woman too scared to listen to her instincts that screamed out for escape from her promise to a man who would never fill her heart with the love she ached for. A man terrified of her yearning for independence, romance, and a love that was not his to give.

There was ash in her stomach. She shivered despite the heat beating down. Then the fury rose, hot and ferocious. She shook with angry tears. The knot in her stomach tightened. She lurched and heaved by the tree. A speck of vomit flecked the hem of her skirt.

"You're sick."

Carmela looked up, startled. Was there drool at the corner of her mouth?

"Water?" the little boy asked, offering his leather pouch hung across his bony body. He squinted in the sun. Carmela fumbled to kick earth over the mess she had made by her feet.

"No." Flick, kick. *"Grazie."* She wiped her lips with the back of her hand.

"You look like my aunt." The young boy was no more than nine years old. His black eyes bored into her.

"She died," he added.

"Paolo?" Carmela replied with a tight swallow. Her throat was acid.

His face cracked into a wily grin. His skin was the same hue as the tree trunks framing him, but he looked more pinched than he had when she and Kavanagh had seen him at Signor Lau's farm a few weeks back.

"You're the talker for *l'Americano,*" he said, giving his head a scratch. It looked as if a blindfolded barber had attacked it with sheep shearing scissors.

Carmela felt naked. How long had he watched her? And how could he stand the heat in those oversized woolen trousers and jacket?

"You don't go to school?"

A raspy cackle. "Nothing to learn there, Signorina. That's what Papa says."

This scrawny shepherd boy was ripping her out of her self-inflicted ravine. What must he think of this woman in a linen suit and smudged lipstick, sobbing and vomiting into the trees?

"Do you have cholera?" he asked.

Carmela burst into laughter. Tears fell off her cheeks, leaving little droplets on her shirt.

"Mamma told me the cholera makes people mad."

Carmela wiped her eyes, a giggle at the end of her breath.

"Maybe a spider bit you? Nonna said she watched a woman die of crazy because of a spider."

"No, it's nothing that will kill me. Or you, for that matter."

Paolo took a step forward. "Did someone else die?"

"How long have you been watching?"

"Signora, I have to go and get these sheep down the hill and back before sunset."

"Good heavens, that's a day away!"

"Not with these lot, Signora. Papa gives me the difficult ones. Teach me a lesson."

"Oh?"

Paolo yanked at a tuft of wild fennel and chewed for a while. "Does your Papa hit you?"

Carmela turned to look at his tiny face. "No."

His twinkling black eyes bore straight through her. "I'm bad," he said.

"Everyone has a bit of bad."

"You don't." He shrugged. "Only a bit of

sick — for someone."

Carmela took the first full breath since leaving the base. "Try not to do bad things. Papa might go easy on you."

Paolo took his gaze toward the sea. A memory flitted across his face. Then his expression fell into studied inscrutable.

"I'm good at keeping secrets, Paolo."

Paolo rolled up his sleeve. A huge gash was across his upper arm. It looked hot with the beginnings of infection.

Carmela gasped, reaching down for his small wrist and clasping it in her hand. "You're coming with me!"

Carmela marched down the hill with a reluctant Paulo dragging behind her, screaming out in protestation. "No, Signora!" he cried, fighting to free himself from her grasp.

"They have medicines," she barked back at him without taking her eyes off the base at the bottom of the hill.

"You'll get me killed, Signora!"

His escalating cries fell on deaf ears. All Carmela could hear was the thumping of her heart and the crunch of her feet on the cooked earth.

Carmela burst through the base doors. Mary-Anne looked up at the clatter. Her eyes landed on the duo. Carmela paid no mind to the scuffs of dried earth on her white linen, the puffy, tear-stained shadows under her eyes, or the hair that looked as if she had slept in the wilderness for months. Nor did she, even for a moment, consider it inappropriate to drag a shepherd's son into the base and demand immediate assistance. Carmela brushed away that little voice, reprimanding her for using this poor wretch as an excuse to step back inside. Mary-Anne sat openmouthed. "This boy needs help!" Carmela yelled.

"Signora! Please!" Paolo spat. "You're holding on too tight!"

"Excuse me?" Mary-Anne asked.

"You heard me! Call a doctor!"

"Miss, is he injured?"

"No, I'm taking him on a tour of America."

"Sorry?"

"Get me a doctor!"

"Signora, you're hurting me!" Paolo pushed at Carmela's wrist, but the vise would not be loosened.

"Are you telling me that you are not going to call a doctor for immediate assistance?"

"Please tell me where the accident happened."

"No accident. This boy was hurt on purpose!"

"Miss, I'm going to ask you to calm down."

"And I'm asking you to open that gate there and lead us through to the ward. Now!"

The tears were rising. Carmela's first night beyond those starched curtains, Kavanagh tending to Salvatore with the tender care of a father, replayed in her mind without pause. "Call Signor Casler!"

"Miss, this is an army base, not the Red Cross!"

Carmela didn't realize she was sobbing. "If Lieutenant Kavanagh were here, he would not turn his back on a sick child!"

"If this is a medical emergency I suggest you take him to the local hospital in town immediately."

Carmela shrieked. An intense pain shot up her wrist. Paulo slipped free of her grasp and flew back out the doors, disappearing into the hills, leaving behind nothing but two little teeth marks on Carmela's hand. Mary-Anne's eyebrow raised, then lowered.

"Where's Casler?!" Carmela yelled.

"I can take a message. If it's urgent."

"Has he gone home now too?!"

"If you do not calm down you will be

escorted out of the base."

"One month you have watched me come in and out of here. Do you have any idea what my work has done for you? You wouldn't have your job without me, do you hear?!" Carmela's arms were flailing now, punching the air with desperate lobs.

Casler snaked in. "Nothing hotter than a pair of gals clawing at each other, right?"

Mary-Anne flushed a deeper shade of pink. "Major, this woman is demanding —"

"Bet she is. Her ride has skipped town. I was trying to forget I lost my right arm. What the hell?!"

Carmela took a breath, but Casler didn't give her a chance to use it.

"You two done scratching, or shall I stay and watch the rest of the show?" He looked from one red-faced woman to the other. He took a final drag of his cigarette, then stubbed it out on the chrome ashtray upon Mary-Anne's desk as he walked past, tipping his hat. Carmela watched him disappear down the corridor for his rounds.

"Good-day, ma'am," Mary-Anne concluded, sorting a batch of files for the fourth time.

"If, in your heart," Carmela began, leaning toward her with a threatening whisper, "you believe Kavanagh would not have helped that poor boy, you will sleep well tonight."

Mary-Anne looked up and met Carmela's gaze squarely. "A skin infection does not warrant military intervention. Your young cousin, with whom you came in previously, was almost maimed by undetonated enemy mines. This young companion did not appear to be in such a position or in danger of dying from malaria, ma'am."

Capital M.

Mary-Anne was not moved by Paulo's plight. Or Carmela's. Or, if she was, she hid it with military precision. Carmela turned on her heel for the second time that morning, paying no mind to her ripped hem, her hands scuffed with earth, or the sniggers of the two nurses who, on hearing the commotion, had approached for a closer look. She wouldn't admit to having used Paolo as a pitiful excuse to return to the place where Kavanagh should be. What did it matter?

America had shut her doors.

Chapter 16

Carmela stared down into the metal skillet, watching the slivers of garlic fizz dark brown in the hot oil.

"It's burned," Piera said, setting down the last plate upon the kitchen table.

Carmela yanked the skillet off the flame and dropped it on an unlit burner with a clang. "And the world still turns."

"Here," Piera said, handing Carmela a pile of cotton napkins. "I'll start a new sauce. Lay these and go change out of your linen suit."

"And miss Icca telling me about the garlic too? Not if you paid me."

"Someone's still recovering from the dance!"

Carmela flung the napkins onto the table. "Someone is not recovering. Someone couldn't care less if the whole lot of you ate donkey's oats for their damned lunch, because, in the end, whether it's good or whether it's bad, it will never be good enough, will it? And we shuffle around, pleasing the queen, while she hides her growing grandchild behind stone walls."

Piera's jaw fell open slightly, but Carmela stormed on before she could even take a breath. "I don't need to feed or please or beg or apologize for a hypocrite, I —"

"A hot cook is best out of the kitchen."

Carmela whipped around to the crooked silhouette of her grandmother in the doorway. "Anything you care to tell me directly, child?" Icca asked. "Or shall I just hold on to the poisonous snippets I caught from the other side of this door?"

Carmela felt woozy. A gray feeling. So quickly had she drifted to the frayed edges of sadness. So fast was she retreating into a numb place, an emotional purgatory, a no-man's-land. Would she let one man push her so far into the deep? Of course she would. His very essence scored her. Every inch of him was committed to memory: his woody scent, the rosy pallor of his pale skin, the way the sunlight set his hair on golden fire, how his blue eyes shone with warmth and honesty.

How could she have let herself mistake the way he looked at her for anything other than decorum? How could she have let her eyes linger a moment too long on his capable, skilled hands at the wheel, on the head of his child, the marble shoulder of his wife. Or let his face, or the imagined weight of him on top of her, be the last thing that would float into her mind before sleep overcame her? Cling to numb, Carmela, she pleaded with herself. There's air there, if a little thin. "Lunch is almost ready," she said.

"Very well," Icca replied.

"Yolanda needs me at the studio. Tell Mamma I will be late this evening."

She glanced at her sister before turning to leave. Piera's eyes appeared to search her own for an explanation, which Carmela doubted she would ever be able to give. How could she turn onto her side at night — their usual sleeping position like the dovetail of fine furniture — wish her sister sweet dreams and say, by the by, that she was engaged to the wrong man and had lost her heart to another? In another world, perhaps. Another life. To burden her sister with anything of the sort was nothing short of unthinkable.

Carmela walked across the concrete terrace. For the first time that day her mind drew a blank. An intermission. She walked down the steps to the lower terrace, passed beneath the mimosa and wisteria without her daily admiration of them, without taking in the little houses encrusting the funnel of her town, toward the cathedral's golden spire. She stepped into the *viccolo* beyond their house in silence and closed the gate behind her.

The lock clicked.

"*Soda alla menta,* please, Antonio." Carmela raised her hip onto one of his bar stools.

"The belle of the ball graces my little cave with her presence! You want me to ask everyone else to leave?"

Carmela's eyes didn't smile.

"Still groggy? Comes with the territory. Princess by night, mortal by day."

Carmela caught a sliver of herself in the mirror behind the army of bottles behind the bar. She looked blank.

"There you are, Signorina," he said, placing a tall glass of green liquid before her. A long, skinny spoon rested inside it. She watched the effervescent bubbles race skyward, their ephemeral existence expiring at the surface with a pop.

"Hey," he pinged, snapping her back to the bar, "is it true that Blue Eyes has done a bunk back to Uncle Sam? Someone said they saw his wife in a fit of tears."

What brittle resolve she had cracked on

meeting his eyes.

He read her. "Carmela," he whispered, "*tesoro,* I'm so sorry." His warmth was disarming. The first drop of a flood hit her hand as she averted his gaze. Antonio whipped around to the front of the bar. "Come with me." He called to a young man serving a couple outside. "Matteo, I'm in the office if you need me." Matteo gave Carmela a sweep, then raised an eyebrow at his boss, which Antonio ignored. He closed the door behind them and signaled for Carmela to take a seat on the tired leather chair at his desk. "No mint soda's going to fix what you have, is it?"

Carmela bit her lips so they would neither lie nor confess. The sobs broke through regardless. Antonio watched her for a moment. Then he wrapped his arms around her. How had his mother taught him to listen so carefully?

"This will hurt," he said, taking her puffy face in his, salty tears trickling down her nose. "For a long time, this will ache. But believe me, Carmela, I have loved where I shouldn't have loved. It's a knife. But it doesn't have to kill you. You can choose."

"What have I done?" she murmured before the second wave washed to shore. She shuddered into the ashen center of her sobs.

Antonio smelled of licorice. She pulled away from the wet patch she left on his lapel. "How did I let this happen?"

"I knew it the moment he walked in here with his little pawns. I watched you at the picnic. You hid it well. Piera doesn't suspect. You kept everything locked away, almost from me, even."

Carmela's reputation lay in the palm of his well-manicured hands. But in the suffused light of his tiny office she felt a brief feeling of lightness. Her breath returned to something close to normal. "They're keeping him there, indefinitely."

Antonio nodded.

She met his eye. "You console me like I'm a widow. So stupid. Nothing happened, Antonio. You believe me, don't you?"

"I believe love when I see it and when I feel it. So you got dealt a good hand on a crappy round? Your future is not in a daydream, Carmela. Everyone has tempting detours on the road, but they just serve to make us clear about where we really need to go. Your future is across the piazza there, a sewing empire for the taking, and you the most talented and beautiful queen they could wish for."

She lifted a stray thread from her skirt. "I shouldn't have said anything."

"You're the sister my mother should have ruined."

Carmela let out a watery laugh, and for a moment they swayed on a hammock of silence. "What happened to her?"

Antonio cocked his head, as if confused.

"You never told me who stole your heart."

His voice quivered. "In hell you know what you're up against. In purgatory there are no exit signs. I don't think I've left yet." Then he straightened, shifting out of the spotlight. "You look like you had a fight with a drunken donkey. Go to the bathroom and splash your face. Walk into that studio like it's yours already."

She nodded.

He wiped a tear from under her eyes with his thumb. "I'm here. Always." And then he left her in the tiny space, alone.

She looked at the faded green paint on the door and, for a breath, the numb feeling disappeared. The image of her five-year-old self skipping up the fountain steps seeped through, then Yolanda hovering over her as she drew her first pattern. Running home to tell Mamma she had qualified for apprenticeship. Helping her papa with the lambing, holding her baby sister for the first time, shelling pine nuts in the shade with Piera, the wailing gramophone on her uncle's starlit terrace, the safety of Zio Raimondo's shoe shop. The pleasure of an orange dawn, the reassurance of a purple sunset, the hopeful white sun of a winter morning. The relentlessness of the wilderness, the seasons, the moon, the winds, the unstoppable pulse of life.

Her breathing edged toward normal.

The enemy of pointlessness is love.

Yolanda's studio was a buzzing hive. Several trousseau orders had been received within days of each other, and the early October deadline loomed. Over the next few weeks there were half a dozen brides on the island who looked forward to a lifetime of wedded bliss with an entire new wardrobe to match. They would look impeccable for their grooms from their virginal first night through the winter ice, spring's victory, and summer's excess. The girls sang to lighten the monotony. As Carmela stepped in, they had reached the third verse of "Non Potho Reposare," at the glissando where the woman cries out to her true love away in the war. She cannot rest, so she says, till he is once more by her side. Carmela stood before the singing seamstresses for a moment. The music ricocheted in warm waves down from the stucco ceilings. She was glad no one noticed her come in. She was relieved that the tears had dried up.

"Carmela, dear," Yolanda greeted her, swinging by with several swathes of material, "I didn't expect you till later this afternoon."

"My interpreting duties are finished," she replied, impressed with her matter-of-fact delivery.

Yolanda tilted her head a little. "Well, that's the best news I've had all week."

Performance accepted.

"It's one thing to be gallivanting in the summer, but it's almost October now, our busiest time of year. I needn't remind you of that."

Carmela nodded and walked to her station. Agnes stopped singing and looked up. Carmela snapped to her, back straight, arms lank by her sides.

"I'm sorry you think I stole your lover," Carmela said. "There are girls who would kill to sit where you are now."

Agnes gaped.

"I am here to work. I don't care enough about you to want to hurt you," Carmela continued. "The past is a trick of the memory. Everything is here."

She didn't pause for a reaction, but tied her apron around her waist and collected her rough sketches of the gowns she had made for the party. As she watched them furl up in the wastebasket, she decided that any memory could be discarded in the same manner if there was enough will behind it. For the first time, she felt honored to descend from a long line of stubborn men and tireless women, Sardinians who could rise at dawn and work till dusk with but a sip of water. Iron ran through their veins, fearlessness in their bones, and a determination that could not be shaken. They were born of the same rock that rose high into the mountains of Barbagia. Ancient. Diffident. Proud.

If not the lover, she would be the fighter.

CHAPTER 17

By October 1952, the rows of vines at the farm hung heavy with plump fruit. Tomas did a bad job of hiding his excitement. "Well, Silvio," he said to Franco's father, patting his back, "no counting chickens and eggs and all that, but my God we are blessed this year!" Silvio adjusted his collar. It was five years since Tomas and Peppe had taken the farm beside his, and this year was the best harvest to date. Carmela lifted a final basket and moved toward the back of the house to place it on top of the others.

The farmer's daughter would soon enough become part of the town's elite — with a life her parents could only have dreamed of. Carmela knew they looked toward her impending future with excitement. Their chests would swell with pride as she flanked the wealthiest young man in town, her head high, her seamstress fingers busy with decorating the wealthy women on their island. When Tomas's back ached, when his fingers were sore from the never-ending swings of the scythe or the grip of a pick, Carmela knew her oncoming marriage gave him the energy to rise with the sun and trudge through his childhood hills to the farm. Because of their tireless work, she would want for nothing. She owed her promised freedom to her parents. She ought to give thanks to God. She ought to feel warmed by their focus on her future. She ought to feel excited that Franco was always ready to offer an extra pair of hands. How he loved to hover around the farm. He and Carmela had left tussled memories among most of the pines surrounding the fields.

Every morning Carmela pretended she hadn't counted the days since Kavanagh left. When Franco tried to reach into her skirts, she would push his hand away with assumed tenderness, offering selfless acts of pleasure on him alone, which he mistook for devotion. She surprised herself at her ability to control her emotions, to the point of feeling nothing whatsoever. In this quiet emptiness it was impossible to summon the strength to change the trajectory of their relationship. It was time to make peace with the man who was intended for her after all. If her mind ran away, she would train herself to draw a complete blank. It cushioned the pain. While she manufactured impeccable performances, in the hopes that she might even convince herself, inside she thought of clouds until everything turned white. There was some semblance of true pleasure in acquiescing to this nothingness, this silence, as if in rehearsal of a peaceful death.

But today was different.

Franco cornered her behind the wine shed where the towers of grape baskets were stacked in preparation for the small crowd of helpers due to arrive to assist with the harvest. Time was of the essence to make wine. The fruit would need to be picked and pressed within hours to extract the full flavor and quality of the juice. The dawn had just peeked over the valley when Carmela felt Franco nuzzle her neck.

"Don't creep up like that!"

Franco placed a hand over mouth and pulled her skirts up with the other.

Carmela wrestled free. "Stop it, Franco! They'll be here any minute!"

"Don't waste time then." He lunged forward and took her buttocks in his hands. "Touch me."

She thrust back. "Not today, it's not safe."

He pushed her hand onto his trousers. Their trysts had become a ritualistic war dance that Franco mistook for passion. "You get wet when you argue. I know you better than you know yourself."

Carmela turned on her heels. He grabbed her wrist and pulled her into him. His tongue was shooting down into her throat when footsteps approached. By the time Piera poked her head around the wall, Franco was bashful personified.

"Oh, I'm sorry," she said, hesitant. "I just wanted to bring around some of the baskets." Piera tapered off, misunderstanding Carmela's pleading look.

"You look out for yourself today, Piera," Franco said, his face stretching into a broad grin. "I heard a certain Luigi is trying his hand at the land just to get a closer look at one of the farm girls."

Piera flushed. Franco had caught her off-guard.

Carmela watched her sister disappear around the corner, perplexed by her decision not to defend herself or brush off Franco's insinuations about Luigi.

Franco stepped behind Carmela and pressed himself against her. A shiver raced up her spine — fear and arousal had become awkward cousins. "I'll taste you later."

By midmorning the vineyard was swarming

with sweaty Simiuns charging up and down the rows with overflowing purple loads in the deep baskets. Tomas stood at the helm, by the press, loading the grapes into the enormous wooden vat. A row of young men sat on squat stools with enamel bowls of warm water on the ground in front of them, where a girl knelt and took great pains to clean their feet. It was a job most fought over since it provided a rare opportunity for intimacy. This year Piera had taken the unusual step of declaring she would wash. Her parents, accustomed to her shrewish attitude, understood this for nothing more than unusual dutiful willingness. When Carmela saw that Luigi was sitting before her, however, all her suspicions were confirmed. When had Piera worn her hair plaited rather than scraped back away from her face like it was some tiresome inconvenience? When had she donned a floral blouse for *Vendemia?*

Carmela looked at Luigi's expression. The other men jeered and teased the women, shouted out mock insults at their cleaning technique or tall tales of what they had stepped in the night before. Piera and Luigi, however, floated in their own impenetrable bubble. She cradled his foot firmly but gently. Her face gave nothing away, not a hint of any feeling, but the way Piera's hands moved was proof of everything Carmela was searching for. Luigi looked down at her, his expression nothing more than a gentleman having his hem measured at a tailor's. And yet, Carmela blushed. It was as if she was watching her sister make love through a half-open door.

"Carmela! Salvatore said a bad word and he won't say sorry!" Vittoria was hopping from foot to foot, slit-eyed with annoyance.

Carmela almost took her eyes off Piera. "Do you need to use the bathroom?"

"I need him to say sorry!"

"Vittoria, stop stomping and start playing. Are you going to waste the day fighting? There's work to do."

By lunchtime, half the rows had been harvested. The raucous crowd, high on sunshine and song, became hungry. Carmela's aunt rang a sheep's bell from the house, and the crowds dropped their last loads into the vat and made their way to the front of the house, to a table flanked by narrow benches. Maria, to cheers, carried out her largest metal pan, full of steaming *gnocchetti*. *Vendemia* was about gratitude. Hope. Nature's bounty, pregnant excess. Carmela's mind flitted into the dark quiet of the farmhouse where Rosa was, hiding in the shadows. What was she feeling as the songs floated in through the shutters? When people asked after her and everyone told part of the lie so as not to take the full responsibility of her sin? When her un-wanted kicked at her sides, clawed at her spine?

Carmela felt nothing. Not until her mother handed out the first plate of *gnoc-chetti* swimming in rich red sauce, oozy *pecorino,* steam spiraling to the cloudless sky. Only then did her mind crash back to Kavanagh's first unexpected visit. She sum-moned her well-rehearsed tricks. She con-centrated on clouds, a complicated pattern for an evening gown, counting the *gnocchetti* on the plate her mother was ladling. Her heart thudded and her palms were clammy. She closed her hands into tight fists, but Kavanagh shuffled up to the party regard-less, his head cocked to one side like he had that day, his eyes smiling. The transparent figure turned his smile to her. She thought he told her he loved her. A deep love that only a soul who has found its heaven-sent match could feel. Complicit. Simple. His eyes turned up to the autumn sun and glistened. Was he sorry? Would he return?

Madness was at the end of the table.

Her breath caught. She slipped away, and,

when the vines sheltered her, her march turned to a run and then a sprint till her ankle gave way over a small rock and she fell. The hard earth was dry on her lips. She lay motionless. Her head pounded. How long had she lain there before easing herself back up? An hour? She turned, stiff. From the far end of the row of vines the hungry gaze of Franco brought her back to stillness. She didn't feign surprise or happiness or desire. He mistook her emptiness for invitation. He was on top of her now, murmuring words she refused to hear. His breath was hot. Her arms flayed, her feet threw fruitless kicks into nowhere. She gave up the fight because his hand was so tight around her throat. She looked beside her at the base of a vine as she rocked back and forth against the ground. Franco took the final piece of her.

The diners' laughter rose and fell in unison.

Her tears were silent.

CHAPTER 18

On the eve of All Souls' Day, all the women in the household prepared to welcome the ghosts of those who had passed. Maria finished clearing the table. Then she moved to the dresser for her best tablecloth — cream-colored cotton with elaborate lacework along the trim. Carmela watched her mother smooth it over the table with care, paying great attention to every crease and fold. When she was satisfied, she signaled to Gianetta and Vittoria to lay the plates. They balanced high towers of the family's finest china and set down a delicate plate at six place settings, with smaller dishes on top. Icca, meanwhile, was counting the napkin rings, the only pieces of silver in the house, and began her fastidious polishing, checking her skewed reflection every now and then as she did.

"But how do they know how to find us?" Vittoria asked.

"They just know, stupid," Gianetta said.

"Language, Gianetta," Maria called from the other side of the kitchen.

"Sorry, Mamma."

"But I mean," Vittoria said, breaking the brief silence, "do you think it's far from heaven? Do they have to have a map or something to get down here?"

"Come and help me wash our dinner plates, Vitto'," Carmela said. Her youngest sister joined her reluctantly. They washed without talking.

As Carmela finished drying the final dish, Piera entered carrying a wide circular basket loaded with almonds, hazelnuts, dried figs, and plums. Under her arm she had a heavy rock, and in the sack hanging from her arm there were more of the same. Several metal hammers lay upon the nuts. The women took their seats around the table. A few moments later they all had a rock before them, a hammer in hand, and were deep into the meticulous work of shelling. The light from the single bulb above suffused the room in a somber glow. It was a well-rehearsed dance, performed each November, before the dead were honored on the second day of the month.

Vittoria, still unconvinced, piped up over

the hammering, "What if they don't like nuts?"

"Who doesn't like nuts?" Piera asked.

"If you're dead you don't get to choose what you eat, do you?" Gianetta said.

"Enough. We will think of them. And we will pray for them. We needn't harp on with this silly talk." Maria closed the conversation.

After a little while, the pile of shells grew, as if a small mountain, and each woman drifted into her own thoughts. Icca suddenly looked up at the ceiling and burst into a fervent wail.

Her grandchildren and daughter-in-law watched, without surprise. Maria wrapped an arm around her.

"Why?!" Icca bellowed. "Why did He rip him from my arms too soon?!"

Carmela wondered how much of her grandmother's performance was simply that. No one doubted she had loved her husband, in her own peculiar stranglehold manner, but it struck Carmela that Icca's well-timed outbursts expressed more than a longing for a lost love. Icca raised her fists, as if Jesus himself were hovering just above her, where she might pelt him. Carmela felt a flicker of sympathy for this gnarled woman. After all, who deserved a daughter who flung herself into the arms of a married man and plunged the entire family into possible ruin?

Perhaps Icca should be thanking Jesus? Wasn't it He who gave her the genius idea of sending her daughter to an imaginary relative in Venice, for whom she would supposedly be a devout assistant in all matters domestic, most especially the care of their young children? Wasn't it He who gave her the idea to make sure her time with this "relative" would last the exact time of her confinement, birthing, and adoption? Carmela tried to picture her manicured aunt, fragrant with the latest Paris scent, perched upon impossible heels, chasing after a handful of these imagined Venetian toddlers. Carmela wondered how adept Rosa would be in creating an elaborate tale of her time there. Would she procure violet essence for the younger girls as a souvenir? Perhaps she would describe St. Mark's Square in detail, reminisce about those canal journeys. The pink dawns, through which she had scurried to collect the fresh bread. The narrow *viccoli* she squeezed through taking the children to their nursery.

What did it matter if all those tales were improbable fiction? The storyteller is the weaver; the listener can choose how they

318

believe. In the end, Carmela reminded herself over and over, the truth is only what we decide. Her brief sojourn at the base was just that, not the beginning of an expansive career that might take her beyond the edges of her island. The warm smile from Kavanagh was nothing more than pleasantry. The eyes of the onlookers pick the story they want to see. Venice exists. Rosa's imagined time there would exist, around this table at least, and that is all that mattered.

The mound of shells continued to rise. Icca's cries faded. She shuffled away from the table and returned with a small photo of her late husband that she kept on the corner shelf above her stool. Then she opened the dresser door, pulled out several glass oil lamps, and adjusted the woven wicks of each so they were the same length. She reached into her apron for a small box of matches and lit each of the lamps. Their flames mesmerized Vittoria. "I'm sorry, Nonna."

"You should be. He was an ox."

Vittoria straightened, braced for more questioning, but Gianetta shot her a furrowed glare and she stayed mute.

"To bed, girls. Nonna needs some rest," Maria said.

Carmela and Piera arranged some of the

dried fruit upon the nuts. From another basket on the counter Carmela pulled out several flat breads, baked especially for All Souls' Eve. They were far smaller and denser than the wide *spianata pane fino*. The dough was fluffier and dotted with fennel seeds, scored several times down its length so that when it was cooked the small, flat loaves looked like baked faces. When Carmela had been Vittoria's age, it had scared her so much that she couldn't sleep. She watched her youngest sister now, eyeing the shadows that the oil lamps cast as the family rose from the table. Across the rough white walls the women looked like itinerant ghosts, creeping around the kitchen.

Before they left, Icca placed several more photos by each of the lamps: her brother, killed in the First World War; her aunts. There was a tiny, damaged photo of Maria's youngest brother, who died in infancy, and another of her father. Carmela wondered how her mother had coped with her father passing a week after Maria and Tomas were married. A broken heart, they had said. And yet Maria was loyal in her devotion to him and to her mother, who had passed when she was a girl. Now the grandparents Carmela would never know were propped up on the kitchen table — tiny, faded ghosts invited to a midnight feast.

That night Carmela couldn't sleep. She was twelve again. Every creak and whisper of wind made her ears prick up. She thought of the ghosts downstairs, chomping on nuts, sharing stories, crying for the living, for their lives. Would they cast shadows across the walls too? A transparent glow, perhaps. She thought about checking on Vittoria: A terror shared is a terror halved. Instead, she drew her knees closer to her chest. She thought about Aunt Rosa asleep at the farm.

Thick, hot tears rolled down her cheeks.

Carmela was haunted by something more terrifying than ghosts.

The following morning, the cemetery was full of people and yellow chrysanthemums. Families wove in and out between the graves shaking hands; kissing each other; offering blessings, condolences, and compliments. Each gravestone was polished and gleaming. The Chirigoni clan stood before Icca's late husband's grave while she rearranged the flowers in the vase upon the marker. The week before, Tomas had refreshed the painted letters of the inscription with a new coat, and the marble shone from scrubbing. Zia Lucia stood beside them with her children gathered around her skirts as she crossed herself. Beside the grandfather's tomb lay her son Bruno, taken by encephalitis at ten years old, and her baby Gina, taken at thirteen months from malaria.

Carmela wanted to cry, but no tears would come. Beside her, Piera wiped her eyes with her handkerchief. Zia Lucia blasphemed a little, told her resting children she counted the days since they had left her, shot a sideways glance at Icca, and then marched off to talk with the neighbors. The men replaced their flat caps upon their heads and gravitated toward their friends, huddling in an evergrowing group by the main gates.

Luigi appeared around one of the larger family mausoleums and took off his hat as he approached the family.

"*Buon giorno,* Signora Maria."

Carmela's mother nodded her head. As the group moved up the muddy path, Carmela noticed Piera hang back a little and exchange a few snatches of a conversation with Luigi before he moved on to another group of people.

"A secret is not a secret if everyone knows, you know," Carmela said as Piera reached her.

Piera's face creased into an involuntary grin.

"That wasn't the official parental meeting, I hope. I shouldn't think it wise to bring
your fiancé to the cemetery on All Souls'
Day to meet his in-laws!"

"Shhh!"

"You're the one who ought to keep a little
quieter, don't you think? Luigi turns up
anytime we set foot out of the house. An
invisible wire connects you two. Only a matter of time before they realize."

"With your wedding in the spring? No one
can think of anything else."

Carmela stopped walking. "There's no
competition here, Piera."

"Never said there was."

"I can hear it under your words."

"What are you talking about?"

Carmela looked into her sister's big brown
eyes, moist with frustration and excitement.
It occurred to her that her sister's happiness
was paramount to her own. An image of
Piera walking up the aisle to Luigi flashed
in her mind. There was nothing she wanted
more than to see feisty Piera soften into a
lifelong love. Life with Franco may not
provide Carmela with this fantasy of romantic love, but in the end it was a sacrifice she
would gladly make, especially if her sister
might have the blessing instead. She had
not found love at an early age. She had not

let her eye and mind drift toward a foreign stranger only to have the illusion shatter before her like brittle glass. Of the two, Piera was the one who deserved life's prize. It abetted any last traces of guilt in Carmela to know that, in some way, her suffering had not been in vain. In the end, it was as if she had paid penance for her sister's happiness. "I would be the first person to offer you the cathedral in my place if you and Luigi don't want to wait till afterward. There's no race to win."

"We've only been — I mean . . . just let's not talk about this."

"You're the one who's suggesting my wedding is somehow eclipsing everyone else's happiness."

"I never said anything like that!"

"That's precisely what you said."

"Not everyone has a fiancé who drools over them or people telling us how talented we are all day long!"

The sisters fell silent. Carmela realized it wasn't her sister she wanted to fight. "I've upset you. I'm sorry. I'm a little off today."

Piera surrendered to a laugh, then planted a light kiss on Carmela's cheek.

"I love you too, Pie'."

They turned toward the path. With quick steps they dodged the thicker clods of mud to catch up to the rest of the family. Just before they reached the entrance to the cemetery, Franco appeared.

"*Buon giorno,* Franco," Piera said. With a nod she left them alone.

"This place gives me the shivers," he said, wrapping his arm around Carmela and planting a soft kiss on her forehead.

"Why? Everyone is at peace."

"You say so? Have you seen any of those photographs on the tombs up that aisle over there? You'd think the family would have chosen pictures of the grandmothers where they don't have a mustache!"

Carmela smiled. "The dead don't have much need for vanity."

"Dignity, at least. Who wants to be remembered as the hairy nonna?"

They walked several synchronized steps along the pathway.

"We will lie side by side one day here too," Franco said, without raising his eyes from the ground. His voice was a warm murmur. It was as if he were inviting her to lie with him for the first time, not thinking about dying.

"And we will crumble into our earth, Franco."

They turned to look at one another.

"I'm not frightened when I look at you,

Carmela. It's impossible, when I lose myself in your eyes."

Carmela touched her cheek to his. "First skeletons give you goose bumps, now they turn you romantic."

"I love you with every part of me, Carmela."

He took her face in her hands and placed his warm mouth on hers. For a moment they were adolescents again. The dank November mist disappeared. The dreadful afternoon of the grape harvest had never happened. It was summer. "Have a good feast day. Papa will be calling for me. I must go before he bursts an artery."

Carmela watched him take wide strides over the damp earth toward the crowds. Her hands were warm again. Had a part of their love resurrected? October had been a mistake. His passion had run away with him. She could have said no, stayed with the group. She had been foolish to run away on her own. If that wasn't an invitation, what would be? Neither of them had spoken about it since. She had made sure of that. As well as making sure they never met alone for any length of time, away from the safety of a crowd. Carmela grasped at the hope that these feelings of forgiveness weren't just passing through, the revisiting of a memory, only to fade alongside her ancestors once tomorrow dawned.

CHAPTER 19

The golden rays of late summer were long forgotten. Now a purple gray haze hung limp and frigid over the plains. Carmela stood outside the farmhouse watching the November fog roll in from the coast. The cork oaks looked like arthritic workers, hunched in pain, toiling the frosty soil. She wrapped her wool scarf tighter around her shoulders. In the field before the cottage, Tomas and Peppe finished planting the garlic. Tiny cloves, like white pawns, stood to attention in straight drills inside their holes. Carmela used to draw some comfort from the ritualistic planting rhythms, the promise and reminder of hibernation before the celebration of spring, but all she felt now was a damp, cold seep into her bones.

Usually at this time of year, the men would take the majority of the work on themselves, often staying for days at a time without any help. As Rosa approached her final few weeks of confinement, however, the women took turns staying with her.

"Carmela?" Rosa's voice called from the dark.

Carmela returned inside. The fire was almost embers. She walked to the hearth and threw on another squat log from the basket. It crackled.

"I need something warm to drink," Rosa whispered from her supine position upon the bed, where she had spent most of the day.

"I'll set some tea if you like, Zia?"

"Yes."

Carmela lifted the iron pot, poured in some water from a terra-cotta jug, then hung the pot above the flames on a metal hook. She took a seat upon the footstool.

"A watched pot never boils," Rosa murmured.

"You really think I have such powers, Zia?"

"I think you like to sit there smug while I roll around this cave like a beached whale."

Carmela looked across the room to her aunt. She was pale. Over the last few days she had eaten like a bird, citing that the growth, as she referred to it, was suffocating her to the point of her not being able to swallow. The dark circles under her eyes told the story of sleepless nights. Her hair was swept back under a black scarf, her delicate face skeletal where once it had been compelling. Her demeanor, pallor, speaking tone, was of a woman locked in grief — not jubilant expectancy. Without her signature coral lipstick she looked washed out. A half-finished sketch.

"Nobody is judging you," Carmela said, almost letting the cup in hand fall to the floor, doing a bad job of avoiding the circular conversation at which Rosa excelled since her imprisonment.

"You're a bad liar. It will get you into trouble one day." And with that she turned onto her other side, moaning as her back arched with the protruding weight.

The noise of a car rattling down the lane reached the house. Carmela moved to the back window to see who was there, but the driver had already jumped out and was headed to the front door. Before Carmela could reach it, it swung open and Silvio's brother, Agostino, strode in. Carmela leaped toward him and stood between him and the bed, grateful that the blankets did a fair job of disguising whom it was covering.

"Signor Falchi! *Buon giorno.* Let me take you to my father," she said, shaking his hand and doing her best to lead him back out while appearing hospitable. He was a meaty man, thick all over. Every movement was assured — his handshake, his stride, even the way his eyes surveyed the land.

Tomas and Peppe, on hearing the noise, were already marching across the cold earth to greet him. "Agostino, so glad you could help us this year!" Tomas bellowed. "It's an honor to have you do this for us!"

His voice reached the sty on the far side of the house. "My brother said there was half a pig in it for me! How could I refuse?"

The men laughed. Carmela noticed how round and pink Agostino's nose was, not a world away from the animals that he slaughtered each day. He had axed his way up the butchery ladder since he was a young man, and now he owned all three of the meat shops in town.

"The Chirigonis and the Falchis will be family soon, no? This will be the first of many!" Agostino boomed.

Carmela watched them walk toward the pig sty, a small stone hut. Muddy remnants of past winters clung to its sides, and moss threatened a silent, slow rebellion. The men disappeared inside. Every year she had managed to miss this event, and every year she had offered prayers of thanks. Having Agostino perform the task could only mean one thing. It would be swift, over in a professional heartbeat. Carmela looked toward the sty, sending a meager apology to an animal she had never shown any particular affection toward.

Suddenly, the sow shot out through the gate as if her hind legs were on fire. She squealed into the fog. The men gave chase. Twice Agostino mounted her over her neck to pin her down and twice she threw him off. As Tomas and Peppe helped him up, she waddled, frantic, out toward the field. Her piglets broke loose next. They trotted concentric circles around their mother as she flayed beneath the men's grasp. In desperation, and perhaps more than a little embarrassment, Agostino lunged at her with his dagger but missed her jugular. She bit at the air with her huge jaws and stampeded around her piglets waddling away from the men. Peppe ran toward the house and brushed by a motionless Carmela.

"We carry on like this, we'll ruin the damned meat!" he muttered. When he reappeared his rifle was under his arm. He stomped toward the sow. As she saw him approach the animal bolted once again in the opposite direction. The two other men jumped on top of her, and when they had gained control they leaned to one side and Peppe pulled the trigger.

The sound of the bullet echoed along the land toward the surrounding hills.

Carmela watched the men drag the carcass inside.

Over the next few days every part of the pig would be cleaned and used: pancetta from the belly, cured ham from the leg. All the innards would be sautéed and eaten fresh with caramelized onions and garlic, suffused with *vernaccia* and rosemary. Every bit of meat would be ripped off the bones to be cooked or ground into cured sausages. The bones, stripped of flesh, would be cleaned and salted and saved for the broad bean stews of February's carnival feasts. The butchery was a symbol of lack of want. At least Carmela knew that's what she ought to be thinking. All she felt was a great sorrow for the tiny piglet that galloped on its short legs around the yard squealing for its mother, now dead on the other side of the shed door. Carmela returned inside the house.

Rosa stood leaning against the hearth. Her head rested in the crook of her elbow. She lifted it slightly when she heard Carmela come in. "It's started." Carmela followed Rosa's gaze down to the floor. Liquid was streaking down her leg, a tiny pool at her feet.

Carmela dashed over to her and covered Rosa's shoulders with her scarf. Then she ran to the stove and grabbed all the dish-towels she could find. She covered the kitchen table with several of the towels and helped her aunt onto them by sitting her down and scooping her legs up and over. She gave others to Rosa to place between her legs. The water on the stove was boiling now, though the tea had since been forgotten. Carmela ripped several other towels and threw them into the boiling water. "Don't do anything, Zia! I'm going to call for Mamma!"

Carmela ran out to the sty and pushed the doors open. "Signor Falchi! You must drive to Simius and bring Mamma. It's an emergency!"

Tomas's eyes flicked toward Peppe. In an instant a story was born. "Our farm girl, Agostino. It's her time. Carmela has assisted in births, but Maria is always there."

"I see," Agostino said, holding up his bloody hands. The sow's belly was sliced open. Carmela could make out part of her liver.

"I could drive maybe?" Tomas asked.

"It wouldn't be wise for me to leave right now," Agostino said. "You drive, you say?"

"Yes."

Carmela saw a look pass across Peppe's face.

"Then you must go." Agostino nodded. "I will stay and Peppe will help."

This was a man to whom negotiation appeared to be a stranger. Tomas flew through the doors and jumped into Agostino's car. He rattled up the lane and screeched through several gears before he was swallowed into the inky night.

Back inside, Rosa's labor progressed fast. She was sweating now, more than Carmela had ever noticed in any other woman at this stage, though the contractions appeared to be sporadic and quite far apart. The color of Rosa's skin was between gray and white. Along with Rosa laboring several weeks earlier than anticipated — no irony had been lost on the fact that her baby might be born on Christmas Day, like the second coming — everything about Rosa's behavior was different from the women Carmela had assisted before. When her breathing became uneven, Carmela squeezed Rosa's hand and murmured in her aunt's ear, reminding her to keep to a rhythm. Several times her aunt arched back as if something sharp were clamping her inside, as if the baby were biting its way out. Her veins swelled beneath her paper skin. This was a woman who looked closer to death than birth. Maria could not come soon enough.

When Carmela's mother finally arrived, Tomas managed to engineer an artful curtailment of Agostino's stay. White from the panic of driving with a husband of little experience through a night fog, Maria rolled her sleeves up and scrubbed them with hot water mixed with a little cool from the jug. Her expression confirmed Carmela's instincts. Nothing about this was going the way it should.

"I have to push, Maria!" Rosa yelled, flailing now, standing up by the table, reaching her hips back and away from it. Her knuckles pushed down into the wood.

"I'm going to feel inside," Maria said.

Rosa sucked in a breath and let out a scream that would have woken the dead.

"I need you to breathe, Rosa. Ready? This is my hand you can feel."

Maria took on a look of deep, faraway concentration. She nodded to Carmela. "I feel the head, Rosa. The baby will be here soon."

She had almost finished the sentence when Rosa howled like a rabid wolf. Her back rose up and arched. Her knees fell open, wider than before, and her whole body bore down. Carmela watched Rosa's

336

nails dig into the side of the table under the cloths. When the contraction ebbed, there were tiny marks in the grain.

Rosa's eyes glazed over for a moment. Maria reached quickly for water. Rosa was hot to the touch and starting to shiver. A trickle of blood traced down her thigh. Carmela ripped the cloths from the table and threw them to the floor for Rosa to stand on. There were small clots by her ankles. Terror flitted across Maria's face.

Rosa's face contorted, and she let out one more guttural howl that shook the room. Her body bore down once again. Maria reacted to the signals and fell to her knees, ready to catch the baby. She knew it was too soon, too rushed, but Rosa had stopped listening. She was in another world now. Her back muscles were flexing, her toes were curling, her fingers clawing at the table again. The head appeared, followed by two tiny shoulders, before the rest of the body slithered out like a fish onto a towel Maria held on her lap. She wrapped up the blue-gray baby. Rosa put her head in her hands. Her legs were shaking. Carmela helped her onto the table and propped up against her so that she could rest while they waited for the afterbirth. Rosa was panting. Carmela wiped her forehead with a damp cloth and rocked her a little as if she were soothing a child. The white sheets beneath her were blotted with droplets of red.

Carmela looked over toward her mother, who had taken the baby to the bed. It was too quiet. She watched her mother massage the baby's chest in firm, circular movements. She lifted it and did the same on its back. After several repetitions of this, Maria lay the bundle back down on the bed. Nothing she could do would wake this baby from its sleep. Carmela stopped swaying.

Rosa let out a deep sigh. After a strong contraction a liverlike mass slithered onto the table.

"If you try to get me to eat that, I'll kill you," Rosa muttered, slurring.

Carmela wrapped up the afterbirth inside several layers of cloth and placed it inside a large bucket by the sink. When she returned to Rosa, she had her hands on top of her knees, with her head hung between them. Her panting was slowing down toward normal breaths. Carmela met her mother's eyes again. Maria shook her head. Her eyes were glassy. She lifted the rosary up off her neck, kissed it, then laid it upon the baby's chest. Carmela wrapped Rosa in a blanket and began wiping her legs and feet.

"Don't touch me!" Rosa said. "I will wash

myself."

Carmela took a step back and watched for a moment. Rosa did not look toward the baby that her body had fought out of her. She fixed her attention on her clammy legs, on her pubic hair, matted together with sweat and congealed blood. Every movement expressed a deep disgust for the entire process. Carmela walked to the bed. There lay an angel, a half smile across its face. The ethereal beauty of its unmoving face was overwhelming. The eyelids were pressed together, forever stolen in a pleasurable dream. Carmela clung to her mother. Maria held her child. She wiped Carmela's tears and whispered, "You are to be strong. Time enough for tears. Not now."

Carmela nodded.

Rosa made light work of removing all evidence of what had just happened. Wet rags were stacked in a heap on the floor. She moved over to her bedside chair, wriggled into her nightgown, and pulled a heavy knit cardigan over the top. Then she stood, facing Maria. "I killed it, didn't I?"

A matter-of-fact exchange.

"No, Rosa. It wasn't his time."

She laughed — a mixture of bitterness and exhaustion. "I spared him. Life is over-rated."

Carmela came to Rosa's aid, helping her slip beneath the covers. Maria placed a hand between her shoulder blades; her fever had subsided.

"Would you like to say good-bye?" Maria asked. Carmela thanked God for sending her mother here in time. What on earth would she have done without her? For certain she would not have been able to find these words. She could barely breathe, let alone string together a thought.

"I never said hello," Rosa replied. Then she turned and drew the covers over her head.

Maria cradled the baby in her arms. She moved toward the back door and reached outside for a basket that they used for collecting eggs. She placed the baby inside and wrapped more cloth around it. Once she had said the rosary three times, Maria instructed Carmela to heat a little broth for her aunt and be sure she drank it all. As she left, Carmela saw her take Peppe's shovel with her.

The fire's warmth did nothing to raise Carmela's temperature. She watched Rosa's shoulders rise and fall with her breath. Where was she now? A dreamless sleep? A nightmare from which she would never wake? A chill spidered up the back of her neck. She walked to the window and cupped her hands over the cold glass. Her mother was a tiny, moonlit silhouette by the cork oaks. She was kneeling now. Placing the basket and everything inside it down into the earth. Carmela wept. She prayed for forgiveness. She prayed for the floating soul of Rosa's boy. Another ghost to light a candle for.

She would never howl upon a kitchen table for a baby born from empty lust. Carmela began to weep again. For her aunt's plight? For this baby that was never born? No. These hot tears that traced her cheeks were born of relief. A torrent of images from the summer ran through her mind. Kavanagh turning up at the farm, their first visit to Signor Lau, the way he had looked at her in that dappled light, the way he had fumbled for words. She pictured him in the shadows of the hospital beside Salvatore. The wide grin he greeted her with when she had turned up to accept his offer of work. Her body began to shake with the tears. But it was not grief that rippled through her body. She didn't weep for the life she would never have, for the man who would not love her with the ferocity with which she had harbored for him. The idea of freedom was what she had fallen in love with, not the man who represented it. Freedom from the expectations imposed on her, freedom to choose a different path. Now, standing in the frigid shadows of the farmhouse, she realized that true freedom was hers already. She was not ensnared by some blind lust. She was not trailing a married man like her aunt had. She was not held captive by irrational longings, by the illusion of something. She was not, and never would be, Rosa.

Kavanagh was where he belonged: home. With a wife he loved and a child he cherished. Carmela didn't love him. She loved the idea of a man like him. And she prayed to God with thanks for her narrow escape.

It was true that defeat, pain, or heartache was indeed a blessing in disguise. A prayer of thanks scored her mind, mumbled mutterings in the night. Gratitude washed over her. Amidst the horror of the evening, there was a flicker of hope in the darkness — far better a Franco than an invisible man like Rosa's doctor, who would leave her to face this carnage alone. That was no man. Imagined men are the stuff of bad dreams — ones you never wake from.

Carmela remembered the way Franco had looked down at her at the cemetery a few days earlier. How his expression of fear had given way to that of love. He had promised himself to her as just a boy. His simple, innocent devotion — if at times childish, unrefined, and controlling, even — was a love that could weather an age. This was the man she was meant to stand beside after all. A summer of questions and doubts and idle distractions had served only to reveal her true path. How glad she was to have met Kavanagh, grateful he had sparked a whirlwind inside her. It had served to prove to her what true marriage meant, and which life she was destined to live.

A quiet peace warmed her. She prayed for that tiny soul, out there in the dark, drifting back up to the stars. Her mother's moon shadow trudged back across the cold field.

CHAPTER 20

Small, uniform pieces of onion began to sizzle and soften at the bottom of the huge metal pan upon the stove. Carmela poured another glug of olive oil over them and added paper-thin slices of garlic. She watched them caramelize, lost in the purity of thoughtlessness that cooking invoked.

The descent into the darkness of November had given way to a peaceful December. A tender equilibrium reverberated throughout the household. After a few weeks of recuperation, Rosa found that her depression ebbed; every day she behaved more like a woman grateful for the people who had stood by her rather than dwelling on those who had fled. Piera floated around with a perpetual half smile in her eyes. Even Icca softened. Carmela spotted her launching the odd snowball during the thick blanket of snow that buried Simius in early December. Then the ice froze the steep cobbled steps, and several of Icca's contemporaries suffered grievous injuries. At this point Icca retook her seat inside and held court from there for the entire month.

Vittoria and Gianetta were allowed to dance through the house, on account of the New Year's Eve festivities; gallop, skip, fight, pout, repeat. Tomas sat on his oversized armchair by a new wireless that took up a significant portion of the glass-topped sideboard. He listened to a broadcast of a choral concert from the capital, Cagliari. Only music would slow her father down to a peaceful stillness. Carmela loved his faraway expression as he did so. Her mother sat beside him, her hair in a bun at the base of her head. She wore the yellow glass drop earrings from her wedding day as her fingers flew through an intricate crochet pattern, the skinny needles clicking together as the doily grew.

Carmela returned her full attention to cubing the sausage upon the thick, wooden board. The memory of this sow's slaughter was from another life. As the meat browned, a rich aroma rose up from the pan, sweet-salt steam thick with oregano, rosemary, thyme, and bay. Before the meat was cooked through, Carmela reached for a brown bottle of *vernaccia* and doused the pan. The alcohol whooshed up into steam, swirling into concentric spirals that filled the kitchen with the reassuring smell of a New Year's feast. As the sugar of the cooking wine seeped into the meat, she scraped the onions and garlic off the bottom of the pan to coat them around the sausage. Then she reached over to the counter for a large enamel bowl and tipped its contents of dried lentils into the pan, each nutty bead like a miniature coin, the symbol for prosperity.

She stirred them around the meat, onions, and garlic. The invocation of prosperity this year was for a spring bountiful not only with material goods or harvests but also with love. Piera and Luigi's courtship had become official, and Carmela's wedding would usher in the fertility of the season. She pictured herself beside Franco by the altar at the cathedral. The way he would hold her hand, assured but tender. He might look at her sideways, with a jaunty glint in his eye, forever that tireless youth who had chased her affections at the cusp of their childhood's end. Then she imagined Piera, luminous in a light summer wedding dress, upon the steps of the same cathedral, perhaps a fine lace mantilla to cover her head and then cascade down her firm back toward her hem. Carmela's heart swelled, even more than when she dreamed up her own wedding day. Tonight was about giving thanks. There was much to be grateful for indeed.

Carmela dipped a ladle into the clear vegetable broth simmering on the back burner. She poured it over the lentils and meat, and continued without haste until the liquid reached halfway up the tall pan. She placed the lid on top and reduced the heat. It would simmer on this gentle flame through the entire afternoon, until Yolanda and her husband joined them after evening mass.

"A toast!" Peppe called out from the end of the table. "To the beautiful cooks and the children we wish them!"

Cheers. Clinks. Carmela felt her cheeks redden. Beneath the table, Franco slipped a hand on top of her knee, and then traced it almost to the tip of her inner thigh. Was this giddy feeling the wine or the unfamiliarity of simple happiness?

All the guests around the table stood up from their seats, raising their glasses heavenward. The candles danced in their eyes. For a moment Carmela could even picture Icca as a young woman. Lucia and Peppe kissed each other. Maria and Tomas stepped closer together. Piera lowered her eyes as Luigi took her hand. The gaggle of cousins squeezed in between the adults and passed *ridotto* glasses between them, dipping their fingers inside, then slurping the droplet of wine from the tips.

Yolanda tapped her glass with the tip of her fork.

The family grew silent.

"And now, if I may, I would like to share some news with you all. Please, you may sit back down. As you are all aware, of course, I have had Carmela beside me as my prized apprentice for several years. She came to me a scrawny goddaughter with no hips and two plaits, declaring her dream of following in my footsteps."

Carmela smiled, bashful.

"To be quite frank, my dear, I did doubt whether you had it in you at all."

Laughter rippled around the table.

"Ten years of dogged determination she has put in, displaying patience with even the most cantankerous customer — and let me tell you, money does not buy you class — together with a diligent approach to every task I have ever set her. And so, it is with great pleasure that I invite you, Carmela, to stand beside me at the studio, no longer as apprentice, but as partner!"

All eyes turned to Carmela. Electricity shot through her, a brief, golden silence.

"Zia Yolanda," Carmela said, finding her voice at last, "I don't know what to say. . . ."

"Say you're the best seamstress this town has seen!" Franco shouted, pulling her into his arms.

More cheers.

Carmela ran around to the other side of the table and squeezed her godmother tight, overcome.

"Come now," Yolanda said with a broad smile, "I expect you to keep hold of your level head, child!" The two women laughed. Yolanda wiped a tear off Carmela's cheek and one off her own. When Carmela returned to her seat, the coffee was passed around, accompanied by a mountain of sweets. *Tiricche* — fig-filled pastries, and *papassini* — moist raisin-dotted cookies, topped with icing painted on in delicate lacelike designs, so fine that everyone agreed it was almost sinful to destroy such art by eating them.

Carmela had never seen her mother and father look so happy.

January slipped by in a mist. Toward the end of February, Simius shook off the endless cold and burst into frenetic preparation for the celebration of Martedi Grasso. The piazza was alive with stallholders pitching their stands along the course of the carnival procession that would take place that night. When Carmela stopped into Antonio's bar, he was shining his polished glasses, certain to exploit the opportunity of having his town filled with salubrious, and most likely wealthy, revelers.

"You'll wear it down to breaking, Anto'!"

"You see if I don't, Carmela. If my ladies want a deluxe crème de menthe they come to me — next best thing to sipping along the Champs-Élysées. I'll give them the service they've traveled half of Sardinia for."

Carmela leaned over the bar and kissed him on the cheek.

"You look beautiful, Carmela. It's like you've thrown off your veil."

"All because of you."

"Nothing to do with a certain partnership whatsoever, or having the wealthiest clod head in town hang off your arm?"

Carmela shook her head with a giggle. "Here, take this tray of sweets. Mamma insisted you have them as a gift." She rose onto the tips of her toes and handed the loaded tray over the bar to him.

"I told her I would pay for them! I'll be

selling them later."

"She wouldn't hear of it. I think she wishes her own son would show as much ambition as you." Carmela leaned onto the bar, lowering her voice, "Would you talk to him, Antonio? No one seems to be able to get through to him at home. From what I can see, my brother cares only about what the actors in Rome are wearing these days. He steals my fashion magazines that Yolanda buys for the studio. Of course Papa won't hear of him training with me, though I've suggested it several times. He insists little Salvatore will take over the farm."

Antonio smirked, but Carmela couldn't tell if it was derogative or complicit. "Tell him to stop in. I'll see what this councilor can't do. Chirigonis are my specialty."

Carmela had never felt such an intimate connection with another man, based on nothing more than an open friendship. Never had there been even the slightest hint of attraction. It puzzled her; he was beautiful, mannered, ambitious — sane. A very private person when it came to it, far more adept at drawing out the secrets of anyone who stepped into his bar than revealing his own: the consummate professional. Everyone needed to talk to Antonio. He would listen with his whole body, making the speaker feel there was nowhere he would rather be, or any other face he would care to gaze upon but theirs. Where had he learned that? His formidable mother couldn't be more opposite. Perhaps years of battering indoors helped him hone a patience known only to saints.

Back on the street, the last clangs of scaffold rung against the stone houses as large teams of builders erected several platforms. On one stood a thick, four-legged iron frame for a gas ring, heating an enormous copper cauldron. Three men took turns stirring the steaming broad bean stew cooking inside, using wooden spoons with handles as long as brooms. The smell was rich with smoked pancetta and the deep flavor of the salted bones from the November slaughters. The first of the aromatic wild fennel balanced the earthy starch of the harvest to perfection.

At the opposite end of the piazza was another platform, upon which Cubeddu, the town's poet, would return from the mainland to spar with hopeful local bards in their much loved poetry competition. This year, an excited customer had told Carmela that the discourse would be on whether each poet would choose his mother or wife to save in a disaster.

Carmela was struck by the way the poets could find humor even in the darkest themes and keep the crowd hanging on every word. She loved to watch them, the bristles of their long beards twitching as they are taken over with the passion of the moment and the desire to win. One stand already had a huge metal vat of melting sugar on the go, in preparation for the almond and hazelnut brittle the confectioner would craft later for the crowd.

In the studio the girls burrowed their heads deep into their work. The faster they sewed, the earlier they might be let go, and the longer they would have to beautify themselves for the parade.

The Martedi Grasso moon, full, fat, and smiling, rose high in a starry, cloudless sky. The dissonant clatter of hundreds of sheep bells suddenly echoed down the *viccoli* toward the piazza. A hush fell over the vast carnival crowd, pressed together like salted anchovies around the perimeter of the main square. The bells rang once again, in unison. The crowd shuffled in anticipation, eyes searching for the noise coming from farther up one of the narrow *viccoli*. Again the bells rang out, closer this time. Several children ran from the front of the crowd to cling to their parents.

Their shadows appeared first, folding around the corner building on the edge of the piazza, rising toward the shutters. Hooded silhouettes bowing under the weight of at least two dozen metal bells attached to their backs, on sheepskins that wrapped around their bodies. Then the Mamuthones appeared, at least fifty local men donning full costume. They wore thick, wooden masks of skewed faces, huge eyes, crooked mouths, and noses that ran almost from the forehead to the chin. Some had high-carved cheeks, and others had grave, sorrowful expressions, turned-down mouths etched deep into the wood; others still had an abstract of surprise, with long, tapered horns. The rich, dark wood lent a woe-stricken undertone to each. It was an army of demons.

Shunt to the right, step step.

Shunt to the left, step step.

As they filled the square, the crowd's expression rippled between fear and wonder. Once they had taken their positions, their leader summoned them into a semicircle and they began an elaborate answer-and-response, the leader performing a movement and the chorus of dark figures echoing. As the tempo accelerated, the cheers began. Faster and faster the macabre dance went, until the entire crowd clapped to the same beat.

The entrance of the horses released the crowd from their frenzy and back into silent awe. Their riders were dressed in thick, woolen trousers; crisp, white shirts trimmed with elaborate lace collars; and black waistcoats embroidered in bright colors along the edges and on the breast. Their buttons were polished gold, some encrusted with coral and turquoise. They too were masked, but unlike the Mamuthones, theirs were bright white, ceramic, and expressionless — impassive faces beneath wide, black hats. Some had scarves that trailed down from the back rim. All wore thick, white gloves.

The Mamuthones fell silent as the horses paraded into the center. It was impossible to tell which was Franco, but the rider toward the center appeared to have a gait Carmela recognized. The horses walked through the semicircle, then led the procession onward down through the cobbled streets beyond the piazza, where Simiuns hung out of their windows, wrapped in their warmest furs, and others crammed into doorways and along the street.

As the riders and Mamuthones left the piazza, some revelers followed, and others stayed to dance as the traditional folk band wheezed into life, having accompanied several dance troupes earlier in the evening. The rituals were over — the party began in earnest.

How very different, Carmela thought, from the celebration at the base. What on earth would Kavanagh have made of all this paganism? How would she have explained the meaning and mysteries behind each of the figures and their place on the eve of Lent? Would a crisp American from a Southern state ever comprehend what it all meant? The Americans were conspicuous in their absence. Carmela couldn't help wondering if they had been ordered by Casler not to fraternize. He was probably riding masked himself, hoping to wind his way into some illicit embrace or other. How liberated she suddenly felt, to be free of all that. She felt proud to be Sardinian.

Vittoria popped out from behind her. "Carmela!" she cried, waving a piece of paper in her hand.

"Whatever is the matter? You said you would be with Gianetta. Where is she?"

"She's with Yolanda, buying brittle. Nonna said I can even have some. Weren't they scary?"

"Yes, I suppose. What have you got there?"

It looked like a letter, a puzzling sight in the midst of the party.

"It's for you! The lady from the post office saw me just as she was closing up, and she said she had something for you. It had been in the post office by mistake for ages, she said, so she gave it to me and this is me giving it to you and —"

Carmela took the letter from her sister's hand. Who on earth would be writing to her? They had distant family in Munich and some in the outskirts of Rome but none accustomed to writing. The stamp was American. Carmela's heart skipped. Maria's sister had settled in Niagara Falls before the war. They wrote regularly. But this letter was not for her mother.

She fought the urge to tear it open right there and then, instead folding it inside her coat pocket.

"Off you go and dance, Vittoria, look, Gianetta is waving to us, see?"

Vittoria dashed off to join her sister and Yolanda. Carmela waved to them but instead of following, her feet twisted her back uphill to where the procession had begun. When she had moved several hundred meters away she found a stone stoop and took the letter out of her pocket. The writing was not her aunt's. She turned the envelope over and over in her hands. Then she ripped it open and pulled out the cream paper. It felt fine milled, expensive. Nothing like the almost translucent stuff her aunt used. She flipped it over and unfolded it. Her eyes raced down to the signature at the bottom of the letter.

Her heart skipped.

Base 16578 — Washington, DC
November 6, 1952

Dear Carmela,

I apologize for my sudden departure, and for not writing sooner. It's one of the hardest letters I've written. My mother lost her life a month ago, in an automobile accident. I hadn't prepared for how grief would tear me to the core, but it has. She was the gentlest, strongest woman I have known. Until I met you.

I am a coward to write this now. But from the moment I saw you, staring at me across your father's field, I did everything I could to forget your face. The way your lips part slightly when you are sizing up a stranger, the courage, curiosity, and intelligence you radiate, your proud stance, childlike verve, and wisdom beyond your years. I wanted to behave with propriety. I wanted to ignore my feelings. But I can't stifle my burning need to tell you the simple truth: I love you, Carmela.

My life is in Washington, DC now. I am stationed here indefinitely. Virginia remains down South with Seymour. We have gone our separate ways. The reasons are not for this letter. The world is quiet and solemn without an infant around.

I am selfish to burden you like this, but I couldn't face never telling you how you have touched me. I want nothing in return. I will not write again. In another life, another time, perhaps things might have been different. I want only to wish you well — health, wealth, and above all else, happiness. These are the riches you deserve more than anyone I know.

Thank you for everything. I couldn't have done it without you.

Joe

CHAPTER 21

The sounds of the carnival whirled around her. She folded the letter and replaced it inside her pocket. Her feet marched her away toward the reverberating celebrations, pounding up the cobble alleys and over the ancient *viccoli*. Once or twice she ducked into narrow corridors only to find Mamuthones and their chosen girls for the night in compromising positions. Was it every Sardinian girl's tawdry dream to make love to a masked bear? Several streets had scantily clad people dancing down them with delirium, oblivious to the cold or decorum — out-of-towners. She felt faint, but couldn't stop walking.

At last, a tiny, deserted alley. She flew down it. At the stone doorframe of the last house, she stopped. She was dizzy now, feeling as if the whole street might tip up and slide everything and anyone on it, helpless pinballs in a loser's game. There was drumming from the piazza and more cheers, warped by the *viccoli* and the pounding in her chest.

In the half shadows, she reached inside her pocket for the letter. Her fingers were white from tightly clutching the paper. She skipped across the words like stepping stones: accident, courage, curiosity. Love.

She felt an explosion, neither happiness nor despair. Rather, a stunned white noise jarred her mind, radio static, a tuneless frequency. The blood returned to her head with the first sting of regret, only to slip into silent confusion. She longed for a deeper breath. As she did, sobs overtook her, an unstoppable wave crashing to shore, washing away resolve and rationale. Her head dropped into her hands. Nothing in her world made any sense.

For a moment she felt invisible, a mist of tears. She surrendered to them. As her breath shuddered through her, in the midst of her fog, she reached an eerie silence. The self-protective numbness of her autumn wafted back, like the coastal clouds before a storm.

Her breath hovered closer to normal. She peeled open the page again, smoothing it over with gentle, apologetic fingers. For a breath or two she allowed his words to take her back to the golden memories of the summer. His bashful smile when he had first met her at the farm was more than the awkwardness of a foreigner outnumbered by formidable islanders. The way he held her gaze past politeness at the hospital. In those twilight shadows, she had chosen to interpret the electric silences as nothing more than her own skittish excitement. His desperate attempt to impress her in the ward's kitchen was more than civil hospitality after all. The way he had stuttered over his clumsy compliments about her cooking at the picnic. The way he had insisted they work alone. That gaze, which Carmela never allowed herself to fall into the way she would have liked, might have revealed more than she could ever have imagined.

The sharp twist of regret's knife.

But what was there to regret? Not having had the courage to tell a married man she had fallen in love with inexplicable passion? That he had touched something deep inside her? What courage would there have been in that? It made her sick to imagine herself back in September pouring out her feelings to him, only to run back to town and finish his wife's hem, the final touches for the perfect couple.

And what courage did he display toward

her? Did he ever even come close to sharing any of these feelings with her? Where was his courage when he was touched by such passion? The sparkle of her intelligence had done nothing but send him running back to the States. Where was the passion in that? Did he fight to return? Five months after the fact he was living a lie — without his wife or child.

And yet.

Much as she tried to paint him with a coward's brush, her heart knew he was the stronger for not burdening her with his feelings. As she wallowed through these murky thoughts, she couldn't stop picturing him nursing his own deeper wounds, his own tragic losses. However she might try, Carmela would never be able to convince herself that he had acted with disrespect of any sort — quite the contrary.

She ran her fingers along the words. He had touched this page. He had thought of her over every word. His tongue had touched the envelope's fold. Those lips she had burned into memory, gazing at them while his attention was directed toward his captain, a farmer, his wife. She ached for them. Had dreamed of them. How long had she spent gazing up at her ceiling at night imagining the feel of them on her own, or on her neck, her hand, her thigh?

What of it now? Carmela knew there to be but one chance at true love in a lifetime. She had let hers slip away. She had clung to safe, to The Plan. What intelligence could he have seen in her? That of a woman so desperate to follow the life others had created for her? Terrified of intuiting what she really wanted? Her weakness disgusted her. First, for falling for someone who was not hers to fall for; second, for watching him drift away while she held up the mask of propriety.

She looked down at the writing. The beautiful penmanship took her breath away. Such care over every word. This was not the scrawl of someone in a downward spiral to irrecoverable despair. This was the hand of a man who never professed what he didn't feel, a man in touch with the undercurrents of his own emotions and those of others. He wrote of being selfish, didn't he? This wasn't a bogus declaration. This was a measured confession.

Carmela's body ached. She looked up and away from the words, though she knew that every one of them would be imprinted in her mind till her dying day. She would walk up to the altar with another man in her heart, an invisible man. The only one who could have ever reached her, the only one who offered her an insight into the woman she could become.

But how could any man believe in her and her future if she didn't herself? If she had looked her future square in the eye, she would have found the strength to be honest with him, with herself, and with Franco. In the end, she could blame only herself for not grasping the life she had fantasized about. She couldn't escape herself — that was the worst pain of all. No sparkling intelligence in not chasing after her dreams, shying away from standing tall in the face of repercussions, holding on to resolve even though others might be hurt. She had allowed herself to be crippled by all those expectations, and this was her punishment: the declaration of love from a man she would never set eyes on again. God had sent her a life of buried regrets to shackle her soul. She had created this mess, and no amount of deft backstitching could fix it.

The oil street lamp at the apex of the alley flickered and then went out. Her tears began to dry on her cheeks. The purple-black night was crisp with winter. She looked up. The stars were bright, scattered across the sky like shards of gemstones. How insignificant everything felt. Nothing mattered indeed. A lifetime flits by, and then we are stardust once again. This pain would fade. This regret would be buried.

The births of her own children would heal this wound. A sewing empire would provide a profitable, all-consuming distraction. She had known this deep attraction, and this was enough. She had felt it score her bones deeply. And now she knew it had been reciprocated all along.

It would have been far sadder to drift through life and never feel this. She ought to be thankful for having met that elusive great love, even if it would be neither consummated nor fulfilled. He would not sit beside her in old age. But what of that? Two people had found each other, if but for a snatched moment in time. Was that not enough? Does the length of time two souls spend together make the encounter more meaningful? Does a lifetime of shared experience always make something more worthwhile? The physical expression of their love would only have been a manifestation of something far deeper, more intimate, than any touch could convey. If anything, the physical would have reduced these powerful feelings, this inexplicable connection, to the carnal, banal even.

Yes, this was enough. She could look her

future daughters in their eyes and tell them that great, burning love is possible, that there is the perfect soul for everyone in the world. She would tell them to be ready to spot it when it came, to not let it slip away. She would tell them not to look back toward their mother on the island but to spread their wings, seek their lives. She would not burden them with her own expectations. She would set them free, because freedom is the most powerful expression of love. Kavanagh had set her free. He had never forced anything on her whatsoever. His love was pure, untainted with demands.

If a life with Franco would give her a safe home, a lifetime wanting for nothing, a brood of children who could learn from her mistakes and rise, like the phoenix, from the ashes of her own failings, her existence would not be wasted or stunted with missed opportunities. What would there be to regret? She would die a fulfilled woman after all.

Carmela clung to the image of those dreamed-up daughters, so bright and clear in her mind's eye, standing proud, bristling with curiosity, ideas, and fiery independence.

Then she wept.

They weren't her daughters. They were her.

She wept for the woman she would never become.

The clumsy clatter of drunken footsteps snatched her out of her head. She froze in the darkness of the doorway. She heard the voices of two men. All these houses were empty, of that she was certain. The inhabitants would all be down in the piazza. Only a couple of meters separated her from two drunks on carnival night.

What was she thinking, tearing herself away down into an abandoned street? And tonight, of all nights, when her town was awash with strangers, unaccountable drinkers in search of a good time whatever the price. Every year stories would set tongues alight about undesirable encounters. It wouldn't be unusual for Agnes or one of her crowd to recount horrific tales of local girls being taken advantage of under the cover of carnival's chaos. All she had cared about was a stupid, out-of-date letter. Was that worth the unspeakable that might happen if these men saw her?

They were laughing now. One sounded a little younger. Her ears pricked up. Something about the laughter was familiar. For a second she thought it might be Franco. She didn't move a muscle, praying they wouldn't walk farther down the alley. What on earth would she say to him? How would she explain hiding in a doorway on carnival night while her sisters danced in the square?

Most likely it would be Franco's younger cousin Cristiano with him. She would wait. No doubt they would soon find their way back to the party. The men's footsteps were getting closer. Her breaths became shallow.

"It's all right," she heard one of them say. "Everyone is in the piazza."

There were a few more murmurs from the younger voice. Then silence.

Carmela's heart pounded.

Out of the quiet a sound grew that she couldn't make out at first. A sort of fumbling. The men's soles scuffed across the cobbles. They stopped talking. What could they be searching for? Perhaps they had stolen some liquor? That wouldn't be unusual for Cristiano. There was no sound of a bottle though, or the glug of liquid. Every fiber in her body willed her to hold her stance, but she burned to see what mischief they were up to. She craned her neck and peeked through a narrow chink in the doorway's stone where the grout had crumbled away. It took a moment to decipher the figures as they dipped in and out of the shadows. When one of the faces caught the only sliver of light along the street, it took her breath away. This was not Franco. This was not Cristiano.

This was Antonio.

What was he doing away from his bar on a night like this, down a darkened alley? He slipped back into the darkness. Out of the silence more movement. The silhouettes were close together now, so much so it was hard to make out where one ended and the other began. Their heads were almost touching. What Carmela saw next made her breath catch.

Antonio had tilted his head to one side. His hands were on either side of the other man's face. She stared, unable to tear her eyes away. The men clasped each other, hands racing over bodies. Carmela froze. Antonio was swallowed into the black.

She heard only the sounds of the two bodies pressed against one another. The figures moved faster. The second man caught the light for a flash before disappearing into the breathy darkness. A stone fell to the pit of her stomach.

She spied him. A tumble of judgment and embarrassment overtook her racing thoughts. The men's lips parted. They held each other's hands for a moment and then dodged behind a corner. Carmela's heart thumped. Then it ached for Antonio. He too would never relish a lifelong love. He, more than anyone she knew, was treading the same unsteady ground.

His secret was one he would not, could not, share. Yet he had been there for her. Two friends stood, chasing after love in the dark. An impossible love. A punishable love. How had he reconciled himself to his duality? Everything he had said to her in the back office of his bar now ricocheted in her memory, more meaningful than at the time. He doled out romantic sagacity because he was still living the nightmare Carmela thought she had escaped. Why was she overcome with pity? Who was she to judge his actions, his choices? She hid in the same shadows as he.

CHAPTER 22

Carmela gazed up at the elaborate frescoes on the ceiling and let the choir's voices wash over her. Swirls of biblical stories in bright colors twirled within the intricate trompe l'oeil of geometric gilt cornice. The choir's hallelujahs modulated higher and higher, vibrating joy throughout the majestic cathedral packed with all of Simius dressed in their Easter fineries. As the verse swelled, Carmela felt a tear run down her cheek. The lyrics were so full of hope and triumph, it was impossible not to feel overcome. The women's voices were bold and brave, their warm vibrato lifted up like sunbeams.

Carmela's eyes scanned her neighbors, every now and then her memory jogged by a coat or skirt that she had made. Then they rested on the marble Madonna cradling her Jesus beneath the raised lectern, her skirts falling in gentle ruffles around her son, forever smiling, forever hopeful. The dark days of winter were behind Carmela and her family. Kavanagh's disappearance and her childish infatuation with him, the gore of Rosa's violent stillbirth, even the disorientation of Kavanagh's ill-timed letter seemed from a distant past. New beginnings were on the horizon.

She looked along the pew at her siblings in their best dresses. Vittoria, prim in navy blue; Gianetta wore Carmela's old yellow A-line skirt; Piera looked luminous in a maroon two-piece that gave gentle curves to her wiry frame. Every now and again Carmela spotted Luigi cast sideways glances at her from the other side of the aisle, where he sat with his family. His face beamed with love. Carmela felt a great wave of happiness for her sister and the life she saw laid out for her and Luigi.

Carmela's mother looked sanguine at the far end of the pew, holding hands with Tomas, letting the music take her into the meditative state that churchgoing induced. Carmela had never known her mother to miss the first mass of the day. Even Icca looked at peace with the world, reveling in the staccato rhythms of the priest's Latin.

Carmela reached over for Franco's hand. He held hers warm in his. There was strength in this hand. Strength she could harness, channel. Directed in the right way this strength could be a powerful source for good. What could they not achieve together? Besides a brood, what limitless possibilities could there be between his contacts and influence and her deft creativity and head for figures?

What were those tears streaming down Carmela's face, other than allowing herself to be overcome with the staggering beauty and potential of life? She would not waste hers. She was ready to roll her own stone away. She was ready to leave her mother speechless at her own rise. Her hand was cradled in Franco's. She allowed the heat of his to penetrate hers. She would be loved and protected. Skepticism was dead. Long live Hope.

Just after the sun spiked the horizon, Lucia and her fruit truck rattled down the *viccoli* to collect her load of passengers. She pulled up at the foot of the harsh incline that lead to the Chirigoni house, where a small army of revelers waited, each holding baskets stuffed for the Easter Monday feast. Luigi and a handful of his closest friends flirted with Piera and several of their cousins. Vittoria, Gianetta, and a gaggle of other squealing girls charged up and down the hill. Icca linked her arm in Maria's as they took their final pigeon steps down from the house.

Franco stood beside Carmela, holding a wrapped lamb flopped over his shoulder. Once upon a time, Carmela would have interpreted this as some kind of warped omen: a dead child, in her eyes, torn from a loving mother, ready to be consumed.

Today though, and every day from now on, Franco would be nothing but the proud provider. This was a man who knew how to look after someone. He wouldn't feed her flattery, fill her head with perfume or fancy words. She wouldn't expect silk lingerie chosen with taste for their anniversaries. What were those things worth? Rosa had a lifetime supply of it all, and where had it left her? Loveless, childless, and scarred.

Carmela would be cared for in the most practical ways a human could want. Their love was not lofty, ethereal, and transient. This was bones-and-flesh love. It started raw and, over time, it would warm, sweeten, just like that lamb, soon to be caramelizing on her father's spit.

"All aboard!" Lucia bellowed from the driver's seat.

Carmela looked up at her aunt and flashed her a warm smile. "Good to be driving again, Zia?"

"And some!" she shouted back. After the first few exhausting months of her youngest son's birth, Lucia had risen back to her usual verve, once again driving the fruit runs for the market. She often took her youngest children with her, and all of Carmela's cousins understood that as soon as they were tall enough to get behind the wheel, they would be expected to perpetuate her legacy. Carmela felt a rush of pride for this gregarious woman. Her aunt shrugged everything off with a joke about her orphanage childhood and the demented nuns there who administered questionable care. Carmela felt blessed to be flanked by such strong women: Yolanda, Lucia, and Maria were an indomitable triumvirate.

"Don't stand there gawping, child! One of you boys help Carmela up!" Lucia shouted. One of Luigi's friends rushed over and held out his hand. His face looked like he'd just passed the first flush of adolescence; his hair was combed to one side with mathematical care, and a vertical crease pressed down the length of his trousers.

"Well, thank you."

"Pleasure's all mine, Signorina." With that, he steadied Carmela up to the small metal step, and she clambered into the open truck. Its canvas sides were pulled down, and the floor was packed with partiers. Icca and her mother took their seats beside Lucia in the cab, Grandmother clutching her rosary, for, as she had proclaimed all night, their lives did indeed depend on it, what with her least favorite daughter-in-law at the helm.

"Easy now," Franco said, his back to the young boy, "she's almost married, you know!" The crowd laughed, and someone yelled that the young boy had discovered only yesterday what all his God-given equipment was for. The truck charged along the dirt roads out of Simius to the farm, lifting clouds of dust, filling the awakening valley, pink orange in the morning light, with song.

By the time the truck pulled into the farm, the fire below the spit was dying down, perfect for roasting. Tomas sat beside it on a squat milking stool, looking at the flames as if they were weaving a captivating story. Peppe leaped past his brother, over to his wife. "They all in one piece?"

"Your wife seems to think it hilarious to rattle her mother-in-law's bones to dust," Icca growled as Peppe opened the passenger door.

"Oh, come now, Ma, plenty of time for that!"

Icca rolled her eyes and, with a begrudging scowl, allowed her son to help her out.

A steady stream of people filed out from the back of the truck. The children raced into the dewy fields, birds that had just found their wings; the women made their way inside the farmhouse to begin preparations while the men crowded around the fire, greeting Tomas with polite salutes, ready to spear the lamb onto the metal rod. Tomas had a jar of olive oil beside him, several cloves of garlic resting at the bottom. A brush made of rosemary and sage stems tied together with twine was dipped inside, infusing the oil with their aromatic scent.

By the time Carmela and Piera reached the house, it was swarming with industrious females. A group of younger women prepared a vat of broth, slicing beef belly at a slanted angle, peeling carrots, cleaning celery and removing the papery skin of onions. All the ingredients were thrown into the pot and covered with cold water, then set upon the stove to boil. When the lid began to rattle, Carmela lifted it slightly, then sprinkled in some peppercorns, fresh parsley, and a sprig of fresh thyme. The onions, placed in whole, bobbed up and down at the surface. It wasn't long before the whole kitchen was filled with its promising aroma.

Others flanked the table, cleaning the rest of the fresh carrots and radishes, slicing them and creating attractive arrangements upon long slabs of cork bark. When several raw vegetable platters were complete, they were placed on the marble counter where the cheese was usually made, to keep cool. Others unwrapped the fresh, sour cheese, which Carmela and her mother had made the week before, from their muslin cases, where they had hung inside wicker baskets. A small group cubed the cheese, ready to be tipped into the broth just before serving. Another group of women folded and tore fresh *pane fino,* still warm from the dawn's baking. They were placed in round, flat baskets and covered with cloths to keep them soft. Carmela watched everyone's happy, busy hands. The kitchen sang with the hum of familiar rituals. A great wave of comfort washed over her.

She pictured Kavanagh's letter wafting up the chimney into swirls of smoke, with neither pain nor love. Then her mind drifted to Antonio, and for a moment she felt the heavy burden of his secret. Yet even he had found a way to lead a full life. He was a successful man, a faultless friend. If he could lead two lives and find happiness in each, who was she to confront him with knowing the truth? What was that in any case? Whatever anyone chose to believe. Today there was only one thing she believed more than ever: this place is where she belonged.

Maria checked the uncooked *seadas* laid inside a huge earthenware dish, perfect discs of thin pastry filled with more of the fresh cheese, ready to be fried after lunch and drizzled with acacia honey. Carmela hadn't tasted them since last summer, the day Kavanagh appeared.

She could look back to that day with a smile now, a maternal nod to her younger self. No thorn in her side, no teenage flutter. Even when a couple of her cousins started murmuring about the young American soldiers they had danced with at the carnival, she didn't feel the slightest twinge. She felt happy for them, that was all. Was there anything sweeter than that first blush of attraction? Or anything more enriching than true love that grew with time and sank roots deeper with each passing year?

The hours drifted by, the spit turned, the meat roasted. The broth darkened. The aromas wafted into the house. The crowd nibbled on fresh, crusty rolls smeared with homemade butter and fig jam. Some of the men took wine bottles and *ridotto* glasses and then headed for the far fields to gossip out of earshot or play cards while the sun promised a warm day. The women warmed the house with tales, old and new, sipping coffee in between filling small bowls with olives from enormous glass jars, where they had marinated over winter in brine and wild fennel.

By the time the sun should have risen to midday brightness, the clouds rolled in from the coast and the temperatures dipped. The fire was stoked in the house and the tables brought inside, arranged next to one another in a long line that stretched the entire width of the kitchen. The women emptied baskets of enamel plates that each had brought for the several dozen guests. The cottage was a clatter of crockery and cutlery, punctuated by the frisson of so many young, lithe bodies in one small space. There was a frisky spring in everyone's step — the men rosy with wine, the women warmed with good company and the pleasure of granting themselves a day to devote to the making and consuming of food. Everyone was immune to Icca's drawl on how everything should or shouldn't have been chopped, and no one even paid attention to the fact that Rosa did little more than change seats and conversation every hour or so.

At last, the meat was ready. It was pulled off the spit and lain upon a bed of myrtle stems along a vast slab of cork bark. With quick hands, Maria removed the dampened paper wrapped around several dozen potatoes that had cooked in the earth beneath the fire and placed them around the meat. She forked the tender meat off the bone, arranging the sprigs of rosemary around it. Then she put the head and brains on a separate plate for Tomas and his brothers, and drizzled olive oil over the roast and the potatoes, before sprinkling coarse salt over it all. Lucia helped her carry it to the center of the table, not without some effort. The sight and smell drew everyone to the table, applauding.

Hurricane lamps were lit and hung from three hooks on the low ceiling, creating a golden bridge of light above the party. The fire crackled. Tomas led a short grace, guests' heads bowed. The swirling steam from their soup bowls warmed their cheeks. There were cheers, raising of glasses, in celebration for surviving winter and for a table loaded with plenty: food, family, and love.

Carmela gazed at the orange glow on everyone's faces. What did people strive for if not this? What was the point of being a sought-after seamstress if not to provide for her family the way her own had all her life? Carmela wondered whether her father, digging Mussolini's roads under the scorching African sun in return for enough money to build a house in Simius, had pictured this scene. She looked at her mother beside her, swirling her soup, fresh cheese oozing off her spoon as she lifted it to her mouth. Did she cling to this promise while he was away?

Tomas stood up. The guests grew quiet. "I'm a man of few words. . . ."

A happy titter.

"But I would like to say this. To the cooks! To many happy years ahead, my friends. Health, wealth, and happiness to you all!"

Everyone stood and reached to one another's glasses once again. Carmela looked across the table and caught the reflection of the fire dancing in Franco's eyes. A rush of warmth rippled up her body. Franco turned toward Tomas; she watched them raise their glasses at one another. Clinks and laughter filled the little house.

The door swung open and crashed against the wall. Salvatore dashed in, only just escaping a hit as it swung back and slammed shut.

"*Gli Americani!*" he squawked.

"Sit down, boy!" Lucia fumed. "Peppe, see to your son!" She huffed and puffed back into her seat. As Peppe made to stand, the party dove into their meal.

"Gli Americani!" Salvatore screeched again. No one except his father paid him any mind. "Sit and eat, boy," Peppe said.

Carmela's eyes darted back to Salvatore. There was a loud knock. Several people twisted around to look.

"I'll go, Signor Chirigoni," Franco called down to Tomas. "It's probably Papa. He said he would be late, remember?"

Tomas nodded, then returned to his soup and lighthearted sparring with his brother. Franco opened the door.

The sight of what lay beyond drew the group into silence.

There, in the doorframe, was the largest chocolate egg any of them had ever seen. It was so big, it covered the bearer's face and half of his torso, with a cascade of pink ribbons twirling down from the apex and over the ebony luster of the shell. At the bottom there was a nest of crepe paper and more ribbons that spiraled down to a pair of shiny boots. Carmela's eyes were drawn to the paper flowers at the base, where two hands held the gift. The egg on legs stepped in

384

and handed its load to Casler, who stood beside.

That face.

Those eyes.

Kavanagh removed his hat. He took a breath and smiled at the crowd. "Signor Chirigoni, I do not mean to interrupt your feast, though I confess I smelled it all the way down at the base, and, as I speak, many of my colleagues are salivating. Signora Chirigoni." He found Maria's eyes. She smiled. "Nevertheless, I feel it my duty to pass on sincere Easter wishes to all of you, from everyone at the base." With that he lifted the gargantuan egg from Casler.

A stunned silence. His Italian was flawless.

Franco turned to Tomas, speechless. Tomas rose and walked toward the soldiers. Lucia lifted the egg out of his hands and placed it on the marble counter.

"Lieutenant, I couldn't have wished for a 'sweeter' surprise!" Tomas declared, to chuckles from the party. "We heard you'd deserted! But you've been hiding away learning to talk!" Tomas shook his hand and patted him on the back. "Come in, please, Maria — lay . . ."

Kavanagh shook his head. "No, no, my father taught me better manners than that!"

His Italian was more staccato now. He had studied his opening patter more than conversational chatter.

"You come to my house? I feed you. No one leaves empty, man — no pride in that!" The guests shunted up and down the long benches accommodating the impromptu additions to the table. Kavanagh took a seat at the far end by Tomas, and Casler sandwiched himself between two of the prettier young ladies, looking from one to the other as his face widened into a smug grin. Franco returned to his seat. Carmela stood up.

"Sit down," he said, face in his bowl. "You're not paid to serve them in your own home."

Carmela paused for a breath. Then her legs walked her toward her mother, who was already at the dresser reaching for another couple of enamel plates, cutlery, and two napkins. "You lay," she said, handing Carmela everything. "I'll bring the glasses."

Carmela looked down at her hands. They felt like they were trembling, but the cutlery wasn't moving. She straightened and steeled herself for the walk to the far end of the table. The house had never seemed so small. What in the world was he doing here? Was this even happening?

His scent reached her before she did him. The woody fragrance he wore, a cologne she didn't know. She had stifled the memory of that, and the smell of fresh air about him, and the unfamiliar soap that left a powdery undertone.

How could this reach her from where she was standing? Impossible. It was the memory of those scents that flooded her senses. Kavanagh came rushing in like a tidal wave. The dam gave out, and the damage was immediate. Her eyes rose from the plate and fixed on her destination. It wasn't his wide, square shoulders, immaculate posture, or the breezy countenance that forced her to hesitate. It was the palpable presence of him, like standing too close to a fire and feeling the heat scorch one's skin. It was the clammy vise around her chest, the acute, wolflike observation of his every tiny movement. She met Piera's eyes. Nothing about the smile she sent Carmela hinted she knew her sister's heart was throbbing. With each step, a deluge of memories, jumbled snapshots of every drowned recollection of him crashing through like the sun-melted ice water of rapids, currents crisscrossing and colliding.

"Carmela has your plate here, Lieutenant," Tomas said, raising a proud arm to his daughter.

Kavanagh twisted around and looked up at her. He didn't cock his head, bashful. He didn't shift in his seat. He looked straight into her. It was all she could do to keep standing.

"Come on, now, Carme'. The man's hungry!"

"Yes," he said, without shifting his gaze.

Carmela couldn't feel the floor.

"It's wonderful to see you again, Carmela."

He didn't wait for a reply but returned to Tomas, and they picked up where they had left. Carmela headed back to her seat, doubting her performance of nonchalance. How could everyone fail to notice her palms clasping into involuntary clammy fists?

She steadied herself as she returned to her place at the end of the bench. Her heart pounded. She swirled her soup, watching the liquid spiral, her reflection a watery abstract. Kavanagh was a few meters away. A thousand scalding pinpricks raced up her body. The room emptied, as if her friends and family had been smudged out of a wet watercolor sketch. All that remained was the presence of two bodies, the air alive between them, like the static of an expectant gray sky before a summer storm, tangible even, should she lift her fingers to touch it. She dare not move her gaze from the strings of melted cheese in the bowl, yet she intuited his every slight move: each time his face angled toward her end of the table, or he shifted in his seat, or his eyes lifted in her direction.

Something had changed while he had been away. Had he hardened? Had she?

"Where's the ghost?"

"What?" Carmela answered, trying to meet Franco's question with her full attention. Kavanagh's outline kept a stubborn hold on her peripheral — he was more compelling than she had dared remember.

Franco's eyes darted toward hers. A bolt of terror shot down her spine. Had he intuited the pounding heat searing through her? Why would he ask such a thing? She was ripped open, feeling the sensation of wanting to snatch at clothes, as in dreams where she found herself naked, on a busy street, with nowhere to hide. He made to speak but was interrupted by Lucia, sending a heaped fork of meat his way. She used the distraction to leave the table and bring another platter of vegetables over from the counter.

The meal lasted an age. Never before had she counted the minutes till she could stand up and help clear the plates. She ached to move, to run, to go outside to the far edge of the fields. Twice her mother had placed a hand on her knee to stop it from knocking against hers. And all the chatter, the noise, the polite and bawdy conversations, were drowned out by the thumping of blood in her ears. She watched her world from inside a tank; a muffled life floated by. Franco spoke to her several more times. She hoped she answered with conviction. It was a queer sensation, the feeling of utter disorientation in a room of people she knew so very well.

She felt a tap on her shoulder. Maria nodded for her to begin collecting the dirty dishes. The heat of surprise edged toward cold panic. Kavanagh's letter fought for her complete attention now — his script, the feel of the paper, the shadows in which she sat to read it in. *I love you, Carmela.* The words wouldn't leave her mind, rushing to the surface like a ball that will not sink, that can be kept down only by force.

She took the first load of dishes to the sink, and as she turned back toward the table, she caught sight of Kavanagh laughing with one of her younger cousins. A pretty girl, with enviable high cheekbones and that blunt gaze Americans went weak for. Her cousin lowered her chin and raised her black eyes at him, thick lashes aflutter. They laughed again. Nothing about the way he looked at her was any different than how he had greeted Carmela.

She felt a sudden, almost unbearable wave of deep embarrassment. The letter was written months ago, steeped in the first stages of grief. He had spoken of Virginia and Seymour having left home. He spoke of his mother's tragic death. How could she have read anything into his greeting or visit other than what it was? Duty.

Something had shifted, yes; his feelings for her. That letter reflected the words of someone in great pain. The moment had past, the madness had evaporated. He would apologize and ask her to forgive his clumsy confession. He would be crippled with embarrassment. Yes, that was what she saw flicker in his eyes.

Piera touched her arm. "How handsome does he look?"

"What?" she replied, jumpy.

"Luigi. I'm falling in love all over again."

Carmela sighed a faint smile.

"Are you all right, Carme'? You look pale."

"I'm fine," she answered, hoping she would be.

"Some of us are headed outside to play bocce. You coming?"

"No. Yes. Go ahead, I'll help Mamma."

Piera left with a small group of cousins after Maria waved them away from clearing up.

"You spoil them, Mari'," Lucia shouted from the other side of the room with a smile. "You wouldn't have lasted five minutes with the Mother Superior at the orphanage!"

"No one wants to hear about the witches who raised you," Peppe said, giving Lucia's bottom a light slap.

"And no one wants to see your hands run amuck, you cheeky bugger!"

The remaining men and women at the table laughed, and Lucia heaved herself up from her seat over to the sink.

"Maria," she began, "give your eldest the day off, in the name of Jesus. She looks like linen before it's dyed!" Maria held her hand to Carmela's cheek. Maria looked at her firstborn. Her eyes smiled.

Carmela sent a thousand silent apologies for the thoughts swirling in her mind. "It's fine, Mamma, I'm glad to help."

"Why don't you and Franco join the others? There's enough of us left inside to make light work of it," Maria said.

Franco reached for Carmela's cold hand. "That sounds like a fine idea." But as he started to lead her out, his father stepped through the doorway. "Papa! Signor Tomas's lamb was superb. We saved you a rib!"

"Well," Tomas interjected, "when the top butcher in town hands you the meat, you know it's going to turn out good! Please, join us."

Franco's father, Silvio, nodded to Maria and Carmela, and then joined Tomas, Peppe, and Kavanagh.

"Franco," he called out, "come drink with your father. I want to hear some American jokes!"

"With pleasure," Kavanagh replied, almost knocking Silvio off his seat with his pronunciation. Franco pulled up a stool next to his father. Casler moved up toward the group, and the men clinked glasses of garnet wine to their health. "And to great beauty, gentlemen!" Casler hollered. "Sure made lunch go down good!"

"Hey, Carmela, what's Americano say?" Franco called over to her.

"He said," Kavanagh began, "that he thinks the ladies here are all *bella!*"

Franco flashed him an indecipherable glance, somewhere in the no-man's-land between pride and affront. "So, Americano, you're *Italiano* now, no?"

Kavanagh's face creased into a wine-warmed grin, and he shook his head.

"No, it's good," Franco said, "because your talker is busy every day sewing her wedding dress."

"What's he say, Kavanagh?" Casler asked. "More food? I couldn't have another bite, unless it's of that little vixen who just stepped outside. Schmanksgiving! Here's to Easter!"

He lifted up his glass and all the men joined him, without knowing they were toasting their cousin.

Franco called out to Carmela, standing at the other end of the table, as his glass touched Kavanagh's. "What's Capitano say?"

The vise tightened. "He enjoyed the feast," she replied.

Kavanagh shot her a fleeting glance, as if he had understood her diplomacy.

"Hey! Capitano, this is no feast," Franco said, stretching his arms out into the air with dancing hands. "You come to the wedding, you'll see a feast, no, Carmela?" With that, Franco rose and snaked his arm around her waist before tipping her chin around to him and placing a soft kiss upon her lips. It was the first time he had kissed her on the mouth before her father. Her cheeks flushed.

Kavanagh twisted back to her. "Congratulations, Carmela."

She ripped her gaze from his face, from those blue eyes, tripping back to Franco's. Off the look that flitted across it, she wasn't sure her feigned normality had convinced her fiancé.

"Before you go out and let us men talk, bring *aqua vitae,*" Franco said.

She nodded and did as he asked. He took the bottle from her and gripped the base.

"Time to find out who's the man here," he said, waving the bottle with a twinkle that Carmela wished was closer to mischievous than menacing.

"Come on, Franco, enough talk, pour!" Tomas said.

"Sì!" Casler echoed, to sniggers from the men. "Whatever the man said!"

Carmela made her escape. Perhaps in the fading afternoon light she could collect her thoughts, dismiss the flash in Kavanagh's eyes. Set aside the fact that every fiber in her body was yearning for him, telling her that he had come back for her, that he had fought Casler for his return every day he had been gone. A little fresh air would bring her back down to earth. Her earth. Not this made-up one, based on a few written lines from a near-broken man.

She took a seat on the bench in front of the house. The air was still damp from the rain but without the winter chill that seeped into the bones. Her cousins looked beautiful out in the fields, laughing, playing carefree. She watched them for a moment, reminding herself that only a few hours ago she was one of them, warmed with the promise of a secure future. She replayed the journey, the singing, the ritual of feast day. She clutched those images. They trickled through her fingers.

"Carmela?"

She turned. It was him.

They held their gaze a beat beyond polite.

"I'm pretending I have to head to our vehicle for something," he began, speaking intoxicating tones under his breath, in English. "Now I'm sitting beside you, pretending we're about to talk about the upcoming farm visits." She met his gaze again. There was a head's distance between their lips, the air thick in that narrow gap. "Now I'm going to look at you straight in the eye, and I'm going to tell you that if you burned my letter and wished me dead, I would understand."

Carmela's lips parted. No sound came out.

This wasn't happening. This couldn't be

happening.

"And if you wished I had never written any of those things, I'd understand. And if you never want to work at the base again, I'd get it. But if you would be happy to work for me again, in the month I'm stationed here before they move me to Munich, I'd be the happiest man on the island."

She looked into him, hoping that neither he nor her cousins nearby could read her longing. Her eyes darted to the door, expecting a bombastic Franco to charge out at any moment and insist on Kavanagh's return inside to drink. She turned back toward the ancient trees at the far end of the field, a boat in distress searching for a place to drop anchor, somewhere back in the reality she knew was out there. The side of his hand brushed hers. The touch pounded in her ears, her belly, her back, leaving a gaping hole where her body had been.

He stood up and looked down at her. Carmela braced herself for another speech. It didn't come. He returned inside, his words left floating in the air behind him.

The axis of her world shifted.

What haunted her was the absence of any desire to shunt it back.

CHAPTER 23

It was dark when Carmela left the house with the flat basket of proven dough for the town ovens. She balanced the wide load on her head while taking care not to slip on the dewy cobbles. The scuff of her shoes on them was the only noise along the silent *viccoli*. She counted each step, as if the order of the numbers might regiment her racing thoughts after a turbulent night's sleep.

On the four hundredth step she reached the ovens and fell into line with the other women. The heat from inside the small bakery reached the chilled street outside. Women stepped outside with cloth bags of baked *spianata*. The smell didn't have its usual comforting effect. The predictability of the line, those familiar faces, the wood-fired oven, the tireless bakers, all seemed locked in another time. Carmela looked at the narrow townhouses with their squat-columned terraces on the upper floors. The beauty of the geraniums in their terra-cotta pots along their sheltered ledges, strewn with hopeful buds, failed to touch her. Even the sky turning from midnight blue to pale yellow left her cold. It was like looking at someone else's past.

The woman behind nudged her. "You going in or just here for the view?" Carmela turned back toward her. She wore several underskirts that added bulk to her already stocky frame. Her hair was pulled back like an afterthought. Her breathing was labored, and she struggled with her heavy load of dough. Only a few years of grueling domestic responsibilities stood between her and this woman. Nothing in Carmela's mind could convince her otherwise.

Is this what a Simius life would amount to?

Is this who she would become?

Carmela turned away from the woman and her thoughts and stepped into the hot room. More familiar faces greeted her. It should have felt like a mother's embrace, that toasted room. It should have felt like a welcome home. It should have served to remind Carmela of all she was grateful for. But she saw only lines and routine and a fire stoked with repetition. The women by the oven moved like machines. Carmela watched them and felt an inexplicable dread. She fixed her eyes on her dough being placed on the wide, round palettes and slid inside the oven by the fire. The rounds ballooned in the heat. The bakers slid the palettes back out just as they began to brown. The air escaped, leaving a perfect round *spianata.* Carmela stacked the bread inside her bag. Back outside the birds had launched into their dawn chorus.

Carmela finished setting the table for breakfast, trying with little success to steady her restless hands. Her sisters began drifting down from upstairs, most of them having slept longer than usual after the excitement of yesterday's feast. She poured large cups of warm milk for Vittoria and Gianetta, then splashed it with a lick of coffee before unwrapping the bread for them to tear. As she made to sit down, the rattle of a vehicle echoed in from the street. They looked up. No car had ever driven up to their door before. Carmela stood and walked across the terrace to peer over the wall. She felt Vittoria and Gianetta squeeze around her to catch a glimpse.

"Go inside! You're in your nightclothes!"

"I want to see!" Vittoria protested.

"You'll see nothing when you catch pneumonia. Get in!"

She waved her sisters back inside. As she looked down over the wall to the street, the eyes of a private caught hers. He saluted.

"Ms. Chirigoni?"

"Yes."

"Message for you, ma'am."

Carmela stepped back from the wall and took a breath. Then she raced down the winding steps to the front gate and opened it. He was a young man, not much older than her brother. He handed her an envelope.

"I've been asked to wait, ma'am."

Carmela looked at him, then back down at the letter. She ripped it open.

Dear Carmela,

Please allow Private Simmons to escort you to the base to discuss our itinerary. I know you have duties at your studio, so I assure you I will take very little of your time, and I will make sure you are escorted back to town immediately.

Or, do not, and I will cease to burden you. Casler is putting me under significant pressure. I'm happy to do this alone if need be.

The feast yesterday was indescribable.

In every way.

Yours,
Joe

Her heart pounded. She asked the private to wait, then ran back up the stairs and dashed through the kitchen and up to her room, ignoring her sister's questions. Piera was finishing getting dressed as Carmela burst in.

"You catch fire?"

"I'll be back," Carmela said, riffling through the lowest drawer of the wardrobe for a shawl.

"Where are you going?"

Carmela straightened and looked at Piera. "I have to go the base for a few hours. Please tell Yolanda I will start a little later today. And tell Mamma not to expect me for dinner. I'll stay on till early evening at the studio."

She turned and flew down the stairs, across the terrace, down the winding garden, and back out into the street. She took her seat beside the private. The vehicle shuddered to attention.

"Take a seat, Ms. Chirigoni."

Carmela thought back to the last time she had stood before this receptionist. Her platinum hair looked fake now, and her smile forced.

She heard his voice from down the corridor. Kavanagh stepped into the light-filled foyer.

"Thank you for coming," he said, all business, holding out a firm, impersonal handshake. "There's a gentleman who has agreed to meet us this morning. If you're ready, we could engage him now?"

"Yes, of course," she said, unable to decipher anything in his tone other than impeccable professionalism.

She followed him out to his vehicle and took her seat beside him. Moments later they were rumbling deep into the countryside, the sun beginning to warm away the night rainfall.

He didn't speak as he drove. Then he took a sudden hard right off the main dirt road and headed down a narrow track deep into a thicket. Onward they bounded down this unfamiliar path. Carmela didn't know of any farms along here. The pines clustered together, blocking the sun. The jeep reached a gradual stop. Kavanagh raised the handbrake and switched off the engine.

They sat in silence for a moment.

She wanted to ask where they were going, though she knew the answer. She considered feigning a disingenuous act. She imagined herself keeping up her frail performance of decorum. But what was that worth now? Instead she just turned her head and looked at him. She watched as his fingers reached for hers. He lifted her hand and unfurled her fingers. He raised her palm to his lips. She thought about saying something. Telling him to stop. Recoiling into safety.

He kissed her wrist and then interlocked his fingers with hers. Her heart raced.

She felt the width of each of his fingers against hers. Her eyes met his. He leaned toward her. She didn't push away. Their lips met.

Soft.

Hungry.

She parted her mouth.

His tongue met hers — this was no stranger's kiss.

Their lips separated as they rested their foreheads against one another.

Their breath fell into a shared rhythm.

"I have dreamed of this, Carmela," he said in a whisper that sent shivers over her body.

She rubbed her cheek softly against his. "There are no farms, are there?"

Kavanagh pressed his lips against hers. Fleshy. Warm. Ardent.

She pulled away. "What are we doing?"

"I don't know."

She looked at Kavanagh, trembling.

"I don't want to hurt you, Carmela, but I can't keep away from you anymore."

"I'm terrified of what I'll say."

"Then say nothing."

He reached in for her mouth again. Then his lips traced her neck.

Kavanagh pulled away, moved around to his trunk, and removed a wide blanket from inside. He set it down on the pine needles of the forest floor. He opened her door, slipped his hands behind and underneath her, and then lifted her toward the darkness below the trees. He lay her down upon the blanket. Neither spoke. There was a time for conscience, but it was not now. He went down on his knees and then eased his weight onto her. Every touch of his fingers, hands, tongue, felt familiar yet uncharted. She fell into the earth and gave in to the sweet exhilaration of surrender.

Just after lunch that day, Franco arrived unexpectedly at the Chirigoni house. He insisted that Carmela ride his motorbike with him to his uncle's villa, where the Curwins spent their summers. The familiar valley of Simius whirred by her, a blur of green noise that failed to divert her guilt. They pulled into the drive, lifting white clouds of dust behind them. Franco slid off and helped her with a gallant hand, wrapped tightly around hers. As they reached the front door, he turned and produced a strip of material, which he tied around her head, covering her eyes.

"I want this to be a surprise," he whispered. Carmela felt him lead her through the door and make a sharp right, walking her up the granite steps. The air was stony and stagnant; she made a mental note to air out the place, even though it would be several months before any guests would arrive. She sensed the runner carpet underfoot as they walked along the corridor, then the creak of the bedroom door, which Carmela judged, from the distance, to be the master bedroom. Franco reached a gentle stop. He traced his fingers down her arm. A shiver spiked the back of her legs. The door closed behind her. She reached up to the blindfold.

"No. Let me do it," he said.

She felt his hands untie the tight knot. The scarf fell away. She squinted in the suffusive light that came in through the shutters in subdued stripes. Across the bed were dozens of rose petals. Carmela glanced at the dresser and the vase upon it, filled with lilies and chrysanthemums. She had never seen those flowers in a bedroom before, only on tombstones or in church. On one of the end tables was a silver wine cooler filled with ice and a bottle of *prosecco.* Her heart lurched.

"You like it, *tesoro?*"

Carmela turned back to him, answerless.

"I said, do you like it?"

"I don't know what to say."

"Say nothing. Just kiss me."

He stepped toward her, clasped her face with his hands, and pulled her into him.

Before she could pull away, he scooped her up and lay her on top of the petals. He fell onto her, smoothing the hair away from her face. "Get used to this, Carmela. This is the bed we'll be waking up in every morning for the rest of our lives."

"What?"

"My uncle, he's giving us the house. Why wait to inherit it, he said." He traced her hair with the tips of his fingers. "You'll never have to serve those English again. Leave hot kitchens to the maids, *tesoro.* You'll be a Falchi soon, not a Chirigoni farm girl."

He dove to her neck, smothering it with his hot lips. She pulled his face up, away from her, "I love working for the Curwins. They are good people. They love this house."

"Not as much as I love you." He pressed his hips against hers. The birth of panic began.

"When were you going to tell me this?" she asked, unable to mask the first quiver of anger.

He yanked himself straight up, the weight of his straddle pressing down on her legs. "You don't sound like a woman whose fiancé just covered a bed with petals to make love to her!"

"I'm sorry."

"You want to live next to pig shit all your life?"

"What's that supposed to mean?"

"I've just told you this is our home, and the first thing you care about is those stuck-up foreigners."

"They've taught me everything I know about English. I owe them more than you'll ever understand."

He started to undo his belt. "No need for English when you're the lady of the house, *tesoro*. You won't have to trail behind anyone ever again."

"I can't do this, not now."

He undid the top buttons of his trousers.

"It doesn't feel right, Franco." Carmela wondered why she was whispering in a deserted house.

He fell down onto her, reaching out for her hands. His grip around her wrists tightened.

"Please, you're hurting me."

She tried to pull away from him, but he twisted her face back toward him. "You love this little game, don't you?" he asked, burying his face in her chest.

"Franco, stop!"

Carmela writhed underneath him.

"Can you feel me, my beautiful? You want me. Say it!"

"Stop!"

Franco pressed his lips on hers as his hand traveled up her skirt. Her knees pressed together. He forced his fingers farther up. Then he let out a cry and jumped to his feet, clutching his hands around his mouth.

"What the hell are you doing?!" he spat.

Carmela sat up. "I told you to stop."

His eyes shot her look of fury. "I'm bleeding, you bitch!"

Beads of blood swelled on his bottom lip.

"I said stop — it's not safe today!"

Franco grabbed her chin, his hand like a vise. "It's not a wife's place."

"I'm not a wife."

Their eyes locked. Carmela couldn't tell whether he was going to strike her. The sheet slid to the floor. A scattering of red petals fell beside it. He let go of her face and walked to the open window. Carmela tried not to think about the Curwins. Or Kavanagh. Or the stinging between her legs.

"I can't do this," she said. "Not here. Not today. I'm sorry."

Franco said nothing. She turned away from him. Above the headboard the Madonna and Jesus sat in a painted garden. A pair of doves fluttered above them.

"They've asked me to go on a trip," she said at last.

"You mean he asked you," he replied, without turning his eyes away from the orchards. This whole escapade was an act of desperation, not romance, Carmela realized with a shudder. He didn't want her to speak English so that she didn't have to trail behind Kavanagh.

"Casler's thinking," Carmela began, purposely emphasizing his name, "that some of the farmers down south might negotiate with them."

Franco twisted back toward her. "What are you talking about?"

"Casler, at the base, wants to go to Cagliari. He's asked me to go."

"And what did you say, little Miss America?"

In the face of his vindictiveness, the guilt

that had trailed her like a phantom since the morning turned to defense. "I said I would be delighted."

"Without asking anyone? Me? Yolanda? Your father, for heaven's sake? What's got into you? You behave like a slut!"

Carmela's eyes studied her lap.

"Go. Have a nice little trip," he said, taking two threatening steps toward her, his body stiffening as he did so. "But don't you set foot back here unless you can promise me that the only bit of land those morons will rent for their weapons tests and little military games is ours — do you hear?"

Carmela looked up at him and answered with defiant silence.

He clamped her chin again. "I said, do you hear?!"

Her breath caught. She swallowed her tears. He let go of her with a flick of his wrist, then walked back to the window.

She watched him without moving, furious that an involuntary tear traced down her face. After forcing the iron lock of the wooden shutters shut, he sat down beside her. *"Tesoro,"* he murmured, tracing a gentle thumb along her wet cheek, "you're a clever woman. And clever women get what they want. And what you want is for me to be happy, no? Not just walk around with a bloody lip."

Carmela looked at him. She gave up the fight against the tears.

"Come here, my darling." He took her in his arms. The man had just presented her with the villa of her dreams, laid out the bed of a princess, and offered to make love to her all afternoon, but her body was cold. Somewhere, in the silences, did he know it wasn't him she wanted to lie beside? Perhaps she ought to finish everything right here, right now. If the tender passion of Kavanagh was nothing but a moment of sheer carelessness that would never be repeated, it couldn't change the fact that Carmela owed it to herself to be honest with Franco.

But she couldn't do it.

Instead, she hid in his arms, feeling his desperation where once there was virile naïveté, the faintest smell of alcohol on his breath. He watched her, misunderstanding her sobs, then smoothed the hair away from her ear and whispered. "I'm sorry I lost my temper. I should have listened. But you drive me wild, Carmela. The only woman I have ever wanted. Will ever want. A man can't feel a passion like that and expect to control it always. It's too powerful."

He eased her face toward his. The only

brightness in the darkened room now was the glint in his eyes — the hardness from but a moment ago softened with well-rehearsed seduction. "Get those Americans paying for my land, do you understand? Our future family deserves that, no?"

He stood up, buttoned his fly, and left her on the crumpled bed.

CHAPTER 24

The lull of the afternoon was Carmela's favorite time of day. Today, although it was three o'clock and the family's cups were filled with the comforting caramel of coffee, she couldn't ignore the knot in her stomach. It tightened with every one of Franco's words as he and her father discussed her upcoming trip.

"So you see, Signor Chirigoni," Franco said, stirring his coffee, "it is important to all of us to make sure Carmela goes on this trip next week."

Carmela picked up her father's cup and refilled it.

"They're not taking their business any other place!" Tomas insisted.

"With respect . . ."

"They've spent months establishing this base. Why would they seek land down south?"

"Signor Chirigoni —"

"Signor Tomas will do. . . ."

Franco lowered his head and smiled, bashful. His performance sent ice down her spine. "Why would they waste time traveling there if this was not their plan?"

"What do you say, Carmela?" Tomas asked.

Carmela looked up from the plate of *papassini* biscuits she was laying on a dish at the counter. She wasn't expecting to be consulted and was loathe to lie to her father. She took a breath, affecting dispassion, as if the decision to let her go would be no more exciting than sewing a hem. "Papa, I think Franco is wise to secure their investment here. I know the captain has expressed interest in our land in particular."

Franco looked at her with the satisfaction of a lion tamer before his obedient beast. She met his gaze and forced herself to soften her expression. The simplicity of her plan became clear. All she had to do was make Casler promise that the Americans would rent their land. She would rather secure her family's finances than maintain this façade with Franco. If they were taken care of, the brutality of a public shaming by Carmela walking away from her wedding would be allayed. There was no way she wouldn't sully their reputation, but at least she would know they would never want for anything. In the fullness of time Carmela's actions would be laid to rest.

She struggled to silence the calculations charging around in her mind; with her family taken care of, she may even be able to flee the town altogether. This gnawing thought was the most terrifying. Since her encounter with Kavanagh she had thought of little else. She clung to the memory of his touch till sleep was victorious. She thought about how few clothes she would need to take with her if they chose to flee. How much money she had saved up over the year from her work at the studio. Try as she might, it was impossible to stop dreaming up their new lives in Munich. The home she would make. The love they would make on their small bed beneath a window that looked out to the surrounding mountains. The unfamiliar faces she would spy on her walk to the baker. Their expressions of delightful indifference, rather than the scrutiny of Simiuns who read her entire family when they greeted her, judged and related to her based on what her brother, sister, aunt, or mother had said or done or failed to. But as the story unfolded in her mind, the lakeside summer retreats, their gaggle of children frolicking in the snow, the handsome clothes she would become well loved for, Carmela felt a sharp wrench of guilt — followed by embarrassment and annoyance at her girlish plans that had no roots in reality.

Two men, whom she ought to have loved and respected the most in all the world, stood between Carmela and her trip with Kavanagh. Now not only Franco but her father too was implicated in her betrayal, for which there would be no forgiveness. But try as her trained conscience might, it could not suffocate her yearning. It was impossible for her to let this opportunity slip between her fingers, for the sake of the men before her now, for the sake of propriety or her future. And what was that? Living a subordinate life beneath a man who would never change? It seemed that propriety offered a man a good life and taught women the art of perseverance and obedience, little more. Carmela watched them as they sipped the coffee. She wondered it did not taste bitter, like the food made by an angry cook.

She made her choice.

They looked up at her, expectant. "It could quadruple the incomings, Papá," she began, appealing to her father's practical nature, "if not more. If I am present at the meetings, I will be party to all the information." She stopped there, in case insisting would make it seem that she was excited about leaving. It was important to make these men think it had been their decision. A passive manipulation on her part — perhaps there was more of Icca in her than she would have liked to admit.

"She speaks sense," Tomas decided.

Franco stood up and held out his hand. "Thank you, Signor Chirigoni. I think this will be a great thing for the family."

"There are greater things than money, boy, remember that. No silk or satin ever made a crop grow. But only a donkey could deny that a coin-filled purse shortens a winter."

Carmela winced. Franco laughed as if he knew what humility was.

There was a ring at the gate. Tomas and Franco turned. Carmela left the kitchen and walked across the terrace to peer down. Kavanagh's jeep was parked below. She ran to the stairs and down along the winding garden. There he stood, his hair golden in the bright May sunshine. Her breath caught. She opened the gate with care, gripping the handle tight as if to stop her hands wandering anywhere else. Kavanagh lifted his hat. "I've come to talk with your father about the trip."

Carmela could only answer with a nod. She wished Kavanagh was asking her father for something else. Then he added with a whisper as he passed, "A day hasn't seemed this long since I was a kid at Christmas." He straightened, and the ardent glint in his eyes disappeared. Kavanagh carried on up the garden and the steps that lead to the terrace with a calm, assured air. Politeness replaced passion.

Kavanagh knocked lightly on the door to the kitchen and then stepped inside.

Carmela followed closely, then placed an extra cup on the table, filling it with coffee. Her heart raced. The men sat down together. Both men stood as Kavanagh entered the room. Carmela's heart raced. Tomas gestured toward a chair. The men sat down together. Carmela tried to ignore the way Franco's eyes darted between her and Kavanagh, as if he was looking for clues, proof even. Her conscience was blurring all sense of truth now, as if she were swimming underwater with her eyes open. For a moment even the sounds of the men's voices seemed warped and distant.

"Welcome, Lieutenant!" Tomas beamed. "We've been talking, and if you are happy to hire Carmela for the job, we are happy to let her go."

"That's wonderful news!" Kavanagh said, shaking Tomas's hand. Then he reached out a hand to Franco. The simplicity of the gesture pierced Carmela. Why did that make Kavanagh seem more of an adulterer than even lying with her? Something about his frank friendliness made what they had done more dreadful. Franco didn't shirk his gaze. "I know you will take care of my fiancée, yes?"

Both men pretended it wasn't a threat.

Carmela looked at Kavanagh. Any trepidation was masked by a steel professionalism. It wasn't hard to picture him, tactical and focused, in the heat of battle.

"Carmela, please explain the following to your father. . . ." Kavanagh launched into a detailed schedule of times and routes. He told of the unit performing several stops along the way, of meetings with a government official down in the capital for which his pigeon Italian would not suffice. He explained that having a local to aid the Americans, who knew the base and its members well, would be of supreme assistance. He clung to the facts, and so did Carmela. Her voice did not waver, nor did his. They both invested in the veil of truth, wove it together. After the comprehensive description of routes and itinerary came to an end, he told Tomas how grateful he was that Carmela could put her studio duties on hold for this short time. Only then did his voice quiver. No one but Carmela appeared to notice. He recovered by taking care to emphasize the increased pay, which appeared to delight Tomas. "The unit leaves before dawn tomorrow and aims to return by nightfall the following day," he added.

"Very well." Tomas stood and shook Kavanagh's hand again. "Carmela will show you out, Lieutenant."

They did not speak as they crossed the terrace, or as they walked down the steps in unison, or as they passed beneath the mauve wisteria blossoms. When they reached the gate, Carmela could think of nothing but the touch of his lips on hers. She opened the gate. He stepped toward his jeep, but when he was almost at his door, he turned. "Thank you, Carmela," he said, but his eyes glistened with anticipation. Together, they had just granted themselves thirty-six uninterrupted hours in one another's company, away from anyone they knew, away from the people they were supposed to be. Side by side they would venture down her beloved coast, onward to unexplored lands. They had given themselves a slice of make-believe. Carmela reassured herself that this would be more than just an escape for a pair of sullied adulterers, groping at one another's bodies.

This time, the heat inside was not the thrill of being someone's prize, the racing excitement of being desired. She had mistaken Franco's chasing for love. She had been too young to know otherwise, too foolish, too vain. Kavanagh looked into her with a tender passion. Was this the man who would offer her the space to blossom into the woman she was meant to be? Was this the man who would become her partner and allow her to stand strong, spread her wings, open her mind, achieve her ambitions? A man who would not be threatened by her resourcefulness, her intelligence, her curiosity? She didn't dare allow herself to think it, but perhaps this was the man she was meant to stand beside until death wrapped her inside the shadows of its cloak.

It was not the perfect way to begin a love affair, but what of that? The beautiful morning glory unfurled purple blossoms even among the ugly debris of war. Is it not my responsibility, Carmela thought, to grasp such moments when they pass me by, recognizing them as the gifts that they are?

She heard footsteps on the terrace. "Many thanks, Lieutenant," she answered, trying for professional when all she wanted to do was wrap her arms around him and hear him promise that he would never be a day away from her.

"Good-bye, Lieutenant," Franco said with a wide grin, slipping in behind Carmela. She could feel his breath on the back of her neck.

Kavanagh nodded and got into his vehicle. Franco put his hand over hers on the gate.

"So," he whispered, sharp, into her ear, "you've got quite a job to do, Signorina." They watched Kavanagh drive down the hill and disappear around the corner.

Carmela's heart was pounding.

Franco traced his tongue behind her ear. "Don't enjoy yourself too much," he whispered.

Then he stepped in front of her, took her face in his hands, and planted the softest kiss on her lips. A tingling of fear slithered down her neck.

The birds called in the dawn as Carmela checked through her small overnight case. She had lost count of how many times she had done it since last night: a pair of knickers she had pulled aside when doing Rosa's laundry, her favorite maroon suede shoes from Zio Raimondo, a tiny bottle of perfume she hoped Rosa wouldn't miss, and Carmela's only evening dress. In the darkened kitchen, she felt the urge to sob. Upon the table was the bag of an adulterer, complete with costumes and accessories. She would look like her aunt, smell like her. Was this what she was yearning for all along? To be dragged along by a married man? Steal moments of pleasure only to be abandoned like old cattle? Wallow in bitterness? It wasn't too late to change her mind. Perhaps there was no business to this trip whatsoever.

She heard a door opening. Carmela looked across toward the hallway, Maria wrapped a shawl around her shoulders. Carmela shut her case and watched her mother walk into the kitchen to begin the morning's bread making.

"*Buon giorno,* Carmela."

"The coffee is set to boil when you are ready."

"You're a good daughter, *tesoro.*"

The words stung.

"Here, take this." Maria opened Carmela's hand and placed a tiny prayer card to St. Christopher inside it. "I will pray for you all. Come back safely." Her eyes took on a faraway look. "When you were born, the seer at the end of our *viccolo* told me she had had a dream. In it, a small child walked

424

toward her and told her she would travel far to find happiness. Then she told me that I would have to prepare for the day that my firstborn would leave, for it would be sooner than I would expect." Her mother's eyes grew misty. "I don't know why I'm telling you this. It came to me just now." She waved off her tears. Carmela wanted to wrap her arms around her mother but out of instinct held back. "I must be older than I think, Carmela, to get soft over such nonsense!" She turned away from the stove, brushing off the moment, and lit the ring beneath the metal coffeepot, dented and smoke stained from a lifetime of use.

"I've always wanted to see Cagliari, Mamma."

"I have also."

"Maybe we could go one day? Together?"

Maria looked back at Carmela and smiled like someone humoring a young child who had asked to fly to the moon.

"I should wait outside." Carmela straightened, walked over to her mother, and took her hands in hers. "I love you, Mamma."

They planted gentle kisses on either cheek. The pot began to whistle.

Carmela stepped out before her mother read any truth or guilt between the lines.

Outside the air was fresh. The black sky

turned midnight blue. Carmela leaned over the wall. Kavanagh was waiting. Her feet trotted down those familiar steps, passed the twinkling lights of Simius beyond her mother's garden. She unlocked the gate and stepped out into the street. Kavanagh raised his hat. She took her place. After several deft maneuvers, considering the size of his vehicle compared to the narrow leveled area in front of their house, Kavanagh led them out of Simius.

There was nowhere in the world she would rather be.

They drove under stars toward the sunrise. Beyond the valley of Simius, winding roads led out from the base to the plains of the surrounding countryside toward the coast. Whenever he could, Kavanagh reached over and took her hand. Carmela traced her fingers along his — kind, strong hands. They reached the coastal route just as the sun rose from behind the water. He slowed down to let them both take in the wide, rugged, deserted beaches of Orosei. On one side, the sight of granite quarries, pink and white stripes of the mountain's harvest; on the other, wide, white sandy shores stretching as far as the eye could see. The town itself lay a little inland, hidden behind the mountainsides that surrounded it, like a precious toy stuffed into a secret crag by a possessive child. It was an intricate warren of *viccoli* and minuscule churches that Carmela knew little of, except for the ramblings of Simiuns who warned of the local women's predisposition for dabbling in magic. After a few more miles Kavanagh pulled over and parked beneath a craggy pine, facing the water. He switched off the engine.

"Is this our first 'unit' stop, Joe?"

"Looks like it."

Carmela turned back toward the sun and enjoyed the warmth on her face. Then she picked up his hand and opened it, tracing her fingers over his wrist and the length of each finger.

He reached over and took her face in his hands. "I've hoped for this on more sleepless nights than I care to think about." He pressed his warm lips against hers. Then he pulled away. "Wait, you must be starving! I've brought breakfast." He jumped out, ran to the trunk, and reached in for a small hamper. He carried it to the front of the jeep and laid out a blanket.

Carmela opened her door and went to him, watching as he set out a selection of fresh pastries, a flask of coffee, and a couple of cups.

"Enough for an army!" Carmela laughed. "Are we pretending there's a convoy after all?" She thought back to his dubious culinary efforts at the base and how she could finally admit to herself that she had fallen in love with him there and then, that night beside Salvatore's bed. He poured a cup for her and one for him. They ate the crème-filled puffs, facing the deepening turquoise of the sea. Beside them, tufts of wild poppies swayed in the spring breeze.

When they finished, Kavanagh cleared everything away and put the hamper to one side. They sat for a moment. He leaned his forehead on hers and breathed in her scent. She turned her lips to his and parted them, inviting him inside. Then his arms searched around her body, which rose and fell to his touch. They lay now, with the ancient sands beneath them, as he ran his fingers up her thighs, as she traced hers along his back, unbuttoning his uniform, pulling it off his shoulders. He moved down past her breasts, the softness of her belly, and tasted her. Her back arched. Every silenced voice and pang of guilt evaporated. No going back now. Now she was the water, the sand, the sky. She was floating high above everything. She gave into him, surrendered fear. Kavanagh cradled her body in his as he searched every part of her. Electricity careened from the tips of her toes to the top of her head as wave after wave of pleasure rippled through her, unlocking her. Her chest rose, her breaths quickened.

Trembling, she reached for his shoulders and pulled his face to hers. His breaths were fast now. She could taste the unfamiliar scent of herself on him. Her hands raced through his hair, down his back, as she urged him inside of her. He inhaled, stopped, and then rose back up onto his hands. She searched his eyes. Had she done something wrong? Had he changed his mind?

He smiled. "I don't want to rush this away." He eased himself down onto his elbows and cradled her head in his hands. Then he rocked into her. Her hips rose to meet his. Her legs wrapped around him. They moved as one, intuiting every shift in rhythm. With every breath, reality faded, like shifting sands trickling down a ravine. His heart beat against hers.

Kavanagh stayed inside her as their breathing returned to normal. He rubbed his lips along hers, then on her cheeks, her forehead, her nose. "Nothing I wrote in that letter has changed."

Carmela looked into his eyes.

"We don't need to talk about real life if you don't want to," he said.

She wanted real earth-and-roots love. She wanted to know every part of him and who he would become. "I want to."

He rolled off her and propped his head on his hand. His chest looked beautiful. She ran her fingers along it, then turned in to him and kissed it. He raised her face to meet his.

"Virginia and I are separated."

"Why?"

"Seymour is not mine."

Carmela sat up.

"Old news back home, I guess."

"Oh, Joe, I'm so sorry." However much she disliked Virginia, she would never have wished this on either of them.

"I'm not. But our love was brittle and I knew it. I was just too scared to admit it. We wrote each other a war of love letters, clinging to memories of one another. You don't let go easy after that."

Carmela watched him relive the pain, wanting to soothe away everything, knowing she would never be able to, not completely. "Of course."

He took her hand in his. "I thought I had

felt this way before," he said, tracing his thumb over hers. "Now I know I didn't. You free me."

The words were a golden light. Carmela acquiesced to the happy tears burning the back of her throat. He took her head in his hands, met her gaze, and held it. Everything about him glowed. His eyes were clearer than she had ever seen them. His cheeks were flushed. If he asked her to jump onto a ship for the mainland right now, she would do it without hesitation. Then her thoughts crashed back to her meeting with her father and Franco. She straightened and wiped her face.

"I want nothing more in this world than you, Joe. I have fought how much I love you. I drowned every memory of you, but the moment you stepped back inside the farmhouse I knew there was no going back."

He wrapped his arms around her. He moved in to kiss her, but she pulled away. "But there is one thing that stands between us and any possible future."

"A fiancé."

She ignored his comment. "I'm here because my father and Franco think that I can convince you to make Casler rent our land instead of the land of people down south."

"Sensible men."

"If I don't go home with the news they're hoping for, I can't say what Franco's going to do. I'm scared, Joe."

Kavanagh kissed her cheek. "No one's going to hurt you, Carmela. I can promise you that."

"You can't promise me anything, Joe," she said, wishing he could.

He tossed aside a pebble. "You know it's not entirely up to me. The consul general in Cagliari is expecting us for dinner this evening to talk about this."

"I thought this was just an elaborate escape plan."

"It is."

They leaned back in toward one another and entwined. Their fingers were on fire now, hungry. Their mouths were hot. Skin pressed against skin so neither could feel where one ended and the other began. Their half-clothed bodies, now woven together, danced under the hopeful rays of a white spring sun.

After almost an entire day of passing through clusters of tiny stone cottages, solitary shepherds guiding their flocks across the coastal mountains, and miles upon miles of dirt roads, the white stone *palazzi* of Cagliari spiked the horizon like an ancient metropolis. It was late afternoon, and they were weary. As Kavanagh's jeep crested the highest point before descending into the maze of *viccoli* before them, Carmela gasped. Huge palms swayed in the soft afternoon light. Beyond the layers of cream buildings lay the wide-open expanse of the south coast.

"Let's find our hotel first. We can explore a little before dinner, if you like," Kavanagh said over the rumble of the engine and surrounding city noise.

Men and women, dressed in their fineries, promenaded along the wide *vias.* Carmela was impressed by their impeccable style. Many looked up at them as they drove on through, but none with the diffident glare of a Simiun. No wonder the army had searched beyond their small town for business.

Kavanagh took a sharp turn that led them toward the pungent cacophony of the port. Here, the *palazzi* narrowed, huddled together, fighting for a slim share of space. Sailors, fishermen, and dubious-looking women swarmed around vast baskets of fresh fish. The jeep rattled through, over the cobbles, and turned toward the high walls of the old town. Carmela had read about the place, but seeing it before her, golden in the afternoon light, was like stepping into a fairy tale. She gaped, gasped, and beamed.

A little way away from the hub of the center, Kavanagh turned down a narrow street and slowed down. Toward the far end he pulled up on the side of the road before a long, blue wooden door.

"This is it," he said, running around to open her door and then back to the trunk for their cases. He moved toward the bell and rang it once. It echoed inside. After a short while there was the sound of a key in the lock and a small, old woman creaked the door open.

"*Buona sera,*" she said, ushering them in. They followed her as she shuffled to her small wooden desk. A large, ornate pink glass globe light was glowing on it beside a ceramic vase laden with bright dahlias. She was dressed in black from head to foot.

"*Nome?*" she croaked, holding her silver fountain pen between arthritic fingers.

"Kavanagh, Signora."

"*E lei, e la moglie?*" she asked, with an expression that told Carmela she would see through any pretense of her being Kavanagh's wife.

"She's asking me if I'm your wife."

"No, *due camere,* Signora," Kavanagh

said, holding up two fingers.

The woman looked down at her book with an almost hidden shake of her head and asked Carmela for her particulars. When she was satisfied she turned to a small hutch of keys hung on the white wall behind her and handed one to each. She launched into a complicated list of directions that Kavanagh struggled to follow.

"She says we're on the top floor, Joe."

"Didn't sound like that's all she said."

"I'm not going to translate all that anti-American slander now, am I?"

"How kind of you."

They flashed a smile at one another. Carmela doubted they would leave the hotel before dinner after all.

They reached the top floor after several flights of steep, uneven steps to find themselves in rooms at the opposite ends of a narrow corridor. An antique credenza stood midway between the rooms, topped with a fine lace doily and a basket with dried maize beside a small vase of dried honesty. They stood, looking in opposite directions.

"I'd like to take a shower," Kavanagh said, "then perhaps we can take a stroll? What do you say?"

"I say I feel alive for the first time in my life."

They stopped themselves from kissing and turned toward their separate rooms.

A few minutes later there was a soft knock at Carmela's door. She opened it wearing nothing but her silk shift. Kavanagh stood before her, taking her in.

"Kinda lonely down there," he said.

Carmela opened her door a little more. He stepped inside, and she closed it behind him. They moved closer. Their noses touched. She listened to his breath, then ran her fingers down his muscular arm and led him to the bed.

A May evening in Cagliari was a lively affair. Outside, the boulevards were busy with people in the finest clothes Carmela had ever seen, so much so that she wondered if there was a particular saints day she had let slip from memory. Kavanagh led them down through some alleys so tight she could reach both sides with her hands. Eventually they arrived at the main piazza lined with an array of delectable boutiques: jewelers, lingerie, stationers, *pasticcerie,* each with window displays packed with abundant displays of luxurious goods. Customers lingered at each of them. Women walked by Carmela with tiny boxes tied with colored ribbons, stacked upon one another. Others stepped out from the *pasticerrie* with pink cardboard trays laden with tiny fruit pastries. Owners walked their diminutive dogs. Children darted across the square, dressed in expensive cotton knit sweaters and leather shoes.

Carmela had to stop herself from gawping several times at the ladies' hats and the elegant cut of their dresses. Her heart ached when she thought back to the dusty cobbles of Simius, of the shoeless children of nearby villages. She felt the painful realization that her town was stuck somewhere in a depressed past. Though they tried to convince themselves that they were unshackled from the austerity of the war, it now seemed they were still victims of it.

But here, among the splendor, the wealth, the sheer abundance of life, Carmela was filled with hope, sadness, and a fiery ambition, unsettling in its ferocity. There was no life in Simius for her. Not the one she would scarce dream of. She thought about snide Agnes, the sideways glances of the others that she had ignored, the petty jealousies for having been chosen to work alongside Kavanagh. So many things she had chosen to brush away. But here, among this genteel version of Sardinia, they careened through her mind with a vengeance. The sooner she could leave Simius, the better. And go where? Munich? She scarce think about it. This wasn't the time to talk of any possible future with Kavanagh. It would break the spell and bring the fairy tale to a crashing halt.

They stopped into a narrow bar for an aperitif. Kavanagh ordered two *aperol* spritzers, and they each took a stool upon the bar. The starched, white-coated waiter laid out several small glass bowls of marinated olives, salted peanuts, and a flat square plate of *stuzzichini* — six or seven thin slices of crisp bread topped with delicate cubes of tomato and mozzarella, drizzled with olive oil and parsley. Others were spread with a coarse olive pâté. There were several stems of creamy *pecorino*.

Carmela had never tasted food in the way she did at this moment. Every sense was heightened, wolflike. A great surge of energy shot through her, this time without admonishment, guilt, or fear. They clinked their glasses, then raised them to their lips, each reliving their lovemaking inside Carmela's shuttered room, the taste of one another, the sweat on their bodies, the tingling in their toes, their backs, their hips. The crumpled linen they left behind, still warm with their scent. Sharing this food was the closest thing to making love in public.

Signor Corosu was waiting for them by the fountain as planned, at eight o'clock on the dot, something that surprised Carmela, unaccustomed to having appointments with any Simiun ever run on time. He was a small, round, sweaty man who made up in girth what he lacked in hair. His eyes scissored all over Carmela's body before he presented himself to Kavanagh. "Dear Americano, I would have picked you up myself! I do hope the travel was easy!"

"Sì," Kavanagh responded with a smile. "This is Carmela, our interpreter."

"Is that what they're calling it these days!" He chuckled, and Kavanagh took the cue to sigh a halfhearted laugh.

"What he say?" he whispered.

"I'm a whore."

Kavanagh beamed past gritted teeth. "So, Signor Corosu, lead the way."

"What he say?" the consul puffed.

"Signore, the lieutenant invites you to show us the way," Carmela replied, impressed by her impassive performance.

The three walked along a maze of narrow *viccoli* until they came to a quiet street. Signor Corosu knocked on a door at the center of a plastered wall. Its pale blue paint was peeling. After a short wait, it opened. A

439

hearty man with a booming voice shook Signor Corosu's arm almost free of its socket and welcomed the group in. He bowed his head in between sentences. Then he led them through a candlelit courtyard into a small dining room that seated a handful of customers. Each table was antique, with a silver candelabrum at its center. The fire was roaring inside an ornate mantel at one end. At the opposite end was a long table with a fine white tablecloth upon it, laden with a rainbow of seafood *antipasti*. Carmela's eyes swept along the delicacies, spying grilled urchins, steamed mussels, a basket of crispy calamari, and a long porcelain dish of grilled whitebait. The maître d' led them to their table, a little way from the fire. Several diners looked up at Signor Corosu and gave respectful nods as he passed.

"Bring us your best, Daniele!" Signor Corosu said. "We'll begin with a *vermentino,* yes? Save the Cannonau for the meat course."

Carmela whispered to Kavanagh. "Pace yourself, this man is a drinker and knows the chef by first name."

Something flickered across Corosu's face, which left Carmela wondering whether he didn't speak better English than was supposed. "What's that?"

"Signore, I'm explaining to the lieutenant how to eat. As you know, little can compare to the cuisine of Cagliari." She met his eyes with a polite smile, feeling her nerves strengthen their grip. How was she expected to behave at this business meal? How would she survive a dinner sitting opposite a man who had decided she was nothing more than a local floozy? After all, this evening, she couldn't win the argument against the fact.

"Where are you from?" he asked.

"Simius."

"I've heard of it. Not too far from bandit country, yes?"

Carmela bristled. "Close enough to intimidate the wrong sort, far enough to be safe."

"Yes. They only chase the rich, those mudheads."

"What's that?" Kavanagh asked, off Carmela's iron body language.

"Pleasantries," she replied. "He is a bigot."

"Mio Italiano, poco . . ." Kavanagh offered with his winning smile.

"*Sì.* But pretty ladies always help, yes?"

Daniele saved the moment with a wine flourish.

Corosu sniffed, sipped, and nodded. "Please, help yourselves!" he said, gesturing toward the table.

Kavanagh and Carmela stood up to sample the delights.

"I don't know what I'm doing here, Joe! He sees right through us," Carmela spat under her breath.

"He's a peacock."

"What if he knows someone in Simius? Did you think of that?" She looked down at her hands, giving an anxious stir of a bowl of steamed octopus with potatoes.

"What could he tell them? He met my beautiful interpreter?"

The colorful selection of grilled shrimp, charred zucchini, sunblushed tomatoes, and marinated anchovies in a light vinegar dressing were no longer tempting. Aside from masquerading as a professional, she was now posing as someone who had the right to eat with the wealthy southern elite. Amongst the dishes were baskets of *pane carusau,* heated in the oven and brushed with garlic and rosemary-infused olive oil. The immeasurable pleasure of eating the finest food would elude her, however, because she was in the wrong place sitting next to the wrong man.

Fresh pasta with a rich lobster cream followed. Then a huge sea bass baked in several inches of rock salt was wheeled to the tableside and forked apart by the skilled waiter, who fileted every piece before serving it, alongside charred radicchio and a fresh salad. Just when they thought the marathon was over, a grilled platter of more seafood and mixed fish found its way to the table, followed by a plate of grilled *porceddu,* suckling pig. What should have been sheer abandon to the delights of great food became a kind of punishment. Was this Corosu's intention? Keep them with him long enough to figure out what they were really doing here? When a bottle of *aqua vitae* and *mirto* was placed upon the table, Kavanagh looked relieved that he didn't have to eat anything more.

"Signor Corosu, I can't thank you enough for your hospitality," Kavanagh said.

"The lieutenant thanks you."

"It's the least I can do," Corosu replied. "These are but the tip of the iceberg. Cagliari has much to offer you. The region is vast, with many untouched areas, as you know. Nothing stands between your needs and our space."

"Signor Corosu is happy to help," Carmela said.

"Is that all?" Signor Corosu asked her.

"Sorry?"

"I spoke for longer than that."

"Yes, Signore. The Americans have a very simple way of talking. I told him that you and your region would be happy to offer the Americans whatever they need."

"Let us not go so far as that, Signorina. 'Whatever' always seems a little vague, does it not? In your line of work I'm sure you can appreciate this." His eyes flashed a mischievous spark that made Carmela sick to her stomach.

She turned to Kavanagh. "Lieutenant, is there anything more you'd like me to add?"

"You see, Signor," Kavanagh began, all business, "my captain has sent me here to explore our possibilities. We are looking for a sizeable area. Somewhere to perform military exercises, an uninhabited space where we can experiment with some exciting advancements in equipment."

"Signor Corosu, the Americans need much space to test new weapons. Kavanagh would like you to understand the risks involved," Carmela said.

"Well, of course there are risks, but the financial benefit would outweigh any of these."

He produced a paper file from his suitcase and pushed it across the table. "Please, take this to your captain. I had hoped to meet him this evening. There are photos of various places we could offer you, and I'm sure we could come to some arrangement to benefit us all."

Carmela turned to Kavanagh to translate, but Corosu plowed on. "It is impolite to talk of money when there is *mirto* to drink, no?" He chuckled, and Kavanagh mirrored him. They clinked, and Corosu sipped from his glass without taking his eyes off Carmela.

"Is he talking about money, Carmela?" Kavanagh asked.

"Joe, we don't speak of money right away. It's not the Sardinian way."

"No, it's not," Kavanagh replied under his breath. "Rather I get to sit and watch you eat, knowing how soft your skin feels at the top of your thigh . . ."

"Signorina?"

"Yes, Signor Corosu?" Carmela replied, hoping she wasn't blushing as much as she thought.

"Tell your friend that I will send a colleague to talk of these matters with care. I find it crass to sully your pretty little head with facts and figures. Let us speak no more of business, yes?"

Carmela turned to Kavanagh. "He will send a colleague up to you at the base. Figures are not for women. What did I tell you, Joe? Everyone's going to find out it was only the two of us here."

"Thank you for this fantastic welcome, Consul." He cleared his throat before launching into his well-rehearsed Italian. "I hope to return your hospitality at our base, Signore."

"And so do I. Your captain and I have corresponded. I look forward to putting a face to the name. It's getting late. I have a wife at home who does not like to wait up for me! May I call a taxi for you?"

"He asks if we need a car to take us back."

"No, thank you, *no, grazie.*"

"Very well," Signor Corosu said, shaking Kavanagh's hand with both of his. "Thank you for allowing me to share the cuisine of Cagliari. Tell him, Signorina, that I look forward to seeing him soon."

Kavanagh smiled and turned toward the courtyard. As he stepped out, Corosu pulled Carmela around to him. "My English is not so bad, but only to talk business. Don't go to any trouble when I meet him next," he said, in the closest thing to an English accent she had heard from anyone in Sardinia. Her heart gave a thud. "From what I can gather, I'm sure you will enjoy the rest of your evening." Then he turned with a crooked half smile and headed back to the dining room.

Carmela walked across the courtyard past Kavanagh, opened the door, and marched down the street. The shadows from sporadic streetlights flickered across her face as she pounded by the closed wooden doors of the narrow stone homes without knowing or caring if she was headed in the right direction for their hotel. Kavanagh caught up to her.

"What's going on?"

"I'm a cheap whore after all!"

"What?" he yelled, stopping her and turning her to face him.

Carmela's eyes stung with angry tears. "This is wrong. All wrong! Take me home, now!"

"What did he say to you?"

"He speaks English, Joe, he heard everything. Do you understand? Everything! This is not how it should be. This is all wrong! I knew it!"

Kavanagh's expression fell.

"Take me home. Now, Joe!"

Carmela watched Kavanagh stream through scenarios in his mind, then straighten with military calm. "What of it, Carmela? I have no intention of doing business with him. We will never see him again. I can promise you that."

"Stop offering empty promises! To love is to give more than air!" As the words escaped she felt the pang of regret. What on earth was she doing, standing here, screaming in the street, making demands? This wasn't the woman she wanted to be.

He took her hand in his. "It was the only way I knew I could be with you."

"So I am a cheap whore? You've paid me to make love to you, haven't you? You going to pay interpreters wherever you end up, to keep your bed hot at night?"

The words flew out before she could stop. This wasn't the evening she wanted. Her pretend world began to warp.

Kavanagh's expression turned stony and solemn. "If you for one moment think all this is nothing more than an adolescent's scam for sex, then we will return to Simius tomorrow and never see one another again."

Carmela looked at him, stunned.

"Do you think I would lure you into all of this," he started before she could reply, "knowing the risks involved, understanding the type of man you have promised yourself to? Finding myself each day more fond of your family?"

"Joe, I —"

His studied calm was ebbing now. "Please don't ever mistake my actions again, Carmela. I am no Franco. I have spoken my heart. I want you, Carmela. All of you. But I don't want to pressure you the way Franco has. I don't want you running back to the Simius valley without a second glance. What we have is precious. At least I thought it was. Perhaps I misunderstood."

It was all the proof she needed. She wouldn't waste his love by testing it. Now was the time to allow herself to express her feelings with the same ardent passion he felt for her. Deceit would damage their love quicker than a tarnished reputation. "I have never loved anyone the way I love you," she said, feeling as if she were both barefoot on the naked earth and soaring above it.

He took her hand. "This isn't easy for either of us, Carmela."

Carmela looked up at him. His eyes sparkled in the orange light. She couldn't imagine not gazing into them.

"I know a place," he began, his tone caressing them both back toward calm. "It's not too far from here. We'll set out early tomorrow before we start back. I want this to be perfect."

Perfection could not be planned. It wasn't under candlelight or at sumptuous feasts or any orchestrated outing. Perfection was no place but here, in this very moment. "It is already."

"I don't want to scare you, Carmela" — his eyes fixed to hers — "but I can't imagine not being able to feel you beside me."

The cool of her tears began to dry on her cheeks. She slipped her hand into the cradle of his. They walked back to the hotel in silence. In the hushed quiet of Carmela's room they made love. Their bodies knotted together and then gave in to sleep.

CHAPTER 25

They rose just before dawn, packed their bags, ruffled the sheets on his untouched bed, and left money upon their dressers with a written apology for not waiting to check out after breakfast. Then they headed out into the star-studded sky wrapped over Cagliari.

The road to Chia was a trail of treacherous curves across the southern cliffs. The fuchsia yellow of the sunrise reminded Carmela of her mother's birthday cakes, light layers of sponge smeared with pale yellow custard, streaked pink with *alchermes* liqueur. Kavanagh's jeep began its descent. His deft driving reassured Carmela, as did the thought that should God decide to send them trailing to their deaths it would not be so great a tragedy. She would have Kavanagh by her side, after all. They turned another bend, and the majesty of the southern coast stretched out beneath them. Unlike the humble, inviting coves of her coast, this sea was immense, profound. Huge rocks rose up from the cobalt water, mossy islands of antiquity.

They approached a long stretch of deserted beach lined with rich fauna. Kavanagh pulled over. For a moment they listened to the dawn. Carmela stepped out onto the cold sand. The horizon sent ripples of excitement through her, its endlessness alluring. She stared out to sea, as if gazing at the infinite would somehow prolong her time alone with Kavanagh. He moved in behind her and wrapped his arms around her waist.

She felt his soft kiss on the back of her neck.

"If we start swimming, we could be in Africa for lunch," he said.

She laughed and turned to face him, breathed his scent. She rubbed her cheek against his, then found his lips. A swirl of starlings swooped overhead. Then their tiny black silhouettes spiraled into a different direction and disappeared toward the hills.

"I'm scared, Joe."

"I know."

"I don't want this to end."

"It can't. Not now."

Carmela took his hand. They walked

toward the water. "I can't lie anymore."

Kavanagh moved around before her, knelt down, and looked up at her. "I don't want you to. And I don't want you to start hating yourself, or me, and that's what will happen if we keep on scurrying around like guilty kids."

"Joe —"

"Carmela, listen. I want to be with you. I want to be old with you. Will you —"

"Stop." She placed a finger on his lips, though those were the precise words she had fantasized hearing from him. Yet to speak of it now, so soon, inside their make-believe bubble on the south coast of her island, felt as if it would jinx what little time they had before Carmela faced reality back home. She knelt down and met his gaze. "I want you to ask what I think you were about to say. I want nothing more than to stand beside you. Forever. But don't ask me to promise anything while I'm still promised to Franco. It feels even more wrong than lying together somehow."

He looked at her with a gentle expression, reassuring her he had not mistaken her words for rejection.

"Let us just be here," Carmela murmured.

He stood up. "Follow me."

Kavanagh walked to the jeep, picked up a

small canvas duffle bag, and paced across the beach, back toward the cliffs. Carmela brushed her skirts free of sand and ran to catch up with him. She slipped her hand into his. They walked in silence. Ahead of them was a small opening in the rock. He led them inside. Carmela hesitated, but Kavanagh's grip was firm and reassuring. "It's okay."

It was dark for the first section of the passage before the tunnel curved around and opened up into a larger space. Kavanagh reached into his bag, pulled out a candle, and lit it. Carmela gasped. All around them, the orange light caught the glistening tips of stalactites and stalagmites. He reached back into his bag and began lighting a dozen more candles. Carmela stood, without moving, watching him let a few drops of wax fall on the smooth floor of the cave. Soon there was a warm glow where they stood. He placed the last candle, straightened, and looked at her, expectant.

Carmela had tears in her eyes. "I think I've died."

"I think you've just been born, my love. And so have I."

"How did you know this place?"

"Casler and I came across it on one of our first reconnaissance trips. We couldn't believe how many rocks are still intact here. Up north, most of them have been stripped."

Kavanagh walked toward her through the candlelight, and then wrapped his arm around her waist. He pulled her into him. Their faces, hearts, and hips pressed against one another.

Carmela leaned back against the cool smoothness of the rock. Kavanagh reached up her thighs. Carmela's breath caught. They stopped, looking into each other.

"Everything, Carmela."

"Take it."

Their pleasure echoed into the blackness of the cave.

It was almost the middle of the day as they reached the town of Dorgali, halfway up the eastern coast toward Simius. They left their cave with reluctance, but once on the road, Kavanagh had wasted little time. The jeep rattled through streets just wide enough for a donkey carrying a load, jerking along the sharp cobbles. The houses were squat, unlike the Simius homes in the center of town that rose several floors high, topped with columned terraces. These homes lined the alleys like a crushed crowd at a fair. Every shutter was snapped tight against the heat.

Not even a stray cat meandered on the hunt. It was as if the entire town had been evacuated for lunch.

"So much for my timing!" Kavanagh yelled over the engine. "I was hoping to find someplace to grab food."

"I'm not much help — it's my first time here. . . . I'm a tourist on my own island!"

A near right angle turn demanded Kavanagh's full attention. The never-ending warren continued downhill until they reached a tiny piazza with views of the jagged turquoise bay below. Along the edges of the dusty square stood a meager choice of establishments: a small bar with one table outside, a closed *tabacchi,* and a narrow building with a sign that read OSTERIA.

"There's our place, Carmela!"

He pulled over. A group of men, the first people they had seen all day, sat beneath the tree in the center of the square. They looked up, squinting from under their flat caps, and their conversation fell silent. Carmela felt their eyes follow them like targets.

Inside, the eight gingham-covered tables of the Osteria lay empty. The door swung shut behind them. The bell sounded a half-hearted jingle. A boy approaching puberty appeared from a door at the back. When he saw unfamiliar faces, his eyes widened and his thick, black eyebrows furrowed.

"Sit where you want," he said.

Kavanagh chose a table by the window, though not much could be seen of the outside through the lace curtains.

"Vino?" the boy asked.

Kavanagh nodded. The boy disappeared again.

Carmela looked around, the corners of her mouth lifting into a secretive smile.

Kavanagh laughed. "Don't say I don't take you places, right?"

The boy reappeared with a cork-covered carafe of garnet liquid that tasted as pungent as it looked and a basket of crispy, warm *pane carusau.* Two sips later, Carmela already felt light-headed.

"Do you think they have menus?" Kavanagh whispered.

Just then, the boy reappeared with two huge enamel bowls of fresh mussels steaming in their *vernaccia*-wine infused juice. He laid them down and vanished again. "I think not," Carmela said, unfolding her napkin.

She looked down at the bowl, breathing in the rich, salty smell. She clasped a shell and forked out the steamed mollusk, then used the empty shell as a pincer to pull out more. The fresh, metallic tang of seafood merged into the earthy garlic and parsley. The delectable intensity of the flavors commanded their full attention. Neither of them spoke as they devoured their lunch.

The trip had been a sensual overload, and she didn't want it to end. When all that was left was a pile of shells, the boy appeared and took everything away. They sat, satisfied, filled with each other and the food. It was excruciating to resist touching one another. Carmela gave a fleeting glance toward the kitchen, then traced her foot up the inside of Kavanagh's thigh, a little shocked at being so forward and not caring. She watched the look on his face and realized no one had ever made her feel quite so beautiful. Only a few days ago, the trajectory of her life was so different. But now her possibilities unfurled in wild tangents, like the spiraling sparkles of fireworks.

The boy opened the back door.

She slammed her foot back to the floor.

He reached the table and laid a steak before each of them, then put down a plate of charred radicchio. He placed a small enamel bowl of coarse salt between them. They sliced their meat and ate it, remembering their morning. On the boy's final visit he presented hot *seadas* with a small espresso cup containing a shot of tarlike coffee. The melted cheese oozed into the warm honey and reminded Carmela of summer, and then her mother. She laid down her fork, unable to think of anything but the expression on her face as she watched her leave yesterday. She couldn't eat another mouthful.

"What's wrong, darling?" Kavanagh asked.

"Nothing." She shook her head, peering out through the lace curtains. The men were still watching. "I'm feeling nervous. The closer we get . . . I don't feel ready. I have to protect my family, Joe." Tears pricked her eyes, which she refused to let fall. "They've given me everything. They're relying on me. I won't be an ungrateful daughter. If they find out anything about this —"

"They mustn't find out."

Her cheeks blushed. "Will we be a secret forever, Joe?"

"Of course not."

"So they will find out."

Kavanagh reached for her hand, but she withdrew it. "I leave for Munich in three weeks."

Carmela looked at him, feeling as if she'd been teetering on a cliff's edge and the sandy bank had just given way.

"Join me?" he asked.

His words hung over the table. Before she

could answer, the humorless waiter was beside them clearing off the last of the dishes. He left a strip of paper with a rough scrawl of sums. Kavanagh laid money on top of it and rose for the door. He held it open for Carmela. They took a moment to adjust to the brightness. Carmela noticed that the men had left their outpost. Lunch, and harried wives, had won out over spying after all.

She stepped up into the jeep. Before he turned the key in the ignition, Kavanagh looked at her. "There's a way."

"You don't know Franco."

"I knew him the minute I set eyes on him."

"You want me to pack a bag and run away from everything?"

Kavanagh let out a faint sigh. "I want to give you the world, Carmela. It might not be as hard as we think. Casler has recommended promoting me." He straightened. "In Germany I'm going to hold a lot more weight than I've had here, though he's offered me a lot more freedom and responsibility than other captains might have."

"He has a lot of nurses to keep him occupied."

He smiled. "I'll go ahead first, arrange for suitable housing for us, and get the lay of the land. After I've been stationed I can mail you your ferry ticket crossing to Rome. From there you catch a train straight to me."

It hurt to not touch him. How she would get through her daily life after this was unimaginable. "It's all happening so fast, Joe."

"I know, but maybe it's for the best. There's no time for fear this way. How could we start a life here in Simius? It would be way harder than being together, out of gossip's way, don't you think?"

"I love my family, Joe."

He wrapped his hand around hers. "They're wonderful people. I felt it the moment I met them."

Carmela shifted in her seat. "So you want to take me away from them?"

Kavanagh's eyes hardened. "I need to be with you, Carmela. And I think you feel the same." He turned to her. "I'll make sure that Casler's plans involve a generous payment to your family in return for the use of their land. I'll have him sign an agreement by next week. Everything else is up to us. It's time to summon our courage, not cave in like deserters. We choose, Carmela. But we have to be honest with ourselves."

"This is not a military offensive, Joe. You can't organize feelings and people like this!"

"Yes, you can. If you want to."

"Is that what you're doing to me?"

He let out a deep sigh.

"I'm sorry, Joe. I'm allowed to feel scared."

"So am I. I'm also allowed to tell you that you're the best thing that's happened to me and I won't sit back and let this slip away. Not ever."

Carmela gave in to the tears. A shutter creaked shut nearby. Who had been listening? The sooner they got out of here, the better.

"Drive, Joe. I'm tired of making an exhibition of myself."

"Look at me, Carmela."

She turned to him, feeling the streaks of fear drip down her face.

"Do you love me, Carmela?"

"More than anything."

"So take the rest of this month I'm stationed here to think. If you believe that what we have is worth chasing after, then I know how to make it happen. I know how to build us a life in a land neither of us understands yet. It'll be strange at first but not as hard as you think. If once you've thought carefully, and you decide the life you want is in Simius, if you can't picture growing old anywhere else — then stay. I won't be the one to take you away against your will. I'd never forgive myself for that."

"So we run away? Live in exile?"

He wiped a tear from her cheek. "At first it might feel that way, but once everyone has got used to the idea we, or at least you, will be able to come back and visit whenever you want. The world is smaller than it used to be."

He pressed his lips against hers with a tender kiss.

The decision was sealed.

He started the engine. After an hour or so, Dorgali and their conversation faded into the distant hillside.

It was late afternoon when the roads grew familiar. They passed along the coast of Orosei once more but didn't stop. The sun dipped toward the water as the jeep rattled toward the road for the base. Kavanagh took an unexpected turn into the woods. Carmela grabbed the handle on the door to steady herself. He stopped, sharp.

"Promise me you'll keep talking to me. The next month will be hard. It might not be as easy to see each other as much as I'd like. But you have to promise me you won't shut me out."

Carmela looked at him.

His face softened. "We can't suffocate what we have. Not now."

"Hold me."

He took a breath, placed her palms in his, and looked into her. "Be my wife."

Those magic words. They ought to feel like lazy afternoon sunshine, a dip in a warm sea. But they stung, a sorrow-tipped arrow. Her heart pounded, but not with delight.

"Yes," she said, wanting to cry, but the tears wouldn't come. She thought about her gown hanging in her mother's wardrobe. She thought about Piera sleeping alone. She thought about the shadow of shame that would hang over her family. She thought about her other sisters, who would have to hear the nuns whisper about Carmela's journey to hell. She thought about her grandmother, who would pummel her parents with her wrath and embarrassment. She thought about Rosa, smiling with twisted revenge. She wanted to think about Kavanagh by her side, his ring on her hand, his heart in hers, but the pictures faded before they could even appear clearly in her mind, shipwrecked treasure floating up to the surface only to sink back into the deep.

The woods ahead of her looked dark. Where were those fairytale trees that had sheltered them, hiding their first tryst? Where was the beach of Orosei? The cave?

Had any of these been real? How long before the consul of Cagliari would be smearing her name around the base? How long before everyone found out that the unit consisted of two lovers, no more? Their interlude had been ill judged. How could Carmela face her reality again after that? It was impossible.

"And Virginia?" she asked suddenly. The name felt cold in her mouth.

"Virginia counts the minutes till our divorce is complete. She and her beau plan to marry." His expression unsettled Carmela. She liked to think those scars would not be tender for the rest of his life, but it was impossible to convince herself of the fact. Virginia's shadow would linger like a faded stain.

Kavanagh took her hand up to his mouth, kissed it, traced a finger with his tongue. She would die without a touch like that. A studio could be established in other places, a language could be learned, a broken engagement would be in the past eventually. But a lie? A lie would kill her. The tip of her finger was inside his mouth. She rose from her seat and straddled him. Tenderness and intimacy gave way to a ferocity that thrilled and terrified each of them. She guided him inside her, gazing into him, unswerving, as he climaxed. His expression of surrender gave way to liberation and desire. But then, for a moment, a glint of hopelessness flashed in his eyes. It sent dread racing through her veins. She folded into him, breathed at his neck, and traced her teeth gently down it. He softened inside her.

"I have never loved anyone like I do you, Joe," she whispered. "I don't care if it kills me."

He looked up at her. "We can do this, my love. The hurt to others will be less than the betrayal of living a lie."

Was this the calm before a storm? "I will talk to Franco."

"I'll talk to Casler."

"Then?" she asked, pushing her forehead against his.

"We'll be free."

Their lips danced together until the garnet sun streaked low in the thicket.

And then Kavanagh started the engine.

CHAPTER 26

A platter of artichokes and potatoes steamed in the center of a Sunday table around which the Chirigoni family sat. The plate's aroma infused the kitchen with garlic and parsley, but the comforting smell had little effect on Carmela. The last few weeks had smudged into an interminable blur. She wished Franco's hand was not on her knee below the table. She looked down at her hands. The artichokes had left tarry marks on her fingertips and under her nails, as if she had been clawing at the earth. The image of herself suffocating underground flashed into her mind, digging herself out of her own grave. She brushed it off with the rest of the night wakings that had forced the much-needed sleep she craved to elude her. There was a tiny bead of dried blood where one of the artichokes spines had poked into her. She turned her palms down onto the tablecloth and bowed her head as her father said a swift grace.

No one spoke as they filled their plates. Her sisters had already asked all their questions about her trip, crammed onto her single bed, bombarding her with demands for intricate descriptions that she was glad to relay. She relived every step of that place and, in between the lines, allowed the memory of Kavanagh to wash over her like a golden light. When her sisters had eventually succumbed to sleep, she was left awake with the thought of him. She considered praying for forgiveness, or at least guidance, but there was little point. Any godliness had left her months ago. Only a hypocrite would turn to divine grace now.

Instead, she stared out her window at the crescent moon — an omen of hope, heralding growth, change, and expansion. The moon offered the peace she sought, not a bearded figure full of wrath and judgment. Then she thought of her mother's daily attendance at mass and the peace it brought her. Perhaps in Carmela's new faraway life in Germany she might fall into the same rhythm after all. God had blessed Maria with health, children, a husband who worked hard, and a home to be proud of. What was so different from what Carmela planned for her own life?

The bell cut through the hungry silence.

"What is wrong with people?" Icca barked. "The only person who would barge through lunch hour on God's day is your sister-in-law, Maria! Tell her to come back later."

Maria stood up and walked toward the terrace. A little while later she returned to the kitchen. Kavanagh was beside her.

Tomas stood up and greeted him, then ushered him toward the table.

"No, Signor Chirigoni, I know it is lunch hour," he began in jagged Italian. "I came only to give you this." He handed Tomas a thick envelope. Everyone watched him open it. His eyes scanned the writing at speed and then he handed it directly to Carmela. She willed her fingers not to tremble.

There it was, her life in black and white. Her family's security signed and sealed. Her ticket to freedom. "It's a contract, Papa, for the use of our land, and of the Falchis' lot beside us. You're to sign it. Here at the bottom."

Tomas and Franco locked eyes. As they did, Carmela found Kavanagh's for a fleeting moment. No turning back.

"Papá, it says here that they will pay twenty thousand lire up front and two thousand every year thereafter for a minimum term of ten years. If they choose to move to a different site, they will give six months' notice. If they choose to extend the term, the rent will be re-negotiated with a minimum of five percent increase."

Tomas's eyes glistened. "Maria, this kind man has just made us a happy family indeed! Feed him!" Tomas grabbed Kavanagh's hand with both of his, shook it with the gruff warmth for which he was well known, and pulled him to the table. Despite Kavanagh's best efforts to refuse, he took a place beside Tomas, opposite Franco. A metallic shiver clawed up Carmela's back.

Franco again reached for Carmela's knee under the table. He gave it a gentle squeeze, and then ran his finger up her thigh. She turned to him. He looked at her, his eyes twinkling with unnerving mischief. "Fine work, *tesoro*."

She feigned warmth, feeling as if she was looking at him through glass.

Carmela watched her family dive into their plates, slurping from hunks of bread, soggy with the fragrant broth of the artichokes. She couldn't taste anything but salt. Her stomach clamped shut. Her food moved from one cheek to the other. She intuited every one of Kavanagh's moves without looking at him, catching the tips of his fingers as they broke the bread, feeling his head turn from Tomas to Maria.

"So, when do you move in, Americano?" Franco called over to him.

Everyone laughed. Carmela remembered to mimic them just before she caught Piera's eye.

Kavanagh smiled, then offered a polite reply. "That's for my captain to decide. Today, I'm his messenger."

"He said —"

"It's all right, Carmela," Franco interrupted, "let the grown man speak for himself!"

"*Grazie,* Franco — *mio Italiano e poco,*" Kavanagh replied.

Tomas chuckled. "He's our guest, Franco, no more teasing. He can speak Russian for all I care!"

Everybody laughed. Carmela noticed Franco shift in his seat. Kavanagh's cool façade was impeccable. Was hers as convincing?

Maria cleared away the plates and placed a bowl full of fresh almonds and *tiricche* in the center of the table. Each mouthful brought Carmela and Kavanagh deeper into the deceit. Her family would look back to this lunch, in the days after her fleeing, with nothing but bitterness. They would think of his smiling face, his carefree charm, and the honest warmth in his eyes. The images would cut like a knife. It might have made her love him less, but even now, with the most precious people in her life surrounding her, she knew she couldn't risk losing him again. It was the biggest sacrifice of her life, but one she wouldn't live without. If she could, in time, forgive herself, then surely they would too.

Kavanagh ate a polite portion before eventually being allowed to stand, his cheeks rosy with wine and *mirto.* Was there a tiny part of him enjoying the masquerade? Was he relishing his victory over Franco? Carmela caught his eye; all doubts were silenced.

"Carmela!" Tomas boomed, a voice hot with a bottle of his own fierce wine. "Show this fine man out and tell him, next time we cook a proper meal, no peasant soup, yes?!" He burst into a cheeky cackle and looked twenty years younger.

Carmela rose, knowing this was the last time Kavanagh would be a welcome guest. They crossed the terrace. The late afternoon had lost its springtime chill. Summer was around the corner.

Kavanagh stopped beneath her mother's wisteria. "I want the best for you and your family."

"Thank you."

"I love you, Carmela."

Piera popped her head over the top of the wall down into the garden. "Carmela!" Her eyes whipped from her sister to Kavanagh. She hesitated for a moment, as if she knew she had interrupted something private. "Papá's dancing! You have to come! He's switched on the wireless and is jumping up and down!" Then, appearing to succumb to a sudden embarrassment, she fled inside.

Kavanagh's face stretched into a wide smile that forced Carmela to forget her sister's unsettling expression.

Carmela mirrored his smile. It took every ounce of determination to stop herself from reaching for his hand. "We are all children today, Joe. Because of you."

He turned and opened the gate, then stepped into his vehicle. "I'll be waiting."

Carmela nodded and watched him disappear down the hill.

As afternoon smudged into evening, Tomas's wine got the better of him and he began warbling up to the ceiling like a demented tenor. Franco rose and offered cordial salutes to his future mother-in-law. Then he kissed Icca on each cheek and departed. Carmela followed and closed the main door quietly behind them. Before they reached the steps he stopped and took her hand.

Carmela took a breath.

He placed a gentle finger on her lips to silence her. "Me first. I have something for you, *tesoro.*" He dug into his pocket and pulled out a dark, velvet box and placed it in her hands. She looked at the blue ribbon across the top, and then lifted the lid. Inside, nestled among ruched satin, was a gold locket. "Read the back," he said.

She lifted up the chain and watched the locket spin around in the moonlight. He reached out and stopped it, turning it so she could read the inscription: *Per Sempre.* Forever. She looked at his thick thumb. He lifted the chain to put it over her head. She twisted away from him. "Franco, I can't . . ."

Franco didn't move. His eyes took a moment to hone in on her. "You don't like it?"

"It's beautiful."

"Here," he said. "Turn around."

Carmela faced the twinkling lights of Simius. The feel of his fumbling fingers at the base of her neck made the little hairs there rise to attention. The clasp closed. He kissed her behind her ear. She flinched. "Sorry, Franco, Mamma and Papa are just over there, it doesn't feel right to —"

"You're right." Before she had a chance to enjoy the surge of relief, he had his hand clasped around hers, pulling her down the stairs toward the lower terrace, hiding them in the shadows of the thick wisteria canopy.

His hands raced around her body.

She was being ransacked.

"Stop, Franco!"

His fingers were pressed into her thighs now.

She pushed her hands against him, but he was stronger.

His palms traced over her breasts.

She pushed her nails into them.

He stopped moving for a moment and put his face level with hers. He looked like that young boy who had chased her through the cherry groves. She wavered, but then found a deep breath, wanting to escape without a fight. "We found ourselves as children!"

"And we will make many more!"

Carmela tried to speak, but the words stuck in her throat. She watched him picture himself a father, a boy playing dress-up with his grandfather's jacket. It was too late to wish he was sober. She willed herself back into the woods with Kavanagh, back on the coast, reminded herself of the future she would gift herself. "Not like this. Not here."

"What did you say?"

"You heard me, Franco."

"I heard some woman speak, but it wasn't you."

Carmela looked down at her hands. She tried to stay calm.

He grabbed her chin. "There she is. Say it."

"Let go of me."

His hand covered her mouth. "You haven't let me touch you in weeks. You think I don't know what's going on?"

Carmela's eyes pleaded with him.

He threw her back against the wall and walked a few paces away, looking out toward the town. His back rose up and down with fast breaths. "Carmela." He shook his head, then turned back to her, menacing. "So you're nervous about the wedding, so what? I am too! What fool wouldn't be?" He moved in closer, slamming his hand by Carmela's head. "Answer me!"

There were footsteps above. Vittoria appeared at the top of the stairs. "Carmela? Are you there?"

Franco nodded, hidden by the shadows, out of Vittoria's view.

"Yes, Vitto'," Carmela called up, her voice shaking, "just getting some air, *tesoro*. Go in to Mamma."

Franco waited for the footsteps to fade.

"We just got the contract we wanted. We're supposed to be celebrating!"

"Move away. I mean it."

"Threats now?"

"Promises."

"Do you even know what they are?"

He grabbed at her skirts. She fought his hands. They scratched her. She slapped him. He clamped his hand onto her underwear. She bit his cheek and lifted her knee deep into his groin. He let out a wail, folded over, and then shuffled backward a few involuntary steps.

"No husband of mine will ever touch me like that. Do you understand me?" she spat, not caring whether her voice was starting to rise.

"You ungrateful bitch!" he panted. "You think anyone will want tainted goods? You're stuck with me and you know it!"

"Get out!" she said, opening the gate. He walked toward it. As he was just outside she slammed it shut.

His foot caught in between. "You've lost your mind!"

Carmela's legs started to tremble.

He pushed the gate open and slammed it shut behind him. Then he lunged into her. His hands tightened around her neck. She watched him watching her, struggling for breath. She started to splutter.

White lights.

Franco let go.

She stood, bent over, panting. Her hand cradled her bruised neck. He took a few paces from side to side and ran a hand through his hair. "We will talk tomorrow. When you have seen sense."

She watched him step out of the gate, and this time shut it quickly behind him.

"Per sempre?!" she called out, wanting everyone to hear, to bear witness.

He stopped, turned, and walked back toward the gate, pushing his face against it. "There's no turning back now."

"This isn't what marriage is, Franco."

"You're tired," he began, changing tack. "You've had a big trip. Get some rest." He looked at her as if nothing had happened, smiling like the lover he thought he was. "I love you, Carmela."

She watched him walk away. When he was almost at the bottom of the hill she shouted out at him, "You don't know what love is!"

He sprinted back up to the gate. She felt like a coward for hiding behind the steel. Why not step out, face him like a lioness? Why barricade herself like this? What could he do, right now, with all the neighbors watching and listening between the slats of their shutters? He could have killed her, right then. He was close. But he had stopped. Now was the time to summon her courage. She flung open the catch. The gate hit the low wall beside it. "Show me what a man you are! Spit at me through my gate! Do it! Do it for everyone to see!"

Franco looked at her, taken aback. "Get inside," he whispered.

"I will stand outside my house if I choose."

Franco's face creased into a snarl of a smile. "You want to play?"

"I want you to stop!"

He walked up to her. She stood, unflinching. He traced his nose over her cheek, then tried to force his tongue inside her mouth, but she clamped her lips shut. His teeth bit down into her. Fast. Sharp. She gasped. She raised her hand and clutched her lip, finding the metallic taste of her own blood.

"I don't play games," he said, turning away. She watched him saunter down the hill.

Carmela retreated into the garden and shut the gate, her legs giving in. She sat down on the wall. Carmela reached inside her pocket and pulled out a handkerchief. She blotted her lip. There was a noise. She looked up.

Vittoria's small face was pale in the sliver

of moonlight. Her eyebrows furrowed. She flew down the stairs. "Did he hurt you, Carmela?"

Carmela bit back her tears. "No."

"You were fighting."

"You're not to worry, you hear?" Carmela reached down and smoothed a hand over Vittoria's cheek. "Fighting is ugly, don't you think?"

Vittoria nodded. The sisters sat in silence while Carmela tried to grapple for some semblance of composure, but she knew her sister saw through it. How long had she been listening?

"I found this," Vittoria said at last. She held up the locket. "It's pretty."

"It's for you," Carmela said, opening her sister's hand and placing it on her palm. "See what it says under here, Vittoria? I want you to remember those words. You and me — *Per sempre.* I was the first person to hold you. Don't forget that, will you? I was the one who cradled you till Mamma took you to her chest." She started smoothing her sister's hair, hating herself for succumbing to the tears. "I watched your puffy eyes open and take in this world. You and me, yes?"

"*Sempre,*" Vittoria uttered with a sad smile.

"Let's not tell Mamma, all right?" Carmela asked, wiping her own face. "We don't want to worry her, do we?"

Vittoria shook her head. Carmela kissed her sister. The unbearable burden of guilt washed over her. She would write to Vittoria. Every day she would write long stories of her new life. She would describe the buildings, the food, the look of the blond tresses of the stylish women. She might go to a *pasticerria* one day and order a cake and sit eating it, thinking of Vittoria, and jot down its every particular. Vittoria wouldn't feel betrayed. She would learn about a new world. It would feel like Vittoria had moved there with her.

"Now, go back upstairs and help Mamma."

A reluctant Vittoria rose. Carmela watched her take pigeon steps up toward the terrace. After she heard the door close, Carmela's eyes drifted skyward. The clouds had rolled in from the coast. She couldn't see the moon.

CHAPTER 27

Carmela squinted at the ornate plaster cornice of the doctor's office ceiling, waiting for faces to reveal themselves as if it were a sky of shifting clouds. Light streamed into the white room from the busy city street outside. Sassari was a half-hour bus ride away from Simius and the closest place a woman could hope for any medical privacy.

The nurse pulled the curtain around Carmela. "You can get dressed now. The doctor is finished." She left the room. Carmela eased herself off the bed, pulled her underwear back on, and stepped into her skirt. Her hands were trembling. She heard the door open and then the doctor's voice. "Signorina Chirigoni, please come out when you're ready."

Carmela opened the curtain and took a seat. The leather felt cold. The doctor's words washed over her as if she were listen-

ing to him speak underwater. Carmela nodded in all the right places, offered what she
hoped were expressions of contentment to
mask the shock and panic. She listened to
herself ask whether she would be able to fit
into her wedding gown in a month's time.
At the same time, she chastised herself for
masquerading a semblance of propriety
before this stranger. The pounding of her
heart didn't relent, even as she left the office and stepped out of the palazzo onto a
wide *via*. She headed toward the central
piazza, where the tables of the café Moka-
dor were filled with men putting the world
to rights.

Rosa spoke of Sassari as if it were the
metropolis of the north, some grand gateway
to a better place, but the wide *palazzi* —
elegant apartment blocks with grand stucco
frontage that lined the square — failed to
impress Carmela. It lacked the richness of
Cagliari, the touch of the exotic. It upheld a
pretense of history, like a replica painting.
Rosa talked of moving to this city. Carmela
had memories of listening to her sermons
about the place, delivered for the eager ears
of Vittoria. Perhaps Rosa had had some
fantasy of being closeted inside a velveteen
boudoir for the doctor to stop in and visit
at leisure. Perhaps she had fashioned some

idea of strutting the piazza in the morning and then again in the afternoon, in different outfits of course, with matching nails on hands that did no work, sipping coffee or an aperitif as the sun would dictate — a life of rhythmical luxury. She would imagine this still, no doubt, till her dying day, but her reality was another world.

Who was Carmela to judge now? Hadn't she just stepped out of a doctor's office much like her aunt did the spring before? But Carmela had a promise. She had a lover who counted the days to take her away to a new place. Across the street, she watched a young couple take a sedate stroll, stopping to look into the attractive shop windows. Franco filled her mind, and the knot in her stomach tightened. The woman slipped her hand into the man's. Carmela watched them, feeling that time, like the fine sands of Chia, was slipping through her fingers, shifting underfoot. A cold panic rippled from her abdomen to the tips of her feet.

She began marching toward the piazza. This child would not slip out of her into a cold farm cottage, lie deep in the earth, unwanted, unloved. She could hear her feet pound against the hot pavement. This child would feel the heat of Carmela and Kavanagh's unconditional love. Her soles scuffed.

Then the thought of giving birth far from her mother sent ice through her veins. The idea of wading through those first forty days with a newborn and no one to cook hearty broths and warm drinks, like every mother in Simius would do for their daughters, made her breath catch. No matter, she tried to comfort herself. Hadn't Maria mothered without her own to watch over her?

Carmela thought about Piera and the joy with which she would have set about caring for her sister and a new nephew or niece. Carmela was robbing her family of the finest moment of her life. But this child was conceived out of wedlock. This child was illegal. This child would be blighted with more than original sin. Her family could never love it. This baby would be an American. German even — an enemy's child.

Carmela's heart ached. Nausea swelled inside her stomach. Here she stood, a stranger in a stranger's city, trying to pant away the panic. Her palms were clammy. Her breasts ached.

She headed across the piazza toward the depot. The bus pulled up. Carmela stepped inside. Franco's younger brother was sitting toward the front. She started. He looked up as she walked past him. "Carmela?"

She turned, feigning pleasant surprise.

"Ciao, Luca, how are you?"

"Better now. Mamma sent me to here to buy a suit for the wedding."

Carmela gave a feeble smile, not knowing what reply to offer.

"She's fussing over Franco like he's the first boy to get married!" He flashed a wide, youthful smile. Luca's features were much like Franco's, only softer. His eyes were a lighter chestnut and sparkled with a bright, endearing energy.

"Luca, I hope you don't mind, I'm going to sit toward the back. I'm not feeling too good."

"I'm sorry to hear that. You got the jitters too, eh? Franco's stomping around like a bull. Mamma's cooked him his favorite meal every night. Bet I won't get the same treatment when it's my time."

Carmela gave a polite nod and took a seat on the hot plastic several rows back.

As the bus pulled into Simius's Piazza Cantareddu, the market was charging into life. There were bellows about artichokes and almonds and salt cellars. Thuds of axes crunched nougat and shanks. Insults were hurled among the men playing a heated round of *murra,* the ancient street game in which two participants stand head to head and call out the sum total of their own, and their opponents', fingers. All this is done while flinging digits into the air between them at implausible speed. Frantic steam from the espresso machines in bars lining the square sent wafts of coffee that smudged into the cheese stall's pungent aromas. Carmela's nausea piqued.

Sun-wizened sellers, fresh off their farms, were held to account by the fat-fingered, fanatical cooks hunting for the best anise they could sniff, the juiciest tomato they could pinch, or the sweetest apricot they could try. The cacophony would evaporate in a couple of hours, when the streets would be deserted and even the most loquacious tongue silenced as inhabitants ensconced themselves in the relative cool of their stone bedrooms.

Strands of Carmela's hair clung to the wetness on the back of her neck. She wound in and out of the crowds and walked uphill, leaving the piazza behind her. She stepped into Yolanda's studio.

It wasn't long before the noise of the other seamstresses' chatter and activity began to ricochet in her head. Carmela leaned on her desk, licked the sore on her lip. The peeling paint on the window frame caught her eye; its age looked just like that today, tired. She met Yolanda by the fabric-cutting table. "I'm taking an early lunch," Carmela said, rubbing her forehead. "I will stay late."

"None of the girls are taking lunch today," Yolanda replied, cool.

"I see."

"We can't get these trousseaus completed without you. You know that."

Carmela's eyes glazed with involuntary tears.

"Whatever's the matter?"

Carmela shook her head. Yolanda took her by the elbow and led her into her tiny office. They stood in the cool dark for a moment. The clock ticktocked the day away in the corner. Yolanda searched her niece for clues, but Carmela was determined to offer none. "You're under a lot of pressure here. Perhaps I've asked too much of you after all."

"Zia, my work has nothing to do with this. I love my work."

"You are a nervous bride. That much is clear."

Carmela looked at the closed window behind her godmother, wondering how to navigate the conversation. For a moment she felt like offering her the unadulterated truth. Then terror gripped her throat and the words refused to surface. "I'm not sure of very much just now," she said at last.

Yolanda straightened. "Carmela, I won't stand here and offer you a shoulder to cry on, because that will do you no good. This is not the time to let personal feelings drag you away from your commitments. A month from now you're going to be one of the most influential women in town. But right now, this business has to come first."

Carmela shifted, wondering why it surprised her that Yolanda tackled personal feelings with the same steel she did her business.

"We need all your energy directed here now, do you understand? We're several girls down too. Many are the youngest girls whose heads are turned at the slightest distraction. I always thought you different, made of stronger stuff. I see my younger self in you, Carmela, I always have, to be frank. Perhaps I was wrong." Her face hardened. "It's because I didn't waste my youth that I stand here today. Could I have done that if I had let my mind flitter? Did I feel the sweet flush of adolescent love for your late godfather when I walked up the aisle under the eyes of God? No! Because those tender kisses of childhood don't build a life, Carmela. You don't marry the boy who first kissed you. You marry the man he will become."

Carmela nodded. She had said too much. "I'll complete my assigned trousseaus. You can be sure of that."

Yolanda kissed her cheek. Carmela's throat tightened, clamping the hidden tears. Yolanda walked past her, back to the floor. Carmela stood like a nervous customer at her first fitting, and hating herself for it.

A wild knock at the door ripped Carmela out of her reverie. As she opened it, a breathless Vittoria stood yelping before her. "You have to come now!"

"What's happened? Who's hurt?"

"No one! You have to go to the post office! A phone call, Carmela!" She panted in between words. "Urgent, they said! Came to the house looking for you! Mamma sent me here."

Carmela swung around to Yolanda. Her godmother gave her a reticent nod. The sisters flew down the steps out into the street. The uneven cobbles poked as their feet pelted the hill to the main square, with the urgency of two gazelles fleeing the clutches of a hungry lion. It was Carmela's first-ever telephone call. Only two families out of the five thousand people of Simius had phones in their homes; one belonged in Franco's uncle's house, the other to the Mayor.

490

Carmela and Vittoria reached the heavy door of the post office. Their cheeks were flushed. They entered. A couple of people in the line looked up, shadow ghosts, as Carmela's eyes struggled to adjust to the darkness of the room.

"Miss Chirigoni?" the clerk asked, sweeping a critical eye over Carmela's tousled demeanor. Carmela nodded. The glaring eyes of the other customers were now visible. Her cheeks flushed a deeper crimson.

Carmela was led into the gloom of what appeared to be a forgotten back room. She took Vittoria's small hand in hers, feeling her fingers tighten. As the clerk closed the tall, wooden door behind them, the last whispers of the folk outside faded into silence. They stared at the phone in the center of the desk.

"It's not going to answer itself," a voice snapped.

Carmela looked to the figure behind the desk. Of all the people in Simius, there was no one she wanted to avoid more at this moment. Her heart sank. Agnes. "Pick it up, then — you've kept him waiting long enough," she continued with a snarl.

Carmela picked up the receiver and placed it to her ear, tentative.

"Carmela Chirigoni?"

The clipped voice of the operator caught her somewhat off-guard. *"Sì."*

"Please hold. Signor Joe Kavanagh is on the line."

There was a click, then the faraway sound of his American voice. "Carmela? Urgent news."

"Are you all right, Joe?"

"I am fine." He paused. Carmela felt her stomach tighten. "Casler is sending me to the mainland tonight."

"What? Why?"

"Business in Rome. I can't talk about it now. It's only for a week. You must meet me this afternoon. We have to discuss our plan."

"Yes," she replied, trying not to think about Yolanda, or Franco, or Agnes, or the butterfly heartbeats of their tiny baby, floating between her hips, swimming to nowhere.

"Meet me at the Roman bridge at three o'clock."

"I'll be there."

"Carmela, repeat what I said so I know you heard right."

Carmela hesitated. Agnes's beady eyes pierced her like sharp pinpricks. Carmela's thoughts spun in concentric circles. What if Agnes could make out the time and place of their meeting? She wouldn't know it was today. She couldn't deduce anything from a time and place. How would she know it wasn't part of a military visit for which she needed to translate?

And yet.

"Carmela? Are you there? Please copy."

"Yes." How naïve Carmela felt, having imagined she would have been offered privacy. She couldn't leave this town soon enough. "Three o'clock. Roman bridge."

"Thank you. I love you, Carmela."

She longed to utter the same words in reply.

"Only for a week, Joe?"

"Yes."

"Can't they ask someone else?"

"They're using me as much as they can before we head up north, darling. Don't worry. Everything is in place. I've secured our new home. I have your ticket. I want to give you everything today just in case. I'll explain everything when I see you. I have to go."

"Joe . . ."

"Yes?"

A dull tone pierced her ear, sending his voice into the past. She listened for a moment, pretending he was still there. Wondering whether to say a formal good-bye, appease her mistrust of Agnes. She could, perhaps, fabricate something to make the appointment seem more official. Instead her hand slipped down from her ear, lank. Carmela tried to muffle her anxiety by imagining what he had been wearing. If his right cheek had smirked into dimples. What story she would have read in his eyes. The pictures faded fast, with each fresh wave of panic, like feeble twirls of steam.

"Another holiday, is it? Or just an order for one of your famous picnics?"

Carmela gave a polite smile and replaced the handset. "I'll see you later, Agnes. Yolanda expects everyone to work late."

Agnes raised an eyebrow. "Nice to have friends at the base though, isn't it?"

"I'm an interpreter." Carmela felt her voice quiver, then her legs hollow.

"I'm surprised you find the time for it all. Franco must be very proud of you."

Carmela was a fly on a sticky web, thankful for Vittoria beside her to stop herself from wiping the sneer off Agnes's face with one swipe. "We aren't all lucky enough to have mothers who work in post offices and give us shift work," Carmela said, immediately regretting her sarcasm.

Their eyes locked for a breath.

"See you at the studio." Carmela took Vittoria's hand and made their escape. As they stomped out, the tail end of a discussion at the counter reverberated around the main hall.

"What do you mean you have no stamps?! This is a damned post office, you imbecile!" yelled an overheated customer.

"I don't know when our next delivery is," the clerk said.

"I'll go to the *tabacchi* then!" the man yelled, brushing out past Carmela.

"It's supplied by us, Signore." The clerk sighed, world-weary sweat glistening on his brow.

Carmela looked down at her sister, her young eyes wide with excitement. "Go home and tell Mamma it was a phone call about work. I must get back to the studio now, and I will stay there late to finish some trousseaus. Do you understand?"

Vittoria nodded. Carmela watched her disappear up the hill in the direction of their house and then headed to Antonio's bar.

"The traveler returns!" Antonio looked radiant. His tables were out for the first time since the winter and occupied with the kind of ladies who spent their husbands' money well.

"What are you doing at two-thirty today?" Carmela asked.

"What I always do." His voice dipped into

a private whisper. "Having a lie down, hoping to dream of someone who embodies perfection."

Off Carmela's serious expression he straightened. "What's happened?"

He caught sight of Carmela's lip. "Franco?"

Carmela looked at him, nothing more to say. She shrugged, silenced by her numbness.

"Shall we go somewhere private?" he asked.

"Nothing private about our fight on the street, so what should I care now?"

Antonio reached for her hand.

"Kavanagh came back," she said, meeting his eyes.

"I know."

She watched Antonio intuit a world of unspeakables. "He's leaving tonight, for one week. I must see him."

"Where?" he asked, without judgment.

"Roman bridge."

"I'll meet you in the piazza at two-thirty. I know a wonderful taxi driver in town. He might be there waiting."

She stiffened.

It hurt to hold the truth from her most treasured friend. It ached not to tell him about their plans for Munich, about the baby, about the whole new world that had just opened up at her feet, but it had to wait. If she had any hope of slipping out later without incurring Yolanda's wrath, she would have to make up significant time now. "Thank you, Antonio."

Carmela tried not to watch the clock. She sewed through a mountain of dresses and their finishing touches. She worked tirelessly, her fingers deft and nimble racing along the fabric. Every stitch inched her toward Kavanagh.

She hung the last dress on a wide wooden hanger by the fitting area. There were nearly twenty outfits beside that one — another woman's new life draped before her. Carmela's eyes traced over the trousseau. What would she be doing as this woman slipped into her yellow summer dress? As this newlywed closed the clasps of her evening gown to delight her new husband, what streets would Carmela be strolling with Kavanagh? At summer's ebb, while this customer donned her demure navy two-piece, how would Carmela be spending her autumnal evenings in Germany? She felt pleased with her work and took a moment to wish the woman well.

Then her thoughts crashed back to Franco

and Luca. While Kavanagh was on the mainland she might reveal her difficult news to her family. It felt safer to wait until Kavanagh's travel arrangements were all in place. She wanted to feel the ticket in her hand. She wanted to know her new address. All the things he had assured her of, which now would have to be delayed at least a week or so. No, it was impossible; her new life must be kept secret until she was safe, beside Kavanagh, in their new world.

She clung to the meticulousness of her work to keep her mind from dashing around memories and doubts like a faulty missile. The sense of being in complete control of her tools, which her work delivered, was satisfying. Yet standing before this fine collection, Carmela felt the powerful realization that very little was under her control after all. She had grasped at this futile need for so long now, in her every action, her speech, her work. But it was only now, having given in to the one thing she could never have controlled, that the world had been set alight. She would return one day, dressed in her new life, filled with stories she would be happy to share. Then she pictured Yolanda's face, aged with betrayal. A bolt of guilt skidded across her waist.

Her lip smarted. Franco spitting with

anger filled her mind. The disappearing adolescence that Yolanda spoke of didn't apply here. Its failure to develop was at the root of the problem. Yet Carmela didn't want to leave with hurt in her heart. She convinced herself she wasn't running away. She brushed fear aside, which frayed the edges of her every thought. Fear was simply another hurdle to leap over to earn her freedom.

More than all this, she longed for Kavanagh not to have to leave. A military wife's life would be tougher than she had thought. There would be three in the relationship after all. The trepidation about Virginia's shadow gave way to the understanding that their lives would be puppeteered forever by Kavanagh's seniors. Even a captain would be answerable to someone.

The clock struck two.

"Zia," Carmela began, walking toward her aunt, "I'm going out to buy some new thread."

"There ought to be plenty, Carmela. Agnes brought in a box this morning, before her shift at the post office."

"It's not quite the right shade."

"Don't be long."

"Of course."

Carmela stepped out of the studio before

her aunt could change her mind. She began the climb uphill using the stairs on the opposite side of the fountain. The sound of clanging pans ricocheted off the walls of the chaotic cluster of homes as the women began their weekly ritual of sauce making, the sweet smell escaping through the heavy shutters. Her nausea shifted to hunger.

Turning the corner she locked eyes with Gepetto Comida, sitting motionless under the dappled shade of his pomegranate tree like a skinny Sardinian Buddha. The octogenarian's wrinkles looked sun-dried in the heat, his hands resting atop his knobbly walking cane.

"*Buon giorno,* Signor Comida," Carmela said, in the customary way younger people were expected to greet the elders.

He squinted in reply, nodding a silent half smile. Carmela wondered if he could read her improbable morning on her face, or if he had simply discovered the secret meaning of life.

Inside the cool quiet of her bedroom Carmela opened her wardrobe. She pulled out her yellow linen dress and slipped into it. Then she reached in for her favorite maroon shoes that Zio Raimondo had made for her twenty-first birthday. Piera stepped in.

"You're home! Vittoria said you wouldn't be back. What's this I hear about a phone call?!"

Carmela closed the wardrobe door. "They needed to reach me from the base urgently."

"Everything all right?"

"Of course. I'm just going out for more thread."

"In Sunday shoes?"

"Yes."

Piera looked at her. Carmela couldn't decipher what she read in her sister's face, but it unsettled her. "I thought the new shoes might refresh me — I'm exhausted. Yolanda's working us to the bone . . ." She stopped herself just short of babbling.

The sisters looked at each other for a moment. Carmela promised herself that every evening this week, before she left for Munich, she would take Piera on a walk to the piazza. She would buy her fresh gelato from the Bar Nazionale, an aperitif even. This week without Kavanagh would be the perfect way to devote time to the siblings she wouldn't see for a while. They would remember this week when they would wake up to their farewell letters. They would let go of their anger, their sense of betrayal, because they would remember the sister who had taken care of them, spoiled them, bought them all the little treats she had always wanted to. They couldn't hate her. They would only remember the love she showered on them.

Carmela stepped forward and planted a soft kiss on each of Piera's cheeks. "I love you so very much, Piera."

Piera's expression shifted between confusion and trepidation. "Are you all right, Carmela? You look . . ."

"What?"

"Frantic."

"I've never been happier in my life, Piera."

Piera nodded, but her smile seemed unsure. "I love you too, Carmela."

Carmela turned for the door and then closed it behind her without looking back, in case her sister's expression would prick her conscience any more than it already had.

The piazza was deserted. All evidence of a market had been cleared away. She thought about the weight of Kavanagh on her, the cool water of the river at her feet, juniper, rosemary, and thyme dancing on the salty air above them. She could see Antonio beside his taxi at the far side. He was leaning against his cab, smoking.

"I didn't know we had a date." The sound of Franco's voice spun her around.

He stood leaning against the wide trunk of an old tree. How had she not seen him?

"You don't look so happy to see your fiancé." He stepped toward her. Behind him she saw Antonio look over at them.

"How do I say sorry, Carmela? How do I tell you that the memories of your hair on my face, your soft skin against mine, the taste of your sweet mouth, keep me awake at night?"

"Franco, stop."

"Stop what?"

He wouldn't hurt her here, not in the square.

"We fell in love before we even knew what it was," she said.

She looked down at his wrist. His watch read almost two-thirty. She needed to get to the other side of the square. Fast. "Why are you all dressed up?"

She hooked a strand of hair behind her ear. Had he seen the slight tremble? "I spilled something all down myself and ran home to change."

He stepped toward her, wrapping his wide hands around her face. His lips pressed against hers. "I am going to love you till the day I die, Carmela. We can't live without each other."

His words didn't match his expression

somehow. It was as if they were coming out of a radio nearby and he mouthed along with them.

"I'll come and see you tomorrow, Franco," she said, doubting whether she sounded as relaxed as she would have liked. *Just get on your bike and ride away.*

Antonio was in her periphery, signaling to hurry. She couldn't wait a moment longer. "Antonio's running me to the shop in the next town for an order for Yolanda," she said, immediately regretting it.

"I'll take you."

"No, it's rolls of fabric. I wouldn't be able to hold them." The saying was true after all: It was impossible to tell *one* lie. She listened to the tales tumble out of her mouth. Who had she become? A storyteller. For a moment she felt dizzy, like looking at her life through the distortion of a shattered mirror. Which parts were real? She felt herself suck air in from deep underfoot, willing herself to feel the ground beneath her.

Seemingly satisfied with her performance, Franco planted a peck on her cheek, straddled his bike, and rode out of the piazza, waving to Antonio as he did. Carmela dashed across the cobbles. When she reached his taxi, he looked at her with panic. "I can't drive you now. Not with

504

Franco around the corner, are you mad?"

"I don't have time."

Antonio looked hesitant.

"I have to see Kavanagh."

Carmela's eyes pleaded.

Antonio nodded. He looked sweaty.

They slipped into the hot taxi. Carmela watched Franco, already several hundred meters away, turn toward the direction of his house. His mother would be wondering why he wasn't home in time for lunch. What lie would he spin?

Carmela took in the cloudless blue above as she stepped out of the car. The sun lit up her face. It took her back to the coast of Orosei, inching her toward some semblance of calm.

"Thank you, Antonio."

"I'll come back for you?"

"No need."

"Sure?"

She nodded.

He stood for a moment, as if he wanted to add something. Then he seemed to think better of it and instead slipped back inside his taxi. Carmela watched him drive away toward the hills that surrounded the valley.

The old Roman bridge stretched across the marshy river below. Its stones were faded by the sun and time. A dozen arches rose from the water, squat and strong. Carmela made her way down the bank and sat by the ancient bricks. Some Roman had stepped here, swum here, made love here. Some Roman had built this bridge, drunk this water. Perhaps some Roman had died here. Right here, beneath this craggy pine, beside these sharp pebbles, in this shallow water.

The river was still. She thought about the May first picnics that she and her family would have along here when her father was in Africa. Before empty promises and wars. Before studios and patterns and futures and marriages. Before she knew love. She promised herself that she would come here every day this week, to remember the smell of wild fennel and the dried pine needle floor, the scent of her sea, the sun-parched dusty roads, the warm wind of her summers, and the aromatic forests of autumn under a Sardinian sky. The feel of her father's farm's earth underfoot, the smell of her mother's kitchen, the sound of Vittoria running through the house singing — even the sour expression of her grandmother's face. All this she would commit to memory, carry it with her during the oncoming months and the challenges and joys it would bring.

She tried to picture Kavanagh's expression as she revealed the news of their child. Her stomach tightened. Perhaps he wouldn't believe it was his. Perhaps it would be best to wait. He would be gone only a week, after all. No sense clouding their move. This would be painful, familiar territory for him. Why had she not thought of all this before? This child would signify everything Kavanagh had left behind. How would he stand by her side when the time came, wondering whether the child was his? He would have nothing but her word to assure him. Was their love sealed with this kind of trust yet? Of course it was. She was ready to walk away from her life in Simius for him, and he for her.

The sun's white rays beat down onto her scalp. She was alone. Her future with Kavanagh seemed fragile all of a sudden. How stupid she felt for dancing around in her fantasies of sublime motherhood away from her motherland, when all along this might be the one thing that would send Kavanagh running in the opposite direction. Why hadn't she been more careful? In all the time she had been with Franco, she had made sure no chances were taken. And yet, for Kavanagh, she had run away on an illicit weekend, silencing all second thoughts. She had fallen into him without reserve. Now he would feel trapped by her. For a moment she considered walking back to town, right then. That way she couldn't be tempted to keep the truth from him. And what way was that to start a lifetime together? With a lie? Every thought was a little tug on the unraveling thread of their supposed lives: a future born of deceit.

Carmela tried to summon the excitement she had felt earlier, as she had pouted and twisted into her dress before her flustered reflection back at the house, but the feelings wouldn't surface. A quiet gray drifted over her, like a fog. Cutting through the haze, a thought reverberated in her mind, clear as a bell: Everyone's life would be simpler if she wasn't there at all. What child would want this woman as a mother? She would have no comforting tales of courtship for endless retelling. All her past would be bottled in a secret place, webbed with murky half truths. What way would that be to raise a proud Sardinian woman? And if he was a boy, how would he not reject her when he learned how he'd been conceived, and deceived? She watched the water trickle by her feet, willing her thoughts to slip down into it and be carried far away. Where was her courage now?

Her family had their sights set on a certain future for their first-born. Her siblings would have to live with the repercussion of being the ones left behind by a sister who had fled with an American. Her parents would never recover. What kind of business partner had she proven to Yolanda? The woman who had taught her everything she knew, who had rolled out the carpet of success only for her to turn her back on it all. How would she ever be able to return with her head held high, having thrown the opportunity of a lifetime back in her godmother's face?

Perhaps Casler would change his mind and keep Kavanagh posted on her island? Then she wouldn't have to shatter her brittle life. But what of that? How would she walk her streets without shame? There may be no life for Kavanagh and her here, but there was no life for her and Franco either. She tried to convince herself that Kavanagh could face a life of fathering a child even if he would never be sure it was his. But she knew that every time those young eyes would look up at him he would silence doubts. If it was a boy? With dark eyes like Franco? What would stop him slowly growing to hate that child?

Carmela looked down into the water. No

answers to be found there. What solution for the mess she had created? She had drawn the people she cared most about toward certain misery. And for what? For the satisfaction of her own pleasure. Never would she have believed, a year ago, when Kavanagh stepped onto the farm, that she would have been capable of such cruelty, of such shameless selfishness. Charging toward her supposed happiness with Kavanagh, she would leave a trail of destruction. What happiness in that?

Carmela scooped up some water and splashed her face, as if the coolness might cleanse the feelings of disgust, of dread, of panic. A few drips fell from her chin onto her dress. She looked at the tiny, wet circles on her skirt. A fish rose to the surface. Carmela watched it dive back into the deep. How she longed to lie on the cold mud of the riverbed for a moment. Hidden from everyone, hidden from her own turbulent thoughts.

The idea of invisibility was seductive.

But the hiding was over. She had found herself out.

A sound from above ripped her out of her thoughts. All worry slipped away. Kavanagh loved her. He would take her in his arms and lay her down by the water. He would slip inside her with promises and hot kisses and feet wet with the river.

She rose, shielding her eyes from the blinding sun.

A silhouette charged down the bank toward her.

It wasn't Kavanagh.

AFTERWORD

Simius, Sardinia — June 2008

Our family home in Simius has only one photo of Carmela. It's in a silver frame, beside an aquamarine telephone, in what my cousins and I used to call the Dolls Room, on the second floor, here in my grandmother's house. The bare bulb casts a blue gloom over the peculiar menagerie inside. The afternoons spent with my cousins in here replay in my mind, as I recall the sensation of being fascinated and spooked by the bizarre stuffed animals and trinkets inside the glass cabinets.

Taxidermy lines the left wall — my clan have a peculiar approach to the deceased. These animals pose in purgatorial freezes. Did my family want to commemorate their passing or existence? Zia Piera's pet Chihuahua is dressed in a puzzling knitted two-piece. I know from pictures that she used to dress him up this way when he was still breathing too. I can only imagine how that felt to that wretch of a dog in the forty-degree heat. His bulging eyes plead with me to free him from the stand poking his genitals. I run a finger across the coarse hair of the wild boar next to him instead — one of Grandfather's prized hunts.

There is a glass-topped table beside the animals. Inside, an array of miniature silver objects has not altered in thirty years. I look over the tiny ornaments: a pacifier, an iron, an elephant, a lamp lighter, and his lamp-post. The everyday items are transformed into precious objects by rendering them silver and minuscule. As a child I remember collating them in my mind with elaborate stories. Now they look banal. Is the viewer to admire the craftsmanship, and therefore, in turn, the magnificence of our everyday habits and gizmos?

My eyes return to Carmela's photo. After all these years of staring at her image, it's still hard to decipher her expression. She looks off camera, struggling toward her smile, and though the corners of her lip curl upward, her eyes remain melancholic. A few days after it was taken she disappeared. Only her clothes were found, folded in a neat pile on the bank beneath the Roman bridge. The premeditated actions, police decided, of a troubled woman preparing to take her own life. Most likely, the authorities argued, her corpse had been washed out to sea after she had jumped off the bridge. She was denied formal burial because of it, and for falling pregnant out of wedlock — information uncovered after questioning at the doctor's office in Sassari. Franco left town in the days that followed, not returning for several weeks. Maria and her brothers demanded investigations that proved fruitless because the body was never found. Carmela's sisters and brother were asked to leave the church youth group on account of their eldest sister's sin and ridiculed at school for the same.

Zia Rosa left for London the following year, after an advertisement in the local paper invited Simiuns to the city to work as either domestic or nurses. She began her training and returned triumphant the following summer. Piera accompanied her on her return to London to take up a post as housekeeper for the Curwins. Over the following three years, one sibling joined them each summer, expanding the domestic team at the Curwins. Tore became their butler, who also gardened and chauffeured. Piera trained Gianetta and Vittoria to be her assistants in the house, until they were old enough to sign up for nurse training. They would visit their parents every summer, with matching suitcases — now stored in the room next to this one — bringing a touch of Brit-chic to sprinkle along the dusty Simius streets where they once lived.

I crank open the bedroom shutters, breathe in the fresh morning air, and take in my Simius. It spirals into the valley, funnel-like, the homes scattered like stony debris. The cathedral spire catches the sun and strikes eight. Later, scooters will charge down the narrow *viccoli* zipping teenage lovers to secret afternoon hideouts on the town's periphery. I know because I used to be one of them. A butcher's son once whizzed me to a pine tree clearing, stuck his tongue too far down my throat, showed me his erect penis, then professed his undying love. The next day he dumped me — in his butcher's shop, no less. He offered me three photos of him from a plastic bag he kept beneath his counter, as a consolation prize. I was so gobsmacked that anyone would have the gall to dump me, let alone someone I hadn't agreed to date, that I found myself taking him up on his offer. I chose three snapshots: posing solo in goal, half naked on the beach, and outside his shop. I've still got them somewhere. He kissed me good-bye on the mouth when I left, but I was mostly paying attention to his bloody fingernails.

The psychedelic housecoat of Great Zia Rosa sweeps around the doorway. "Morning, ducky!" she croaks, pinching my cheeks, planting a powdery kiss on each. "Breakfast time, my bubala," she adds with a wave of her arthritic hand, which she hooks into my arm, leading me downstairs. I've always loved the way my Sardinian relatives scatter their broken English with Yiddishisms. Their decade of working as that small domestic army for the Jewish Curwins in 1950s London left its mark. Growing up I became educated on the Jewish holidays by the food Zia Piera would bring home, the perfect balance, in my view, to a Catholic schooling. Yet somehow I've managed to escape both obesity and crippling guilt.

We spent last night going through Zia Rosa's collection of rings, each with semiprecious stones as big as an eyeball. She retold her stories about traveling solo to the east, on organized tours. After a few hours she had started to slur again and began to warn me about my mother and Zia Gianetta, who, according to her, were itching to steal everything. Her dementia comes and goes like the northeastern maestrale wind, brutal and unbridled.

"You'll end up with a fat belly like your father," she adds, though we both know that wouldn't happen however hard I might try. And I've tried very hard. No amount of carbohydrate appears to grow curves on me — I will be the closest thing to a son my mother will ever hope to have. My sister, on the other hand, more than makes up for it. She's in the bedroom now, coaxing her son into appropriate clothing for Zia Piera's memorial mass later this morning. Her husband is calling it the memorial chase because he knows he will spend it running after their toddler, Nicoló, in the square outside while friends and family pay their respects to Zia Piera within.

"Gianetta's gone for bread," my mother says, bringing a pot of coffee from the stove to the table. Mum's hair has grown back in chemical curls; we like to refer to it as her chemo souvenir. Her cheeks are rosy again. She's wearing one of the colorful silk shirts she bought last week, having celebrated her remission with an overhaul of her wardrobe and a small spending spree on a new one. My mother appears to have affronted the mortal threat with grace and good humor; she's even risen to top student in her watercolor and mosaic classes. Her reward is an extended lease on earth and renewed zeal for life on it.

A mouthwatering waft of freshly baked *pane fino* heralds Zia Gianetta's arrival. "Must be hungry, yes?" Zia Gianetta smiles, dropping her wide bread parcel onto the table. "Still eat anchovies for breakfast?"

I smirk. " 'Course."

"I have some ready."

She makes her way to the larder, surfacing with jars of anchovies marinated in herbs and lustrous green olive oil, home-grown mini bell peppers stuffed with soft cheese, and a generous slab of smoked ricotta. It's good to be with the feeders again, even if Zia Piera's favorite chair by the stove is empty, tucked in under the table.

Incense hangs in the aromatic, stony air of the church of Santa Lucia. There is a picture of Zia Piera, the same that will go onto her headstone, upon the steps before the altar, flanked by half a florist's shop's worth of white lilies and chrysanthemums. No memorial is complete without chrysanthemums in Simius. My mother, passionate and knowledgeable about almost every flower, especially her beloved orchids that she nurtures like small children on her windowsill back in London, cannot abide them.

She's the one who insisted that a dozen lush red roses were scattered among the white, because Piera loved them. It's a scandalous move, but one that none of her cousins will challenge the bereaved over.

The priest is young and witty; he wouldn't look out of place bopping at the local discothèque to Ministry of Sound anthems. He'd talked us through the order of things a few days earlier, inviting us into one of the cavernous antechambers, its high walls lined with paintings of past priests, all looking down on us, thin lipped and scowling.

My cousin was married here a few years ago. She was a radiant bride dressed in a simple modern take on traditional Sardinian costume. Along the length of her cream tunic, wheat sheaths were embroidered in soft, golden thread. Her fringed cream headscarf reminded me of a demure Arabian princess. The traditional chaos had started at her parents' home with plate smashing (to ward off the evil eye), grain throwing (to augur fertility), and petal strewing (for happiness). Then a caravan of fifty cars honked through the skinny streets to this church. There was a lot of singing and crying, followed by the consumption of enough food for the Russian army: *antipasti,* two pastas, one seafood risotto, grilled king prawns, fresh mussels, oven-baked sea bass, grilled suckling pig, fruit salad, sorbet, and *semifreddo* — a dessert somewhere in between cake and ice cream. The hours of dancing that followed helped everyone digest, before trays of *pecorino,* olives, and salami were pushed out to the floor as the newlyweds spooned sugared almonds into little sacks for the guests.

I remember how even Zia Piera had danced that day, the first time I had seen her do so in my life. She had thrown her hands in the air, joining in with the women as they shuffled traditional steps to the accordion player's music. Then I remember an older man taking her gently by the elbow. I had watched them speak in a corner. When she returned to our table, she looked pale. After some persuasion on my part and reluctance on hers, she said, "That was Franco's brother."

I didn't reply, knowing that more prodding would likely have the opposite effect.

"He wanted to apologize."

I remained silent, hoping she would continue.

"He told me that all he remembers was our families being close and then suddenly never seeing any of us again. He never knew why. He told me . . ."

She stopped, tears in her eyes, which she rarely let fall. I watched her dab them with a serviette from the table. "He just wanted to say sorry. That is all." And with that she closed the conversation.

It was futile to bombard her with whys. A short lifetime of them had never led me anywhere in particular other than familiar dead ends. Everyone clammed up on the subject, from my closest relatives to distant aunts and neighbors.

These memories float away as the congregation inside the cool church stands to sing. It's in a minor key, a musical heritage line to the Arab invaders of years gone by, coupled with the haunting Byzantium chords of a time when Sardinia was its own kingdom. I can't follow all the words — my Sardinian is no way near as fluent as my Italian — but I catch the gist: There is wailing about loss, love, and salvation.

My mother wanted me to wear black. The idea of mourning being represented by attire doesn't chime with me. I remember writing a piece on Bali, where I had witnessed a funeral. The entire family danced around a huge pyre, in the middle of the woods, all dressed in light layers of white. They watched their loved one's body being consumed by the flames, an idea of cleansing and release that moved me. As did their open expressions — void of pain; no loss could be read there. What a world away from our weary Western idea of death — life's failure.

The singing ends and everyone takes their seats. Many of the women are wiping their eyes. After Communion, it's not long before the whole ritual is over and we start to file out of the huge doors. I stay behind a moment and let the rest of the family go on, watching the sea of people flow outside.

A crooked man on the opposite side of the aisle catches my eye. I do a double take, thinking him an uncle, but something about the profile tells me otherwise. His stubble is white. He shuffles instead of walking, dragging one of his legs behind like a weight. He turns toward the altar. That's when I recognize him. My heart begins to gallop. Before I can move toward him there's a tug at my arm. It's my sister, Antonia. "Mina, stop dawdling. Mum needs us out there. We're supposed to be in line."

She takes my hand. I look back for the man. He's gone.

Only immediate family come with us to the cemetery. We watch a fine demonstration of physical comedy as the gravediggers try to hoe a hole big enough for the urn to slide down into the family tomb — and fail. An aunt speaks in stage whispers to her husband, ordering him to get down and help the imbeciles. When he doesn't spring into action she kneels down herself, clawing at the earth alongside the workers. A few minutes later, everyone in the group offers a hand. Turns out it's not something they are used to doing around these parts, shunting an urn inside a tomb, but I welcome our sobs being forced into chuckles. Her death has been one of the most surreal moments of my life, so it is only fitting that her burial elicits the same feeling. Eventually, after some pushing and shoving, the magic dust version of her lies in the ground next to her parents. Their photos are next to one another on the tombstone, reunited at last.

As we tear ourselves away and toward the feast at an aunt's house, I meet Zio Bacchisio, my mother's cousin, and give him a gentle tap on the shoulder.

He turns. "Mina, so sad am I to see this day. No tears now, girl. Piera was a fierce woman in life as in death."

"*Grazie,* Zio. May I ask you something?"

He stops for a moment and faces me straight on. His beard is something to behold, several kilos of thick, black curls —

something no hipster in East London could even begin to aspire to, let alone cultivate.

"You once told me that Franco lived near here," I say.

His face drops. "Mina, this is a day of rest."

"That's why I'm asking you which house it is."

He shifts from foot to foot. "I thought we had buried all this. I told you last time, let sleeping dogs lie. What sense in dragging up the past? For what? For who? Think of your family."

"I am. Please, Zio, no one will know it's you who told me, I promise."

"You promised you'd let this go."

"I promised I wouldn't hurt anyone. I leave tomorrow. It would mean everything to me."

He begins to relent, and then mutters the address. I tell my sister I'm taking a moment alone. Off her frown I assure her I will not miss all of the lunch. Then I turn out of the cemetery gates and head downhill toward Franco's villa.

I pass three or four ostentatious homes on my way downhill. This is the part of town that families move to for more space, a sense of living in the country while being close to town. There are houses with three floors and several terraces, long driveways, and as many testaments to success as they can buy: elaborate railings, large cars, strips of lawn. I reach his home — a square, concrete, 1960s build, which I find neither palatial nor garish. It's the kind of house that doesn't invite attention, sanitary almost. Metal roll-up shutters are closed tight. It's painted a pale mustard color. There are no pots of flowers on the gray-tiled pathway to the door but a meager terra-cotta dish with a few succulents fighting for life. I ring the bell, imagining my sister's expression if she knew I were here. The gray silhouette of a figure shuffles toward the mottled glass door. My hands are clammy. The door opens.

There he is.

Bent over.

Cheeks hollowing.

He looks at me, confused. *"Sì?"*

"Franco?"

"Signor Falchi."

Is this the man who had so terrified Zia Piera? Who had so slanted her lifelong view of men, to where she had never felt able to trust a man, even Luigi, ever again? Wasn't Franco the reason she had broken all of her engagements? Wasn't Franco the one responsible for Carmela's death — a view not held by the courts but by everyone else I'd ever met.

"*Sono* Mina. Piera's niece." I thought I would feel panic, vehemence, anguish, but none of these emotions surface. A surprising calm takes their place. His eyes give away nothing. I don't know what I'd expected from him. Some kind of dramatic reaction I could commit to word? None materializes. "I saw you in church today."

His eyes narrow.

Now or never, Mina. "I have something for you." I hold it out. His eyebrows furrow again. "Please, Signore, take it. We have no use for it now."

He reaches out a hesitant palm. I place the locket in his hand. He pulls up the thin chain and squints. The inscription is minuscule and beginning to fade. I can see he is struggling to make it out. It's two words, in Italian italics: *Per Sempre.* Forever.

I have kept it with me since my mother gave it to me as a teenager. I had been romancing the kind of boy who needed to know my whereabouts every minute of the day. Something my naïve younger self mistook for love. On the day he stormed out of the house after a stupid (loud) argument over nothing, she had sat me down and did a stunning job of warning a young girl about the perils of domineering young men. My admiration for her mastery stays with me to this day. Knowing the kind of headstrong, contrary person I was, she was artful to not send me running straight back into his arms out of rebellion against my parents. It's the sole possession we have of Carmela.

I only know he has recognized it when he loses his footing. I step forward out of instinct. He is, after all, a frail man, but he waves me off.

I watch him crumble.

The Bronx — September 2008

It's reassuring to find Arthur Avenue bustling with the same Italian American verve it had from when I last visited. Some years back I signed up for a three-month writing course here in New York City and used every spare slice of time I had to lose myself around it. My yearning for my mother's pasta sauce had brought me up here to the Bronx, on recommendation. Every time I'm back in the city I devote an entire afternoon to pacing myself through several courses. Today I've taken a spot on the corner of one of the huge wooden tables at the center of Arthur Avenue Italian Deli, a vast hangar of salty prosciutto and mature cheese air.

Open barrels of olives, artichokes, and stuffed peppers line the aisles. Sausages hang from metal bars above the counters, along the edges of the huge space. It echoes with office workers getting an authentic slice of Italy on their lunch hour.

I'm visiting my favorite merchant, Salvatore, whose *antipasti* I have paid worship to for several years now, and who is the subject of my latest article for a broadsheet back home.

"Usual, Mina?"

"Of course!"

"You know the wife got me to wear my best shirt for you today."

"You look as good as I remember — but the photographer won't be here till tomorrow, you know."

"So I got to look like this two days in a row? That hurts."

His face creases into a wide grin and his black eyes twinkle. I watch him disappear behind his counter. It won't be long before I can dive into three types of cheese — one Sardinian, especially for me — paper-thin twirls of prosciutto and stuffed calamari. Three small portions of homemade pastas will follow, each with different sauces: usually a marinara, a pesto, and a wild card — ricotta and toasted walnuts maybe, or crushed hazelnuts with *pecorino.* Sometimes he throws in a small taste of whatever risotto he's created that morning. I lose all sense of reality when it's a saffron risotto day, though I feel a traitor for considering it even better than my Zia Piera's. I always eat here early. That way I might even have digested this feast before I collapse into whichever friend's couch has been loaned for the duration of my trip.

My plates are wiped clean. My wineglass is empty. I kick back a strong, creamy espresso and straighten up for work. Salvatore is the perfect subject. Like most people, with some gentle probing he loves to talk about himself, his life, his family, and most important his roots. Sellers here are passionate about their Italian heritage and snub any mention of Little Italy down on Mulberry Street — a brash of Russian mafia imitation. The real deal is right here.

I'm standing by his counter, listening to his stories, watching his hands dance in the air, when something catches my eye. Behind the stacks of huge, fresh loaves there is a painting I had never noticed before. I interrupt his flow — "Sorry, Salvatore, that picture is beautiful. I can't take my eyes off of it."

"I bet — it's Sardinia."

"I know that place!"

" 'Course you do."

"No, I mean, I know that exact view. It's a huge rock of an island off the coast."

"I forget the name, my friend told me — he painted it."

"It's called Tavolara. You can see it from the beach where my family always goes in the summers. I mean, it's *right* in front."

"Oh yeah? I just loved the colors when he showed it to me, and he let me have it."

I walk toward the picture. It's the exact view that's etched into my memory from childhood. The turquoise water is dashed with flecks of sun. Every year my family and I would take a boat trip out there. My sister and I learned to dive in the deep, crystal-clear waters that surround it. We could see right to the rocky depths. Every year we'd spend the whole day out at sea, grab a bowl of linguini twisted around fresh clams doused in garlic along the shore of the singular tavern upon the rock before steering our rented boat back to Simius.

I'm right beside the picture now, the quick, thick brushstrokes a mess of color. My eye darts to the signature on the bottom right corner: J. CRUICKSHANK.

"Not a very Italian name, Salvatore."

"He was a friend of my father's. Captain

Joe, we called him. Loved Sardinia, as if he were born there!"

"Captain Joe?"

"Yeah. I guess his mother was quite the painter. He changed his name to hers after he came back to the States. Some guys are never the same after their mammas go. I don't even like to think about it."

I nod. Something's stirring in my mind I don't want to even admit.

"You know what name he went by before that?"

"Now you're asking — I knew it. . . ." A frown creases his olive-skinned brow. He looks up to answer, but a customer commands his attention. "I know he lives up north, some place called Ogunquit, Maine — all the rich Boston guys head up there, I guess. Fancy stores and overpriced gelato, he'd say." Salvatore talks, all the while wrapping a hunk of fresh Parmesan in waxed paper, handing it over to the woman. "Sorry, Mina, I'm no good with names."

"If you do remember, text me, okay? I'd really like to know."

"You got it."

When we finish the interview we give each other a hug and, like always, I promise to eat at his place on my next visit. I step through the damp wall of August humidity outside, hoping to silence the improbable scenarios playing out in my mind. Inside a sliver of a bar, I indulge in a couple minutes of air conditioning and order a liqueur. Leaving this area is never easy. As I swirl my Sambuca around the hunks of ice my phone buzzes. It's a message from Salvatore. I read the solitary word he's written.

My heart skips:

KAVANAGH

It's early evening by the time I'm pounding up Ogunquit's Main Street. My mind flits like a moth, alternating between an inventory of everything it sees and a flurry of numbing doubts; the smear of warm chocolate upon the marble slab at the homemade candy shop, the wooden ticket booth of the old movie theatre, a tiny dressmaking shop with miniature shoes dressing the window, the shuffle steps of the vacationers, the smell of fried clams. I make a flimsy attempt at steadying my mind by focusing on the cigarette paper I'm twisting around a pinch of tobacco. It fails. Uncertainty takes over. Will he wish I'd never come? Is the grief too much to bear? Does his family know about his time in Sardinia? Should I have come here at all?

I could have called first. I could have taken a moment before I jumped on that train heading north. Too late now. Number 52 Main Street stands before me. It's a modest Cape Cod painted cornflower blue. The hanging baskets below the white-shuttered windows are picture perfect. Everything is in its place. This is a home of a person who thrives on military precision in all things. I would have expected nothing less.

I have been trawling the Internet and asking favors for years, and all that time Kavanagh had literally disappeared. On return to his homeland, Cruickshank took his place. Why had I never thought to search for different names? My stupidity irritates me. Of course nothing surfaced on him. Of course every line of inquiry came to an abrupt halt. Of course it wasn't as simple as tracking Franco. And what would I have gained from a visit anyway? Someone who changes his name doesn't want to be found. And someone who doesn't want to be found has something to hide.

He may have been one of the last people to see my aunt. Perhaps he's the only person on the planet that can shed any truth on her mysterious disappearance. I'm standing before the door of the man who can help my family put this story to bed. I press the doorbell. Twice. Nothing.

I look around, figuring it will get dark soon and I ought to be thinking about where I'm staying. Yet I can't tear myself away. I stub out my cigarette on the ground and flick the end into a drain by the curb. After the fifth failed attempt, I sigh in frustration. I'm overheard. I turn away from the door to catch the friendly neighbor beaming at me. Her blusher has been reapplied too many times, each more orange than the first. Her hairspray is so thick, in preparation, I assume, for any oncoming storms the area is known for.

"Well, hello there, miss." She smiles.

"Hi."

"I'm Betty. Are you a friend of Mr. Kavanagh's, honey?"

I let her question hang for a moment, taking in her big, smiling eyes and the flutter of her blue mascara eyelashes.

"I'm — a fan of his paintings. He was a friend of the family."

"Isn't it awful?"

I feel my eyebrows squeeze into a small frown.

"We knew he was sick, but he never let on quite how bad. But that was Joe through and through."

"Is he . . . ?"

"Yes, honey. A week ago today, in fact. His wife was by his side. Thank the Lord for small mercies."

"His wife?"

"Beautiful woman. Never knew she was over eighty! God bless her heart. How she found the strength to take the trip I'll never know!" I watch her yank her crisp, pink shirt down over her ample girth.

"A trip?"

"Aha — you do have the most charming voice, you know that? Why don't you come on in for some iced tea 'stead of sweating in this god-awful heat?"

"That would be nice, thank you."

I follow her into her house, tiptoeing through the assault of dolls lining what must have at one time been clear, open space. Each figure looks in the near distance with the demonic gaze I always associate with these vulgar ceramic creations.

She mistakes my glare for admiration. "Do you like my lifetime's collection? Joe's wife made quite a number of their outfits, you know. The women around here do a lot of crafts. The winter is brutal."

"So I've heard."

She leads me to a wicker table at the back of her kitchen, then places a cold glass of tea before me. I wait for her to sit down.

"Would you tell me about the trip? I'd like to send my condolences."

"I feel like I've been there myself — they'd talk about this special place all the time, you know. Wanted his ashes sprinkled in his favorite sea, I guess. She's a good woman to do that, at her age and all."

"Where is this island?"

"In Italy someplace."

"Sardinia?"

"Yes! That's right — I've got an old woman's memory!"

"Do you know where in Sardinia?"

"I don't know the name or anything, but he gave me this painting of it." She reaches over for a miniature upon her sideboard. "He took it up after retiring. Isn't it beautiful?"

I can't be sure I said a polite good-bye or closed the door behind me. I cannot remember the blur of travel to Logan International Airport, or taking off, or the twinkling lights of the city below me.

Tavolara — two days later
The nose of the boat lifts and dips into the water, cutting through the deep teal. Half an hour from the shore behind me, the rock looms up into the sky, warding us off and daring us to approach. Suddenly a warning

536

blasts out of a hidden speaker: "WARN-ING! Alter your course immediately! You are approaching military waters!" My driver swerves to the left, away from the mountain-ous island, home to a not-so-secret NATO base. We're back on a straight course for the shore of Tavolara.

I haven't slept in twenty-four hours, yet every sense has returned to its heightened feral state. My body is on high alert. The taste of the salty spray on my face is sharper than I can ever remember, the beating sun harsher. The driver drops anchor. I hold my flip-flops in one hand, jump into the water, and wade up to the glare of white sand on the shore. I turn back to the driver. "Please wait here until I return." He gives me a sun-cracked nod, which makes me wonder whether I might not be marooned here tonight after all.

I stomp up the sandy walkway lined with a driftwood fence, past the small groups of day tourists reddened by the vacation sun. Inside the singular bed-and-breakfast on the island, I hold my ground by the deserted reception. A reluctant receptionist shuffles to something close to attention.

"I'm here for the American guest. Mrs. Cruickshank. She's expecting me."

I don't care that I'm blurting and using

brusque, informal Italian.

"Sorry? We have no Americans here," she replies with a disappointed shrug.

"Yes, you do. She came a few days ago."

"No — I know Americans when I hear them. And I would remember a crazy name like that."

"Well, memories play tricks on us, no? Do me a favor and have a look along the list of guests for me?"

"Honestly," she replies, trailing a lazy finger down some scrawl, "there's no one here by that name."

I feel like I'm about to burst into tears. The tiredness and adrenaline is getting the better of me, and it's not a battle I want to lose in front of this woman.

"Thanks," I mutter, storming out onto the terrace for some hot air.

I lean against the wooden railings. I'm not sure what I would be crying about anyway should I surrender to the feeling. For following a ridiculous hunch? For hoping that some stranger could enlighten me about her late husband and his passion for an island he once loved — oh and, by the way, do you know what really happened to his fleeting sometime lover?

I'm so disappointed by my wild-goose chase. There are worse places to feel the bitter regret of stupidity, I suppose. I'll take refuge at Grandmother's house back in Simius for a while, maybe travel back with my mother, who has stayed on after Piera's burial. I walk away from the terrace toward the shore, hoping the open space and expanse of Mediterranean will somehow lull me back to calm. I know this view well. The rosemary and wild thyme air is so familiar, the smell of sun-toasted wild fennel so comforting. I'm a child in an instant. I taste that sense of utter freedom and limitless possibility.

I think I've centered myself, when a wave of tears shudders through me. Tiredness is brutal. Then it occurs to me that I have been trying to stay so very strong for my mother. These are the tears I could have shed at Zia Piera's funeral perhaps, or her memorial. I find a spot where I'm alone and protected from the nosy stares of day visitors.

I've not done too good of a job, because I feel a kind hand on my shoulder. I turn. A small, old woman is handing a tissue to me. Her hair is white but for a few streaks of stubborn black, clinging to another age. Her huge, dark glasses cover most of her face. She has few lines that I can see and the familiar, warm glow of a local's skin.

"Grazie," I say, mopping up my tears and embarrassment.

"My pleasure," she answers in Italian but with an unfamiliar lilt. My Sardinian accent is closer to English, and I always recognize foreign origins in others' Italian too.

"Signora is not from here — like me?" I ask.

"I live abroad now."

That's when I hear the unmistakable twang. I've come all this way in a crazed dash — no sense tiptoeing around etiquette. "I'd guess the States?"

She sighs a faint laugh. "You're a very good listener!"

"I'm nosy — for a living. Journalist."

"Do you have a name, journalist?" she asks, in English this time.

"Mina."

"A beautiful name. I had thought about that name for one of my children."

"What did you choose instead?"

"Anna. She never lived to learn it."

A shiver scissors through me. I'm sure Mrs. Cruickshank had not planned on a stranger wading through her grief.

"I'm so sorry."

"She found peace. Isn't that what we all want?"

I watch her turn her head toward the sea.

I take in her proud profile, wide jaw. It's her posture that captures me the most. She is small, and thanks to Betty I know her approximate age, but I hadn't imagined someone with such a straight, strong back. She has the élan of someone who might just spring into a sprint should the need arise, coupled with the poise of a dancer — elegant, open, beautiful. I tear my eyes away from her so she doesn't feel my stare.

"It's good to cry, Mina."

I feel my own hand involuntary stroke the tears off my cheek.

"That's what they say." I shrug.

"Even when you think you've shed more tears than you can bear, there will be more. And it's okay. Good, even."

"My aunt died recently. I've not been myself. She was my second mother."

"She was lucky to have had you."

"More like the other way around."

"Is that why you're here? I know a Sardinian when I see one — whatever accent they have."

A chuckle escapes before I realize. I've never felt quite so at ease with a stranger before. She is leading the conversation. I had a list of questions for this woman about her husband, but they seem unimportant all of a sudden.

"My mother is from that town back on the shore. This is the home I carry with me. Especially when the London rain is slashing down."

"I've always wanted to go to London."

"Betty, your neighbor in Ogunquit, said you were a fearless traveler."

Her head jerks toward me. She stiffens.

"She told me you had come here," I continue, regretting my heavy-handed introduction, "with your husband's ashes. I think he may have known my aunt. I was trying to find him to ask more about her."

I notice her back lengthen. She freezes with the stillness of a cat, alert, poised, waiting. "Who is your aunt?" she asks, her voice close to a whisper now.

"Her name was Carmela. She worked for him for a little while."

I notice her swallow. I ought to stop. This is an elderly woman grieving. What right have I to do this? But I can't stop now. I may never see this woman again.

"All I have are snippets of stories," I continue, as gentle as I can, "tattered fables of what she might have been like. My mother, Vittoria, was so young when she disappeared. Everyone is deeply Sardinian about the whole thing. I ask questions and everyone I know slams shut. She is a taboo subject. All families have them, don't they? Only I've been obsessed with her for as long as I can remember. I have a feeling she and I were similar in a lot of ways."

Her gaze returns to the rippling water. We stand in silence for a little while. I hear the gentle memory of waves lap up onto the wet sand.

"What did you want to ask me about her?"

"Anything you might have heard him say about her or his time here."

"I know some things. She loved Joe dearly. And he, her." She pauses for a moment. I am a callous intruder. The pain streaks across what little of her face I can see around the glasses. She smooths the hair off her face, stands tall once again, regal almost. There's a fearless quality to her gait. One that comes for some with age, but I suspect the woman before me is made of a particular strain of courage that can only be inherited, not learned. "I heard she was a brave woman. But one with many regrets."

"Thank you — I know this must be very difficult for you. I'm touched Captain Kavanagh — sorry, Cruickshank — shared this with you."

"We had no secrets."

"That's beautiful. And rare."

I feel her hand slip into mine, and I stop

myself from flinching. British habits die hard. Her hand is strong. For a moment our breaths synchronize. The past forty-eight hours have left me floating a little beside my body, like a blurred photo in the hands of an unskilled photographer. She lifts my hand and studies it. I notice I don't feel strange. I'm trying to guess who is doing the comforting.

"When he died," she begins, "I thought there would be nothing. Now you've found me. I know that your aunt took many risks. I know that Joe found her lying by the Roman bridge minutes from death. She had fallen on a boulder, running away from her fiancé, who had his hands around her throat. I know the last thing she remembers is the stone racing up to her face. Then blackness. When she awoke, the first face she saw was Joe's and she knew right then and there that she could never go back home. Not ever. That night she chose to disappear. There was no other choice. Joe took her to a hospital in Rome, where they nursed her back to health. They married soon after. She fell pregnant three times, but each of those babies were born sleeping. Sometimes they'd think that was their punishment for leaving the people she had loved most in the world."

Her head tips down. She is crying. The tears trail down her cheeks and drip onto her blouse. My hand squeezes hers.

"It's okay," she says, breathy. "I want you to know all of this. I need you to know all of this."

I search her eyes but see only my skewed reflection in her shades.

"Many years passed till she could return home again. Now it seems like a dream she dare not wake up from."

There's a galloping in my chest.

She lifts her glasses.

I would know that face anywhere. It's the face etched into my imagination from a singular photo. It's the black eyes full of expression described to me by anyone who had ever known her.

"Zia Carmela?"

There are no words. Only her shuddered cries in my ears, against my chest. Only the tightness of our winding arms. All space between has gone. Her hands are around my face now. Her eyes are boring deep into me, familiar and new, searching and yearning. She is full of longing and fear and courage and joy. Still no words. The summer breeze whips up around us, playing with the strands of our tear-streaked hair. She presses her wet cheek against mine. We hold the space for a moment into the quiet center of our tears. The sun begins its gentle descent. Her skin turns golden in the setting rays of rose.

"Please, Mina," she whispers, pulling away a mat of my curls from my ear, folding the hair gently behind it, "would you take me home?"

ACKNOWLEDGMENTS

Firstly my thanks go to the wonderful Sardinian clan from which I sprung, who all spun their tales with pride and passion. Huge amount of gratitude for the tireless guidance and encouragement of my agent, Jeff Ourvan, at Jennifer Lyons Literary Agency, without which this story would have stayed rattling around my imagination for another decade. Deepest thanks to John Scognamiglio at Kensington Books for his positivity and incisive suggestions, and to his team, who have brought this story into being. It has taken a small army of people to help me weave this tale, headed by the energetic boys I live with, one adult and two small, who never complained when I edited these chapters at the foot of their beds as they fell asleep, and always reminded me to never give up.

■ ■ ■ ■

A Reading Group Guide: Under a Sardinian Sky

Sara Alexander

■ ■ ■ ■

About This Guide

The suggested questions are included to enhance your group's reading of Sara Alexander's *Under a Sardinian Sky*.

DISCUSSION QUESTIONS

1. Do you think Carmela had any choice in the way the relationship progressed with Kavanagh? Could the tragedy have been averted? How? Why? Would Carmela's dilemma be so very different today?

2. How realistic is the theme of thwarted love explored in the story? What are the differences/similarities between Antonio's hidden sexuality and Carmela's journey? Rosa's infidelity and Carmela's?

3. How do you feel about Carmela's decision to stay away all those years? Why did she decide to inflict that pain on herself and her family? Is it forgivable? Where will they all go from here?

4. Were there other ways that Carmela might have dealt with the pressures she

put on herself/received from her family and social norms?

5. Is Carmela's decision to relinquish everything about her life to be with Kavanagh courageous or selfish? Ultimately does the decision liberate or imprison her?

6. Which aspects of the Sardinian world affected you the most, or struck you as very different from what you know of other cultures in the same period?

7. How would the Simius people have reacted if they had known the truth about Antonio's homosexuality? Would it have been received in the same/different way as a woman committing adultery, and why? Are there parallels? How well do you think Antonio dealt with the burden of living a secret life?

8. Does the Sardinian culture offer a rich background for a story that is, in essence, about secrets? Does the culture add/reflect to the theme or juxtapose it?

9. How well do you think the role of women and the strengths/ challenges of womanhood are explored in the story? Do the

female characters fall under one of the aforementioned categories only, or do they embody both at different times?

10. Is the fear of an abusive partner explored in a realistic way? Is it any different from the millions of women in abusive relationships today? If so, why? If not, why?

11. Which scene embodies the main themes of the story the most for you? Why did it move you? What aspects of it did you love?

12. Does the character of Mina add or detract from the story? Does she help us identify with Carmela? What traits do they share? Does Mina's relationship with her "invisible" aunt underline the theme of inherited stories and histories? Why does Mina feel compelled to write Carmela's story?

ABOUT THE AUTHOR

Sara Alexander graduated from Hampstead School in London and went on to attend the University of Bristol, graduating with a BA hons. in Theatre, Film & TV. She followed on to complete her postgraduate diploma in acting from Drama Studio London. She has worked extensively in the theatre, film and television industries, including roles in much loved productions such as *Harry Potter & the Deathly Hallows, Dr. Who* and *Franco Zeffirelli's Sparrow.*